After nearly fifteen years as a software engineer, Karen Sandler returned to her real love — writing. She enjoys working across the writing spectrum, including novels, screenplays, and short stories.

Karen lives with her husband and two sons in northern California. You can write to her at P.O. Box 165, Rescue, CA 95672, or email her at karen@karensandler.net

UNFORGETTABLE

Randon Bolton walks into Kyra Aimes' junkyard and she can't resist the pain in his eyes that only she is able to see. Then a 1955 Ford Fairlane is put in the yard, and visions appear to both Kyra and Randon whenever they are near the car. Two teens plead for their help — then disappear. It seems only they can help these ghostly young lovers find the truth about their death, and give them eternal rest together. Can this quest also bring Kyra and Randon hope for happiness?

KAREN SANDLER

UNFORGETTABLE

Complete and Unabridged

ULVERSCROFT
Leicester

First published in the
United States of America in 1999

First Large Print Edition
published 2006

British Library CIP Data

Sandler, Karen
    Unforgettable.—Large print ed.—
    Ulverscroft large print series: romance
    1. Romantic suspense novels
    2. Large type books
    I. Title
    813.6 [F]

    ISBN 1–84617–215–2

Published by
F. A. Thorpe (Publishing)
Anstey, Leicestershire
Set by Words & Graphics Ltd.
Anstey, Leicestershire
Printed and bound in Great Britain by
T. J. International Ltd., Padstow, Cornwall

This book is printed on acid-free paper

This one's for you, Dad, and for all the cars you've owned and loved.
And to Gary, my real-life romantic hero.

Prologue

She'd never tire of his crooked smile.

Laura leaned against the door of the '55 Ford Fairlane and let her gaze trace Johnny's face. His warm brown eyes met hers, the soft glow in them a companion to his rakish smile.

'*Come and kiss me, Laura,*' he growled in that half-man, half-boy voice. A shiver skittered down Laura's spine at the sound.

She hesitated, just to let him know she wasn't about to let him order her around. Then she inched away from the door, sliding slowly across the Ford's vinyl bench seat. The skirt of her frothy homecoming dress slithered across her knees, reminding her of Johnny's fingers skimming her calf, dipping just beneath the hem of her dress.

Her breath caught at the memory of his touch, in anticipation of feeling it again. As he slid out from behind the steering wheel, his gaze fixed on hers, intense, filled with a power reflected in her own eyes, her own heart. He tipped his head down, a thick lock of brown hair dropping across his brow.

She paused just as she reached the center

of the big bench seat, waiting for him to close the distance.

Oh please, let it happen this time, oh please.

She trembled, waiting, head tipped up in invitation. He bent lower, eyes shutting.

A sizzle and a flash sputtered between them, driving Johnny back. As he stared at her, anger and frustration playing across his face, phantom tears pooled in Laura's eyes. She, who'd cried at nothing while alive, felt new grief all these years after hers and Johnny's death.

Johnny's fist smashed against the unseen barrier between them, sending up a fountain of sparks. Laura jumped back, although she knew from long experience the fireworks were all show and couldn't hurt her.

'I thought it'd be different this time,' Johnny said angrily.

'*Me, too,*' Laura said, her words a sigh.

Johnny looked around, out the black windows of the Ford. '*It feels different.*'

Laura peered through the expansive front windshield, straining to see something, anything in the endless darkness. But she saw only shadows, black on black nearly as dark as the nothing that filled her eyes during the in-between times, when she didn't even have this car, when she didn't have Johnny.

2

Johnny fixed his gaze back on her. '*Can you feel it?*' he asked fiercely.

She wanted to say yes, tried to push the lie past her throat. But Johnny knew what a lousy liar she was. The silvery tears that never wet her face gathered again in her eyes, spilled over as she shook her head.

'*Well, I can,*' Johnny insisted. He thrust his chin up the way he always did when he was certain he was right. She saw the little boy in him then, the sixteen-year-old young man giving way to a child.

A well-loved child. Laura smiled and leaned closer to the unseen barrier. '*Can you feel me?*'

Johnny's face changed and the young man returned. '*I can.*' He spread his hand on his chest. '*Right here.*'

He tipped his head, bringing it inches from her, and held himself there, waiting. With a sigh, Laura closed the distance as best she could, feeling the energy of the barrier scudding across her brow. She shut her eyes, not wanting to see the space that still separated them.

A steady thrum sounded in her ears, the ghost of her heart, the phantom of her love for Johnny. The sound soothed her, sustained her through the long in-between times, when even her memories were black and empty.

The barrier between them seemed to thicken, to stiffen. Something pulled at Laura, pulled her away from Johnny. '*What's happening?*'

'*We can't be going back yet,*' Johnny said. '*It's too soon.*'

Terrified of the black limbo that awaited, desperate to say the words, Laura shouted, '*I love you, Johnny!*'

His hands came up, reaching for her. '*I love you, Laura.*'

'*Next time, Johnny.*' Her eyes never leaving his face, she waited for the gray that would segue into the interminable black of in-between.

But although the endless night outside the car window changed, lightened, the color of the ether seemed more rose than gray. And now Laura could discern shapes beyond the broad sweep of the Fairlane's windshield, irregular edges and broken curves.

'*What is it, Johnny?*' she murmured as tantalizing glimpses materialized beyond the Ford.

'*Another chance,*' he said, a familiar, long-forgotten glow lighting his face.

In the next moment, Laura was alone, and standing in the brilliance of an ordinary summer morning.

1

Kyra Aimes bent over in her chair and tightened the laces on her heavy tan work boots. She rose from the wheeled office chair and shoved it under the chipped Formica desk, upsetting a precarious stack of paperwork. She grabbed for the slithering sheets, barely resisting the urge to ball them all up and toss them into the trash.

Dumping the heap back on the desk, she left the windowless office for the service room beyond. Old Jackson stood alone, fielding the queries and purchases of the early morning visitors to Kyra's wrecking yard. He turned briefly from the six-deep queue at his payment window, a smile creasing deeper seams in his dark brown face.

'Looks like that girl's late again,' Jackson said.

Damn Trish and her teenage unpredictability, Kyra thought as she stepped up to the second window. She pulled the CLOSED sign from it and nodded to the next customer in line. The wispy-haired seventy-something man, his faded blue coverall splotched with oil, clunked a carburetor from a '74 Granada on the counter in front of Kyra. He nodded at her, pale blue eyes intense as he pushed the grease-encrusted part closer to her.

'How are you this morning, Mr. Carson?' Kyra asked as she searched for the carburetor price in her computer.

He didn't answer Kyra's query; he hadn't yet in the half dozen odd times she'd seen him. Trish had told her he rebuilt carburetors and alternators in his garage, then sold them to the local auto shops.

'Hot as blazes out there already, isn't it?' Kyra said, keeping up the one-side conversation.

Kyra looked past him at the heat shimmering off the rows of wrecked cars. Late August in the Sacramento Valley rivaled anything Mephistopheles could conjure up. Nine A.M. and it was already toasting in the mid-eighties, cooking along to a three-digit climax by late afternoon. They were predicting a high of one-thirteen, and the asphalt and sheet metal of Kyra's wrecking yard would add ten degrees to that.

The swamp cooler above Kyra coughed out gusts of cool air, fighting a battle it would lose by four o'clock. It didn't matter anyway; Kyra would be out in the yard by then, continuing her endless cycle of environmental paperwork, making sure FourStar Pick-n-Pull

6

dotted every T and crossed every I the state asked for.

As Mr. Carson dug out the wrinkled bills for the carburetor, Kyra heard Trish's high, sweet voice call out to Jackson. Kyra turned to see her errant clerk effervesce into the room.

'Morning, Kyra. Hey, Mr. Carson,' the eighteen-year-old said as she slung a book bag under the counter. Mr. Carson gave the girl a sour look in response before snatching up the carburetor and sidling off.

'You're late,' Kyra said, stating the obvious. She tossed the change from Mr. Carson's transaction into the till and shut the drawer. 'Again.'

Trish scruffed up her spiky hair, tossing Kyra a placating grin. 'Car wouldn't start.'

Excuse number twenty-nine, used three times this month already. 'Jackson's backed up. Give him a hand.' Kyra gestured to the queue that had swelled to eight.

Kyra waited until Trish was shouldering her load before she headed out into the broiling sunshine. She fidgeted with the clipboard she carried, tapping it against her thigh as she wove through the rows of cars. Her boots crunched on the gravelly asphalt as she passed the '83 Chevys, bits of broken chrome and shattered side view mirrors

7

giving off an eye-hurting glare.

She ran a mental list of everything she had to do today, anxiety creeping up on her. The unfinished, overwhelming details from yesterday, from last week, from last month, piled heavily on her, dragging her down like Marley's chains. Her conscience took the form of her late unlamented husband, his snarling voice ringing in her mind's ear.

Got those payables done yet, lazybones? I had to finish those state reports, then work the service window . . . Don't give me your damn excuses. How the hell we s'posed to stay in business if we don't pay the damn bills?

The Snake. Kyra hadn't referred to her husband by his real name, either verbally or mentally, since he committed the ultimate act of betrayal by dying.

Kyra hunched her shoulders in reaction to his memory, then threw them back again irritably. She'd never missed paying a bill out of neglect. Only when the Snake had run through the month's receipts in booze and trips to the Indian casinos.

She turned left at the rank of '91 Olds and serpentined her way to the back gate where the auction purchases had been delivered. Eight new totaled vehicles fresh from the insurance company auction crowded together against the cyclone fencing. She scanned them, taking a quick mental inventory of body panels and windshields, headlights and front grills.

When she'd first started working at the FourStar wrecking yard, a new bride still snowed by her husband's charm, surveying the damaged cars always gave her a chill. Had there been a family in this one, piled into the car for a Sunday drive? A young man in that pick-up truck, on his way to work? What had happened to them? Had they survived the crash, had they walked away, grateful to be alive?

The increasing bitterness over her marriage only added to the hard shell she'd grown over those empathetic concerns. Now, when she viewed the line of twisted metal, she shut off those thoughts before they started, shunted them into the same dark abyss she'd routed her hopes for a happy marriage.

Instead, she focused on the eight sets of tires her mechanic, Mario, would have to pull for disposal, the eight radiators full of antifreeze to be drained and the contents discarded safely. Not to mention the used motor oil in the engine case and Freon from the air conditioners, all accompanied by the mountain of paperwork the state of California demanded.

Kyra swiped a line of sweat from her brow as she worked, the sun beating brutally on the back of her neck and shoulders where her navy tank top didn't cover. She'd forgotten her hat, and though her thick, short-cropped black hair protected her ears, she missed the shade the ball cap's bill provided her eyes.

Damn, she'd give a month's receipts for a day of winter right about now. Even a bitter cold December storm would be welcome. Fat drops of rain hammering the asphalt, Alaska chill cutting to the bone. Of course, any decent rain chased away her customers and flooded half the south end of the yard.

Maybe summer wasn't so bad, she thought wryly as she hoisted herself up on the running board of a jacked-up pickup. She peered at the interior, checking the condition of the upholstery. A half-dozen beer cans littered the foot well of the passenger seat and a faint odor of hops lingered.

She dropped back down to the pavement with a grim smile, remembering the same collection of empties in her husband's car. Thank God her misbegotten spouse had died in a drunken fall down a flight of stairs, not in a car crash on Highway 50. At least the Snake didn't take anyone with him when he went.

Just a piece of her soul, Kyra thought. She scrubbed at her face, wiping away the ugly memories. She'd be damned if she'd let the no-good louse harass her in death the way he had in life. The grief she'd felt at his passing had shocked her — until she'd realized her sorrow hadn't been for the Snake's expiration as much as it had been for the death of her dreams.

She moved away from the pickup and scanned the line of cars again. The invoice had read eight vehicles, but she only counted seven. She turned slowly, looking around her, trying to spot the missing vehicle.

The glint of chrome caught her eye and she turned back. She sought out the tell-tale glare. There, back behind the row of '78 Toyotas, almost wedged in between the Toys and the fence. A pair of fins and round red taillights peeking out from behind a battered Corolla.

Kyra's brow creased as she moved closer to the car. A '55 Fairlane? She glanced at the list on her clipboard, but the car she hadn't yet located was a late-model Chevy, not a vintage Fairlane. Yet the notation at the top said *eight* cars.

When she neared the car, she was even more puzzled. The rear end was nearly pristine, with only a few minor dents. The worst of the damage was a broad smear of mud sullying the strawberry-ice cream pink

11

of the plump front fenders.

How did Jackson manage to snap up a nearly cherry classic '55 at the auction? He knew her budget, had assured her he'd kept it to the penny. How could he have outbid the competition on such a prize?

Kyra shook her head, sending off a shower of sweat from her hair. Her tongue felt glued to her mouth, and she cursed herself for forgetting to bring out her water bottle. She had to find the damn Chevy and get back inside before she expired of heatstroke. She'd leave the puzzle of the Fairlane for later, when she could ask Jackson.

She turned to go, but something drew her back. Sunlight glared brilliantly off the white trunk of the two-tone car, tempting her to touch it, to soak up the heat of the sun-warmed metal. The line of chrome separating the pink from the sweep of white winked at her, a teasing glitter of silver. She reached out, pressed her palm against the trunk.

The metal was cold.

She snatched her hand back, staring down at the car, eyes fixed on the trunk lock just above the empty license plate frame. Her hand trembled, remembering the chill centered in it. A cool streak of sensation shivered down her spine.

Before she realized what she was doing, she'd hurried several steps away, fear goosing her. Feeling ridiculous, she turned back to the car, retraced her steps. She put out her hand, held it above the Fairlane's trunk lid. Waves of heat radiated from the white metal. Jaw set with determination, she lowered her hand to the lid.

The warmth of the metal nearly burned her. As it should, as it would with any other car in the lot, baking in the late morning heat. What she'd felt before . . . well, she hadn't felt it. She'd imagined it. No doubt a product of her wistful wish for winter, for the cool rains of December.

Chin high, she moved away from the Fairlane. Her eyes again scanning the row of new arrivals, she finally spotted the Chevy. With a purposeful stride, she headed over to inventory the last car on her invoice.

★　★　★

Randon Bolton let his pickup coast down Highway 50's Bass Lake grade, his eyes fixed on the haze of the Sacramento Valley below. He'd meant to get an earlier start today, before the sun rose to its zenith and pinned all beneath it with its fire. The A/C on the truck had long ago given up the ghost, and the gust of tepid air from the vent did nothing to cool him.

He'd been through Sacramento before, a good fifteen years ago as a wet-behind-the-ears nineteen-year-old. Rachelle was a senior in high school by then and had had two years to recover from the death of their parents. Randon figured the neighbor woman would do as well as him taking care of his younger sister, maybe better.

So he'd left her behind. He'd called her every day he worked the California State Fair as a carny, checking to be sure she was eating right, keeping safe. Had she gotten the check he'd sent? he'd ask. Had she bought herself some school clothes?

That lasted for five years, Randon eking out an income with this job or that, always on the move, never spending more than a fraction of his paycheck so that Rachelle could reap the benefits. He couldn't be with her anymore, couldn't stand to be in one place that long, but he could assuage his guilt by making sure she was provided for.

Until that day he received his check back with a polite note from Rachelle's husband — husband? Randon hadn't even known his sister had married — that *he* would be supporting Rachelle from here on out, and Randon should keep the money for himself.

Except that Randon hadn't a clue how to spend money on himself. So he continued his frugal ways and put the extra into something a rodeo wrangler had called a 'mutual fund.' He had a vague idea of giving the money to Rachelle's kids. But from what he heard from his sister, the few times her letters caught up with him, her husband Tom had done well for himself. Their two boys wouldn't be needing Uncle Randon's money as much as they would Uncle Randon himself.

Randon tipped back his cowboy hat to rub away a line of sweat, then settled the hat back on his head. The temperature seemed to rise with each foot he descended into the valley. A prickle started in the back of his neck, not so much from the heat, but from that persistent nag of guilt that he'd given so little of himself to his nephews.

Especially now, since that phone call from Rachelle's husband, when he told Randon about her . . . problem.

He couldn't even say the word, not even in his mind.

I'll make it up to them, he swore silently as he pulled off the highway at Sunrise. *Maybe when I've finished this job, I'll go pay them all a visit.*

He'd promised himself that very thing just a month ago when he'd finished his stint on a

Carson City ranch. And at the tail end of last year, when he'd wound up that flood control work just before Christmas, he'd had every intention of dropping by Rachelle's. But somehow a stack of presents made its way to Rachelle's Redding home without him. And as much as he might tell himself that that was enough, he couldn't ignore the sharp tug of pain when he received the boys' thank you note, complete with a photo of the two wearing the twin cowboy hats he'd sent.

Randon continued south down Sunrise, eyes scanning either side of the boulevard, watching for the wrecking yards. The movie's production designer, Jeffrey Evans, had torn two pages from the motel phone book and handed them to him, along with the Polaroid camera. An effete little man with a gray-streaked ponytail, Evans had given Randon his directions in his mincing, flighty way, although Randon knew the man was straight as an arrow. The way he flitted around would have made the gay cowboys Randon had met squirm with embarrassment.

All part of the act, Randon supposed. Evans saw himself as an 'artiste,' never mind the rock-bottom budget and the raunchy script for the grade B horror movie.

Randon reached the stretch of Sunrise lined with wrecking yards on either side. No way of knowing where to start. No way of knowing what would satisfy the self-satisfied pretender he worked for. He'd make a random choice, snap a few pictures, then move on to the next one. He had five packs of film, fifty shots. If he was lucky, he could finish this today.

Something glittered off to the left, catching his eye. Sunlight off a car mirror, no doubt, or a bit of chrome. Randon looked back over his shoulder at the place he'd just passed, decided it was just as good a choice as any.

He slowed the pickup and made a U-turn at the next intersection, heading back up Sunrise. He pulled the pickup into the parking lot and found himself a scarce patch of shade in which to leave the truck.

★   ★   ★

'It was just some guy,' Trish said, counting out change to hand to a waiting customer. 'He had the Fairlane. He had his paperwork.'

Kyra tapped the clipboard against her palm in a steady staccato. 'But people don't just sell vintage cars to a wrecking yard for scrap value.'

'He showed me his salvage license,' Trish insisted. 'He had his paperwork from the state. You tell me not to be nosy. I didn't ask questions.'

'Maybe you should have this time,' Kyra said. Irritation bubbled up at Trish's negligent shrug of her shoulder, and Kyra knew it was time she isolated herself in her office. Haranguing the girl who had only done as Kyra had asked would only cause hurt feelings.

Kyra tossed the clipboard on her desk and shut the office door. She'd just as soon collapse on the worn sofa crowded in the corner, lumpy as it was, but if she lay down, she doubted she'd be up again before dark. She didn't sleep well in her tiny Placerville Victorian. She often spent the early morning hours wandering the narrow rooms of her house, seeking a bit of cool peace to rest in.

Somehow the sultry heat of her office acted as a soporific, tempting her to put aside the oppressive stress of her life in an afternoon of slumber. But sleeping away her day wouldn't get the bills paid, wouldn't answer the question of the '55 Fairlane ensconced in the back of her yard. Ignoring the sofa, she sank into her office chair.

She'd have to call the county sheriff and check to see if the car was stolen. It wouldn't be the first time an inept thief had towed in a vehicle, hoping to make a little money off the scrap value. They weren't the professionals of stolen car rings and chop shops, but the hapless bumblers or the estranged husbands whose idea of revenge was to sell their wife's transportation for parts.

Another fine endorsement of marriage, Kyra thought sourly, then shook her head at her own bitterness. The institution had worked well enough for her parents they had loved each other dearly before her mother died. It was just she who had been inept in matrimony, who couldn't discern the difference between love and charm, ambition and deviousness.

She dialed the number for the sheriff and waded patiently through the voice mail system. When she hung up the phone a few minutes later, she kept her hand on the receiver a long moment, puzzled. No record of a stolen '55 Fairlane. She owned the car, fair and square.

Kyra reached for the stack of bills, determined to get them out in the mail today. She'd just flipped to the first one when the office door rattled with the 'Shave and a Haircut' of Trish's knock.

'Someone to see you, Kyra,' Trish called through the door.

'Who?' Kyra called back.

'Some guy,' Trish said. 'A real hunk. He

asked to see the owner.'

'Salesman,' Kyra muttered as she pushed back her chair and rose. She already had a ton of junk in the back storeroom, stuff the Snake couldn't resist buying. Boxes of pens with their address misprinted, car sun shades emblazoned with the lascivious silhouette of a nude woman.

'I don't think he's a salesman,' Trish said as Kyra strode from her office. 'Not this guy.'

Kyra stepped into the service room, eyes roving the three windows. When her gaze fell on the man waiting at window three, she stopped abruptly.

The long tall drink of water in a battered white cowboy hat bore no resemblance to a salesman. His faded blue T-shirt had seen better days. The muscles in his tanned arms were ropy, no doubt from real work, not from lifting samples cases. He fidgeted with what looked like a Polaroid camera, passing it from hand to hand as if he wasn't quite sure what to do with it.

She'd known men who styled themselves as men of power. They piled up stacks of money and influence, flaunted their affluence, flexed their riches instead of their muscles. But the man who stood in the broiling midday heat, waiting with edgy energy, exuded a true power — that of his own self-confidence. His

20

authority sprang from his own fingertips, encompassed not only what lay within his grasp, but what lay beyond, within his reach.

Kyra experienced a fleeting urge to let Jackson handle him. She could justify it — that growing mountain of paperwork in her office wouldn't process itself. Jackson knew every inch of the business; he could handle whatever the man wanted as well as she.

She'd nearly opened her mouth to call Jackson's name when the stranger outside leaned into the service window and shifted his gaze to her. The gray eyes, deep-set in the sharp planes of the man's face, fixed on her. They widened, as if to enfold her image, as if to pull her in to him.

He wouldn't be the first man to study her with that avid interest. Although she was small of stature, Kyra had long ago resolved herself to being what one man had crudely described as 'stacked.' She'd given up trying to hide her generous bustline back in her twenties, instead relying on a cold stare to discourage rude perusals of her anatomy. But the man wasn't studying the line of her breasts filling the tank top. His gunmetal-gray gaze fixed on her face, traced the curve of her jaw, settled on her lips. When Kyra flicked a tongue out to wet them, his eyes narrowed, darkened.

Angry, flustered, irritated, Kyra turned on her heel and headed for the door to the outside. She ignored the temptation to confront the man with the barrier of the service counter between them, and strode out to meet him face-to-face.

Damn, he was taller than she'd thought. Short as she was, she had to crane her neck to look up at him. And the way those blue jeans hugged his body was downright indecent.

She pasted a pleasant smile on her face. 'Can I help you?'

'I was looking for the owner,' he said with the slightest hint of a drawl.

She maintained her smile with an effort. 'You're looking at her.'

He gazed down at her doubtfully, then flicked a quick glance inside the service room. 'Your husband not in today?'

Anger knotted in Kyra's throat and she tamped it down impatiently. 'I said, I'm the owner,' she said tightly. 'What can I do for you?'

A moment's hesitation, then he juggled the camera into his left hand and thrust out his right. 'I'm Randon Bolton.'

As much as she might like to, she couldn't refuse his proffered hand. 'Kyra Aimes.' She pressed her palm to his.

Despite herself, she found she liked the firmness of his grip. It wasn't the limp gathering of her fingers in a pseudo-handshake so many men used greeting a woman. The calluses on his fingertips brushed the back of her hand and something curled low in her belly in reaction. She pulled her hand back, shoved it into the pocket of her shorts.

'What can I help you with?' she asked again.

He stared at her a long moment, the gray eyes puzzled. Then he seemed to come back to himself. He gestured with the camera. 'I need some cars. For a movie.'

Kyra narrowed her gaze on the tall stranger, her perspective of him shifting 180 degrees. 'You're making a movie?'

'I'm just the propmaster.' He grinned, his face going from zero to sixty on the devastating scale in seconds. 'Or at least that's what the guy I'm working for calls me.'

Kyra felt the immediate peril of that heart-lifting smile, felt a warmth spread within her. She thrust the threatening softness aside. 'This is a wrecking yard. Nothing out there runs.'

He'd seen the moment of weakness in her; she could see it in his speculative gaze. 'They don't have to run.' He shifted the black plastic case of the camera from one callused palm to the other. 'They don't even need engines.'

Nothing in his tone suggested he was coming on to her. His eyes remained fixed on her face, not once flicking down to her chest. But Kyra could feel a heat rise in her cheeks nonetheless.

She edged back a step. 'I can't pull engines for you.'

His grin had faded to a faint smile, its wistfulness just as compelling. 'I'll just take them as they come. With engines, without.' He hesitated, just a heartbeat. 'I only need the bodies.'

Irritation rose in Kyra, making her edgy. He wasn't trying to be suggestive, was he? That she couldn't tell for certain; that she reacted with a pleasurable warmth instead of cold disdain as she did with other men only unsettled her more.

She'd been out in the damn sun too long, that was all. Imagining, maybe even hoping for some interest from a good-looking cowboy. There had been no one since the Snake died last year — and little enough when he'd been alive. She was allowed a little fantasizing.

She pushed back her hair with her fingers, putting more distance between herself and the cowboy in the process. 'You pay for whatever's left on the car.' She looked out over the yard rather than at him. 'I won't have you leaving a damn mess.'

'I won't.' An edge had crept into his voice.

Kyra turned back to him, lifting her chin in response to his annoyance. 'And you'll have to pay Mario to tow them.'

'No problem.' He leaned toward her so that the brim of his hat shadowed his face. 'You know I could go to one of the other places just as easy.'

The words were out before Kyra could stop them. 'No one's keeping you here, cowboy.'

His gray eyes darkened in his shadowed face. 'I would think you'd be glad to get the business.'

She took a step toward him. 'Not if I have to deal with an attitude.'

His eyes widened as if he couldn't believe what she'd said. 'Lady, the only attitude here is yours.'

She advanced on him another step. 'And I damn well don't need you leering at me like some pervert!'

He barked out a laugh. 'You're sure as hell overestimating your attraction.' He grinned as if the very thought of her appeal were amusing.

Heat rose in Kyra's cheeks, mortification

urging her to look away. But she stubbornly kept her eyes on his.

'There are a half dozen other wrecking yards along Sunrise,' she said evenly. 'I suggest you check them out.'

For a long moment, he glared down at her. Something burned in his eyes, something like rage, something like fire.

'Fine,' he snapped, then turned on his booted heel. Ten long strides and he'd reached his pickup in the lot beyond. The roar of his engine and the spitting of gravel signaled his departure.

Hell, why had she done that? She'd just thrown away God knew how many hundreds of dollars. Enough to pay off a few of the bills she'd been juggling since Peter ran out of money to pay Paul.

With a sigh at her own stupidity and a wry grin for Trish, who watched, rapt, from the service window, Kyra headed back to her office.

★　★　★

Johnny! Oh, God, Johnny, where are you?

Laura turned in place, looking around her at the tumbled wreckage of cars. Her gaze fell on the '55 Fairlane an arm's length away. She bent to peer inside the front windshield

26

again, but he wasn't there.

A dark head moved between the rows of cars and her heart lifted until the man moved closer — not Johnny. The man called out to a blonde woman near him and the two walked past Laura, close enough for her to reach out to them. But they never looked her way, as if she didn't exist.

Well, of course you don't exist, silly. You're dead.

Dead, but in the real world again. Real sunshine spilled down, would have warmed her shoulders if she could still feel. And a real sky arched overhead, brilliant blue hazed faintly with clouds. But no one could see her. Not the dark-haired man and his blonde companion, not the older couple meandering down the rows, nor the Mexican man leaning under the hood of the car three feet away. If no one saw her, heard her, returning was pointless.

Oh, where was Johnny? Every time before, they'd come back together. Never able to touch, but side by side. It had made the long dark times in between tolerable. How could she bear to be back in the world without him?

She would wait for him, that was it. She would climb inside the Ford and curl up on the seat and wait for Johnny.

But when she moved toward the car, a

most peculiar thing happened. Sparkles of light surrounded her like crazy fireflies, and the air grew thick as cotton candy. The more she pushed toward the car, the heavier the air became until it stood firm as an implacable brick wall. She could not even reach her hand through it to touch the pale pink fender of the Fairlane.

Her heart wrenched inside her chest as if the living organ still beat there. '*Johnny!*' she cried again, her whole being in the call. '*Johnny!*'

Then a wonderful thing happened. Three people standing nearby, the old folks and the Mexican man, turned their heads toward her, eyes alert. They peered in her direction, listening a moment before returning to their business.

There was hope, then. She might well be able to reach one of them, to ask them what she and Johnny had been asking for so very long. And maybe this time, they'd find an answer.

★ ★ ★

Randon caught up with Kyra first thing the next morning, just as she was heading out into the yard. His hat literally in his hands, the camera slung over his shoulder, he called out her name, halting her before she'd reached the first row of cars.

He hesitated a moment before striding over to her, his face set. He stopped a decorous three feet away.

'Could I please look around your yard?' he asked, eyes on her.

A long night of pondering past due notices had dissipated any lingering pride. 'Of course. I'm sorry if I was rude yesterday.'

He nodded. 'Me too, ma'am.'

She tipped her head in return, then gestured out to the yard. 'Help yourself.'

He planted his hat back on his head and slid the camera from his shoulder. 'Thank you.'

Another long look, then he moved away from her, heading toward the first row of cars.

'Randon!' she called out, the question nagging at her. He turned back, attentive.

'Why did you come back?' she asked.

He waited a beat before he answered. 'I couldn't find what I wanted.'

A chill skittered up Kyra's spine, a sudden premonition. But before she could put her finger on it, Randon disappeared among the wreckage and the sensation dissolved in the summer heat.

2

Randon couldn't shake her image. He caught glimpses of her across the yard, moving gracefully between the rows of trucks and cars, her petite, curvaceous form winking in and out of sight. But even when he couldn't see her, she remained in his mind like an afterimage, the short, glossy, dark hair slipping into her eyes, scooped back with slender fingers, the sleeveless cherry-red blouse hugging her curves. He liked women, enjoyed thinking about them, but this woman — she was an obsession.

Why *had* he come back? He'd prowled three other wrecking yards yesterday after-noon, the sun's heat dragging after him like an unwieldy cloak. He found several cars amongst the endless lines of wrecks that surely would have satisfied the production designer. But each time Randon raised his camera, his finger on the shutter release, her face intruded. The dew of sweat on her brow, her wide, angry hazel eyes, the soft curve of her lower lip that he couldn't seem to pull his gaze away from.

And he wouldn't snap the picture. In fact,

each time, he'd had to stifle the urge to fling the damn camera across the lot, or smash it into a windshield. Somehow Kyra had grabbed hold of him and he knew he had to go back. Had to tease out the reason for the attraction, then dismiss it and go on as he always had. So here he stood at FourStar Pick-n-Pull mooning over a prickly, stiff-backed woman he had not the slightest inclination to get to know better. That her curves would tempt a saint was beside the point. There was something behind her frank gaze that tugged at him, lured him, and that should be enough to set his feet running in the other direction.

Damn, he was looking for her. He'd stopped walking, had cocked his hip against a white Toyota with a streak of primer gray and was scanning the tops of the cars. He pushed himself away from the battered fender and cast his gaze resolutely down, closing his line of vision to a narrow few feet. He moved away from the Toyota. A cool chill raised gooseflesh on his arm. He snapped his gaze up, stopped in his tracks. A classic Ford Fairlane stood stoutly against the cyclone fencing. Mud caked the hood and front fenders, concealing the pink-and-white paint job dulled by years of oxidation.

He stepped closer and felt the chill again. A

prickly sensation danced along the hairs on his arms and he shuddered. His feet didn't seem to want to approach the car; they remained rooted to the pavement. What the hell? Randon looked around him, seeking a culvert or a drain pipe nearby. Even in the height of summer, a little water flowing in a nearby ditch would produce a gust of coolness. But there was nothing beyond the gravel and asphalt of the wrecking yard except acres of scrub and hip-high dried grass.

Shaking off the tension in his shoulders, Randon pushed himself forward. As he stepped up to the passenger side door of the Fairlane, he felt nothing but the ordinary heat of day radiating from the two-tone pink and white metal of the car. An odor drifted from the interior, faint as a memory, nagging at him to identify it. But then the sun seemed to bake it away, consigning it to his imagination.

He reached for the silver-bright chrome door handle, curved his fingers around it. His thumb hovered over the release button and his arm tensed, ready to pull the door open. The door lock was down, and he reached through the open window to pull it up. Coolness danced across his arm.

He looked up, left, right, searching for the source of the chill breeze. The scrub in the empty fields beyond lay motionless, not a twig touched by moving air. Yet he felt it, skimming along his arm, skittering up his neck. He looked back down, at the door lock. It was up.

The door handle seared his hand and he jumped back, releasing it. He could feel a line of warmth, sketched across his palm by the sun-heated metal of the handle. He checked his hand, surprised it was unmarked, then shook his head at his own flight of fancy. He looked sidelong at the car. The door lock was down, as it had been all along. That he'd seen otherwise was a trick of heat, of light and shadow. Nevertheless, he'd lost all inclination to open the Fairlane's door.

'Randon.'

He whirled at the soft-spoken sound of his name, his heart suddenly hammering in his chest. *It's only Kyra*, he thought, his heart taking a brief respite, then racing again like a thoroughbred when it realized 'only' would never apply to Kyra.

He took off his hat and scraped back the sweat-curled hair falling across his brow. 'Hello,' he said, settling the hat back into place.

'Finding what you need?' She hugged a clipboard across her chest.

What would it be like to have her hold him like that? His face buried in her softness, his flesh burned by the heat of her. The sweet comfort of her woman's body easing away the long years of loneliness — He slammed a lid on that line of thought, as if it were a yearling colt jerked to a stop with a stud chain. Lord, if she had a clue to what he was thinking, she'd throw him out of here on his ass. *But wouldn't that be better — to get away from her?* She drew at him, tugged at his emotions, at the empty place inside him. If he had a teaspoonful of sense, he'd run the other way. And yet he'd come back.

He rubbed a hand over his face, wiping away his stray fantasies. 'I've found a few,' he said, finally answering her question. 'Snapped some pictures to show the production designer. He'll have to approve my choices.'

'Then you won't be taking the cars today?' She didn't seem too happy about that.

'In a hurry to get your money, sugar?' He drew out the endearment, knowing the verbal caress would rile her. 'Or just wanting to get rid of me?'

Her jaw worked, but her face remained neutral. 'I couldn't care less whether you're here or not. I just can't guarantee the cars will be here when you return.'

'How about I leave a deposit for the cars I

choose?' he suggested. 'You can mark 'em sold.'

'That should be acceptable,' she said, although she looked as though she wished she could have found fault with his recommendation. She tilted her head up at him, narrow-eyed. 'What're you doing working on a movie, anyway?'

She must have realized how rude she sounded, because she flushed. He grinned at her discomfort. 'I don't look like the Hollywood type?'

'I wouldn't know,' she said, shifting to lean against a Chevy 4×4. A scent floated from her, tempting him to seek its source. 'But film making wouldn't have been my first guess of your profession.'

'I wouldn't say I have a profession, exactly.' He shrugged, resisting the urge to drag in a lungful of her fragrance. 'This is just a job that came along.'

She tugged a lock of dark hair off her forehead. 'What kind of movie is it?'

'Depends on who you ask, me or the director.' He cocked a hip against the truck, a few inches away from her. 'He calls it art. I'd call it a cheap slasher flick.'

She had to raise her chin higher to meet his eyes. 'Then why'd you take the job?'

'It pays for beer.' He watched for her frown

35

of disapproval. She didn't disappoint him.

'I suppose that would be enough for a man like you,' she said with a prissy tilt of the chin.

He felt himself lean toward her, like a skittish horse easing toward a grain bucket. 'And what kind of man would that be?' he asked softly.

If she had an answer, it was trapped in her eyes, a message he couldn't quite translate. Her face entranced him, the curve of her cheek, her moist lower lip. He itched to draw his thumb over her chin, to see if she would open her mouth, to see if she would let him kiss her . . .

He straightened abruptly, taking a step or two away from the pickup, away from her. What the hell had happened to his sense of self-preservation? Burned in the fire of that longing in her eyes.

'I don't really have time to talk, sugar,' he said harshly, gesturing with the camera. 'I'd just as soon get this done today.'

She stiffened, irritation washing away the heat, the imagined passion. He figured that was just as well.

She backed away. 'I'll need a record of the cars you pick. The number off the windshield.'

He nodded agreement, then turned his back on her. He could feel her gaze on him, as palpable as an angry touch. Then the sound of her brisk strides away from him rasped at his ears.

Perfect. Great. He'd just go take his damn pictures and get the hell out. He'd give her tow driver the numbers on the cars and let him handle transporting them.

He moved blindly through the lot, snapping shots left and right. He finished the pack of film, tucked the snapshots in his jeans pocket and headed for the exit at a halfrun. Good riddance, Kyra Aimes, he thought as he gunned his truck out of the lot. Good riddance and good-bye.

*   *   *

Johnny hung close by the chain-link fence and watched the woman storm toward him. She sure looked mad, just like Laura that time she caught him talking to the homecoming queen. He saw in the woman's face the same balance between anger and tears. It wouldn't take much to tip a woman over to brimming eyes that could drive a dagger of guilt into a man quicker than lightning.

The woman reached the row of cars lining the fence, started to pass Johnny. She lurched to a stop, one hand outstretched as if feeling something in the air. Then she snatched her

37

hand back and held it close to her. She looked around wildly, searching for . . . Was she looking for him? Had she somehow sensed him, recognized that something unseen occupied the ether near her?

Johnny stepped away from the fence, approached the woman. What had the man called her? Kyra? What if he called her name? Could he get her attention? Would she hear him?

Kyra! He willed the name, shouted it in his mind. It sounded loudly around him, but the word wouldn't shape in his mouth, only inside him. It was clear Kyra hadn't heard. She'd already closed herself off to the possibility of him, had taken a half step away.

Kyra! he called again, this time with his very soul. But Kyra walked away without hesitation, no doubt dismissing the very notion of Johnny.

Aching to his depths, Johnny cried out again, this time a name as familiar as his own heart. *Laura!*

He imagined her answer — *I love you, Johnny* — soothing his fear, his pain. Johnny returned to the fence, staring out across the auto graveyard, holding that fragment of Laura close inside him.

★   ★   ★

Randon stared at the production designer in disbelief. 'What do you mean, none of them will do?'

Evans waved a hand at the fan of Polaroids he held out before him. 'They aren't what I was looking for.'

Randon turned to examine the photos again. 'They're late-model cars, all with extensive damage.' Randon gestured to one shot. 'Look at this one — bashed front end, shattered windshield. It's what you asked for.'

'But now that I see them, they're not what I want,' the production designer said adamantly. He plopped the stack of photos in Randon's hand. 'I want older cars. Find them.'

Randon crumpled the stiff squares, suppressing the urge to shove the handful down Evans's throat. 'I thought we were on a tight schedule.'

The diminutive man fluttered his fingers. 'Art can't be rushed.' Then he minced off toward the grove of black oaks where the cinematographer had set up a late afternoon shot.

Randon glared after Evans darkly, then turned on his booted heel toward his truck. Along the way, he tossed the ruined photos into a trash can near the folding aluminum tables the assistant director had arranged.

Randon dug into his pocket for his keys, longing for a cold shower at the tatty motor inn down in Placerville.

'Hey, Randon.'

He whirled to see the assistant director stepping down from one of the trailers parked at the location. Melinda tossed back a hank of shoulder-length light brown hair, and made her way sinuously toward him.

The A.D. had made it clear from the moment Randon had arrived that she was ready for action. No doubt she was the reason Joe, his stuntman buddy down in L.A., had recommended Randon for this job. Randon had heard Joe's wife nag him to hook Randon up with this female friend or that. Melinda must be their latest choice.

'Where ya headed?' Melinda all but batted her blue eyes at him.

She was willowy, her slender waist begging a man to span it with his hands. Her breasts crowded the V-necked knit top she wore, drawing his eyes to her deep cleavage. The scent of musk wafted from her warm flesh, suggesting tangled sheets and enthusiastic sex.

'To the motel,' he told her.

Her eyes lit up, somehow reading an invitation in his neutral tone. 'I'm done for the day. We could have dinner.'

He smiled, shaking his head. 'I'm pretty beat, Melinda. I thought I'd grab a burger and eat it in my room.'

She took a step closer, her musk scent growing thicker. The smudge of blue on her eyelids seemed to weigh them down.

'So we grab two burgers,' she murmured, 'and we eat them together.'

He gazed down at her, willing a yes from his lips. He had only to accept her offer and for the next few hours he could chase away the emptiness, distracted by Melinda's lithe, willing body. He tried to picture Melinda's long legs wrapped around him, her lush lips pressed against his flesh. But instead he saw Kyra, her hazel eyes meeting his, angry one moment, clouded with sadness the next. The fragility of her, sheathed in steel.

He retreated, out of reach of Melinda's cloying scent. 'I don't think so, sugar. Maybe some other time.' He turned and continued on to his truck.

'Then I'll see you tomorrow?' she called out after him.

He waved without turning; the ambiguous gesture could mean anything she wanted it to. If he didn't look at her, he wouldn't see if it were anger or hurt in her face. He'd damn well caused the latter enough times.

He started the truck and gunned away

41

from the location site, guiding the truck toward Highway 50. The glare of the setting sun nearly opaqued his windshield as he headed west toward Placerville, driving a needle of brilliance between his eyes. Setting his teeth against the pain, he focused on his own spreading loneliness, the familiar sense of isolation. But despite all efforts to the contrary, Kyra's sweet, wary face intruded in his mind's eye, until the blast of the sun was a welcome distraction.

★ ★ ★

Kyra leaned her elbows on the top of the washer and buried her face in her hands. She tried to ignore the water lapping around her stocking feet and spreading across the floor, but the soapy wetness oozed between her toes and sopped her socks. The grinding roar of the washing machine finishing its spin cycle punctuated her despair, and she bowed her head lower to rest it on her arms.

A flooded floor wasn't the end of the world. But teamed with a failing refrigerator and a stove with only two working burners, it was all just too much to bear. She'd kissed the microwave good-bye three weeks ago and had resigned herself to giving up toast when the toaster went, but damn, she needed a working washer.

A questioning yowl brought her gaze slanting to the left. Her cat, Bubba, speared her with his golden gaze, the expression in his jet-black face unsympathetic. There were issues of greater import than washing machines in Bubba's universe — crunchies in a food dish, gophers in the yard, a soft nest on the bed. An empty, lonely bed. Unbidden, an image seeped into her mind of Randon Bolton stretched out between her sheets. He would dominate the narrow double bed she'd purchased to replace the one she'd slept in with the Snake. If comfort could be doled out by size alone, Randon Bolton would certainly provide a generous measure.

Dangerous, dangerous thoughts. She slept alone because that was the way she wanted it, to avoid another disaster like her marriage. She was just feeling down over the series of catastrophes plaguing her, vulnerable to trouble in a well-muscled six-foot-plus package.

Kyra lifted her head and gazed out the window into the backyard. The sun neared the horizon, but still hung stubbornly above it, unwilling to release its heated grip on the Sacramento Valley and the nearby foothills. The air-conditioning in Kyra's tiny house was thankfully new; its efforts coupled with the shade of the massive oaks in her yard lent a blessed coolness.

So at least she could mop the laundry room floor in relative comfort. Kyra sloshed across the floor and grabbed the sponge mop and bucket. Leaning the mop against the washer, she peeled off her socks and tossed them on top of the dryer.

The sun had finally surrendered to the early evening dusk by the time Kyra finished swabbing the laundry room. After putting the mop away, she pried the sodden load of clothes from the washer and tossed them into the dryer. At least the machine had completed its rinse cycle, forestalling a trip to the Laundromat for a day.

She filled a pot with water and set it on a back burner, one of the two that still worked. She'd throw in some rotini after she'd showered and toss it together with some veggies for a pasta salad.

But when she padded out barefoot, skin damp, hair dripping from her shower, the water still hadn't boiled. Cinching her robe tighter, Kyra held her hand close to the burner under the pot. The black coil was stone cold.

With a sense of inevitability, Kyra turned the knob for what should have been the last operating burner. She waited a full five minutes, her hand hovering over the coil. Maybe she'd lost her sense of touch, she thought whimsically as the black metal refused to yield heat. Then with a growl that sent Bubba skittering out his kitty door, Kyra snapped both knobs into the off position and stomped off to her bedroom. Shedding her robe and tossing it onto the bed, she dug a tank top and shorts from the dresser.

Kyra tugged on her clothes, then grabbed her purse as she headed out the door. If she couldn't scrape together enough money for dinner at Mama D's, she'd beg Mama for a meal. Damned if she'd eat half-gone milk on Frosted Flakes another night.

* * *

Randon hung up the phone, dropping the receiver from nerveless fingers. He lay back on the lumpy mattress of the motel bed and stared at the wall of the tiny, shabby room. A weighted fist had taken hold of his middle, each finger etched with the words his brother-in-law Tom had just spoken. *Her test came back positive.*

He wanted to roar at the four walls of his room, to wrench the damn phone from its cord and slam it against the floor. He wanted to erase those words, to force them back into

45

Tom's throat, to turn the truth of them into a lie. *God, how could You?* No answer from that quarter. Randon didn't doubt the Almighty's existence, he only recognized that God's priorities didn't include the life and sorrows of a worthless wanderer. But Rachelle . . . Rachelle was another matter.

Randon scrubbed at his face, surprised at the moisture wetting his cheeks. Since he damn well didn't cry, it had to be something left from his shower or sweat from the stifling warmth of the room. Not tears. He couldn't let it be tears.

Rolling off the bed, he hit the floor with his bare feet and prowled the four square feet of empty space beside the bed. A scream of rage bubbled in his chest, clawing to get out, goading him to put a fist through a wall. He hadn't trashed a motel room in years, and back then it was from sheer drunken idiocy, not this creature of fear that had sprung into life inside him with those five simple words. *Her test came back positive.*

He had to get out. He looked around him frantically for his clothes. He scrambled into a worn T-shirt, shoved bare feet into boots, grabbed up his wallet. He didn't bother with the keys to his pickup. He had to walk, to work off this terror blooming inside for Rachelle.

As he strode across the parking lot of the motel toward Broadway, he forced back the panic, the urge to run. He would keep himself under control. He would walk from one end of town to the other, once, twice, three times if necessary. And he'd beat back the five little demons that danced at his heels. *Her test came back positive*. Randon swallowed a groan and walked a little faster.

★ ★ ★

Kyra mopped up the last of the gravy on her plate with a bit of roll and popped it into her mouth. Sliding her plate across the counter, she leaned back in her seat with a sigh and smiled up at Mama.

'Fabulous,' she told the narrow-faced woman behind the counter, 'as usual.'

Mama nodded her miserly approval, then slapped down the check next to Kyra's plate. 'Pie comes with the special,' the older woman said, one hand on a cocked hip.

Kyra flicked a glance at the specials board; it said no such thing. Mama kept her sharp gaze riveted on Kyra, daring her to contradict.

Kyra just smiled. 'I'd love some pie. Apple if you've got it.'

Mama gave her a look before turning back

to the pie case. Of course they had apple. Didn't Mama's brother own an orchard up in Apple Hill? Mama even put apples in the pancakes.

'What kinda ice cream you want on it?' Mama asked, a plate of warm apple pie in one hand, ice cream scoop in the other. As if Kyra had a choice. 'Vanilla.' Mama mounded on the ice cream, then set the plate and a fork before Kyra. Kyra picked up her fork and contemplated the golden brown pie, the puddle of melted ice cream. An emotion welled up in her, gratitude for Mama's kindness, so sparingly doled out. The small gesture brought back to Kyra memories of her own father, a quiet, gentle man whose love and caring she lost the day she married the Snake.

She shook off the ridiculous, incipient tears, and forked up a big bite of pie. The flavor of the delicate pastry coupled with creamy vanilla exploded in her mouth. She closed her eyes, reveling in the tastes and textures.

'Boyfriend of yours?' Mama asked, intruding on Kyra's sybaritic pleasure.

'What?' Kyra's head bobbed up, she looked around her. 'Who?'

Mama pointed out toward the street. 'The one at the window. The long, tall one lookin' like a lost puppy.'

Kyra swiveled her seat, turning toward the front of the coffee shop. Looked past the hanging plastic ferns, the other customers.

And saw Randon, at the window. Staring in at her like a lost soul who's just found salvation.

★   ★   ★

Laura drifted between the rows of cars, gazing up at the black arch of sky littered with stars. A dull ache fisted in her chest, never mind that she was long dead, that there was nothing left of her body to pain her. Johnny was lost to her, and she was alone in this ugly, alien place. The thought of a second night without him was unbearable.

She traced the hood of the car next to her with her fingertips, watched her hand pass palm deep into the solid metal as she moved. A silvery glitter followed the path of her touch, skittering off the hood. *Johnny*, her heart cried, *Johnny!*

She continued down the row of cars, looking inside each one. The other times she and Johnny had come back, they'd returned to that spot on the river, to the tomb of mud and trash and deadfall. They'd never had a chance to see how the world had moved on in the years since their deaths. The changes were beyond her imaginings. The strange lines of the cars, the gadgets displayed across their dashboards. People didn't even dress the same. How many years had passed? *Johnny!*

She tipped her head up, looking around her. Where was the Fairlane now? Much as she'd tried, she'd found it hard to stay close to the car. Something always seemed to force her away. Back to the man. He was tall, and he wore a cowboy hat. She supposed he was handsome, for an old guy, but half the time he scowled as if he were angry about something. It especially seemed to make him mad when she drew near him. Laura suspected the man could sense her presence and he didn't like the feeling. *Was he the one?*

He was gone now, along with all the others that had wandered the junk yard. Her only company was a restless German shepherd that looked like Rin-Tin-Tin. And the dog wouldn't go near her.

She had to find the Fairlane again. If she couldn't be with Johnny, she needed the comfort of something she knew, something real. She could curl up on the seat and dream of him, picture his sweet kisses, the feel of his hand in hers.

Looking around her again to get her

bearings, she chose a direction that seemed right and threaded her way between the cars. A breeze sighed across the yard and she pretended it sifted through her long blonde hair, lifting the strands off her neck. Just like Johnny's touch, right before he kissed her.

When she saw the Ford, she started to run, afraid some unseen hand would snatch her away, toss her to the other side of the yard. But each step brought her nearer, until she could see the glare of moonlight off the windshield and the brilliant white of the hood. Now, rather than push her away, the car seemed to pull her to it, like the welcoming porch light of home.

Laughing with excitement, Laura rounded the front of the car to the passenger side. She grabbed at the door handle, tugging the shiny metal to open it, but her fingers slithered through the handle in a shower of sparks.

She stared at the door in frustration, wondering if she'd have to climb through the broken window to get inside. Then the realization came to her in a shock of awareness.

She didn't have to open the door.

She gazed down at the car, the windshield opaque in the moonlight. Moving tentatively, Laura reached out, fingertips brushing the stark white. Ignoring the glittering display, she pushed her hand farther, knuckle deep in the door, wrist deep. She thrust her arm in up to the elbow.

When she paused, the gentle tingle grew sharper, more painful. So she continued to press herself through the car, shifting her body as she would if she'd been climbing through an open door. She wondered fancifully if her bottom would slip through the car seat when she tried to sit, if she would find herself dropping onto the rough gravel beneath the Fairlane. But as soon as she'd passed inside, the car seemed to solidify around her. The vinyl seat bounced as she dropped onto it, and her hand banged the inside of the door when she reached out in reaction.

She leaned against the seat in satisfaction, closing her eyes. She lifted her chest as if taking a breath, imagining Johnny's scent in her nostrils. Then she let it out in a sigh.

'*Laura*.'

She froze at the sound, hoping against hope. Then she opened her eyes and turned slowly so as not to frighten away a miracle. She screamed in jubilation. There was Johnny, big as life, sitting on the seat beside her.

3

The naked need in Randon's face frightened Kyra, and she swallowed back the urge to bolt. It wasn't a sexual need; Kyra had been stared at, leered at enough times to recognize the difference. This was stark vulnerability she saw in Randon, made all the more poignant by the power and strength of the man.

If Kyra's head said to run, her heart had other plans. Without thinking, she'd risen from the vinyl stool and moved quickly through the cafe, keeping her gaze locked on his. He broke that intimacy only once, to glance up, then down Main Street as if seeking an escape. Hurrying through the glass door of Mama D's, Kyra closed the distance between them.

He didn't give up the nervous energy easily. His arms tensed stiffly at his sides, his hands fisting, then releasing. Despair burned in his eyes, and a yearning hope for comfort. For an instant, Kyra thought he would pull her into his arms and hold her against his heart. She swayed closer to him in response. Then he shifted, turning his body slightly away, and the moment passed.

'Were you hungry?' she asked to cover up the awkwardness. 'Did you want something to eat?'

He stared at her as if she'd spoken Greek. 'What? Oh. I already ate.' He scrubbed at his face. 'No, I didn't. Lord, I don't know.'

Moving slowly, as if coaxing a chary wolf to accept her hand, she took his arm. 'Mama's got a great special tonight.' She urged him back inside the cafe.

As she wended her way through the crowded tables, toward the counter, she saw Mama had staked out a booth for them. Kyra changed directions and seated herself at the booth; Randon lowered himself onto the bench opposite her. He picked up the menu Mama placed before him and opened it, but Kyra could see he didn't read it.

'Just bring him the special.' Kyra smiled up at the scowl of sympathy on Mama's face. 'I'll have the rest of my pie.'

Mama plucked the menu from Randon's fingers and flounced off, barking out the order to the cook. Kyra gazed up at Randon, into his now shuttered gray eyes and waited for him to speak. As if he would. He stared down at his work-hardened hands as if they held a desperately needed answer, if only he could interpret it. Kyra realized that any conversation between them would have to be initiated by her.

'Want to tell me about it?' she asked.

His eyes swung up to meet hers. 'What?'

Kyra shrugged. 'Whatever it is that's bothering you.'

His spoke quickly. 'Nothing.'

'Could have fooled me,' she said mildly. 'You look like a man pursued.'

He took in a sharp breath, then as swiftly concealed whatever strong emotion drove him. 'Nobody's chasing me.' But the words didn't quite ring true.

A sudden thought occurred to Kyra — what if Randon were in trouble? He could be on the run from the law for all she knew. He didn't have the sleazy quality of the creeps that tried to sell her stolen cars. But hell, hadn't the Snake taught her that even the most charming men could be jerks?

Kyra glanced across the cafe at the sheriff's deputy seated three tables over. 'Then you wouldn't mind if I stepped over there and had a word with Jack.'

Randon spared the deputy a quick look. 'I'm not in trouble with the law, Kyra.'

He sounded so tired, so empty, that guilt lanced Kyra for even suggesting it. 'Then what?' she said softly.

He dragged in another breath, his hands

55

shifting on the table like two wrestlers. He opened his mouth, seemed to urge the words out. Then the emotions in his eyes muted. 'The production designer didn't like any of my choices,' he said.

That wasn't what he'd intended to say. He knew she knew it, too; she could see it in the look in his eyes, as if he dared her to object. She wanted to, wanted to pull the secret agony out of him, to share it, to soothe it. But she had no right to. 'Why not?' she asked, keeping a neutral tone.

Randon shook his head, his smile rueful. 'The man's an idiot. He doesn't know what he wants. But he's the boss and he doesn't need a reason to say no.'

'You're coming back to the yard, then.' Kyra wasn't sure if that was good or bad. 'To scout out some more?'

'Tomorrow,' he said. 'First thing.'

He leaned back as Mama arrived with his dinner. The sour-faced woman had stacked a double serving of meat loaf on Randon's plate and mounded a mountain of gravy-flooded mashed potatoes. She slid a newly cut piece of apple pie in front of Kyra, the warm pastry crowned with a fresh scoop of ice cream.

Randon dug into his meal, eating rapidly as if surprised to discover he was hungry. Kyra savored her pie, her sensual enjoyment of the dessert sharpened by Randon's presence across the table. She pushed it aside when she simply couldn't take another bite. She sat back, eyeing Randon. 'I'll have to pull the tags on that first set you chose. I'd marked them all as sold.'

He stroked the roll across his plate, soaking up the gravy. 'I can do that. I'll pull them as I go.'

She nodded, mesmerized by the motions of his strong hands, by the sight of his tongue licking a bit of gravy off his thumb. He caught her watching him and he stilled, then took one last deliberate taste of his finger.

She felt the stroke of his tongue on her own flesh as surely as if he had touched her. She should wrench her eyes away from his, should break the sudden, exquisite intimacy of their visual contact. But she kept her gaze steady on him, her own tongue stealing out to wet her lips as she ached to have him do.

His eyes darkened, their gray depths turning stormy. A sudden, intense image invaded her senses — Randon making love to her, his hands on her body, slow and thorough instead of rushed and impatient as the Snake had been. Her pleasure intensifying under those competent hands, his fingers strumming her nerve endings to a fevered

57

explosion of sensation.

He smiled, his mouth stretching in a sensuous curve. God, he knew every thought that danced through her head, could see every image. The heat of mortification washed over her cheeks and she tore her gaze from his to look away, anywhere but at him.

Her shaky, skittering hand banged against the dish of apple pie. 'Would you like the rest?' She gave the bowl a nervous shove toward him.

At that moment, Mama arrived with a huge plate of pie à la mode. Whisking away Randon's dirty dishes, she plopped the pie before him, then stomped off.

'Guess you don't need it,' Kyra muttered, her hand sneaking out to pull back her offering.

He laid his hand on hers to stop her. 'I might want both.'

She fixed her eyes on his fingers crossing the back of her hand. She willed them to move, to break contact, to stroke her flesh. She chanced a look up at him and he seemed as stunned as she at the feel of skin against skin.

He snatched his hand away, turned his attention to the pie. 'Looks good,' he said, shoveling a forkful into his mouth.

Kyra removed her hands to the safety of

her lap. Her thoughts tumbled over each other like mismatched socks in a dryer. She tried to grasp one, struggling for something to say, some safe topic of conversation.

A picture of ice cream pink and white formed in her mind, and a chill chased down her spine. 'Did you see the Fairlane?' she blurted.

Randon slowly lifted his gaze from his pie. 'Fairlane?'

'The '55 Ford in the back of the yard.' She shivered, remembering the icy feel of the car. 'It's a two-tone, pink and white.'

His gaze turned wary. 'What about it?'

'Have you seen it?' Kyra asked.

'I have,' he said carefully.

'That production guy you're working for might like it,' Kyra suggested.

'No,' Randon said flatly.

'But, it's a classic.'

Randon dropped his fork on his empty dessert dish. 'He won't want it.'

'Why not?' His adamant attitude puzzled her, as did her own urgency in mentioning the car.

'Because it isn't right for him.' He swiped at his mouth with a napkin, as if to close off the line of conversation.

'But how would you know unless you showed it to him?' Kyra persisted.

'I know. He won't want it.'

He rose, reaching in his back pocket for his wallet. Mama arrived at that moment to hand him a check.

Kyra scooted from the booth. 'Where's mine?' she asked Mama.

'I don't do separate checks,' Mama huffed, although Kyra knew she did when it suited her.

Kyra turned to Randon. 'What do I owe you?'

'My treat.' He slapped a generous tip down on the table, eliciting a rare smile from Mama.

Kyra followed him to the register. 'I can't let you pay for me.'

'You don't have a choice.' He handed Mama a twenty.

Anger simmered at the back of Kyra's throat. 'I want to pay my part of the check.'

'Too bad,' he said, taking back his change.

Kyra gave Mama an exasperated look, but she was beaming at Randon, her homely face lit up like a Christmas tree. Kyra would receive no help from that quarter.

'I don't want you paying for my dinner,' Kyra gritted out.

He stuffed his wallet into his back pocket, drawing Kyra's eye to his well-muscled backside. 'Then you buy next time.'

It took a moment for his words to sink in, then she popped her gaze up to his face. 'I can't afford to take you out to dinner.'

He laid his fingertips lightly on her shoulders, turning her toward the exit. 'Then cook for me.'

Kyra spun to face him. 'What?'

'Make me dinner.' He urged her out onto the sidewalk. The sultry air closed in on them like a caress. 'It's been too damn long since I had a home-cooked meal.'

Kyra tossed her head, tried to shake the feel of him from her shoulders. 'I can't,' she said, tipping her chin up.

He thrust his fingers into his thick, curly hair, and she realized for the first time that he wasn't wearing his cowboy hat. He hesitated, then glanced inside the cafe as if wondering if he'd left it there. Then he seemed to remember where and why he'd left the hat, and a flash of pain flared in his eyes, then was gone.

He shoved his hands into the front pockets of his jeans. 'You can't cook?'

She lifted her chin higher. 'Of course I can cook. I just can't cook for you.'

He cocked an eyebrow at her. 'Can't or won't?'

'Can't,' she said emphatically, glad for an excuse. 'My stove is broken.'

The beginnings of a smile curved the corners of his mouth. He thought she was lying!

'It *is*,' she asserted, not sure why she even cared if he believed her. 'None of the burners work.'

'What about the oven?'

'I gave up on the oven the day I put in biscuits and ended up with charcoal. Something wrong with the thermostat.'

'Microwave?'

'Dead.'

'Toaster?' he asked hopefully.

She didn't bother answering, just tipped her thumb down. His faint smile deepened, creasing two dimples in his cheeks.

Good Lord, dimples. The Snake had had dimples.

Although . . . Kyra gazed up at Randon, at the light of humor in his steel-gray eyes. The Snake had only smiled when he'd wanted something from her. Somehow Randon's dimples seemed so much more honest.

'I'm sorry,' she said, not exactly sure what she regretted. 'I can't cook you a meal. But thank you for dinner,' she added belatedly.

His hand went up to his head again, as if to take off the hat he'd forgotten. He dropped his hand. 'Can I walk you to your car?'

She gestured to the yellow Hornet on the

opposite side of Main. 'It's just across the street.'

He nodded, took a step back from her. 'See you tomorrow, then.'

She glanced up and down Main. 'Can I drop you at your truck?'

He shook his head. 'I walked down from the motel.'

'Then I could drive you there.'

'I . . . ' He looked back over his shoulder, and Kyra got the sense again of a man seeking escape. When he turned back to her his expression was grim. 'Thank you, but I'd rather walk.'

'Okay,' she said. 'See you tomorrow, then.'

She headed up Main to the crosswalk, then made her way across the street and to the Hornet. As she tugged open the car door, she looked back at him. He hadn't moved, just stood staring at the sidewalk.

Kyra started the reluctant Hornet, pulled out and guided the car up Main Street. She made a U-turn at the Bell Tower, then doubled back toward home. As she drove slowly past Mama D's, she was surprised to see Randon still there. She raised a hand to wave, then dropped it when she saw his face. His head bowed, gaze fixed on the sidewalk, one emotion stood out starkly. Grief.

Johnny gazed at Laura, drank in the sight of her. Her blue eyes glowed in the shadows cast by a flood light that towered above the junk yard. The sweep of her pale blonde hair tantalized him, made his fingers itch to touch her.

With a sense of inevitability, Johnny reached for her across the car as he always did. Again his fingers hit the barrier, again a shower of sparks glittered between them.

But different.

He pulled his hand back, then tested again. Laura followed the motion of his hand, her eyes fixed on the streaks of light.

She glanced up at his face. *'What is it, Johnny?'*

He didn't want to say yet, afraid he'd imagined the change. *'Feel it. From your side.'*

Her small, slender hand moved to mirror his. Her brow furrowed as she mimicked his movements, the tip of her tongue stealing out as she concentrated. The sight of her pink tongue blew away Johnny's focus with the power of a hand grenade. Memories of Laura's touch surged into his mind, burning him as surely as it had his living flesh.

'It feels different,' she finally said, dragging

Johnny back from a thousand wayward fantasies.

'How?' He wanted to know if her perception was the same as his.

She pursed her lips slightly, threatening to distract Johnny again. Then her eyes widened. '*Softer. Thinner. Almost as if . . .* '

He put a finger to his lips to stop the words. '*Let's try,*' he told her.

She nodded. Then, her fingers trembling, she pushed against the barrier from her side as he did from his. The glitter of sparks became more intense, brighter, flaring into fire. He could feel the heat as if he still had skin and bones and nerves to feel. He became afraid for Laura as the pain shone sharply in her face, as she pushed and pushed and pushed from her side of the barrier. *He could feel her fingers!*

Just for an instant, then he shouted, '*Stop!*' as the phantom tears stood out in Laura's eyes. She snatched back her hand and fell back against the car door, cradling her arm.

She tipped her head up to him. '*I felt you,*' she whispered.

'*Me, too.*' He rubbed away the scalding heat.

'*But it hurt,*' she scraped out, and the words knifed at Johnny's heart.

He swallowed hard, fixing his gaze with hers. *'We might have to do it again. If we ever want to be together.'*

She hesitated, then she gave him a small nod. *'I want to be with you, Johnny.'*

An agony of emotions roiled in him, a phenomenon he'd never understood. He was *dead*, damn it! How could he feel, how could he hurt? How could he love? And yet that last emotion, the miracle of loving Laura, and holding her heart in return, was worth any trial, any torture. Except that of seeing her hurt.

She sat with head bowed now, still nursing the ethereal pain in her hand. Her silver-gold ponytail lay against her pale throat, shining in the lamplight. Gleaming tears coursed down her cheeks.

He couldn't bear her tears, his inability to soothe them. He tore his gaze away, to look out over the phantasmagoric shapes of the junkyard, half lit by the series of flood lights. *'I guess we have another chance.'*

She swiped at her face. *'It'll work out this time. I'm sure of it.'*

He tried to share her hope, but the weight of their imprisonment squeezed it out of him. *'Did you find someone?'*

'A man,' she said. *'Kind of a cowboy.'*

He nodded. *'And I found a woman.'*

'They're the ones, Johnny. The ones meant to help us.'

Doubt swamped him. 'I don't know, Laura.'

She tipped her face up to his, tears threatening to gather again. 'It has to be, Johnny. God couldn't be so cruel to keep bringing us back, to give us hope — '

'Where was God when we died?' Johnny asked savagely. 'Where has He been all these years when we've been trapped in the in-between, kept apart from one another?'

'I don't know, Johnny, I don't know,' she said softly. 'But I have to believe.'

Johnny tried to hold onto his anger, but in the face of Laura's hope, he couldn't. 'Then I'll believe, too.'

Laura chewed on her lower lip, reminding Johnny of a long-gone moment of passion, when his own teeth grazed her lip. His heart contracted.

She swung her head up to look at him. 'We have to get their attention. Find a way to talk to them.'

'But how?'

Laura's eyes snapped with impatience. 'I don't know, Johnny. We'll figure out a way. Are you going along, or are you going to fight me on this?'

If Johnny hated seeing Laura hurt, he

absolutely loathed arousing her ire. 'Whatever you say, Laura,' he said tamely, eliciting a suspicious glance from her. He smiled innocently.

After a moment's scrutiny, she turned to gaze out toward the East, where the faintest blush of dawn painted the horizon. 'I don't know when we'll have a chance to — '

The answer to her unfinished question came sooner than she might have expected. Because as the sun eased above the horizon, the Fairlane's interior grew dimmer. Laura faded along with the car. When Johnny looked down at his own self, he too became insubstantial. Until he found himself standing again in the junkyard, alone, facing a new day.

★   ★   ★

She really wasn't watching for him. Kyra sat rigidly upright as she signed the next check in her register, then neatly tore it from the two others on the page. As she stuffed the check into the return envelope, she resisted the urge to rise from her desk, step into the hall, and search outside for Randon. She knew he was here. Trish had announced his arrival when she'd brought Kyra a cup of coffee two hours ago. Kyra assumed he was still here, roaming the wrecking yard in the noonday heat, swinging the Polaroid at the end of its strap as he searched for just the right cars.

She should be outside as well, inventorying the three new wrecks Jackson had purchased yesterday. She'd also intended to supervise the transfer of several cars from the auxiliary lot to the main yard. Not to mention her providing an extra pair of eyes to prevent the theft of small parts off the cars. She didn't like to think of how much inventory 'walked out' each day. But still she remained in her office, proving to herself that she didn't need to see Randon. She'd be just as happy if they didn't cross paths at all today. Wouldn't she be?

Somehow, she'd risen to her feet and had walked to the door of her office. With an impatient sigh, she returned to her desk and to the task of paying her bills. Forcing herself to focus, she worked through the bill-paying process with meticulous care, ignoring the distraction of her fertile imagination.

An hour later, a neat stack of paid bills lay alongside her checkbook with its near-zero balance. She held a fan of six more envelopes in her hand and performed some mental arithmetic on the past due amounts. They totaled to a staggering sum. She flipped through them, despairing over the mounting finance charges, feeling the weight of her financial instability heavy on her shoulders.

A month ago she'd contacted all her creditors, the ones she'd had no hope of paying in full, and offered them a token, good-faith sum each month. All had agreed except one — the lowdown, pitiless company that had extended a half-dozen loans at heart-stopping interest rates to the Snake during their marriage.

Kyra rubbed at the furrows between her brows, lines put there by eight years of marriage to a compulsive gambler. She had to find a way to pay off the loans. If she lost the business — it didn't bear thinking about. Her employees counted on their weekly paycheck — Jackson to support his grandkids, Trish for college, Mario to send funds to his family in Mexico. There had to be a way . . .

Her thoughts strayed back to Randon. She couldn't put off going outside any longer. She had a clipboard stacked high with state environmental forms that needed her attention. She rose, stripping off the ratty sweater she'd donned in defense of the icy cold of the peripatetic swamp cooler. Tugging the straps of her teal tank top over her bra straps, she scooped up the clipboard and a pen and pushed open the door to her office.

Head down as she strode down the hall

toward the exit, she saw the cowboy boots an instant before she collided with their wearer. Clipboard clutched to her chest like a barrier, the muscles of Randon's lean belly pressed against the back of her arm fleetingly before she retreated again.

'What do you want?' she asked him, the jangling of her nerve endings making her impatient.

He lifted his hat from his head and scooped back the sweaty brown curls. 'To talk to you,' he said, replacing the hat.

'What about?' She snapped out the words, knowing she was being rude, but it seemed the only self-defense she had.

He seemed to see through her brusqueness. He smiled, his mouth stretching into an appealing grin. 'About your problems.'

For a brief moment, she thought he referred to her financial situation and anger flared that he had somehow discovered her plight. Then she realized the ridiculousness of that notion and she tamped back her fury.

'What problems would those be?' she asked.

He hefted the ubiquitous camera, tossing it lightly from hand to hand. 'Your broken stove. And the toaster. The microwave is out of my league, though.'

She narrowed her gaze on him. 'What are

71

you talking about?'

He turned to lean against the wall, cocking one booted foot behind him. 'I'm offering to fix them. I have a toolbox in the truck. You throw together a salad and I'll spring for pizza. I can fix the stove after dinner.'

Good God, this was a gift from heaven! But she couldn't possibly accept. 'Look, I appreciate the offer, but — '

'Don't say no,' he cut in. 'You'd be doing me a favor.'

She grew suspicious again. 'What favor would that be?'

He broadened his smile. 'The chance to eat somewhere other than a motel room or a restaurant. A place to kick back and watch a little T.V. after dinner.'

'And after you fix the stove and you watch T.V.?' she asked.

'I leave,' he assured her. 'Go back to my lonely motel room.'

She ought to say no. She ought to politely decline, fabricate a story of how she'd lined up a repairman for later in the week. She didn't need him to solve her problems. And yet . . . She gazed up at him, at his rough, yet appealing face, his compelling gray eyes. Those eyes were bright with humor, but grief lingered behind the lightness, sadness that tugged at Kyra's heart. And she couldn't say no. 'I'd appreciate your help.'

Emotions flickered in his eyes — relief and something else she couldn't quite put a finger on. Then he dipped his head down to his booted toes. 'Six o'clock okay?' he asked.

She thought quickly. Jackson could stay the extra hour to close up so she could get out of here in time to shower and change . . .

'Six would be perfect,' she said. Tearing a corner off one of the forms on her clipboard, she scribbled her address.

He took the scrap of paper then turned away, camera tucked under his arm. Kyra watched him amble across the yard, her gaze fixed shamelessly on his narrow hips and broad shoulders. She felt foolish and giddy and happy all at once.

She was grinning like an idiot, not even sure why the thought of a man — this man — coming to dinner delighted her so. Maybe because it was a step outside herself, a step outside her life and her problems.

She gripped the clipboard more tightly, and the unyielding edge of the pressboard nudged her back toward reality. This wasn't a fairy tale, she reminded herself, and Randon Bolton was no hero. She'd have her dinner with him, have an hour or two of adult conversation, then she'd escort him back out of her life.

Her heart resting heavily again in her chest, she moved down the hall toward the exit. Two steps into the glaring afternoon sunshine, the heat dropped onto her shoulders like a fiery blanket.

★ ★ ★

Randon struggled to contain a smile. *She said yes!* Why it pleased him so damn much, he hadn't a clue. Nor why a thirty-four-year-old man like him should feel like a teenager anticipating his first date. It wasn't even a date, for God's sake. He raised the Polaroid to capture the image of an '89 Accord with a buckled front end, then cut across the row of Hondas toward the back of the lot. He'd taken twenty shots; surely there would be ten amongst them that would satisfy the production designer.

Randon fingered the third packet of film he had tucked into the back pocket of his jeans. The mid-afternoon sun blasted down, its glare sending brilliant fire along the bits of chrome trim on each car. A sensible person would pack it in for the day and head for shade. And yet . . . He gazed across the wrecking yard until he could make out the figure of Kyra moving among the cars. He would see her tonight, in only a handful of hours, yet he was loath to leave her.

He tugged the packet of film from his pocket and loaded it into the camera. He'd make one last sweep along the back fence amongst the older cars and see if he could find something really eye-catching. Although, he thought as his gaze strayed again to Kyra, there was nothing in the wrecking yard as eye-catching as her.

He skirted a last row of cars and reached the chain-link fence that separated the lot from the empty fields beyond. He looked up along the fence, then down. And felt it again. Chill fingers dancing up his spine, brushing his cheeks. Just like yesterday, but even stronger. A heat-induced mirage, that's all it was. He tried to ignore the feeling as he had before, shrugging off the sensation of coolness. He threw back his shoulders, casting off the illusory touch as he would an unwelcome hand. Gooseflesh raised on his arms, prickled up the back of his neck. Confused and angry, he turned, looking around for the source of his unreasonable fear, searching for an answer.

His gaze fell on the '55 Ford Fairlane just beyond him. The cold closed tightly around him, constricted frigidly in his gut. A girl sat on the hood of the Fairlane, chin in hand, elbow on her knee, her vivid blue eyes fixed on Randon.

4

Randon gaped at the impish teenage girl
smiling at him from the Fairlane's hood. Her
fingers drummed along her chin as if from
barely suppressed excitement, and her legs
shifted beneath the froth of aqua skirt nearly
covering them. She sat up straighter,
propping her slender arms behind her on the
hood.

Randon narrowed his gaze on the girl.
'Who are you?' he asked, taking a step closer.

She smiled more broadly, tapping together
the toes of her bare feet. Then her mouth
moved, shaping a word.

'I can't hear you,' Randon said, annoyance
warring with the tickle of fear. 'I want to
know your name.'

Her mouth moved again, forming silent
syllables. She smiled again, and Randon
realized she was playing a game with him. An
irritating game.

'You don't belong in here,' he told her. 'If
you don't tell me your name and what you're
doing here, I'm calling the owner over.'

The girl pursed her lips and glared at him
crossly. Then she took a breath — at least it

seemed she did, although her chest didn't rise and Randon couldn't hear even a whisper of her breathing. Something like caution scraped at the back of Randon's neck.

She moved her lips again, in the slow exaggerated pace the hearing sometimes do with the deaf. He could almost read what the girl was trying to say, thought he saw the word 'my' and 'name.' She looked at him hopefully when she'd finished, pale blonde brows raised.

Randon shrugged, feeling guilty now for his irritation. Obviously, the girl was mute, unable to speak, although she knew how to shape the words.

Randon smiled apologetically. 'I'm sorry, I still don't understand.'

The girl's mouth tightened, vexation darkening her pretty features. Her toes tapped faster.

Randon slapped his pockets for a pencil, for a bit of paper. 'Maybe you could write down what you want to say.'

She shook her head, her blonde ponytail bobbing behind her. Randon could see the vitality of the young girl, her slim body nearly glowing with energy.

Then with a shock, Randon realized the girl *was* glowing, light lining her pale arms, haloing her head. She looked up at him beseechingly, then down at her nervous feet.

Except her feet were gone. Mouth open in shock, Randon stared down at the slender ankles edged in brilliant silver. The girl held her legs out before her, seeming more annoyed than frightened. As Randon watched, the line of light at her ankles moved up to encompass her calves, and they vanished along with the girl's feet.

The girl folded her arms over her chest in a huff of irritation, squirming on the car hood as the swirl of her skirt disappeared beneath her. The light hesitated at her waist, then moved on with a flourish, taking the folded arms with it. The blue eyes went last, their cerulean brilliance hanging on the air an instant before they flashed away.

Randon swayed in the blast of summer heat, his hat suddenly seeming much too tight. He tugged it off and scraped his fingers through his sweaty hair. When he brought his hand down, it trembled and he nearly dropped the hat when he tried to raise it to his head again.

Too much damn sun, that's what it was. Too much sun and too damn long without the comfort of a woman. The heat combined with his yearning for Kyra had conspired to make him crazy, to make him see impossible things. He hadn't really seen the girl, he had concocted her from sunshine and fantasy.

Randon swiped a hand across his face and backed away from the Fairlane. He kept his eyes anywhere but on the car. Last damn thing he wanted to see was the imprint of a young girl's behind in the dust on the hood.

With his back resolutely turned toward the Ford, Randon retraced his path to the exit of the wrecking yard. He forced himself to stop at the service window and give Jackson the ID numbers of the cars he'd photographed, just as he'd promised Kyra.

As he headed for his truck, Randon let thoughts of Kyra catch up with him again, wiping away the bizarre vision of the girl. His attention centered safely in his groin, Randon climbed into his truck and gunned out of the parking lot.

★   ★   ★

Kyra let the chill water of the shower wash over her, sighing as it cooled her overheated skin. She'd made it home in record time, dodging the worst of the Highway 50 rush hour traffic on the twists and turns of White Rock Road. Nevertheless, she had only twenty minutes to shower and dress before Randon arrived for their . . . For their what? Date? No, it couldn't be that. *Date* implied he interested her in a romantic way, which he most certainly did not. Their dinner? That sounded safe enough. Dinner in exchange for a favor, although since he was paying for the pizza, it didn't seem like a very fair exchange. Which could mean he'd expect something more. Something intimate. A kiss, a caress. Rough-gentle hands stroking sensitive flesh, trailing dark passion and heat —

Kyra twisted the shower faucet to a colder setting and gasped as even icier water drenched her. Her heart beat wildly, an aftermath of her straying thoughts coupled with the shock of cold water. Throwing back her head, she rinsed the last of the shampoo from her hair and turned off the shower. The hell with putting a label on tonight. She would eat dinner with the man, take advantage of his expertise at repair, fend off any unwanted advances and say goodnight. She didn't have to call it anything.

Kyra had just pulled the lettuce and tomatoes from the refrigerator when she heard the knock on the door. She clutched the head of iceberg and the bag of romas indecisively a moment before setting them on the counter. Wiping her hands on her denim shorts, she tucked her sleeveless shirt more securely into the waistband.

She should have blow-dried her hair. She

put a hand to the thick mass and felt only the slightest dampness. She rarely got the results she wanted when she blow-dried her hair, but she should have at least taken a stab at taming her recalcitrant hair.

When the knock sounded again, Kyra shook off her concerns for her hair and strode toward the door. This wasn't a date, for heaven's sake, it was just a . . . well, whatever it was it didn't matter what her hair looked like. If Randon Bolton didn't like how she looked, he could take his pizza and his tools and go back to his motel.

Kyra swung open the door. Randon stood on her porch, pizza box balanced in one hand, the other raised as if to knock again. A battered red metal toolbox rested beside him.

'Hi.' His gaze roamed her face. His perusal continued down the line of her throat, bringing back the heat she'd thought she'd left behind in the cold shower.

'Hello,' she said, stepping aside to let him in.

He stooped to pick up the toolbox, his gaze fixed on her shirt. Kyra resisted the urge to cross her arms over her chest, angry at his frank appraisal, at her swift reaction to it. She prayed he wouldn't see the pebbling of her nipples beneath the cotton fabric of the shirt and the silky nylon of her bra.

'What color is that?' he asked, eyes still on her shirt.

His unexpected question stopped Kyra in the act of shutting the front door. She felt the early evening heat seep in from the porch, pushing against the air conditioner's cold front.

She closed the door and turned away from him. Heading for the kitchen, she looked behind her, prompting him to follow.

'I don't know — aqua maybe?' She opened the oven so he could put the pizza inside.

He still seemed transfixed by the blue of her shirt. Frowning, he shook his head and looked at the open oven.

'I thought you said it didn't work.'

Kyra shrugged. 'It doesn't, but the pizza might stay warmer there while I make the salad.'

He dropped the flat cardboard square on the top rack and stepped back so she could close the oven door. Setting his toolbox to one side, he pulled off his cowboy hat. He leaned back against the counter, combing through his hair with his fingers. Then he set the hat aside on the counter.

Kyra turned her attention to the salad makings. She stripped the plastic wrapping from the lettuce and cored it. Laying the head in the sink, she ran water over it and the tomatoes, all the while conscious of him watching her.

She tried to will away the sense of awareness that tingled along her nerve endings. But his gaze on her seemed as palpable as a touch. She searched for something to say.

'Why did you ask about the color of my blouse?'

She heard him shift his feet. She tore the lettuce into chunks as she waited for his answer. More feet shifting. Finally, she looked expectantly over her shoulder. Whatever she might have anticipated in his face, it wasn't embarrassment. He looked down at his booted toes, then mumbled, 'Just wondering.'

Kyra eyed him, perplexed, suspicious. His awkwardness made him seem vulnerable, almost boyish. Never mind the well-muscled chest and broad shoulders, their all too tempting lines stretching the knit of his T-shirt advertising a Carson City feed store. In that moment, Randon seemed open to her in a way that both drew her and frightened her.

Then he pushed away from the counter and restlessly crossed the kitchen. His face seemed shuttered now, closed. 'Can I help you with anything?'

Kyra stared at him, wondering at the

transformation. 'You could get the dressing out of the fridge. There are a couple of bottles in the door.'

As she turned back to making the salad, she heard him rummaging through the refrigerator. 'How about these olives?' he asked holding up the can he'd found.

'Sure,' she told him, taking the olives from him. Her fingers brushed his, and she nearly dropped the can at the brief contact.

'Peppers?' he asked, brandishing a bottle of pepperoncini.

'Okay.' She took the bottle, more careful this time to avoid his fingers.

Pulling out a large glass bowl, she filled it with the torn lettuce. She drained the last of the liquid from the half-filled can of olives, then dumped them onto the lettuce. The sliced romas added a touch of brilliant red, and the pepperoncini garnished the top.

All the while she could feel the intensity of Randon's gaze. She'd had other men stare at her, their avid eyes stripping her of her clothes, their fantasies of what lay beneath clear in their faces. But if Randon's gaze stripped anything bare, it was her very soul.

Damn him. Kyra stomped across the kitchen and nearly slammed the salad bowl on the kitchen table. If Randon sensed her agitation, he didn't comment on it. He merely pulled the pizza from the oven and set it on the table beside the salad.

Kyra skirted him as she recrossed the kitchen to retrieve plates and silverware. She set the dishes on the table with a clatter, then returned to the refrigerator and wrenched it open.

'What do you want to drink?' she asked ungraciously. 'I have sodas, beer, water, milk — '

'I'll take a beer, if you don't mind,' he said mildly.

Kyra grabbed a can of beer and a Coke and delivered them to the table. She flicked a glance at him, saw puzzlement in his expression. No doubt he wondered at her rude behavior.

Kyra dragged in a deep, calming breath, berating herself for her ridiculous temper. Randon was here to help her; she owed him at least a modicum of courtesy.

She forced a more polite tone. 'Have a seat.'

But rather than sit, he pulled her chair out for her. Kyra's gaze fell on his large hand on the chair back, trying to remember the last time a man seated her before himself. Certainly the Snake had never done it, even before their marriage when he still seemed charming. She remembered only one man

85

— her father, when he took her to dinner to celebrate her sixteenth birthday.

Tears briefly tightened her throat as she lowered herself in the kitchen chair and scooted toward the table. She was acutely aware of Randon's hands on the chair back, his fingertips perilously close to her bare arms.

Then he moved to his own chair opposite her and sat down. He opened the pizza box and gestured for her to take a slice first. Tugging a fat wedge from the circle of pizza, she brought it to her plate, then retrieved the sausage bits she'd left behind.

Licking the last of the sausage from her fingers, she lifted her gaze to Randon. He sat motionless, his eyes fixed on her mouth. A compulsion washed over Kyra, to curl her tongue around her fingertip again, to watch him react. Then to brush that finger against his lip, to feel him taste her.

Heat rising in her cheeks, she lowered her eyes to her plate and gave her full attention to the pizza. She'd eaten nearly half of it, bite by methodical bite, before she chanced to look Randon's way again. She flushed at the sight of him holding out the salad bowl. He'd obviously called her name more than once; she could see it in his face.

She took the bowl from him and set it

down at her place. 'Good pizza,' she said, shoveling salad onto her plate.

'You seem to be enjoying it.' She heard a trace of humor in his tone.

She glanced up at him again as she reached for the bottle of salad dressing. 'How'd you do today at the yard?'

Something flickered in his eyes — alarm, or wariness. Then he smiled. 'Got another twenty shots. The production designer's bound to find ten he likes.'

Kyra nodded, relieved to have him finished and gone. And faintly disappointed at the lost opportunity to see what might have developed between them. She stabbed a bit of lettuce and tomato with her fork. 'Do you do much work for the movies?'

He swallowed a mouthful of pizza before he spoke, the motion of his brown throat entrancing. 'Did some work as an extra down in L.A. once — herding cattle in a western. Made friends with one of the stuntmen. He got me this job.'

Kyra wiped her hands on a napkin, then took a sip of Coke. 'Do you like it? The movie business?'

He shrugged. 'It's a job. It's easier than ranch work. But I miss the horses.' He tipped the can of beer to his lips and drank. 'How about you?'

'What about me?'

He pulled another slice of pizza from the box. 'Do you like the wrecking business?'

'Auto dismantling,' she corrected him. At his questioning look, she said, 'The state calls it 'auto dismantling'.'

His mouth curved into a smile. 'Just so no one thinks you're out there wrecking cars for a living.'

He has a heartbreaking smile, Kyra thought, and it's infinitely dangerous. Even the Snake didn't pack that much wallop into a smile.

'Do you like it?' he asked again.

It was her turn to shrug. 'It's a job.'

He grinned. 'But how did you get into it? I mean, a woman . . .'

She narrowed her gaze on him. 'A woman, what?'

He sat up straighter, sensing her simmering temper. 'It doesn't strike me as a woman's first choice of profession.'

She considered the usual rant about equality between the sexes and how women could do as good a job as men, but somehow it didn't seem worth the effort. She was just damn tired of justifying herself.

'It wasn't my choice at all,' she said. 'It was my husband's idea to buy the business.'

Surprise flickered in his eyes. 'You're married?'

She laughed. 'No, thank God.' Then she sobered, realizing how cold that sounded in the face of the truth. 'He died a year ago.'

His fingers tightened around the beer can and he slid it back and forth on the table. 'You don't seem much broken up about it.'

She lifted her chin, facing him full on. 'It wasn't a good marriage.'

He looked ready to probe further, but Kyra forestalled him by gathering up her plate and silverware and heading for the sink. 'How about you, ever been married?'

'No,' he said, then added deliberately, 'thank God.'

Her shoulders tensed, but she kept her attention on washing and rinsing her plate. 'Where are you from?'

'Here and there,' he said. 'I doubt you're going to get that plate any cleaner.'

She stopped scrubbing and set the rinsed plate in the drainer. She dried her hands, then returned to the table. 'No family at all?'

He stopped chewing for a moment and set aside his slice of pizza. He made a great show of finishing the bite before he answered.

'A sister,' he said finally. 'Lives up in Redding.'

Kyra sat again and took another drink of soda. 'Are you close?'

'We don't see each other much.' He fished

in his salad for a pepper. 'She's married. Got a couple of kids.'

'Boys or girls?' Kyra asked.

'Two boys.' He bit off a big mouthful of pizza, then bent to his plate, forking up salad, eating pizza and drinking down his beer as if he were ravenous. He glanced at her once as if to make certain he'd thrown her off the scent. But the look in his eye, wariness mixed with a deep sorrow, only teased her to want to know more. She would have pushed him, except that she was no more eager to lay open her own past, the secrets of her own disastrous marriage.

He popped the last of his pizza into his mouth and rose, wiping his hands on a napkin. 'Better get to work,' he said, closing the pizza box and picking up his plate.

'I'll clean up.' Kyra reached for his plate. He resisted a moment, not quite letting go as she tugged, so that she looked up at him. The intensity was back, that viscerally deep awareness of each other. Then he released the plate and turned away from her. She trembled as she cleared the table, carried his plate to the sink. She felt held together with gossamer that threatened to tear at the slightest glance or touch from him.

He dragged the stove from the wall, the sound of the rattling metal loud in the small kitchen. Squeezing his large body back behind the stove, he reached a strong hand out for his toolbox. Kyra watched him, her hand wiping the same spot on the table over and over until she realized what she was doing.

She finished her quick clean up, then escaped to the backyard on the pretext of throwing the pizza box into the outside trash. As she stood in the blessed evening coolness, she dithered over what to do next. She'd like nothing more than to hide in her bedroom, but her mother's childhood lessons in courtesy were too ingrained.

She rubbed her eyes, trying to think. The atmosphere in the kitchen was explosive; she needed something to distract her. A vision of her sewing basket came to mind and the slacks that had needed mending for a good six months. She hated sewing and was so bad at it, it always required her full attention. The perfect chore to keep her mind off Randon.

She went back inside, leaving the backdoor open to the cool night air, then breezed through the kitchen. 'Be right back,' she said, heading for the spare room.

Randon straightened from behind the stove just as she returned to the kitchen. In one fluid motion he pulled off his T-shirt and tossed it to the floor. About to bend to his task again, he stopped when he saw her standing mesmerized in the doorway.

'Too hot,' he said by way of explanation.

Way too hot, Kyra thought irreverently. She squeezed her eyes shut a moment, then continued on past him, clutching her sewing basket and the black slacks. By the time she sat down at the kitchen table, he'd crouched behind the stove again, but nothing could wipe the image of his naked chest from her mind.

She'd always thought she hated hairy chests. The Snake had been hairless, with muscles gone soft with too much alcohol. She tried to remember what it had felt like to run her hand over his bare skin, smooth as a teenage boy's.

But another picture intruded — the pale brown hair covering the taut muscles of Randon's chest, her fingers tangling in the soft curls. She could almost feel the tickling against her palm, the heat of his flesh beneath.

God, she wanted to touch him. She wanted to hear the catch of his breath as she stroked his skin, his low moan as her fingertips traced the path of hair to the waistband of his jeans.

Kyra snatched up her Coke and gulped down the last of it. She put a trembling hand to her cheek, trying to cool it with the moisture from the Coke can. Then she dug in her sewing basket for a needle and black thread.

It took her three tries to poke the thread through the needle's eye. Then she dropped needle and thread when she picked up the slacks and had to search on the floor to find it. She pricked her finger twice as she ran the needle along the seam, closing the tear with crooked, irregular stitches.

She just had her heartbeat under control when Randon rose from behind the stove again. Sweat sheened his chest, darkened his hair. The muscles in his arms rippled as he worked with a bundle of wires in his hands. He must have felt her watching him because he paused, looked up. Her heart rate exploded into a frenzy and she could hear her own breathing rasping in her ears.

He didn't look away. She could feel his gaze pull her as surely as the needle pulled the thread through a fabric. The frank desire in his face pricked her as sharply as the needle had, plunged even more deeply. She felt seared by his heat, every inch of her excruciatingly sensitive.

Fight or flight, her mind urged, and she took the coward's way out. Shoving back her chair so hard it banged against the wall, she scrambled to her feet. Grabbing up her sewing, Kyra fled from the room.

5

Randon dragged in a breath, eyes still on the doorway through which Kyra had fled. The sudden rise in temperature in the kitchen had damned little to do with the summer heat and everything to do with how delectable Kyra looked in shorts and a sleeveless shirt. And if he thought having her leave the room would calm his libido, he didn't reckon on the hyperactivity of his imagination.

He took another breath, his hand gripping a pair of needlenose pliers so tightly they cut across his palm. This had been a hell of a bad idea — offering his help, coming to her house and placing himself in temptation's way. He knew better, but he'd been thinking with the part of his anatomy that had no business making suggestions.

Randon bent again into the cramped confines behind the stove. He had to finish this, complete his repairs and get the hell out. He tugged free the wire he'd identified as having the short and clipped it just below where the insulation had worn through. He spliced on a clean piece of wire from his toolbox and covered it with black electrical tape.

Damned lucky that short didn't spark a fire. He shuddered at the thought of Kyra trapped by a conflagration, overcome by smoke, unable to escape. He would have felt a clutching feeling in his gut for anyone in that terrifying situation. It certainly wasn't any stronger or any more horrifying just because it was Kyra.

Although the kitchen had cooled considerably with the deepening of night, sweat broke out on his brow at the thought of Kyra in such danger. Just to be certain, he examined the bundle of wires behind the stove one more time, searching for weaknesses. When he was satisfied that the electrical system of the stove was as safe as he could make it, he plugged the appliance in for a test.

Gathering up his tools, he squeezed out from behind the stove and flipped on the burners. All four coils warmed, then glowed bright red as they heated to the top setting. Turning off the burners, he switched on the oven and waited until it was hot. As a final precaution, he leaned over the back of the stove, sniffing for the telltale acrid scent of burning wiring.

Everything seemed fine. Which meant he was done. He could leave now, head back to his motel room. Or maybe go out somewhere for a beer and keep company with the local drunks for an hour or two.

Or he could stay. The teasing proposition settled in his brain, sapping his resolve. He could stay here a while with Kyra, relax with her on the sofa, watch a little television or listen to some music. He could tuck her body close to his, curve his arm around her shoulders. He could lean over, brush his lips in her silky hair, stroke along her slender throat with his fingertips . . .

When he turned off the oven, Randon wrenched the knob so hard it came off in his hand. His hand trembled slightly as he fit the knob onto its post, then manhandled the stove back into its corner. Snatching up his shirt, he tugged it on, then tossed the pliers, wirecutters, and screwdriver into his toolbox.

He slammed the lid on the toolbox just as if he were slamming the lid on his wayward thoughts. He didn't need a complication like Kyra Aimes in his life. He knew that. And he damn well wasn't staying here any longer with her, just as he wouldn't be making any more offers of help.

Scooping back his hair with his fingers, he grabbed his hat and secured it on his head. He picked up the toolbox, then stepped out into the small formal dining room off the kitchen.

Where was Kyra? He couldn't just leave without saying good-bye. But he sure didn't want to blunder around the house in search of her, either.

He carried the toolbox over to the front door and set it down. Returning to the dining room, he poked his head into the hallway that he figured led to her bedroom. The house was small, all the public rooms opened to one another; if she'd gone anywhere but into her bedroom, he'd have known it.

'Kyra,' he called softly down the hallway. He listened for a response. 'Kyra,' he said more loudly as he stepped fully into the hall. Just before he called again, the door at the end of the hall opened. Kyra stepped through the doorway, giving him a tantalizing glimpse of frills and soft pastels in her bedroom before she shut the door behind her. Her eyes were wide, watchful as she approached him.

The heat in those wary hazel eyes struck him dumb. He had a hazy impression of having something to say to her, something about being finished, that he had to leave. But the smooth curve of her cheek, the narrow vee where her shirt parted scrambled any sense in his brain. All he could comprehend was that she stood before him, a faint sheen of sweat on her brow dampening her hair, the slight trembling of her bare shoulders where the sleeveless shirt ended.

He had to touch her. The immediacy of that impulse closed in on him, cocooning them both in its urgency. If he simply touched her, everything would be right again, his world back in balance, restarted on its track. He lifted his hand. Every luscious inch of Kyra beckoned to him, clamoring to be first. Like a package that begged to be opened, her womanly form called to him. His gaze fixed on hers, he reached for what seemed closest, most tempting . . . the soft line of her cheek. As he drew his fingertips along her satiny flesh, Kyra made a sound, half sigh, half moan. He followed the line of her cheekbone toward the shell of her ear, barely teasing that sensitive flesh before moving back across her face toward her parted lips.

He could touch her lips with his, press his mouth against hers, dive inside that welcoming warmth with his tongue. Would she fight him at first, refuse him entry, then sigh with surrender? Or would she give in to him easily, first her lush mouth, then the softness of her generous breasts . . . Without conscious thought, his hand had slipped along her throat, traced along the opening of her blouse, edged inside toward her breast. The warmth of her body shot straight through him, jolting him as if he'd gripped a live wire. Everything screamed inside him to close his hand over her breast. A stiffening in her body transmitted itself dimly to his fogged brain. His gaze met hers, and he registered a dark anger battling with her own desire. He snatched his hand from her, backing away a step. 'I'm sorry,' he muttered. 'Damn, I'm sorry.'

He turned and headed for the living room to put some distance between them. He picked up his toolbox by the front door, then chanced a look back at her. 'Stove's fixed,' he said, settling his hat more squarely on his head.

She stood ramrod straight, as prim and proper as the Victorian lady that might have owned this house a hundred years ago. 'Thank you.'

'I — ' he began, intending to throw out another apology, but a certain mortification had taken hold of her face and he could see she'd just as soon have him gone. 'Good-bye,' he said instead, then let himself out the door.

He dumped the toolbox in the back of his pickup with a bang, the sound ringing along the quiet streets. He put all his pent-up frustration into starting the old Chevy, gunning its engine as he ripped away from the curb. At the stoplight at the bottom of the hill, he shoved his foot on the accelerator a few more times, taking a perverse pleasure in the engine's roar as if it were his own.

When the light flicked green, he turned left on Highway 50 with a squeal of tires. He raced up the highway, quickly hitting the speed limit, barely holding onto the urge to exceed it. He passed the exit for his motel without a glance, then continued on up the hill toward Lake Tahoe. What the hell did he think he was doing, touching Kyra? He'd thought he had at least enough conscience not to involve himself with a woman like her. He was a drifter, a here-for-now, see-you-later kind of man. He wanted a good-timing woman, someone to enjoy the moment with, someone who wouldn't be moaning and groaning when he left her behind.

But Kyra . . . Kyra deserved a commitment. Kyra deserved tomorrows. Kyra deserved love. Everything he couldn't give her. All the things he had no capacity for. No desire for. Never mind that empty place in his heart that nagged every once in a while. That burned right now at the thought of leaving Kyra behind.

What he needed right now had nothing to do with commitment. It had everything to do with scratching an itch, with finding momentary comfort in the arms of a passionate woman. A woman who wouldn't mind saying good-bye. A woman like Melinda, the assistant director.

Randon saw the Camino exit up ahead, the turn that would take him to the shooting location. Melinda was staying there, in the trailer, to keep an eye on things. He could head on up to the location, knock on her door, and she'd be more than happy to share the night with him. He made the turn off of Highway 50, then headed down the narrow country road that led to the location. Ponderosa pines and gnarled oaks loomed on either side of him as the pickup's headlights illuminated them. He slowed at the gravel driveway that led to the property the location manager had leased for the shoot.

He turned onto the driveway and the pickup jounced along the rutted track. A roil of emotions tumbled inside him as he slowed the truck. To quiet the jumble of feelings inside, he tried to picture Melinda, her willowy body tight against his, her long brown hair brushing his face. But the images faded before he could hold them in his mind, replaced by a curvier figure, lush and generous, short dark hair like silk against his palm. The ache started up again in his groin at the thought of that soft body pressed against his hardness, of Kyra's sweet scent.

He slammed on the brakes and the truck slid to a stop in a spray of gravel. His heart thundering, Randon leaned his head on the Chevy's wheel, eyes shut. That he could have even thought to pump his need into Melinda when he felt nothing for her disgusted him. She might not ask for commitment at the end of it, but he damn well had to respect her more than to use her as a surrogate.

Jerking the truck into reverse, Randon backed onto the shoulder and turned around. He retraced his path onto Highway 50 and guided the pickup back to the motel.

As he stood under the sluicing chill of a cold shower, he blanked his mind, shutting out Kyra, shutting out Rachelle, closing out the bitter misery of his own lonely heart.

★   ★   ★

Laura gazed across the Ford at Johnny, drinking in his every feature. It had been easier today separated from him, guessing that by nightfall they would be together again. She'd found the Fairlane more easily this time, too, arriving here a few moments before him.

Johnny stared out the windshield of the car,

102

his expression serious. Laura wanted his attention on her, to have him look at her during the few short hours they would be together.

'*Johnny.*' She waited for him to turn.

He smiled at her, brown eyes filled with love. '*What, sweetheart?*'

Laura enjoyed the warm glow his words brought. '*Did you try to talk to the woman today?*'

He shook his head. '*I couldn't even find her.*'

'*But did you try, Johnny?*'

'*Of course I did. She just wasn't around.*'

Worry gnawed inside Laura. Johnny had never believed as she did, that they had a way out of here. And each time they returned without finding answers, he lost a little more of his faith.

'*I've been thinking.*' Johnny's expression turned serious. '*About why you've made contact and I haven't.*'

'*What?*' Laura asked, Johnny's ominous tone sending a skitter of dread up her back.

He fixed his gaze on her, his eyes intense. '*That we came back this time just for you.*'

Dread blossomed into fear. '*What do you mean?*'

'*This time is meant just for you,*' Johnny said. '*The man will help set you free, help* send you along to . . . to paradise or heaven or wherever it is sweet, loving girls go.'

Laura's heart wrenched at the adoration, the grief in Johnny's face. 'God wouldn't take me and leave you behind.'

Johnny's face hardened. 'There is no God.'

Laura's eyes widened in alarm. 'Don't say that, Johnny. You know it isn't true.'

'It is. At least for me there isn't.'

He turned back to the windshield, stared out at the shadows beyond. When he turned toward her again, his cocky, crooked grin was back in place. He flicked a finger at the barrier that lay between them, sending sparks glittering against his face.

'Try to talk to the man again, Laura,' he said, as if the dark moment had never been. 'I'll look for the woman. Then, tomorrow night — '

But tomorrow had come before he could finish, a pearlescent dawn again pulling Laura from Johnny, from the car. She stood again in the warmth of the new day, longing for the sweet boy who loved her nearly more than she could bear.

★ ★ ★

Randon drove to the movie location first thing the next morning, determined to get

104

the production designer's approval for the latest collection of photos. It was long past the time Randon should have finished this job and moved on. In fact, if the production designer didn't approve this set of cars, Randon decided he'd suggest the task be turned over to the P.A., leaving Randon free to go.

Randon pulled up next to Melinda's trailer and climbed from the truck. Melinda sat at one of the folding aluminum tables, studying the script. He felt a twitch of guilt remembering his intentions last night and squirmed when Melinda looked up at him and smiled.

'Where is he?' he asked her roughly, hoping to dampen the spark of interest in her eyes.

Melinda's smile faded, replaced by tight-lipped irritation. 'Back behind those oak trees,' she said, pointing. 'The director's already torn into me once today. I'd just as soon not get it from you, too.'

Guilt lanced a little deeper as he muttered a thank you and headed off toward the grove of black and live oak. Shade and sunlight dappled his back as he traversed the woods, cool and hot in turn. One lone robin chirped out a half-hearted note, the morning's building heat even stifling the birds' energy.

Randon found Evans and the director

leaning against the trunk of a massive fallen oak. The director spoke into a cell phone, scrawling changes on the script, splayed open on the tree trunk. Evans looked over his shoulder.

Randon heard the crunch of leaves and pine needles behind him as someone followed him into the grove of oaks. He turned to see Aaron Cutter, the screenwriter, slapping aside saplings as he stomped up the path. A wet-behind-the-ears young black man when the production had started, Aaron had already seen the director slash-and-burn his creation several times.

'You can't do this!' Aaron shouted at the director, his lanky body radiating rage.

The director glanced at the enraged young man and kept up his rapid patter into the phone. While the agitated screenwriter hopped from side to side like a boxer, spewing a string of curses that surprised even Randon, the director ignored him. Evans just smirked in his supercilious way.

Finally the director snapped the phone shut. 'I'm the director. I can do anything.'

'But you're adding all this . . . this . . . filth,' Aaron sputtered.

'Sex sells.' The director handed the script to Aaron. 'I need these changes by this afternoon.'

The director headed off, beckoning Evans to follow. Aaron stood with the screenplay gripped tightly in his hand, his dark brown eyes a study in frustration. He stared down at the brad-bound stack of paper and Randon could see he wanted nothing more than to fling it into the woods.

Randon approached and laid a hand on Aaron's shoulder. 'Sometimes you gotta eat crap to get anywhere,' he said to the young man.

'The director is an ass,' Aaron growled.

Randon couldn't argue with that. He thought the same of Evans. 'Just do what you have to,' he said. 'Maybe someday you'll be telling him what to do.'

Aaron looked dubious, but he tucked the screenplay under his arm and headed back toward the trailer. Randon went after Evans, following the narrow deer trail the director and production designer had taken deeper into the woods. He found the two men by an old, half-collapsed lean-to. The director was chattering on and on about his 'vision' for the next shot while Evans nodded in eager agreement.

'Here.' Randon held out to Evans the stack of photos he'd taken the day before. 'There's twenty shots. Should be ten good ones.'

Evans flipped through the Polaroids rapidly, barely glancing at each one. Then he plucked two from the stack. 'These will do. I still need eight more.'

Randon gaped at him, automatically taking the rejected photos from the production designer. 'Two? You only found two you like?' He rifled through the pile of castoffs, pulling out four. 'What about these? They're older cars. You wanted older cars.'

The director flicked a finger at the photos. 'I just spoke to the producer. We've changed our concept for the film.'

Randon ground his teeth, feeling a keener sympathy for the screenwriter. 'What is it you want this time?'

The director spread out his hands as if sketching his world view on the air. 'We want to show how life sullies the pristine, how innocence withers.'

It sounded like the director's justification for turning a simple horror film into a soft-porn flick. Randon swiped the side of his hand across his brow to keep from knocking the director's and production designer's heads together. 'And just how does the choice of cars play into this?'

'They all need to be white,' Evans said, 'like these two.' He brandished the Polaroids of the acceptable cars.

Randon struggled to keep his tone even. 'Any particular model year?'

'It doesn't matter,' Evans said, then added, 'for now. And I'll need the first two on location by tomorrow morning.'

Planting a fist in the production designer's face seemed even more appealing. Randon shook his head, annoyed that the temper he'd learned to control in his youth had come back to haunt him. Kyra's face floated into his mind's eye and he realized a good deal of his edginess sprang from the sharp, frustrated ache he felt for her. He snatched the two photos from the production designer's hand and shoved them into the back pocket of his jeans. He kept his fingers closed around the other set to keep his hands busy until Evans was out of his reach. Randon didn't take an easy breath until he'd reached the clearing by the trailer and had tossed the rejected photos into the trash.

Aaron sat at the folding table, hunched over his laptop computer. Melinda stood behind him, rubbing his shoulders soothingly. Although she had several years on Aaron, the comfort she offered him was anything but big-sisterly. Aaron relaxed under her ministrations, his broad smile showing his pleasure at her attentions.

When she saw Randon approach, she

looked up, her expression telling him, 'This is what you turned down.' Randon supposed he should feel a twinge of jealousy, but he felt only relief that her amorous intentions were directed elsewhere.

As he headed west down Highway 50, he tried to tamp back the anticipation he felt at seeing Kyra again. Even if he continued his search at another wrecking yard, he had to arrange to tow the two cars Evans had approved up to Camino. Which meant he had to speak to Kyra at least once more.

As he descended into the valley, the sweltering heat closed in, reminding him of the searing moments last night in Kyra's kitchen, then later outside her bedroom. Images crowded in — of the intensity of her gaze as she stood before him, the feel of her damp flesh as his fingers brushed against it, the catch in her breathing as he stroked — He cut off that line of thought as he took the Sunrise exit, realizing his own rampant imagination had added to the memories, made them even more powerful. If he had any hope of facing Kyra with any semblance of neutrality, he'd damn well better get his libido under control.

As he waited at a stoplight, he felt a different kind of burning in his belly and remembered he'd gone out to the location without eating breakfast. As the light changed to green, he spied a big family restaurant up ahead on the right. That was what he needed, some food in his stomach, something good and greasy. Food and a couple pots of coffee to counteract the restless night he'd spent thinking of Kyra.

The restaurant was big and noisy, busy even after the early morning rush. Randon downed an entire cup of jet-black coffee before the matronly, no-nonsense waitress returned to take his breakfast order. He leaned back in the booth as he waited for his food, eyes closed. Kyra's face immediately intruded. Hell, why couldn't he shake her? She was pretty enough, with her delicate features and tempting curves. Although he'd done his best not to stare at her bountiful chest, he'd sure noticed it. But he'd known other women just as well put together and hadn't spent nearly every waking moment obsessing about them.

He'd known two kinds of women in his life — the no-strings and the strings-attached kind. Everything about Kyra spoke of strings and commitment and hearth and home — all the things he'd avoided in a woman since he left home.

Randon's father had welcomed those ties that held him down, had linked him to

Randon's mother. His dad had said the strongest tie was the one between his heart and his wife's, a tie he'd felt blessed to be snared by. But not Randon. When a woman looked at him with commitment in her eyes, he looked the other way. When he felt the entanglements of strings, he cut loose and made himself scarce. His restless feet always found a better place to be, and if he felt a little lonesome at times, there was always a no-strings woman around to ease him. Until now. Until Kyra.

When the waitress returned, he opened his eyes again. The woman set down a full pot of coffee, then slid his plate of bacon and three sunnyside-up eggs before him on the table. She followed with the toast, then refilled his cup before departing.

Randon dug into his breakfast, ravenously shoveling in eggs and hash browns. Minutes later he was cleaning the last of the egg yolk from his plate with a wedge of wheat toast. He sat back, satisfied.

When his coffee cup was nearly to his lips, a flash of blue caught his eye. He jerked his hand, startled at the blonde, ponytailed girl in a turquoise dress standing with her back to him. The girl turned and started for the cash register, swiveling her head briefly to look at him with disinterested brown eyes. Randon's heart resumed a regular rhythm. It wasn't her, it wasn't the girl from the wrecking yard. Carefully setting down his cup, he wiped the coffee from his hand with his napkin. Digging into his pocket for his wallet, he threw a tip down on the table. He rose slowly, keeping one eye on the ponytailed girl, half-expecting her to vanish. She did, in a more prosaic way, walking out the front door with her family. Nevertheless, Randon waited until she was gone before approaching the cash register to pay his check.

6

Kyra hung up the phone and rubbed at the bridge of her nose. *Hell*, she thought, *now what?*

'We're sorry, Ms. Aimes,' her bank's loan officer had said, 'but the appraisal came back low.'

It had been a long shot, but she'd had to try. The thought of refinancing the mortgage on her tiny Victorian and pulling enough out to pay off the Snake's loans had terrified her. She could easily lose her house as well as her business if her finances continued their downward spiral. But she hadn't seen another choice. And now even that grand sacrifice wasn't enough. They'd barely managed to buy the house two years ago, right before the Snake died. He'd used a gambling windfall as a down payment, money that should have gone to pay off debts. In hindsight, Kyra was grateful; the house was perhaps the only thing she could thank her late husband for.

But she didn't have nearly enough equity in her home to pull any money out. So short of selling — which would scarcely net her enough to pay broker's fees, anyway — her house wouldn't save her. Would anything? She thought of Randon, his broad, strong shoulders, the power in his hands when he turned a wrench or stroked her cheek. Something within her longed to turn all her troubles over to the tall cowboy, to let him fix her life just as he fixed her stove.

Of course, she couldn't — wouldn't — give herself over to a man that way. She'd done that with her husband, let him run the business, run her every waking moment when he couldn't go even one day without getting himself into trouble. She'd been so hungry to fill the space left by the absence of her father, she'd allowed her husband to dictate her life in a vain hope of justifying the mistake that was her marriage. But she'd wised up. She learned soon after the Snake died that men didn't fill the emptiness, they only made new holes to fill.

She shook away the image of Randon in her mind's eye. She had more important things to think about than one oversexed cowboy. She shuddered, remembering his gray gaze on her, his fingertip brushing her heated flesh, the rasping of his breathing teasing her even more than his touch. Even as anger roiled within her at his straying fingers, she'd wanted to step closer, to draw his warm palm over her breast, feel him graze her nipple . . .

Agitated, she shoved back her chair and rose. Pacing the tiny office, she glanced up at the fly-specked clock on the wall. Eleven-fifteen. She'd told Jackson she'd relieve him at the service window at noon so he could do some shopping. He had a birthday present to buy for his youngest granddaughter. Might as well go out there now, give Jackson the extra half hour. It had to be tough for a sixty-year-old to find just the right gift for a six-year-old girl; he'd probably appreciate the extra time.

Kyra dug in her purse for her brush and a lipstick and came across a pair of hair combs nestled in the bottom. Running the brush through her hair, she swept it back with the combs and fixed them behind her ears. Her hands trembled. *Not eagerness*, she told herself. *I'm just in a hurry*. It wasn't until she was squinting in the tiny mirror she'd also found in the bottom of her purse, swiping on lipstick, that she realized what she was doing. Primping. Not for Jackson, not for Trish, not, certainly, for herself. But for Randon, on the off chance that the tall cowboy would amble over to the service window in search of her.

She grabbed a tissue to swipe off the lipstick, stopped with the wadded paper nearly to her mouth, angry and indecisive.

116

Why shouldn't she make herself look halfway decent for once? There was nothing wrong with wanting to look like a woman, to feel feminine. It didn't have to be for Randon. She dropped the tissue in the waste basket, then tossed brush, mirror, and lipstick into her purse. Tucking her raspberry shell top into her denim shorts, she headed out to the service area.

'Hey, Jackson, take off,' Kyra said as she entered the outer room. 'Go find something good and frilly for your granddaughter.'

Jackson glanced at the clock, then quickly handed change to the customer on the other side of the window. 'Thanks, Kyra.' He backed away to let her take his place. 'Be back in an hour.'

'Take your time,' Kyra called out after him, trying to squelch the giddiness that seemed to have come over her. Jeez, a little lipstick and she was acting like a teenager.

Trish turned to her with a grin, gum snapping as she said, 'Lookin' good, boss.'

'Thank you.' Kyra willed herself not to blush. 'Lose the gum, Trish.'

Trish spit the gum out and returned her attention to the next customer in one fluid move. Kyra chanced a sidelong glance at her, narrowing her gaze at the girl's smug grin. Kyra bit back any further comment, knowing it would only make things worse.

Ignoring Trish, Kyra smiled pleasantly at the young man standing at her window. 'Can I help you?'

He set down the locking mechanism for a glove box on the counter. 'It's from an '88 Olds Cutlass.'

Kyra nodded and turned to the computer to her left. She brought up the inventory window, grateful she'd invested in the software after the Snake had died. 'Two dollars and eighty-nine cents,' she read from the screen.

After the young man ambled off, Kyra put up her 'closed' sign to give her a moment to check the computer. Last night she'd blocked out the IDs for the twenty cars Jackson had said he'd gotten from Randon. She wanted to check on their status. Not to check on Randon, of course, to see if he'd arrived in the yard yet this morning. But just to see whether that inventory was available or not. And she couldn't ask Trish. Lord only knew what the teenager would make of such an innocent question.

A quick check told her that eighteen of the twenty cars had been released for sale. Something quivery passed through her as she realized Randon had indeed already been in this morning. Kyra set her teeth against the annoying pang of disappointment that he hadn't sought her out, that he had perhaps already left again.

She burned to know if he was still here. As nonchalantly as she could, Kyra scanned the yard. She saw a tall, lanky figure striding between the cars, but the man disappeared behind a Plymouth Voyager before she could be sure.

'Hey, Kyra,' Trish said.

Kyra tensed, sure her profound interest in Randon's whereabouts was plainly written on her face. She bent over the computer screen, as if the display was vitally important. 'Yes?'

'What's the equivalent for a '69 Vette timing cover?' Trish asked.

Kyra forced her shoulders to relax. 'Check the Hollander interchange.' The computerized index listed hundreds of interchangeable parts between one car model and another.

'Can't. ROM drive's down,' Trish reminded her.

Kyra remembered now — the CD-ROM drive had crashed yesterday. And all the Hollander data was on compact disc.

Kyra sighed. 'Did you get hold of the computer tech?'

'He's coming tomorrow morning,' Trish said. 'Had to promise a batch of double

119

chocolate brownies to get him here that soon.'

Damn. They wouldn't be able to access the Hollander interchange until the tech replaced the drive. And she no more knew the equivalent for the Vette's timing cover than she knew the derivation of Einstein's theory of relativity.

She glanced over at the customer waiting impatiently at Trish's window and her heart fell. Ed Wilkens, an old buddy of the Snake's. Ed was of the opinion that a woman didn't belong in the wrecking business, a view the beefy blowhard loved to expound upon in her hearing. It didn't help that she'd flatly rejected his many passes, several of them even before the Snake had died. He'd like nothing better than to watch her falter. The Snake, damn his eyes, would have known the answer to Trish's question off the top of his head. His encyclopedic knowledge of cars had been his only asset in the business. That and his gender, by Ed Wilkens's reckoning.

'A 1969 Corvette,' Kyra repeated, stalling, hoping her brain would miraculously kick in with the answer. She kept her gaze down, as much to appear thoughtful as to ignore Ed's supercilious leer. 'Timing cover for a '69 Vette.'

'Nineteen-ninety Chevy truck,' a deep male

voice said softly from the other side of the service window.

Kyra looked up, startled and excited all at once when she saw Randon standing there. In faded black T-shirt and black denim jeans, he used his broad, confident male grin to devastating effect.

Her thoughts scrambled, her breath hitching. 'What?'

'The timing cover,' he said, still keeping his voice low.

She narrowed her gaze on him, irritated at her out-of-control reaction to him. 'How do you know?'

He brought a finger up to his lips to quiet her, tipping his head slightly toward Ed. 'You'll have to trust me.'

She gave him a measuring look. Trust him? Lord, she wasn't even sure she liked him. And after last night . . .

'Hey!' Ed called out, 'I ain't got all day.'

She turned to the other man, resolute. 'Ninety Chevy truck. We have several in inventory. Trish can tell you where to find them.'

Ed scowled at her. 'I know my way around.' He turned from the window and stomped off into the yard.

Kyra turned back to Randon. 'Thank you.'

He shrugged. 'Glad to help, sweetheart.'

She ground her teeth against the fluttering in her heart at the endearment. He meant nothing by it, it was ridiculous to respond as if he did.

'Can we talk a minute?' he asked.

She bit her bottom lip, uncertain she wanted to hear what he might have to say. 'What about?'

'Why don't you come on out here, sugar, so we can talk more privately?' he asked, the devilish smile still in place.

She stole a glance at Trish, who listened in fascination even as she collected money from the next customer in line. Two more stood in Trish's queue. FourStar usually did a brisk business during the weekday noon hour, but the broiling sun had chased away all but the hardiest. She didn't have the excuse of a heavy workload to deny his request.

She looked up at him again, at his up-to-no-good smile and the mischievous glint in his eyes. He was just a man, after all. She could handle him. No problem. But as she repositioned the CLOSED placard more squarely in her window and turned to exit the service room, she couldn't shake the feeling that she was walking into a lion's den.

* * *

122

A muddle of emotions roiled in Randon's belly as he strode over to the exit door and waited for Kyra to appear. His impatience seemed to extend the moments until he simply couldn't stand it and he jerked open the door. Kyra stood in the hallway, arms raised, slender fingers resetting the combs in her hair. There was something impossibly erotic about her graceful pose. She blushed, caught in that intimate moment. He wanted to pull her hands down, release her hair from the combs, and smooth the silky strands behind her ears.

Damn. He'd sworn he would keep this light and easy, that he'd resist the powerful pull he felt for her. He forced a cocky smile back on his face and stepped back as she slipped past him into the blast of summer heat. Then with his cowboy hat tipped down to shade his eyes, he moved closer to her, intentionally invading her space.

Kyra's mouth tightened, but to her credit, she held her ground. 'Are you here to apologize?'

He relaxed his face into a broader grin. 'For what, sugar?'

Her hazel eyes flashed. 'For last night.'

As if he could think of anything but last night. He leaned one shoulder against the hot stucco wall, looming over her. 'What's there to apologize for?'

Confusion threaded through her anger. 'Because you . . . you were . . . you . . . ' She pressed her lips together as if she didn't trust the words coming from her mouth. Then she tilted her head up. 'I think you know.'

He knew, all right. He'd touched her, without her encouragement, without her permission. A touch that stopped far short of what he'd done with other women dozens of times and yet . . . And yet there'd been more power, more heat, more connection in that simple contact that was anything but simple. Because now he felt her strings running all through him, tangling in his gut, wrapping around his heart.

He reared back from her, startled at the thought. Damn it, his heart had nothing to do with this. This was about attraction, sex, lust. Why this particular woman had thrown him for such a loop he'd yet to figure out. The summer heat, maybe, or his wrenching worry over Rachelle made him more vulnerable. But as soon as he teased out the reason for Kyra's elusive appeal, he'd be able to walk away from her without a second thought.

She was still glaring up at him, waiting. He nudged his hat back slightly to rub his brow, tried to jumpstart a few brain cells.

'I wanted to ask a favor.' He remembered

the little speech he'd rehearsed on the way over here.

Her eyes narrowed. 'What?'

'Dinner tonight.' He smiled. 'Home cooked.'

As she worried her lower lip, her white teeth flashed into sight briefly. 'I suppose I owe you.'

'You don't. I just wanted to . . . ' What the hell had he wanted? To be with her, get to know her better? He didn't like the sound of that.

This had all seemed so reasonable when he'd first arrived and found out from Jackson that Kyra was hard at work in her office. Randon hadn't wanted to disturb her, so he'd headed out into the lot instead. But as he wandered among the wrecked cars, he couldn't squelch his disappointment at the delay in seeing her. His idea had seemed brilliant at the time — he would persuade her to cook for him, give himself another night with her so he could puzzle out exactly why she fascinated him so.

'You wanted to what?' she prompted, suspicion clear in her tone.

'Just spend a little time with you.' He gave her what he hoped was an innocent look.

She crossed her arms over her chest. 'Spend a little time or make a little time?'

Her cleavage deepened above the curve of

125

her scoop-neck top, drawing his eyes to the lush mounds of her breasts. He imagined burying his face there, running the tip of his tongue along that deep valley. He jerked his gaze back up to her face. If her eyes had been lasers, her anger would have incinerated him on the spot, leaving nothing but a pair of smoking leather boots. He forced himself to grin.

'My intentions are purely honorable,' he said, although his body insisted they were anything but.

She bit her lower lip again, and he wondered how it would feel to nibble that tender flesh with his own teeth. 'Okay,' she said finally, 'I'll make you dinner.'

He rocked back on his heels, happier than he had any business being. 'Tonight then. Six o'clock?'

Doubt clouded her eyes and she seemed on the verge of changing her mind. She opened her mouth as if to say so, but to his surprise said, 'Better make it seven-thirty. I have to help Jackson close up, then hit the market on the way home.'

He nodded and stepped away, swinging the Polaroid camera on its strap. He plowed his way back through the cars on the lot, heat battering him on all sides. Mission accomplished, he thought.

Unable to resist the impulse, he looked back at her, grinning when he saw her still watching him. He turned back just in time to avoid a collision with an old man who appeared suddenly from behind an Econoline van. Randon bent to the wispy-haired old man, ready to apologize.

The man glared, venom in his gaze. 'It wasn't my fault!'

Taken aback, Randon stood speechless a moment. 'Of course not. It was mine. Sorry.'

Muttering under his breath, the man resumed his high-speed walk across the yard. Randon laughed off his faint irritation, then continued on through the blast of summer heat.

★   ★   ★

Kyra watched as Mr. Carson threw a dark glance over his shoulder at Randon after their near collision. The old man's mood seemed to grow fouler every time she saw him, as if the sheer fact of life made him angry. When he did open his mouth to speak, it was to complain. Kyra wondered why he bothered coming to her yard at all. Then her gaze left the slight figure of Mr. Carson and drifted in the direction of Randon: She sighed, raking her bangs back from her forehead. What had possessed her to say yes to him? True, she probably owed him a meal, but to risk the intimacy of him in her home again after what had happened last night . . .

She ducked back into the corridor and then into the service room. The customers at Trish's window had dwindled to none, and the girl leaned against the counter flipping through a hot rod magazine. She flicked a glance in Kyra's direction.

'Gonna see him again?' she asked around a new wad of gum.

Kyra wanted to deny it, but knew that would only make things worse. Trish would ferret out the truth anyway. She had a fine-honed talent for digging.

Kyra picked up the paperwork on the cars that had arrived the previous day. 'He fixed my stove last night.' She turned to the computer. 'I'm making dinner for him as a thank you.'

'Hmm,' Trish said in response, the snap-snap-snap of her gum a counterpoint to the no-doubt feverish workings of her brain.

Kyra looked at her sidelong, saw the questions forming in the girl's mind. 'I'm going to finish this in my office. If you need my help before Jackson gets back, let me know.'

Safe in her office, she turned on her

computer and connected with the local network. Bent over the keyboard, she let the tedious work of breaking down and inventorying the newly arrived cars drive out her persistent thoughts of Randon. She heard Jackson's return through the thin office wall, was dimly aware of the swamp cooler gasping out gusts of cool air.

She knew when Randon reappeared at the service window, could hear his deep voice vibrating through the Sheetrock separating her office from the service area. She couldn't make out his words as he spoke to Jackson; no doubt he was reporting on the latest set of cars he'd photographed. Then the rumble of his voice quieted and she imagined him striding off to his pickup. The memory of his lazy grin sent a shiver up her spine that had nothing to do with the swamp cooler's efforts.

When she finally looked up at the clock again, it was 5:30. The excitement she'd tried so hard to smother returned as she realized how soon she would be seeing Randon again. She stretched in her chair, her spine popping with the effort. Rising, she headed to the service area to help Jackson close out the registers.

'Slow day,' Jackson said as she entered. Two stragglers stood at his window. Kyra began ringing out the second register.

Her ebullience fizzled as she counted out the slim pickings in the cash drawer. She hoped Jackson's register had a better take. There was barely enough here to pay for Jackson's and Trish's time, let alone the half-day Mario had worked.

Kyra pushed aside the anxiety. 'Find something nice for your granddaughter?'

Jackson grinned, his smile a slash of white in his dark face. 'Barbie doll and a mess of clothes. Lady at the mall helped me pick them out.'

'I'm sure she'll love it.' She turned to carry the cash drawer to the office safe.

'Not going to make the bank deposit tonight?' Jackson asked before she reached the door.

'Damn.' She turned back. 'I forgot it was Friday.' Then she hastily added, 'I have an appointment tonight. Not sure I have time for the bank.'

As Jackson handed change to the last customer, she could see the glimmer of a smile. She wondered what Randon had said before he left today, burned to know if he'd mentioned that she was making him dinner.

'Tell you what, Kyra,' Jackson said, starting his register on its final ring-out, 'you do the patrol and lock-up, I'll take care of the deposit.'

'But your grandkids . . . ' Kyra protested.

'At my sister's. We're having dinner together tonight.'

At the mention of dinner, a new anxiety popped up, that Kyra had no idea what she would fix for Randon.

'Thanks,' she told Jackson, suddenly feeling the urgency to leave.

Returning to her office, she slung her purse over her shoulder and headed out to the yard. She locked up first, scanning the parking lot to be sure her and Jackson's cars were the only ones left. Then she went to the dog run where Gertie, the German shepherd watchdog, spent her days lolling in the shade.

'Hey, love,' she said softly as she approached. Gertie leapt to her feet, tail wagging in excitement. She'd been another of the Snake's purchases, with a sterling bloodline and the best training money could buy, money they could ill afford at the time. She gave Gertie a scratch behind the ears before releasing her from the dog run. She ought to consider selling the dog, in fact had received more than one offer to buy her. But she'd grown attached to Gertie's single-minded devotion, and it still gratified her that when the Snake brought the dog home, it was Kyra Gertie had looked to and not her ex-husband.

Gertie trotted off into the yard, tail held high like a flag, attention everywhere at once. Kyra took another direction, crisscrossing the lot in search of stragglers that she might have locked in. She soon lost track of the German shepherd in amongst the cars. A trickle of sweat worked its way down her spine as she reached the fence at the rear of the yard. She stood motionless a moment, listening. She heard the dim roar of a motorcycle tearing down Sunrise, a desultory call from a bird. A jangle of chainlink brought her focus to the front — Jackson leaving with the deposit. Then silence.

One corner of the yard left to patrol — the far corner where the old Fairlane sat. She could eyeball it from here. No one was moving between the cars. She couldn't hear the sound of anyone moving. But she'd caught kids hiding in the wrecks more than once, and she ought to go over there, make her presence known.

She ordered her feet to move, and they did so reluctantly. It was silly, really, the eerie tickle she felt when she found herself near that car. All because of the unrelenting heat coupled with an overactive imagination. She glanced up and down the rows as she moved along, peering inside car windows and truck beds. Gertie barked and Kyra nearly leaped out of her hiking shoes. Her heart rattling, she forced herself around the last car between her and the Fairlane.

A boy stood leaning against the hood of the Ford.

A host of sensations crawled over Kyra like a mass of ants. The heat seemed to intensify, then she realized it was only because an icy curtain of air had pressed against the front of her from head to toe. The sun still broiled her back, the contrast driving a shudder through her body. Her brain tried to parse out what terrified her so about this boy. His stance, as he stood with one black pant leg crossed over the other, was insolent but not threatening. His long-sleeved white shirt seemed out of place in the heat, but she couldn't see even a drop of sweat on his face or in his slicked-back brown hair.

She tried to speak, but the words seemed trapped in her dust-dry throat. He grinned, the picture of male arrogance. Anger flooded Kyra, and she opened her mouth, ready to give the boy a dressing down.

'Hello, Kyra,' the boy said.

His quiet greeting knocked the air from her lungs, sent a shiver down her spine. The boy hadn't brandished a knife, hadn't gotten in her face with foul language or violent gesture. She had no reason to be afraid of him. *How*

133

did he know her name?

She swallowed, forcing words out. 'The yard is closed. You have to leave.'

His smile dimmed slightly. A trace of sadness flickered in his brown eyes. 'Wish I could.'

As Kyra tried to puzzle over his response, she heard the faint scritch of Gertie's claws. A sudden need to have the dog near her made Kyra turn away from the boy and call out, 'Gertie! Come!'

She watched as Gertie galloped around the end of the nearest car and gamboled around Kyra in circles. Comforted by the presence of the German shepherd, Kyra turned back to the Fairlane.

The boy was gone.

She quickly scanned the Ford, looked up and down the rows of nearby cars. There was no figure racing to escape, no pounding of feet across the gravel and asphalt.

Alarm gripped the back of Kyra's neck. Was he still hiding somewhere in the yard? How could he have moved out of her sight and hearing so quickly?

'Gertie, heel,' she said to the dog.

With obedient Gertie at her left side, Kyra moved among the cars closest to the Fairlane, watching the dog for a clue that she sensed an intruder. But although Gertie sniffed at each car they passed, she showed no sign of detecting anything amiss.

They returned to the old Ford and Kyra made a quick check of its interior. She eyed the trunk, snaked out a trembling hand to try the lock. Shut tight. Surely she would have heard the sound of it opening, heard the slam of the lid.

A low, guttural sound tore Kyra's attention from the trunk. Gertie stood beside the Fairlane, her yellow gaze fixed on the passenger side door, the hairs on the back of her neck upraised. She growled again, baring her teeth slightly. Shaking, Kyra edged around the car. Holding her breath, she peered inside, scanning the seats, the footwells. The car was as empty as before.

A gust of cold air passed over her. With a yelp, Gertie bounded away from the car. After one last look inside, Kyra followed, forcing herself to move at a normal pace. But she didn't breathe easy until she'd climbed into her car and driven away.

7

Randon turned up on her doorstep at twenty after seven with his toolbox in hand. He grinned, hefting the red metal box. 'Thought I'd check your washer.'

Kyra stepped aside to let him in, drinking in the sight of him, his lean legs encased in softly worn jeans, the muscles of his chest flexing beneath his T-shirt. She tried to work up a little annoyance that he'd shown up ten minutes early. But even though the groceries still sat in their bags on the kitchen counter and she hadn't changed out of her work clothes, she couldn't hold back the leap of excitement within her. She scooped back her bangs, acutely conscious of the disarray of her hair and clothes.

'If you'd like to sit down . . . ' She gestured toward the living room sofa. 'I'll just be a minute.'

He took off his hat and tossed it on the sofa. 'Why don't I take a look at the washer while you change?' He didn't wait for a reply. She watched him, bemused, as he strode toward the kitchen and the service porch beyond. She followed him as far as the kitchen and quickly put away the items in the grocery bags that needed to be refrigerated. Then she hurried to her room and shed her sweaty clothes.

She turned her face up to the cool spray of the shower and tried to ease away the edginess she felt. Barely settled from her peculiar experience with the boy at the wrecking yard, Randon's arrival had reactivated all her jangling nerve endings. Although her reaction to Randon was entirely more pleasant than the shaft of fear the boy had sent through her.

She'd decided at the market that there must be a break in the fence, and the boy had slipped out through it while she was distracted calling Gertie. While she contemplated menu choices, changing her mind a dozen times, she made a mental note to have Jackson inspect the fence tomorrow.

She shut off the shower and slicked back her hair to force the excess water from it. Drying herself hurriedly, she tossed the towel on the floor. She took one step toward the bedroom, then stopped to pick up the towel and lay it neatly over the shower door.

She pulled open her dresser drawer and dug through it for a decent pair of shorts. The lack of a washer had taken a toll on her

137

clothing supply. She hadn't had time yet this week to visit the Laundromat in town, and she was down to the dregs. What she had left she would scarcely wear to work, let alone to have dinner with a man she wanted to . . . Wanted to what? Impress? Surely not. But she couldn't dress like a slob either, simply out of courtesy. She ought to at least be neat for a dinner guest, male or female.

That resolved, she turned to her closet and slid open the mirrored door. There in the back, behind her winter coat and flannel shirts was a dress. A light, summery floral print, it hung from its hanger by slender straps. She tugged it out of the closet and held it out before her. She would have to wear a strapless bra with it, but it would be blessedly cool to wear. Tossing the dress on the bed, she dug in her drawer for the bra.

Dressed, she stood before the mirror. The skirt nipped in at her waist and fell just past her knees. Even with the spaghetti straps, the dress bared less skin than her usual shorts and tank tops. But her customary clothes didn't flow over her body like this, now concealing, now revealing a rounded curve, stroking her legs and hips as she moved. She nearly wrenched the thing off, would have if Randon hadn't called her at that moment from the hallway.

138

'Kyra?' he said a second time when she didn't answer.

She moved closer to the shut door. 'Yes?'

'I have to get something else from the truck. I'll be right back.' His booted footsteps retreated down the hallway.

Lord, even his voice sent sensation prickling over her skin. She ran a hand over her wet hair, then returned to the bathroom to blow-dry it. Once her hair was in order, she contemplated the drawer of rarely used makeup. She conceded a little lipstick, a touch of mascara and shadow, then left it at that. She hardly recognized herself when she was done.

To her relief, Randon was busy with the washer when she returned to the kitchen. 'I hope chicken's okay,' she called out as she pulled the boneless breasts from the fridge.

'Anything's fine,' he said, his tone distracted.

Cooking in the summer always proved to be a challenge. When the thermometer stubbornly clung to the high nineties or low hundreds, the last thing Kyra wanted to do was turn on a stove. The boneless chicken breasts would broil quickly. While they cooked, she would sauté peppers and onions to serve over them. Then she'd sprinkle it all with grated Monterey Jack cheese, using the last of the broiler heat to melt it.

She laid the three breasts on the broiler pan, one for her, two for Randon. A quick shake of seasoning, then she slid the pan into the oven. She tossed the sliced onion and red bell pepper into a pan with a little olive oil. She alternated her time between stirring the vegetables and putting away the rest of the groceries.

'Something smells great out there,' Randon said from the service porch.

Kyra couldn't help but smile. It had been a long time since a man had complimented her on her cooking. The Snake had been lavish with his praise before they married. Afterward, when charm was no longer needed, his only commentary was negative.

She pulled the long loaf of fresh-baked French bread from its paper sack and laid it on the cutting board. The peppers and onions were nearly finished and the chicken ready for turning. 'About ten minutes until dinner,' she told Randon.

'I'll need a couple minutes to clean up.'

She leaned over the open oven, flipping the chicken with a pair of metal tongs. 'I'll give you a two-minute warning.'

She gave the veggies a last stir, then took them off the heat. Pulling down a seldom-used bread basket, she lined it with a cloth

140

napkin, then sliced the bread. She laid the slices neatly in the basket.

'Two minutes.' she called out as she lifted the broiler pan from the oven. She laid it on the stove top, then turned off the broiler.

She heard a clatter of tools, then Randon climbed the two steps from the service porch into the kitchen. Inexplicably nervous, she tugged off the oven mitts and laid them neatly on the counter. She raised her eyes to meet his gaze. A gentle smile played on his lips as his eyes roved over her. She felt herself blush and had to resist the urge to cross her arms over her chest. When he continued to gaze at her, she felt warmth pool in her middle and she caught her breath.

'Just be a minute.' As he stepped past her, his heat brushed against her as surely as if he had touched her.

Kyra took a deep breath as he disappeared into the bathroom. Every nerve ending seemed alive, dancing along her flesh. The soft folds of the dress added to the confusion of sensation and she regretted putting it on. How would she sit across from Randon with the scant fabric of the dress outlining her every curve, revealing far more than she was willing to disclose?

She tossed her head with impatience and turned back to the stove to finish dinner. She spooned vegetables on the broiled chicken, sprinkled a generous handful of grated cheese on each, then slid the pan back into the still-warm oven. By the time Randon returned from the bathroom, she had the chicken arranged on two plates, each with a cluster of fat red flame grapes.

She set the plates on the table, then turned to face him. 'I hope you like peppers and — ' Her voice trailed off at the sight of him hesitating in the doorway. Dampness darkened the hair at his temples as if he'd tossed water on his face. He must have combed the thick curls back with his fingers. His effort at making himself presentable touched her, set off a sweet yearning inside her.

Then she saw the hot look in his eyes and simple yearning exploded into something more powerful. She could feel his gaze tracing the lines of her face, resting briefly on her mouth before dropping to the pulse at her throat. Without meaning to, she raised her hand, as if to shield herself from his scrutiny. 'Shall we . . . ' She cleared her throat. 'Shall we eat?'

A long silent moment passed, then he moved to pull out her chair. She leaned forward as he helped scoot her closer to the table, but nevertheless, she felt his hand brush her bare shoulder. She took a sip of ice water to cool herself, to wash away the rampant fantasies.

He seated himself across from her and shook a cloth napkin into his lap. 'Looks great.'

Kyra watched him as he ate the first bite of chicken, waiting for his response. She'd become inured to the Snake's criticism of her cooking — eventually it hadn't mattered anymore. But Randon's opinion mattered very much, although she didn't want to explore the reason why.

Randon's eyes closed in apparent bliss as he chewed the mouthful: 'Delicious.' He cut another bite. 'Thank you.'

Kyra smiled, the simple joy of his compliment overwhelming her. 'You're welcome. Thank you for your help.'

He took a sip of the beer she'd set out for him. 'Not quite done, yet. I think it's your standing pipe that's clogged. With all those trees in the back, there are bound to be roots in the pipe.'

She held out the bread basket, offering it to him. As he reached in, the backs of his fingers brushed against hers, slowly, deliberately. He took several slices, bending his head to slather them with butter. Then he devoured a slice of bread in three bites.

Kyra struggled for normalcy, cast about for

something mundane to say. 'Can you fix it?' she asked, cutting her chicken with trembling fingers.

He finished one chicken breast, then turned his attention to the other. 'If I can snake out the clog.'

He made his way steadily through the chicken and fruit, wolfing down half the loaf of French bread while she nibbled on one slice. He drained the last of the beer, then sat back with a sigh. 'Best meal I've had in years.'

His blue-jeaned legs stretched out alongside hers, so close she could have rubbed her ankle along his calf. His gray eyes warmed and she realized the positioning of his legs was no accident.

He smiled. 'Did I tell you yet how pretty you look?'

His quiet tone of voice, the appreciation in his eyes conspired to set her to trembling. She wanted terribly to reach across the table and lay her fingertips on the back of his hand, to explore the rough sinews and strong bones there. The Snake might have been male by an accident of nature; Randon was a man in every line of body and soul.

'Thank you.' She turned her hand over, extending her fingers slightly toward him. He caught the gesture, the faint invitation and his hand closed over hers. His palm lay hot

144

against hers. He pressed his leg against hers, the denim scraping her bare calf. His gaze roamed her face, pausing at her mouth, dipping to her bare shoulders, fixing on the shadow of her cleavage.

'Kyra,' he said raggedly. He raised his eyes to hers again. 'When I first saw you — that dress — your skin like creamy white silk . . . damn.' He looked away a moment, then back. 'I want to kiss you.'

His words slammed into her with the impact of high summer heat. She wasn't sure which of them moved first, only that they were both standing inches apart. She tipped her head up, her lips parting slightly, aching, begging for his kiss. His palm curved against her jaw as he lowered his head. Her eyes fluttered closed as she felt the first brush of his lips against hers, a contact that drove the air from her lungs. He kissed her again, pressing more firmly, stroking with his lips. She swayed slightly, then reached up to rest one hand against his chest as an anchor. She waited for the invasion of his tongue, expected it since that was how the Snake had always kissed her. But she should have known Randon would do nothing the same way as her late husband. He used his mouth alone to kiss her, tease her, send sensation rocketing through her.

His mouth left hers, moved along her jaw to the shell of her ear. The feel of his breath spilling out in that sensitive place made her knees wobbly, and she had to grip his shirt for support. A soft moan escaped her throat as his mouth continued its exploration of her ear then dipped behind it to nuzzle in her hair. She gripped his shirt tighter, wanting to pull him closer, frustrated when he held his body away from hers. She took a step toward him, her other hand reaching tentatively for his waist, aching to feel him pressed against her. She felt hot and shameless, knew she would later regret her boldness. But she didn't care. For the moment she wanted only to immerse herself in feelings Randon's touch brought.

It was Randon who finally pulled away. He stepped back, looming down at her in the bright glare of the kitchen light. His arousal was a palpable thing, a throbbing beat in the air between them. In the next instant he turned and headed for the service porch. Kyra stood trembling in the wake of his sensual assault, burning, longing for the feel of his mouth on her. God forgive her, she wanted his mouth, his hands everywhere on her body, wanted him to reawaken that part of her she was sure had died. A low cry sifted from her throat as mortification settled in, sending a chill flood over her body. Gritting her teeth ruthlessly against the shaking in her hands, she cleared the table, dropping the plates so hard in the sink she chipped the edge of one.

Taking a deep breath, she wrapped her fingers around the cool tile of the counter. She could still feel Randon's soft knit shirt against her palm, the warm, firm muscle beneath it. Damn, if he came in here right now, she would go to him again, wrap herself around him and give him anything he wanted.

She turned on the faucet and let the sink fill with hot soapy water. As she washed the dishes, she heard the harsh grating of the plumber's snake scraping its way through her pipes. The guttural noise resonated in counterpoint to her own roiling emotions. She couldn't begin to guess what might be going through Randon's mind, why he'd asked to kiss her, why he'd stopped. But as she rinsed the broiler pan and leaned it against the backsplash to drain, she wanted more than anything for him to leave. She needed him gone, needed some solitude to reorder the tumult inside her.

The clatter of the snake stopped and was replaced by the sound of water filling her washer. She wiped the table with a wet sponge, imagining Randon standing over the machine, watching it fill. She could see his capable hands on the controls, the same hands that had touched her, stroked her.

She tossed the sponge into the sink and jerked the stopper out to empty it. As she watched the soapy mounds disappear down the drain, she listened to Randon moving about in the next room. She wanted to go in and watch him work, to feel relaxed and at ease being in the same room with him. She hated this constant awareness of him, the yearning made worse by the very sight of him.

Randon must have adjusted the controls on the washer because she heard the grind of the tub spinning and the hiss of the water pouring into the standing pipe. The pitch of the water flow changed as the level in the pipe grew higher; she listened for the sound of it brimming then spilling on the floor. Overflowing like her emotions. But then the water receded as the washer tub emptied. He turned the washer off, then tossed his tools in the toolbox. She could hear the bang of each piece. She took a breath, preparing herself for his reappearance in the kitchen.

She grabbed a dish towel and picked up an already dry plate, wiping at it with her back to the door. She turned when he entered, the plate still in her hands.

'Were you able to fix it?' she asked, her smile forced. She opened the cupboard and set the plate inside.

'Yeah.' He set the toolbox down on the floor, the snake beside it. 'It's good for now.'

She picked up the second plate, scrubbed at it with the dish towel. 'Great. Thanks.' *Now leave. Go.* She put the plate away, keeping her back to him. She sensed his eyes on her. Everything in her shouted at her to turn, to face him, but she ordered herself to stay where she was.

'Kyra.'

His quiet voice insinuated itself inside of her like the touch of his fingers. She set the dish towel down, her hands trembling. She heard his footsteps moving closer.

'Kyra, I'm sorry,' he said from just behind her. 'I shouldn't have — '

'You don't have to apologize.' She pushed past him, careful not to touch him. 'You wanted to kiss me, I let you do it. Not even enough to get my dad out here with a shotgun.'

He raked his fingers through his hair, his agitation clear in the gesture. 'I shouldn't have asked in the first place. You're not the kind of woman who — '

'How the hell do you know what kind of woman I am?' she broke in. 'You don't know a damn thing about me.'

He looked stunned and angry all at once. 'No, I don't. But I . . . ' He seemed to swallow back whatever he'd been about to say. 'I have to go. Thank you for dinner.'

She gave him a curt nod. 'Thank you for fixing the washer. I appreciate it.'

He picked up the toolbox and plumber's snake, then headed out the kitchen door. Kyra watched him go, feeling scattered in a hundred directions at once. Then she forced herself to go into the living room, knowing that at the least she had to see him out.

He had his back to her when she entered the living room, his hat in his hand. He was staring down, as if studying the hat, or the toes of his boots, or the fabric of the carpet. He turned the hat once, twice, then his shoulders heaved with a long breath of air. When he finally settled his hat on his head, Kyra could see his dark brown hair was just a little too long in the back, so that the hat pushed the thick curls onto the nape of his neck. Lord, she ached to plunge her fingers into that silky nest, to feel the warmth of the strong neck beneath. He turned to see her watching him. She wanted to smile at him, to say something that would soothe the breach between them. He stared at her, intent, waiting.

'Thank you again.'

She moved to the door to open it.

He picked up his tools, walked to the door. 'You're welcome.'

He pushed open the screen door and stepped outside. Kyra felt his heat scud against her. 'Will you be at the yard tomorrow?' Now that he was going, she felt perversely desperate to draw out his leaving.

He looked back at her over his shoulder. 'Don't know yet. If the production designer approves the photos, I'm done.'

Done. Gone. That set up a hollow ache inside her. 'You'd still have to come get the cars.'

He nodded. 'I should be there tomorrow, then.'

He hesitated, as if waiting to see if she was finished. Kyra leaned on the door jamb, wishing she could touch him one more time. 'Good night.'

'Good night.' He headed down the walk.

She watched him go, one hand covering her mouth, afraid she would call him back. She didn't move away from the door until his pickup truck disappeared into the night.

★ ★ ★

Randon lay on the bed, his gaze fixed on the cottage cheese ceiling of his motel room.

Despite his efforts to relax, every muscle in his body sang with tension. Kyra's heat still seared him from head to toe like the afterimage of an atomic blast. Damn, why had he kissed her? It had only strengthened the attraction between them, heightened his awareness of her to a fever pitch. He'd thought a taste of her would satisfy his body's curiosity, slake the need enough to put it behind him. But kissing her had turned out to be a mistake of monumental proportions.

God, he wanted her. He wanted her with a desperation he'd never felt with another woman. He shifted restlessly on the bed, the urgency thrumming through him. If it wasn't for his damn conscience, he'd go back there now, tease her into bed with him, satisfy his need for her.

But what if it wasn't enough? What if he slept with her, took his fill of her body and only wanted her more? Then what? He would leave her; there was no doubt of that. But could he walk away if he knew he was leaving her hurting, feeling used? Kyra needed a commitment. She needed stability, love, and forever kinds of promises. Not a one-night stand with a drifter who would take what he could and offer her nothing in return.

He shifted on the bed, guilt and arousal making him restless. Thoughts tumbled over one another in his mind, jumbled with erotic images of Kyra lying beside him, her naked body sheened with sweat, legs twined with his as he thrust into her body. One thought kept tipping toward the surface of his consciousness, nagging at him, trying to slip past the barriers deep in his soul. When it finally flared into awareness, it drove him bolt upright. He shook his head, trying to toss away the notion as so much nonsense. But the thought persisted. *What if he didn't want to walk away?*

★ ★ ★

'*But you talked to her,*' Laura said to Johnny, gazing at him across the car from her. '*She heard you.*'

'*I said her name, that was all,*' Johnny said. '*Then that damn dog came and I faded out.*'

'*I wish you wouldn't curse,*' Laura said, anxiously.

Johnny gripped the big white steering wheel, his fingers glittering against the plastic. '*It's taking too damn long.*'

An explosion seemed to simmer inside Johnny, just below the surface. Laura had seen that edginess, the razor sharp emotion once before — the night Billy Hart tried to put his hand down her blouse behind the school gym. Billy had a good six inches on Johnny, but he never had a chance. Johnny had him floored in the space of a heartbeat.

Johnny turned to her, anger brimming to the surface. '*We're running out of time.*'

Anxiety sharpened into the beginnings of despair. '*You don't know that.*'

'*I do,*' he said. '*Each time we've come back has been shorter. This time* — '

'*This time will be different,*' Laura insisted, although she'd felt the moments spilling from her fingers, tangible as dust. '*This time we have two people to help.*'

'*Two won't matter if they don't listen,*' he said, '*if they don't believe.*'

'*They will.*' Laura ached to push past the barrier between them, to touch Johnny again.

He gazed at her, his doubt, his dwindling faith clear in his face. He opened his mouth to speak, his denial of her fragile hope on his lips.

She put up a hand to stop him. '*I can't go back again, Johnny,*' Laura whispered. '*I can't go back to the black between.*'

His anger fell away then, replaced by a harsh, haunted pain. '*I know, baby, I know.*'

They spent the rest of the summer-short night face-to-face, silently speaking all the love in their hearts.

8

Laura rounded the front of the Fairlane and scanned the junkyard again, her gaze seeking out Randon. From the moment night had faded to day and she'd been pulled away from Johnny, from the car, she'd been searching for the tall cowboy. Now the sun beat down directly overhead and she still hadn't found him. As she stood in the brilliant sun, the heat seemed to sap her very essence. She'd felt it yesterday as well, in fact each day since they'd returned. She'd wanted to tell Johnny last night, but when he started talking about running out of time, it had frightened her to acknowledge that it might be true.

Anyway, the weakness, the sense of fading away, might not mean anything at all. She was a ghost, after all, someone long dead and lost to this world. It didn't have to mean that their time was short. She didn't have to feel quite so desperate to find the lanky cowboy who she knew was hers and Johnny's salvation.

When she finally saw Randon ambling through the junkyard, she cried out loud in relief. The sound of her voice, so clear to her own ears, seemed to crisp away in the sun. Hopelessness bubbled up inside her, a despair that she pushed ruthlessly aside. She would speak to Randon this time, would find a way to make him see her, hear her. As he moved closer, she saw he carried the thing she'd guessed yesterday was a camera. He occasionally raised it to his face to snap a picture of a car and a square of cardboard would pop from the front of the black case. She wondered if that was the picture and marveled at how the camera could make it so fast.

He stopped two rows over from Laura, close enough that she could see his face. He lifted one booted foot to the bumper of a nearby car and his gaze strayed over to the Fairlane. He was looking for her, Laura realized. She stood straighter, as tall as she could stretch her five-foot-two frame. His gaze seemed to pass right through her. She waved her arms above her head, jumped up and down, called his name. He stared a moment more, then turned away.

Laura could have screamed her frustration. She watched him swipe a hand across his face; he seemed as angry and irritable as she. He knew she was there, he sensed her, and it made him mad that he couldn't see her. His dark expression reminded Laura of how her father would look when she used to sass him. Thunderclouds, her mother called that look of her father's, a storm about to break.

She leaned against the Fairlane with a sigh, fighting off the ache that the memory of her parents started up inside her. Tears burned at the back of her throat. If there were anything she wanted nearly as much as to hold Johnny in her arms, it was to see her mother and father again. Were they still in this world? Had they moved on to the next? She would never know until she was somehow liberated from captivity.

Randon stuffed the stack of pictures into his back pocket and pushed off from the car he'd been resting against. He paused, looking first away from Laura, then toward her. She saw the unease in his face and he seemed to lean away as if about to go in the other direction. Laura couldn't let him do that. He had to come closer. Drawing deep inside herself, pulling strength from her love for Johnny, her powerful need to be with him again, she called out.

'Randon!'

He stopped, one foot half lifted to step away. He stood poised, listening. Laura gripped her hands into fists, fought against the lassitude of the sun, of her own dwindling hope. 'Randon!' she nearly screamed.

Her voice seemed to echo around the junkyard, rattled the metal fenders of the Ford. If Randon couldn't hear her shout, he somehow heard the clatter of the car. He took a step closer, another.

Laura gathered herself up again, shut her eyes briefly against the blinding sunlight. She pictured Johnny's face, her love for him replacing the white-hot glare. This time, when she spoke, the word came out in a whisper.

'*Randon.*'

He heard her. He turned.

He saw her.

*   ★   ★

Stunned, Randon stared at the girl standing before the old Fairlane. My God, he thought. It's her again. He moved slowly toward her, as if fording a river of molasses. As he neared the blonde-haired girl, he waited for the figment of light and searing heat to fade as it had the day before. He'd convinced himself he'd hallucinated the whole thing — the girl, the disappearing act. But now that she was here again, he wasn't sure which part of his encounter yesterday was real and what he'd only imagined.

'Who are you?' he asked, not liking the

hoarseness in his voice. 'How do you know my name?'

The girl tipped up her chin and grinned, her impish smile lighting her blue eyes. '*I'm Laura.*' Her voice seemed less substantial than the thick summer air.

He glanced down at her bare feet, wondered briefly how she could stand on the hot asphalt. 'How do you know me?'

She shrugged, her ponytail bouncing. '*I've heard her call your name.*'

'Her . . . you mean Kyra?' Randon guessed.

The girl nodded. Her eyes were so bright and she seemed so happy, even beyond the buoyancy of youth. Randon couldn't remember ever feeling so joyous. Except when he was with Kyra. Those few moments when he let himself feel happiness, feel joy. He thrust aside those dangerous thoughts and focused back on the girl. 'I thought you had to be sixteen to come in here without an adult.' He scanned the near vicinity. 'Are you here with your folks?'

A bleak look passed briefly over her young face, then she tipped her chin up higher. '*I am sixteen*,' she said haughtily.

Just barely, Randon conjectured. With a faint smile, he studied the girl, wondering what it was about her that drew him, that made him want to tease her and make her smile. She reminded him a bit of Rachelle in that last year before he left her. A young woman teetering between childhood and maturity. Yet there was a quality about Laura that Rachelle had never had. Something that nagged at Randon, like an alarm barely on the periphery of awareness. As if there were something he should know about her. He felt a sudden impulse to find out more about her. 'What's your last name, Laura?'

She opened her mouth to answer, her shoulders lifting as she took a breath. Her brow creased as if the question were more difficult than it should be. She couldn't remember her last name? Then something changed in her eyes and she gave him a crafty look. '*Is Kyra your girl?*'

So she didn't want to tell him her last name. Randon let it rest for the moment. 'I don't have a girlfriend.'

'*Why not?*' she asked with all the frankness of youth.

Randon crossed his arms over his chest. 'I don't want one.'

She tossed her head. '*Every guy wants a girl.*'

'Not this one.' He took a breath, intending to ask her again about her name.

'*Do you love her?*' she blurted. '*Kyra, I mean.*'

He laughed. 'No. Why would you ask such a thing?'

She eyed him speculatively. *'Because I've seen the way you look at her.'*

Irritation boiled up in Randon at the thought of this girl watching him, guessing things about him he would just as soon not know. 'I'm not in love with anyone. And it's time you told me who you are and what you're doing here.'

'I said my name is Laura,' she said. *'And I'm here because I need . . . I need . . . '* Her eyes grew wide and she flung her arms out as if to save herself from a fall. A moan of frustration escaped from her throat as she bent her head down to her feet. Randon followed her gaze with his own and shock rocketed through him.

Her feet were gone. As he watched, her ankles vanished, then her knees, in exactly the same fashion as they had the day before. She held her hands up as if to save them from the invisible wave. She stared up at him, frantic.

Her urgency struck him, as compelling as the blast of summer heat. 'What do you need?' he asked as the strange force drifted up her body. Nothing but her face remained. He almost thought he saw the glitter of tears in her eyes.

In the instant before she was gone, she

cried out, '*I need your help!*'

Randon stared at the empty space before him, her sweet young voice echoing inside him like a sob.

★   ★   ★

Kyra glanced up at the clock in her office. Another hour to closing time. Another hour to pretend Randon wasn't somewhere in the yard, to pretend it didn't matter that he was here. To agonize over what she would say if he came to see her, to torture herself with the fact that he hadn't tried to see her at all. She'd been out in the yard when he'd arrived, had sensed his presence the moment he walked through the gates. Even without seeing the hat — and he wasn't the only man wearing a cowboy hat as protection against the heat — she'd known it was him striding toward the service window.

He'd stepped up to Jackson's window, apparently to identify to the older man which cars had been found suitable and which had not. She saw him turn once to look out over the yard, but if he was looking for her or just idly scanning the rows of cars she couldn't tell: His gaze passed right over her where she stood behind the bed of a monster pickup. Then he started out into the yard, moving

162

away from where she stood. That he might have done it to avoid her had pricked more deeply than Kyra cared to admit. She had decided in that moment that she'd had enough of the heat and had headed back to her office, where she'd found more than enough to occupy her for the afternoon. Especially since the work went slower than usual because she couldn't seem to put two thoughts together without Randon intruding.

Thank God it was Saturday, that she'd have tomorrow off. She needed a day to regroup, to bring her life back into the balance that had been upset the day Randon had appeared.

She pushed back from her desk, the 'whys' and 'what ifs' whirling in her head. Why had she worn the dress last night? Why had he asked to kiss her? Why had she let him? What if they hadn't stopped, had let things progress to their natural conclusion? She knew the answer to the final question. If she had fallen into bed with Randon Bolton last night, she would have been dealing with more than awkward embarrassment this morning. She would have been irrevocably changed, her life wrenched on a different path.

Because she couldn't have slept with Randon last night and then let him go. She couldn't bear it. And they both knew he would leave. He would leave and, if they'd taken things any further, it would have broken her heart. She might have denied that he knew anything about her, what kind of woman she was and what she wanted, but he was right. She couldn't have sex with him unless it was making love. And it wouldn't be making love unless —

She jumped to her feet, paced the small confines of her office. She didn't love him. She hadn't gone that far over the deep end. But there was more to what she felt for Randon than physical attraction. She could easily live without sex — look at the sterile final months of her marriage to the Snake and the two loveless years since. But caring, affection — she craved that tender attention, wept for it sometimes in the long, lonely nights. But it didn't have to be Randon that provided it. Maybe she'd ignored that side of herself, her needs as a woman, as a human being. Maybe it was time she found a partner, someone to help shoulder her burdens, to reach for during the bleak times. But not Randon. He would only pile more heartache onto her life. Were she to give anything more of herself to him, her body, her heart, the pain of his leaving would be beyond bearing. There were other men, steady men she could set her sights on. As for Randon, it was just as well he leave as soon as possible.

She rubbed at the bridge of her nose, a jumpy energy suddenly skittering along her bare arms. It was time she got out of this tiny room. She turned to the door, laid her hand on the handle. She froze at the rumble of Randon's voice through the thin office wall.

'Hey, Jackson,' he said from the direction of the service window. 'Here's the latest batch.'

Kyra gripped the doorknob. She should simply go out there, give him a cool greeting and get on with ringing out the register. But she waited, breath held, listening. She only made out a word or two of Jackson's soft reply. Then she caught the tail end of Randon's response.

' . . . pick them all up tomorrow.'

A peculiar sensation spilled through Kyra's body. Pick them all up? Did that mean he'd found the last of the cars he needed, that he would soon be gone? Despite her lecture to herself, a dull ache settled inside her at the thought of him gone. Lord, he already meant more to her than he should.

She felt a sudden urgency to see him, to talk to him once more before he left. She pulled open the door and stepped through, listening for his voice. But when she entered the service room, a stranger stood at Jackson's window. An inexplicable feeling of

165

loss washed over her. She stepped up to Jackson. 'I heard Randon out here.' She tried to keep her tone noncommittal.

He glanced over at her as he handed the customer his change. 'He took off.'

Kyra worried the inside of her lower lip, not wanting to ask, not able to stop herself. 'Will he be back tomorrow?'

Jackson shut the register. 'Think so. Got to pick up the cars that director fellow wants.'

Relief flooded her. 'Great. Okay.' She turned to the idle register. Her hands shook as she opened the drawer and began the ring out.

'Thought he might ask about you,' Jackson said.

Her fingers faltered and she dropped a quarter from the handful she was counting. She went chasing after the silver disk, caught up with it just behind Jackson's feet.

'Why would you think that?' Kyra asked as she straightened.

Jackson shrugged. 'Thought you two been seeing a little bit of each other.'

Kyra dumped the counted quarters back into the tray.

'He fixed my stove and my washer. I made him dinner. That's all.'

Jackson stepped back from the empty window. 'Seems like a good man.'

'He's a drifter, Jackson.' Kyra scooped up the dimes, stacked them in tens on the counter. 'Just passing through.'

'S'pose so,' Jackson said, then turned to an approaching customer.

Mr. Carson stood at the window, a grease-encrusted alternator clutched in his hands. He peered up at Jackson suspiciously.

Jackson smiled down at the diminutive man. 'What you got there, Mr. Carson?'

Mr. Carson shoved the part across the counter. 'Alternator. Eighty-nine Lumina sedan.'

As she finished the ring-out, Kyra listened with half an ear to Jackson's one-way conversation with Mr. Carson. She scanned the yard. Ten minutes to closing and it looked deserted. Lifting the money tray from the register to put it in the safe, she turned to Mr. Carson. 'Did you see anyone else out there?'

The old man's ruddy pinched face paled. 'What do you mean?' he said belligerently.

Kyra puzzled over his reaction. 'I have to lock up in a few minutes. I just wondered if there are any stragglers in the yard.'

His rheumy blue eyes narrowed to slits. 'Didn't see anyone.'

'Fine. Thanks.' Kyra turned and carried the money tray to the office. She opened the safe and shoved the money inside. She left the safe door open so that Jackson could put in the second tray.

'I'll check the yard,' she called to Jackson as she passed the service room on her way out.

A thick wall of humidity pushed against her as she stepped outside. Dense gray clouds clustered overhead, portending a summer storm. Electricity seemed to cling to the gummy air, setting Kyra even more on edge. By the time she'd reached Gertie's run and released the dog, her sleeveless cotton shirt was soaked. She couldn't help but remember the boy from yesterday. This morning, she'd described him to Trish and Jackson, asked them to keep an eye out for him.

She gazed out across the yard toward the corner where the old Fairlane sat. Maybe she ought to ask Jackson if he'd seen the boy. She chewed the inside of her lip, indecisive. Jackson would have told her right away if the boy had wandered in. His sharp eyes didn't miss much. She caught sight of Gertie as the shepherd quartered the yard as she'd been trained. The dog would have barked or growled by now if she sensed anything. The yard was certainly just as empty of customers as it looked.

Lightning speared the ground off to the East just as Jackson clanged the front gate shut. Shaking off her jittery nerves, Kyra strode out into the yard to the accompaniment of thunder. As she scanned the lot a section at a time, she worried over the lightning in the distance. If this storm had only fireworks and no rain in store, there was a real danger of those bolts setting off the tinder dry grass in the foothills. Floods in the winter, wildfire in the summer. She didn't know which was worse.

Fat raindrops hit just as Kyra came up against the back fence. She worked her way along the chainlink, reveling in the scattering of rain as it splattered on the ground and on the cars. A clap of thunder nearly startled her out of her work boots and she laughed, relief born of the cool, wet rain.

An instant later, Gertie barked, the deep guttural sound setting off Kyra's anxiety again. The dog might only be reacting to the thunder, but Kyra had to check. She followed the sound of the dog, caution roiling in her when she realized Gertie was near the Fairlane. Kyra blinked away raindrops, squinted at Gertie where the dog alternately barked and growled at the old Ford. There was nothing, no one there. Lightning streaked down off to her right, followed almost immediately by a thunderous boom. A gust of rain slapped Kyra in the face, forcing her to close her eyes. She swiped off her face,

169

opened her eyes again.

He was there.

Kyra stood gaping at the grinning boy leaning against the Fairlane. She worked her mouth, opening it once, twice, trying to shape words. Rain battered the ground, rattled on car hoods. Gertie fell silent, head down, tail low.

Kyra swallowed and forced out a question. 'Who are you?'

'*Johnny.*' The boy lifted a foot up on the Fairlane's bumper and propped his elbow on his raised knee. '*You're Kyra, aren't you?*'

She swiped rain from her brow, her hand shaking. 'How do you know my name?'

He shrugged. '*I've been around.*' He looked out over the yard. '*So, you own this place?*'

'I do.' Kyra advanced a step. 'And you're trespassing.'

'*Hey, if I had a choice, I wouldn't be here at all.*'

There was a wrongness here, Kyra realized as she stared at Johnny. Something off balance in this picture of a cocky young man in her wrecking yard. She didn't feel threatened by him — he was too open and friendly for that. But she felt uneasy, as if her subconscious saw what was askew, but refused to share the information.

170

Kyra chanced to look away, quickly scanning the yard. 'Did you come with your parents?' She looked back at him, was relieved to see he still stood there.

He looked down at the wet pavement, then up at her, the brassy grin gone. 'No, *I didn't.*'

He seemed too young to wear that haunted look. Was he a runaway? Homeless? Good God, was he hiding out, living in one of her wrecks? She speared him with her best authority-figure glare. 'What are you doing here, Johnny?'

He shrugged. '*This is where we ended up this time.*'

We? There was someone else with him here? Good Lord, if anyone found out she was harboring a couple of runaway minors on her lot . . .

'You can't stay,' she blurted, then hastily added, 'I'll help however I can, call your folks or the police.'

'No.' He shook his head.

'But your parents would want to know you're safe,' Kyra insisted.

'*No!*' He pushed away from the car, angry and agitated. '*Damn!*'

In that moment, the downpour ceased, the summer squall spent. Kyra shook raindrops from her hair and took another step toward

171

Johnny, wondering what she could say to calm him.

Then her subconscious finally lobbed out the information it had withheld. 'Your clothes are dry.' Kyra stared at the crisp white shirt, the neat black slacks. Her own shorts and sleeveless shirt clung wetly to her body. 'How can your clothes be dry?'

He didn't answer, too busy glaring down at his feet. Kyra followed the direction of his gaze and her heart skipped a beat before racing again in a double-time rhythm. His feet had disappeared. The wet pavement shone dully just below a pair of ankles. Then whatever force had taken his feet swallowed Johnny's ankles and continued hungrily up his body.

'Oh, my God,' Kyra whispered. She looked up at him. 'What's happening? What's going on?'

'*I can't* — ' His hands fisted. '*Can't stop it.*'

He disappeared swiftly then, his desperate brown eyes fading last. He stared at her, his anguish cutting straight to Kyra's soul. Then nothing remained but the thick, humid air.

As Gertie's frenzied barking resumed, Kyra stepped forward on trembling legs. There should be a mark on the car, a streak across the Fairlane's hood where Johnny had been leaning. But the thick layer of muddy dust was undisturbed. She drew a finger across the hood, came away with a black smudge on her fingertip. She stared at that white line inscribed in the dust for an endless moment, frightened, excited, and agonized all at once. When Gertie finally quieted, Kyra crouched and wrapped an arm around the dog's neck. Her face buried in the wet fur, she willed her heart to slow, her breathing to steady.

When she finally headed to the exit and let herself out, she worried over the questions that tumbled in her mind. Who was Johnny? Why was he there in her yard? Who was with him? And would he be back?

9

Randon gave the rain-wet aluminum picnic table another swipe with the wad of paper towels he'd cadged from the location trailer, then arranged the day's photos in four neat rows. The brilliant blue of the storm-washed sky shouldered aside the thick gray clouds, and the sun beat down again, sizzling away the moisture.

Randon resisted the urge to correct the alignment of one crooked photo as Evans pondered the day's selection. Randon had given up the notion that he had a clue as to what Evans was looking for. He'd just shot at random, hoping the production designer would find something acceptable. He held his breath as Evans lifted first one, then another photo from the table. A long pause, then he selected a third.

'I like these.' Evans handed the photos to Randon.

Randon stuffed the snapshots into his back jeans pocket, then scooped up the rejected photos. 'You want them towed to the same spot as the other two?' Mario had brought Evans's first choices over earlier that day.

'I haven't decided,' Evans said. 'I'll let you know Monday.'

Randon turned to go, then stopped at the sound of Evans's voice. 'Just a minute, Bolton.'

Randon looked back to see Evans pulling the *Sacramento Bee* from his briefcase. He flipped to the classified ads and tore a corner from the page.

'I want you to check this out,' Evans said, pointing to an ad circled in ink. 'Sounds like what I'm looking for.'

Randon quickly scanned the five lines of text. *'71 Ford Ranchero, blown head gasket, take all or part . . .* 'How the hell do I figure out it's what you want?'

Evans gave him a look that clearly indicated he didn't credit Randon with having the brains to walk and spit at the same time. 'I've outlined my vision,' Evans said, tugging a sheet of paper from the briefcase, 'which I obviously should have done at the outset.'

Randon felt the tension in his jaw grow as he swallowed back his anger. Evans's damn vision had changed a dozen times since filming started. He flapped the piece of paper at Randon. 'You just read those over, and if the car fits the profile — '

'Where is it?' Randon asked.

'A ranch up near Redding,' Evans said. 'I've already called to set it up. He's expecting you tomorrow at two.'

Irritation rolled down Randon's spine at the way Evans had commandeered his Sunday. He'd planned on a day off, a day to relax, to regroup. A day to put Kyra Aimes and her all too tempting charms out of his mind, to drive the memory of her touch out of his body.

'I wrote down the directions.' Evans handed him a scribbled Post-it. Then he pulled a fat business-sized envelope from the briefcase. 'Try not to spend it all.'

Randon took the envelope and the neatly typewritten 'vision statement.' 'How do I get the car back here?'

'Pay that tow driver a few bucks to pick it up,' Evans said. 'He looked like he could use the extra money.'

Randon had to turn and walk away then or he would have flattened Evans. He decided in that moment that if Mario towed the car, Randon would make sure the young man demanded a fee that would leave Evans gasping for air. He was so caught up in his aggravation over Evans, Randon didn't realize the significance of the next day's destination until he was turning into the motel parking lot. Redding. He was going up

176

to Redding tomorrow.

Nosing the pickup into the parking slot by his room, he hauled a dog-eared Thomas Brothers map from under the seat. Deciphering Evans's scrawl, he found the location of the ranch. He tapped the map page. There, not five miles from the ranch, was his sister's place. Randon ran a hand over his face. How could he drive two hundred miles tomorrow and not hop on over to see his sister? Even if she never found out — and there was really no way for her to find out — he didn't think he could live with the guilt if he didn't pay her a visit.

Okay, so he'd just go inside and give Rachelle a call. He stepped out of the truck. His feet seemed to drag on the pavement as he headed for his room. He had to dial twice to get the number right and then it was busy. That was nearly enough to persuade him to change his mind. He waited five minutes, then picked up the phone a third time and carefully punched out the numbers. When the phone rang he thought his heart would thump out of his chest. When Tom answered instead of Rachelle, Randon felt sharp relief.

'Tom, it's Randon.'

A long pause in which Randon could feel Tom's silent indictment, then his brother-in-law growled, 'Damn well time you called.'

'I've been busy.' Randon felt like the worst kind of liar. 'How is she?'

'Scared. Hurting. Feeling damned alone.'

Each word went through Randon like the kick of a half-crazed bronc. 'Is she there?'

'Napping,' Tom said. 'I'll get her — '

'No! I don't want to disturb her.' Tom's angry disapproval seemed to sing through the phone wires. 'Anyway, I'm coming up there tomorrow. For the job. Thought I'd drop in if you folks aren't busy.'

'She'd like that,' Tom said quietly. 'Hell, the boys'll be over the moon to see you. You should hear the stories Rachelle tells them about you.'

'Okay, then,' Randon said. 'I should be there around three.'

'Plan to stay for dinner,' Tom said.

'I wouldn't want to put you out — '

'Plan to stay,' Tom repeated, then he hung up the phone.

Randon laid the receiver down, his hand trembling. Damn, what was wrong with him? He was only going to visit his sister, the little girl he'd helped to raise, long distance, anyway. Why should he feel gut-punched at the thought of seeing her again? But he very well knew why. It was because of her . . . problem. Because she was hurting, because she had something eating away at

178

her, something that could kill her. Something he had no earthly control over.

Sending her a packet of money wouldn't make the problem go away. This wasn't school clothes that needed buying or college fees that needed paying. This was disaster looming, a peril that he couldn't fight with his will or his fists. He could only offer Rachelle his heart, his love. And he knew, with bone-chilling certainty, that his love, his heart would fall short. It wouldn't be enough.

He sank to the edge of the bed, feeling hopelessness wash over him. Maybe he should call Tom back and tell him his plans had changed, that he wouldn't be able to make it tomorrow. He reached for the phone, lifted the receiver. Guilt pummeled him, forced the phone from his hand. He couldn't back out. He couldn't go see her. What the hell was he going to do?

Like a sweet shaft of sunlight punching through storm clouds, he saw Kyra's face. It was like a miracle seeing her in his mind's eye and a rush of emotion flooded him. Without realizing what he was doing, he pushed to his feet and grabbed up his truck keys from the nightstand. The need to escape overwhelmed him — to run from his unwelcome feelings for Kyra, his sense of helplessness for his sister.

As he pulled from the motel lot, he punched the pickup's accelerator pedal, as if the roar of the engine could frighten away his demons. A futile effort, because the demons lived inside him.

★ ★ ★

Just past midnight, Kyra switched off her front porch light and crossed the darkened living room to shut the front miniblinds. Her hand stilled when she looked outside and saw the truck parked at the curb. Moonlight reflected off the windshield, reducing the pickup's occupant to an insubstantial silhouette.

She closed the blinds and sat on the arm of the recliner beside the window. How long had he been out there? She hadn't heard him pull up, but then she'd been watching television in her bedroom at the back of the house. If he was here, why hadn't he come to the door? She rose and poked her hand through the slats of the miniblinds to take another look. There was something terribly lonely about Randon's truck parked there in the moonlight. Should she go out and talk to him, ask him why he was there? But if he'd wanted to speak with her, he would have come to the door.

She caught a glimpse of his face in the passenger side window as he leaned over to look at the house. She let go of the slats, not wanting him to see her watching him. He must not want her to know he was there. And yet she couldn't help but sense there was something terribly wrong.

Just as she was about to take another look, she heard the sound of his truck engine starting up. Without conscious thought, she quickly rounded the recliner and pulled open the front door. She slapped on the porch light as she stepped outside.

She still couldn't see him through the windshield, but he must have seen her. The truck didn't move, and in another moment, Randon killed the engine. Another long beat and he climbed from the pickup, gazed at her over the roof of the cab. He was bareheaded, and the missing cowboy hat added to the sense of wrongness.

'Was there something you wanted?' she asked, feeling breathless. She stepped off the porch and down the front walk as far as the light would reach.

A thousand emotions seemed to chase across his face. He backed away from the truck and slammed the door. He moved slowly around the hood and approached her.

'I didn't see you today,' he said, gazing down at her.

'We were both busy.' She tugged at the cropped tank top she wore, wishing she'd changed into something nicer after work. 'Jackson said you'd be back tomorrow.'

'Just to pick up cars.' He raked his fingers through his hair. 'I don't suppose you work on a Sunday.'

'Not if I can help it.'

He shoved his hands into his jeans pockets, rocked back on his heels. He seemed interested in the moon-cast shadows of photinia stretching across the lawn, in the gnarled branches of the oak that shaded her house. She wanted to touch him, run her fingers along his arm, soothe his strange agitation. 'Was there something you needed?'

He opened his mouth, took a breath, looked away again. She did touch him then, bare contact on his forearm before she withdrew. It seemed to steady him.

'I need to drive up to Redding tomorrow.' He seemed in a rush to get the words out. 'There's a car the production designer wants me to take a look at.'

'Did you want Mario to go up with you, drive the tow truck?' A chill breeze curled along her bare midriff and she hugged herself for warmth. 'He doesn't work on Sundays either. He has church, and family obligations.'

He seemed to be struggling again. 'Could you?' he asked finally. 'Go with me?'

'Drive the truck, you mean?'

He nodded and Kyra felt a mix of emotions — disappointment that he only wanted her along to drive the tow truck, a niggling suspicion that there was more behind his request. She did a quick mental inventory of what she'd had planned on her one day off, although she already knew she'd say yes. Randon watched her intently, as if her response were crucially important.

'Sure, why not,' she told him. 'I haven't been to Redding in a while.'

A smile spread across his face, the sweetness of it bursting brilliantly inside her. Somehow she'd lightened his load, and she felt a joy inside at the privilege.

'Meet you at the yard?' he asked. 'Eleven o'clock?'

She laughed, feeling lighter herself. 'Eleven sounds fine.'

'I'll pick up a couple of sandwiches. We can eat lunch on the way.' He backed away, his hands restless at his sides. 'See you then.'

He rounded his truck again and tugged open the door. But he didn't climb in, just looked at her.

'What?' Kyra asked.

He gripped the top of the pickup's door, seemed to measure his words. 'I need to make a stop after we check on the car. My sister's. If that's okay.'

She wondered at his tension. 'No problem.'

'I said we'd stay for dinner.'

The turbulence had returned to his face. Kyra burned to know what it was about his sister that put those emotions there.

She smiled. 'I never turn down a free meal.'

'Great. See you tomorrow.'

He swung down into the truck, slammed the door. The engine roared to life. When he waited at the curb, Kyra realized he wanted to see her safe in the house before he left. She waved and made her way back up the walk. She watched from her front door as his truck pulled away into the night.

* * *

Sipping from his cardboard cup of coffee, Randon leaned against the bed of his pickup, watching for Kyra's car. He'd arrived a few minutes early and pulled the truck under the shade of a spreading mimosa, a scrap of coolness in the already searing heat. He hoped to hell the tow truck was air-conditioned or they'd have a damned hot ride up to Redding.

He took another swallow of the strong black brew and set the cup down in the truck bed next to the bags filled with sandwiches, chips, and soda. He didn't like to think about how desperately he needed Kyra with him today. He felt like a damned coward asking her along to act as a buffer for his visit with his sister. Especially since he'd told her nothing about Rachelle's problem.

He spotted Kyra's car traveling along Sunrise and tipped up his hat slightly to follow it with his eyes. She pulled into the lot and parked next to him. When she climbed out, she smiled up at him, looking cool and comfortable in a sleeveless white blouse and denim cutoffs. God, he was so damned glad to see her and that joy made him feel even weaker.

She gestured to his cup. 'Any chance you brought one of those for me? Didn't quite get my quota today.'

'We can share. You drink it black?'

'I like it with sugar, but I'll live.' She took the cup from him, sipped from it twice. She pursed her lips at the bitter taste. The action sent a curl of heat straight to his groin. He turned away from her to hide his response and grabbed their lunch from the pickup.

'I hope turkey's okay.' He tugged at his

jeans with one hand, his other arm gripping the bags.

'It's fine.' She set the coffee on the bumper. 'Give me a minute. I have to take care of a couple things.'

She strode off toward the entrance gate, the sleek line of her legs beguiling. Picking up his coffee, he followed and watched her as she disappeared into the cinderblock building housing her office.

He leaned against the chain-link fence, his gaze idly roving the yard. Heat came off the twisted metal of the cars in waves, a simmering illusion of motion. Then he did see something move in the distance, an early morning customer, or . . . He stood bolt upright when he realized it was Laura, waving at him from across the yard. He tipped down his hat brim to better shade his eyes and narrowed his gaze. Laura fluttered her hand at him, gesturing to him to come closer. He glanced over at the service window where Trish chomped her gum and flipped through a magazine. She looked up once, stared out at the yard, but if she saw Laura, she gave no indication.

Laura waved again, this time with both arms. No doubt she wanted to talk to him, to madden him with more unanswerable questions. He took a step away from the fence, eyes fixed on Laura —

'Ready,' Kyra said behind him, turning him away from the girl. She brandished a handful of sugar packages. 'For the coffee. Do you mind?'

'No problem.' He handed the coffee to her, then scanned the yard again. Laura had vanished.

Irritation warred with the cold chill Laura's sudden disappearance chased up his spine. He considered describing Laura to Kyra, to ask her casually if she'd ever seen the young girl with a ponytail, but he couldn't come up with a reasonable way to ask the question.

'What is it?' Kyra drew his attention back to her. She sipped at the coffee, gazing up at him expectantly.

He sidestepped her query by moving off toward the tow truck. 'Let's go.'

Randon couldn't resist one last look as Kyra pulled the truck through the double front gate. If Laura was out there, he couldn't see her.

'Forget something?' Kyra asked.

He picked up the bags he'd set at his feet. 'Just wondering where to put these.'

'There's room behind the seat.' She shifted expertly, eyes on the road. 'So is your sister younger than you? Older?'

He set the bags down, faced forward again.

'Couple years younger.'

Kyra pulled onto Highway 50 heading west. 'You get together much?'

The casual question shouldn't have made him feel defensive, but it did. 'I travel quite a bit. Don't get around here much.'

Kyra glanced over at him. 'When did you see her last?'

He stirred uneasily in his seat. 'Four — no, five years.'

'Five years!' She turned briefly to face him, her eyes wide with surprise. 'You haven't seen your sister in five years?'

An unreasonable anger rose in him at Kyra's question. Somehow, he could hear his mother's lecturing tone in the words. His mother had asked only one thing before she died, that he take care of Rachelle. So far, he'd done a damned poor job of it.

He took a calming breath. 'I keep in touch. Send her letters sometimes.' Once a year, maybe. 'Presents for her boys.'

He tightened his jaw, waiting for further censure from Kyra. A long, silent beat passed, then she said, 'But you're going now.'

A knot loosened inside him. He released a pent-up breath. 'I had to. Being so close and all.'

'I'm sure you'll be glad to see your nephews, too. How old are they?'

'Chris is six and Daniel's eight.'

Kyra changed lanes as they approached the Interstate 5 interchange. 'So they were just babies when you saw them last.'

'I've seen pictures since,' Randon said, feeling defensive again. 'Rachelle sends me letters. I keep track of them.'

'That's good, then.'

Kyra fell silent as they headed north on I-5, and Randon sank back into his seat in relief. He knew she only asked her questions out of idle curiosity, but every mention of Rachelle brought back his fears for her, his sense of helplessness.

It occurred to him he ought to tell Kyra the rest, the part about Rachelle's problem. No doubt it would come up during their visit and he should prepare her, to make it less awkward. When he tried to form the words, he realized that Kyra would be the first person Randon had talked to about Rachelle. A new fear tickled inside him, that speaking of Rachelle's diagnosis out loud would make the horror of it seem more real and infinitely more deadly.

He rubbed his hands over his face, telling himself he was being ridiculous. Talking about Rachelle's problem wouldn't change anything or make it worse. He shifted in his seat, glancing over at Kyra, then out at the window. He cleared his throat and took a breath . . .

'What is it?' Kyra asked.

Her question hung between them and he knew he had to say something. But not about Rachelle, not yet. He'd tell her that later, when they were closer to Redding, when he'd figured out a way to say it that wouldn't make the horror greater.

'I am a little worried,' he said.

'About?'

'The boys,' he said. 'They don't know me at all. They might not like me. They could even be afraid of me.'

Kyra turned a brief smile toward him. 'Your sister's told them about you, right?'

'I suppose so.'

'About all your traveling, the rodeos, working in the movies.'

He nodded, smiling. 'No doubt exaggerating a bit.'

'Take my word for it. They'll love you.' She reached over and squeezed his upper arm lightly. 'You're the stuff little boys' dreams are made of.'

Another brief caress, then Kyra withdrew to focus on her driving. He wanted her hand back, to link her fingers with his, maybe have their joined hands rest on his knee. Not as a sexual gesture, but to draw more comfort from her to ease away the still-nagging worries, about the boys, about Rachelle.

But just sitting with her here in the truck was enough. Now that the conversation was safely away from Rachelle and her problem, he talked about the passing scenery, the Sacramento River winding along beside I-5, the endless, dusty flat expanses. He told her about the small-time rodeos he'd ridden in up and down California and into Nevada, the wrangling jobs he'd taken in between rides. He liked to hear her laugh, liked the way she tipped her head back, her short hair brushing the collar of her sleeveless white shirt. So he made the stories as funny as he could, wrenching humor out of the time he got dumped by a bull and nearly ended up singing soprano.

He was damned glad he had her along today, so glad it worried him. He tried to convince himself that if he'd driven up with Mario he'd have enjoyed the man's company just as much, but he knew he was fooling himself. Kyra was beginning to mean far too much to him. To start feeling anything for her would be a mistake. Just the thought of settling down to stay with this one woman set off alarms inside him, weighted him down with needs and responsibilities.

He got tired of talking and let the quiet

stretch between them. When he glanced over at her, a sheen of sweat had settled on her brow as the morning's heat overcame the blast of cool air from the air conditioner. Damned if he didn't want to brush his fingers along her skin there, press his lips against hers.

He took in a breath and she turned at the sound. She must have seen something in his face because her lips parted and her eyes widened. It was all he could do to keep from tracing the line of her cheek with his fingertips, to stroke away the moisture there. He forced his hand to his hat instead, repositioning it on his head. He drummed his fingers on the door, casting about for something to say, to chase away the dangerous silence.

'How about you?' he blurted. 'Any brothers or sisters?'

If she was surprised by the abrupt question, she didn't show it. 'No. I'm an only child.'

Doggedly, he persisted. 'What about your folks? Do they live near here?'

She compressed her lips and her eyes narrowed slightly. 'My mother's dead.'

Randon wondered if he'd blundered into forbidden territory. 'I'm sorry.'

She sighed and shrugged. 'I was young. I

don't remember very much about her.'

'But I bet you still miss her.'

'Yeah,' she said softly. 'Even though sometimes I can't even remember what she looked like.'

'My folks died when I was seventeen,' Randon told her. 'Car accident. Mom hung on a few days after Dad.'

'Oh, I'm sorry, Randon.' She reached out to him again, stroking his arm in a soothing gesture that was nevertheless erotic.

He could feel the first stirrings of an erection and he felt like a fool reacting so strongly to such a simple touch. He tried to think of something to say, remembered her mentioning a husband, a bad marriage. The last damn thing he should talk about.

The words slipped out before he could stop himself. 'So how long were you married?'

She snatched her hand back as if he'd bitten it. 'Too long.' She had an edge to her voice. She laughed, a humorless sound. 'He shouldn't make me angry anymore, but thinking of the Snake still gets my back up.'

'The Snake?'

She gave him a wry smile. 'He had a name. I just don't choose to use it.' She flexed her hands on the steering wheel. 'The most charming man you'd ever care to meet. As long as you didn't cross him.'

She said the words lightly, but he sensed old hurts behind them. 'I suppose you crossed him once or twice.'

'I couldn't please the man.' She got a stubborn set to her chin. 'He never laid a hand on me, but by God, he found other ways. I almost would have preferred a beating.'

He wanted to rage at a long-dead man for his cruelty, he wanted to reach out and offer comfort to Kyra. But touching her seemed far too risky and he couldn't seem to find words adequate to express his feelings.

She must have seen something of his dilemma in his face because she flashed him a smile. 'He's gone. It's over. I like to think that I would have thrown the bum out by now if he hadn't died.'

He closed his hand over her shoulder, just the slightest pressure of his fingers, then he retreated. She sighed, as if releasing tension.

'Got any more rodeo stories, cowboy?' she asked, stretching out the syllables in a ridiculous drawl.

'A few,' he said, then proceeded to tell her the one about the saddle bronc that wouldn't buck and the roping calf that ate his favorite hat.

As the tow truck traveled the long highway miles to Redding, Kyra's laughter, just for those precious moments, held fear and despair at bay.

10

'I think we missed the turnoff,' Kyra said as another mile passed without a crossroad in sight.

'Better turn around.' The edginess was back in Randon's voice.

Kyra had sensed his agitation mounting with the silence between them in the last twenty miles or so. She supposed it could just be that they were expected at two and he didn't want to be late. But she suspected there was something more to it and wondered if it had anything to do with her outburst about the Snake. She tried not to talk about her late husband — hell, she didn't even like to think about him. Maybe Randon felt awkward with her revelations about her marriage. She remembered his tentative touch, as if he wanted to comfort but didn't know how.

She pulled the tow truck into a turnout and reversed direction, then kept her eyes peeled for the narrow dirt road with a hand-lettered sign that read 'Saddleback Ranch.' As they bumped along the ruts, kicking up dust in their wake, her stomach rumbled, loud enough for Randon to hear. He grabbed the dash as the truck pitched into another pothole. 'I guess we forgot about the sandwiches. You want to stop and eat?'

She spied a low-slung house in the distance. 'I can wait until we're done here.' She glanced at the dashboard clock, saw it was nearly two-thirty. 'Or we could just skip it and go straight to your sister's. You said you wanted to be there at three.'

'We can be a little late.' He said the words quickly, as if he had to convince her. 'I wouldn't want to show up hungry, expect them to feed us right away.'

She glanced over at him; he had a troubled look. 'Sure. We'll eat before we head over.'

They pulled up to the ranch house, parking the truck on the sparse grass in the front yard. An old man spied them from the barn, waved them over. They followed him behind the barn where a rusted-out Ranchero sat in the knee-high weeds. A corral lay just beyond it where two sorrel mares watched the proceedings with interest.

Kyra circled the Ranchero, dodging star thistle stickers and the noses of the inquisitive horses. 'She looks pretty rusted out.'

The old man shrugged. 'I want five hundred for her.'

Kyra opened her mouth to protest; the car

wasn't worth even half that. But Randon forestalled her.

'Sounds fair,' he said, pulling an envelope from his back pocket.

She touched his arm to get his attention, gave her head a slight shake. 'That's too much,' she whispered.

He grinned. 'It isn't my money.' He fished five hundreds from the envelope and handed them over without blinking.

'Your funeral,' Kyra said, bemused.

She could hear the old rancher's cackle as she headed back to the tow truck. She spent a few tense moments backing it up to the Ranchero, navigating the narrow alley between barn and corral with bare inches to spare on either side. The tall weeds surrounding the vehicle obscured the underside of the car, making it a real trick to get the tow chain across. Working with Randon, she managed to secure the Ranchero to the tow truck.

She gave the rig one last check, then climbed back into the truck where Randon waited. She started the engine.

'Where do you want to eat?' she asked.

He reached behind the seat for the sandwiches. 'How about that park we passed right past the freeway exit?'

'The park it is.' She edged the truck out

from behind the barn, careful of her cargo behind. Then she slowly made her way down the rutted dirt road. They didn't talk as they retraced their path back to the small community park. Randon sat stiffly, bags of food in his lap, his big hands gripping them as if he was afraid they'd escape. When she parked the truck alongside the road beside playground equipment, Randon didn't move, even when she turned off the engine.

'Thinking about your sister?' she asked.

He turned to her, looking as if he'd forgotten she was there. Wrapping one arm around their lunch, he rubbed at his brow with his thumb.

'I don't think of much else these days,' he said. 'Much else except . . .' He slanted her a quick look.

'Except what?' she prodded.

He smiled, a faint curving of his strong mouth. 'Never mind.'

Of course, she wouldn't be able to forget his tantalizing unfinished statement. She let it be for the moment, opening the door and jumping down to the pavement. He waited for her on the other side of the truck. Giving her one of the sacks he carried, he settled one hand in the middle of her back. 'How about under those trees?'

He guided her toward a group of picnic

tables where several adults sat watching children on the playground. The weight of his hand on her back felt good, made her want his arm across her shoulders, his body snugged up alongside hers. She edged away from him when they reached the one empty table. The shade cooled the air considerably, making the ninety-degree plus temperature almost tolerable. Kyra seated herself with a sigh, for a moment just gazing around her at the patch of lawn, oak trees clustered around them.

By the time Kyra had pulled her lunch from the bag, Randon was already halfway through his sandwich. He took a long swallow of Coke, then gestured with the can.

'Soda's pretty warm,' he said. 'Sorry about that.'

Kyra shrugged, her mouth full of sandwich. She washed it down with Coke, watching Randon over the rim of the can. The way he ate his food, she wondered if he tasted anything.

She finished her sandwich, then tore open a bag of chips. Across the way, on the other side of the small grassy space, a group of children shrieked as they swarmed the play structure. She nibbled a chip. 'So who took care of you and Rachelle after your folks died?'

The question seemed to catch him off guard, as if she'd pulled him from someplace distant. 'I did.' He grabbed a handful of chips.

'But who did you live with?'

'We lived with each other.'

She tried to understand what he was saying. 'By yourselves?' He nodded. 'But where?'

He chewed the mouthful of chips before answering. 'My folks' place. Or at least the house they rented.'

Kyra stared at him. 'The landlord let you stay? I thought you said you were seventeen.'

'I was.' He drank some Coke. 'I lied to the landlord. Said I was eighteen. He let me sign another year's lease.'

'But how did you pay the rent?'

'Quit school. Took the GED.' He gathered up his trash, stuffed it in the bag. 'Worked as a stock boy during the day, dishwasher at night.'

Kyra ached inside for that 17-year-old, that he had to face what must have seemed an overwhelming responsibility. 'What about Rachelle?'

Randon pitched his trash into a nearby garbage can. 'She stayed in school, graduated with honors. I was gone by then, though.'

'Gone where?'

'On the road.' He shifted, stretching his long legs along the bench, resting an elbow on the table. 'Landlord sold the house, so we had to move anyway. Rachelle went to stay with a neighbor.'

'So you left her?'

He got that defensive look in his eyes he'd gotten earlier. 'I sent her money every week. Called her, sometimes every day. I didn't desert her.'

She covered his hand with her own. 'I know you didn't.'

He gazed off into the middle distance. 'I just couldn't stay. I felt all pent up, as if I'd explode if I didn't get out of that house, that town. I knew I had to take care of Rachelle, I'd promised, but once she was old enough . . . '

Kyra rubbed her palm against the back of his hand, liking the feel of him. 'I'm sure she did fine.'

He turned his hand, slowly, as if afraid he'd spook her, and linked his fingers with hers. 'I know she did, but sometimes I wonder . . . '

As his voice trailed off, his grip on her hand tightened. He swallowed once, twice, his gaze growing more intense. 'Kyra.'

Alarm rippled in Kyra's stomach. 'What?'

'There's something I have to tell you.' His thumb pressed almost painfully into the back of her hand. 'About Rachelle.'

Alarm turned to dread. 'What is it, Randon?'

He seemed to squeeze the words out. 'She has cancer.'

Warm sympathy filled her. 'Oh, Randon, I'm so sorry.'

'Ovarian cancer,' he told her, his voice ragged.

Kyra knew how deadly ovarian cancer could be. Jackson had told her about a woman from his church who had died of it within a year of the diagnosis. She brought her other hand to enclose Randon's. 'What's her prognosis?'

'She's lucky really,' Randon said. 'She'd gone in to get her tubes tied and the doctor could see something wrong with her ovary. He removed it, and when they tested it . . . ' He couldn't seem to say any more.

Kyra stroked with her thumb, trying to offer a measure of comfort. 'I'm sure it will work out.'

He captured her other hand in his, so that their linked hands crossed on the table. 'I just thought you should know. In case it comes up.'

His gray eyes seemed to burn into her, hotter than the sun punching through the breaks in the trees. Energy skittered up her arms, as if his hands were a conduit for his heat.

'I'm glad you told me,' she whispered.

She thought she could see clear to his soul in his eyes and it was more than she could take. She dropped her gaze down to the tangle of their intertwined fingers. An irresistible urge rose within her to lift his hands to her mouth, to feel his skin against her lips.

She tugged her hands free. 'We'd better go. We're late as it is.'

'Right,' he said, rising to his feet.

She threw away the remains of her lunch, then headed for the tow truck. Ten minutes later they pulled up to his sister's neat two-story house.

★ ★ ★

Aimless and restless, Laura completed another circuit of the junkyard. If anyone noticed her passage, they didn't show it. One woman had brushed right up against her without even the slightest reaction. What did it mean? That now that she and Johnny had made contact with Randon and Kyra, all their energy was directed at those two? Or was their time growing shorter here and their power to impact this world already becoming weaker?

Here on Earth, time seemed to sift through her fingers like dust, more insubstantial than even her and Johnny. Only when they were in the in-between did time stand like a massive immovable block between her and her love.

Laura continued on, zigzagging between the cars. Randon had left with Kyra hours ago. With both of them gone, she and Johnny were stuck. A wasted day, precious time they couldn't call back.

She neared the front of the yard again, where the girl with the chewing gum worked. Desperate for something to do, she moved along the six-deep line of people waiting at the customer window. She bent to inspect the greasy car parts they carried, put out a finger to touch one . . .

The old man holding it leaped back with a cry. He looked all around him, eyes wide with fear, then turned toward Laura, seemed to stare right at her.

She knew him.

Terror exploded inside Laura as she watched the bitter-faced man take another quick look around before sidling back into line. She knew those eyes, that harsh mouth. The mean, narrow look on his face. She knew him and it scared her to her core. But she couldn't remember his name. Couldn't even recall why he was so familiar to her. Only that he was very dangerous and if he did see her there, it would put both her and Johnny in terrible peril.

She backed away, trembling, as the man moved to the front of the line. Just before she turned away, when she was barely within earshot, she heard the gum-chewing girl behind the counter greet the frightening old man.

'How ya doin', Mr. Carson?' the girl asked. 'Whatcha got today?'

The name meant nothing, absolutely nothing to her. But the terror was all too real. Fear goading her, she hurried to the back of the yard and prayed for night to come quickly, to bring her back to Johnny.

* * *

Kyra liked Randon's sister immediately. Despite the shadows in Rachelle's gray eyes, the stark paleness of her face, Kyra felt welcomed into her house from the moment they entered. Rachelle could almost be twins to her older brother, with the same stubborn chin, identical eyes. Not as tall as Randon, Rachelle nevertheless towered over Kyra. Her light brown hair hung to her waist.

Rachelle's husband, Tom, shook Kyra's

hand warmly, his strong plain face transformed by a smile. The smile faded when Tom turned to Randon and gave him a perfunctory handshake. The look he gave Randon was more measuring than welcoming and Kyra wondered at the tension that hung between the two men.

The two boys stormed in with pounding feet and clamoring voices. Kyra was gratified to see she'd been right — the boys were awestruck by their wayfaring uncle, taking in every inch of Randon from his cowboy hat to his booted toes. When he dropped to one knee and solemnly offered them his hand to shake, the older boy took it gravely. Chris, the younger one, threw his arms around Randon instead, offering an enthusiastic hug.

Kyra wished she could have packaged the joy she saw in Randon's face and held it close to her heart. If he'd had any lingering fears as to how Chris and Daniel would respond to him, surely they'd disappeared with the boys' enthusiastic welcome.

Releasing his uncle, Chris tugged at Randon's hand. 'We want to show you our room, Uncle Randon.'

Randon rose and ruffled Chris's hair. 'In a minute, boys. I haven't even given your mother a proper hello.' He swept off his hat, handed it to Daniel. 'Do you think you could take care of this?'

'Yes, sir.' Daniel took the hat carefully in his hands and the two boys headed off for their room.

Randon turned to his sister. 'How are you doing?'

She smiled briefly. 'Sore as hell.'

'Too sore for a hug?' Randon asked.

Rachelle shook her head and Randon wrapped his arms around her, holding her carefully. Tears glittered in Rachelle's eyes, and Kyra's throat tightened as she watched her bury her face in her brother's shoulder. There was a mix of emotions in Tom's face — frustration, anger, grief. He raked his fingers through his dark hair, eyes on the wife he so obviously adored.

Randon let go of his sister and took a step back. His eyes were dry, but red-rimmed, as if he'd only barely held back tears.

Tom grabbed a tissue for Rachelle and handed it to her. He glared at Randon while Rachelle dried her eyes.

'About damn time you showed up,' Tom said.

'Tom, don't start,' Rachelle said, stuffing the tissue in her shorts pocket.

Randon stood poised on the balls of his feet, like a fighter waiting for the first blow. Tom looked more than ready to oblige his brother-in-law. A long, silent moment passed, then Tom let out a long sigh, the tension in his shoulders relaxing.

'The boys are waiting for you.' Tom gestured in the direction Daniel and Chris had gone. 'You won't get any peace until they show you their room.'

Randon nodded. 'After that, anything I can help you with?'

Tom hesitated, then he said, 'Yeah. Come outside and give me a hand with the barbecue.'

Randon turned to Kyra. 'Come with me?'

'I'm sure the boys would like to have their uncle all to themselves,' Kyra said. 'And I'd love to see your house, Rachelle, if you don't mind.'

Rachelle smiled, seeming relieved at such an everyday request. 'It's not much, but I'd be glad to show you around.'

While Randon headed off toward the boys' room, Rachelle led Kyra through the house, showing her first the kitchen, then the family room, and the boys' playroom.

'They could have each had their own room.' Rachelle leaned against a ceiling-high bookshelf laden with toys. 'But they wanted to share. They like having one room for playing and one for quieter activities.'

'Did Tom build these?' Kyra ran her hand

along the sturdy pine shelves.

'All of it,' Rachelle said. 'The shelving, the craft table, that desk in the corner. Woodworking's his hobby.'

She sighed, one hand going to her abdomen. Wincing, she rubbed herself lightly.

'I'm sorry,' Kyra said. 'You must be hurting. Do you want to lie down?'

She had a pinched look around her mouth and she'd gone even paler. 'I think that would be good.' Her gaze met Kyra's. 'Would you mind coming with me? I'd appreciate the company.'

'Sure. Of course.'

When Kyra took Rachelle's hand, the other woman didn't protest. Although Kyra was sure Rachelle was trying not to, she leaned against Kyra as they walked down the hall.

When they reached the master bedroom, Rachelle lay down with a sigh of relief. She nudged off her shoes and flung an arm over her eyes.

'Sit with me on the bed,' she told Kyra.

Kyra pushed off her own shoes and climbed up onto the other side. 'How are you feeling?'

'Sore. Crotchety.' She took in a long, ragged breath. 'And scared to death.'

Kyra reached out and rubbed awkwardly at Rachelle's shoulder. 'I'm so sorry.'

Rachelle dropped her arm and looked over at Kyra. 'I'm sorry for dumping this on you five minutes after you've met me.'

'Don't worry about it,' Kyra said. 'You're entitled.'

'It's just that . . . ' Rachelle spread her hand on her abdomen. 'I can't seem to talk to Tom about it. He doesn't want to hear how scared I am. And I know he's scared, too. But every time I bring the subject up, he just tells me it will be all right. But what if it isn't?'

Kyra felt entirely inadequate to deal with Rachelle's anguish, but she knew Randon's sister desperately needed someone to be honest with her.

'What have the doctors said?' Kyra asked.

Rachelle hesitated, lips pressed together as if she held something back. Her gaze slid away from Kyra. 'They won't know anything for sure until after the surgery.'

Unease settled in Kyra's stomach at what Rachelle didn't say. 'I thought they already removed the ovary.'

Blindly Rachelle reached out and Kyra clasped her hand tightly. 'They have to cut me open, from here to here.' She gestured from her breastbone down to her pubis. 'From one side to the other.' Then she traced a line from one side of her pelvis to the other.

Kyra was horrified at the image. 'Then what?'

Rachelle laughed grimly. 'They check every square inch for cancer. Every organ, every bit of tissue. Let's just say they get pretty damned personal.'

Kyra gave her hand a squeeze. 'I'm sure the doctors know what they're doing.'

Rachelle nodded. 'They're the best. I'm having it done down at the Davis Med Center.'

'Then it will work out.'

Rachelle's gray eyes met Kyra's, the intense look reminding her of Randon. 'It might not. It could all go wrong. I could die.' She took a ragged breath. 'God, sometimes I think — ' Her hand flew up to cover her mouth.

'Think what?' Kyra prodded gently.

Rachelle looked away, evasive. 'Never mind.'

She squeezed her eyes shut then, and the tears flowed, sobs shaking her slender body. Kyra sat and held Rachelle's hand, comforting her as well as she could, waiting for the storm to pass.

★ ★ ★

Randon found Tom sitting in the shade of the patio overhang, staring out over his wide backyard. He had a box of matches, and he passed them back and forth from hand to hand. An unopened bag of briquettes leaned against the Weber barbecue. Randon shut the sliding glass door behind him and headed for the patio chair next to Tom. Tom didn't even glance at him when he seated himself, just kept fiddling with the matchbox, staring off at the shrubbery separating his property from the one behind.

Randon could see Tom's jaw working and he wondered if his brother-in-law was going to pop him one. Then Tom muttered, 'Damn it all to hell,' and Randon braced himself, ready to ward off a blow. But Tom didn't throw a punch, just pushed to his feet and started to pace. 'I don't know what to do for her.'

'Isn't much you can do.' Randon's insides wrenched at the reality of that. 'Just love her. Hold her.'

Tom rounded on Randon, looking again like he wanted to hit him. His hands tightened into fists.

'But that's just the problem. She won't let me hold her.' Tom turned away, shoulders held stiffly against some inner pain. 'I don't even know if she wants me to love her.'

Randon didn't like the sound of this. He felt entirely out of his element. 'What do you mean?'

'I mean, brother-in-law . . . ' Tom paused, then swore an oath Randon was sure he would never dare say in Rachelle's presence. 'Rachelle and I . . . even before this, Rachelle and I have been having problems.'

'Problems? What the hell does that mean?'

Tom rocked back on his heels. 'We've been growing apart.'

'Meaning what?' Randon jumped to his feet, grabbed Tom's arm, and turned him to face him. 'Have you been stepping out on her? Have you been cheating on my sister?'

Tom snatched his arm free. 'Hell, no! It's nothing like that. And you have a hell of a lot of nerve showing up after five years away and storming around here with accusations.'

Tom met his eyes, until Randon took a step back. 'Okay.' Randon made an effort to calm himself. 'So tell me. What's wrong?'

Tom swiped a hand across his face. 'I wish I knew. It might have started back when I was working all that overtime. She'd already be asleep half the time when I got home and weekends we just never seemed to connect.'

'You still working the long hours?' Randon asked.

'Not since April. But even when I'd get home early, she'd hardly talk to me. I even started to wonder if she was having an affair.'

'Could she be?'

Randon might have expected Tom to fly off the handle at that, but he gave the question some thought. 'I don't think so. It happened to some friends of ours and she was just so damn pissed off . . . ' Tom smiled. 'I just can't see her doing that.'

Randon put a hand on Tom's shoulder. 'I'm sure you're right.'

'Maybe you could talk to her.' Tom bent to pick up the briquettes, then straightened, and faced Randon. 'She thinks the world of you. She might tell you something she wouldn't tell me.'

The very thought terrified Randon. What if she wanted something from him, something more than he could give.

'I can't see her telling her brother anything she wouldn't tell her own husband.' He looked down at the toes of his boots, not wanting to meet Tom's eyes. 'You keep at her. She'll come around.'

There was a long, quiet pause. Then Randon watched as Tom tore off the top of the briquette bag and dumped the coals into the Weber.

'So what's with you and Kyra?' Tom set a burning match to the briquettes, watched the flames lick across the coals. 'Anything we should know about?'

The shift of topic caught Randon off

215

guard. 'No,' he said, too quickly.

Tom gave him a sidelong glance. 'You want there to be?'

Inexplicably, Randon's heart began to race. 'I hardly know her. She's just doing me a favor today.'

Tom looked at him full on, as if he knew just what was happening inside Randon, every little thought and desire. He smirked. 'Like that, is it?'

'What the hell does that mean?' Randon asked.

Tom just smiled, turning back to the flaming pile of coals. 'So what's this I hear about you doing a movie?' With that, the subject of Kyra was dropped.

* * *

Kyra guided the tow truck back onto Interstate 5, still unsettled over her conversation with Rachelle. Randon's sister had put on a bright face when she left the bedroom with Kyra, had bustled around the kitchen as if everything was right in her world. But Kyra could see the fear chasing Rachelle, just waiting for a chance to cloak her in darkness.

Tom would try to touch her, to put a hand on her shoulder or wrap his arms around her waist. But she seemed to sidestep his caresses, always moving out of his reach. Kyra could see the longing in Tom's face as he watched his wife, and she grieved for them both.

Randon shifted in the seat beside her, as if trying to get his long legs comfortable in the cramped cab. She debated inwardly over whether she should talk to him about Rachelle. She really was an outsider and had only been asked along because Randon needed her to pick up the car. That she joined him for dinner with his family was incidental. But Rachelle was hurting, and although she was a virtual stranger, Kyra had to talk to Randon. She glanced at him, his face silhouetted by the setting sun. He must have sensed her looking at him because he turned.

Before she returned to her driving, she saw something in his eyes, something she'd seen earlier that day when she'd emerged from the bedroom with Rachelle. It was a rebellious look, as if she'd challenged him and he was ready to do battle against her. If she hadn't been so preoccupied with Rachelle, she might have laughed at his pugnacious look. She wanted to ask him about it now, but she was preoccupied with Rachelle's problems. 'Your sister's a lovely lady,' she said as she glanced in her sideview mirror and changed lanes.

He removed his hat, dropping it on the seat

between them. 'Yeah,' he said softly.

Kyra massaged the steering wheel with her palms, trying to work out what to say. 'She seems to be taking the cancer in stride.'

Rubbing at his brow, he closed his eyes against the brilliant setting sun. 'I suppose.'

'Actually,' Kyra said, worrying the steering wheel some more, 'actually, I'm a little bit worried about her.'

'It's not your concern,' he snapped. Then she heard him drag in a long breath. 'I mean, you don't need to worry about her. She's got Tom to take care of her.'

'That's just it,' Kyra persisted. 'I'm really afraid she — '

'Leave it, Kyra.' He raked his hair back, then settled his hat back on his head. 'You said your mom died. You never mentioned your dad.'

She saw his change of subject for what it was — a way to avoid talking about his sister. He couldn't know how painful it was discussing her father.

'He's still alive.' She hoped Randon wouldn't press the issue.

'You see him much?' Randon asked.

She shook her head as the old pain roiled within her. Damn, she'd thought she'd put all that behind her. But the day spent with Rachelle, with Randon, with Tom, their

218

problems, their concerns, seemed to have made her emotional.

Randon seemed oblivious to her turmoil. 'Does he live close by?'

Hell, she thought as her throat tightened. She took a breath. 'Sacramento.'

'Oh,' Randon said. 'You two don't get along?'

Memories rushed back of her father's arms comforting her when her mother died, of the joy they were able to carve out in the years afterward. He would have given her anything she asked for if it was within his power. She would have given anything to him that was hers to give. She'd adored her father so. Anything, except one thing.

'We had,' she said hoarsely, 'a falling out.'

For the first time, Randon seemed to sense her threatening tears. He reached across the seat, placed his warm hand on her shoulder.

'Pull over, sweetheart,' he said.

'What?'

'Pull over,' he repeated. 'You're shaking. Pull over and let's get this out.'

11

Kyra obeyed, easing over to the right lane and taking the next exit. It was just as well, because as soon as she had the truck parked, the dam burst, releasing a flood of tears. Somehow, Randon was holding her close, pressing her face into his shoulder, letting her sob out the old grief.

When she could take a breath, she didn't move right away. It felt too exquisite holding him close. Her hands were spread at his waist, her brow nestled against his neck. She would only need to shift her head slightly and she could brush her lips against the warm skin of his throat.

Before she could consider putting the thought into action, he set her away from him. 'Tell me about your father,' he said gently.

She wiped away the wetness on her cheeks. 'He didn't want me to marry. At least not the Snake. But I knew so much better than Dad. I knew he was wrong, that he just didn't know Robbie like I did.' She managed a weak grin. 'Damn, I said his name.'

'I'm sure we can forgive this once.' He

stroked the hair back from her face. 'So what happened?'

Feeling more in control, she edged away from him. He slid back to his side of the cab.

'We had a huge blowup,' Kyra said. 'Dad told me my marriage would only come to grief, that the Snake was a no-good, low down . . . ' She shrugged. 'Snake.'

Kyra sighed, remembering that night. 'Dad said he was only trying to protect me. He told me Robbie would break my heart. I told him — ' Her breath caught on another sob. 'I told him . . . ' She looked up at Randon. 'I told my dad, that *he* was breaking my heart. That if he loved me as much as he said, he'd be glad for me. That if he wasn't, maybe he just didn't love me at all.'

He touched her again, this time just gathering her hand in his. 'You didn't mean that.'

'Of course not!' She gripped Randon's hand. 'But I hurt my dad so badly.'

She looked out the window, at the swath of coral at the horizon, the brilliant orange fire of the setting sun. 'By the time I'd wised up about the Snake, those words had festered inside my dad for a good two years. I tried calling him to talk, to apologize. Even went to his house once.'

'He wouldn't talk to you?'

She met Randon's gaze. 'He's a proud man. And I'd cut him so deeply.'

'When was the last time you called?'

She sighed. 'Two years ago, when the Snake died. He heard my voice and he hung up the phone.'

He rubbed the back of her hand with his thumb, a distracting heat. 'Maybe it's time to try again.'

She gave him a wry grin. 'This from a man who until today hadn't seen his sister for five years.'

'But I've kept in touch!' he said defensively.

She laughed, pulling her hand free. She started the truck again. 'Let's get going or we'll never make it back.'

They pulled onto the freeway and eased into traffic. Kyra stared at the stick-straight ribbon of highway before her, feeling drained from her tears, but somehow cleansed.

'Thank you,' she said quietly.

'You're welcome.'

Feeling lighter than she had in years, Kyra focused on getting them home.

* * *

Kyra sent Randon out to unlock the gate to the wrecking yard, then towed the Ranchero inside. Climbing wearily from the truck, she

222

decided to just leave the rig as is.

Randon closed and locked the big double gate, leaving the pedestrian gate open. Kyra watched as he walked toward her, looking as exhausted as she.

'Mario can take the Ranchero up to the movie location tomorrow,' she told him.

'Fine.' He pulled off his hat, raked his fingers through his hair. He didn't put it on again, just tapped the hat against his leg, watching her. He looked troubled, as if something were eating at him. He'd been quiet the last leg of their trip, and Kyra wondered if his thoughts had gone back to his sister. She knew if she brought up the subject, he'd sidestep it again. But she wished she could help him, could comfort him the way he had her.

'Kyra.' He took a step closer.

She could feel his heat, curling toward her in the cool night air. 'Yes?'

He closed the distance between them. 'Kyra.'

He pulled her into his arms and against his hard body before she could even react. His mouth was on hers before she could bring her own arms up to hold him. She could feel the desperation in his kiss, the overwhelming need for release from his pain. His tongue plunged into her mouth as his hand curved around the back of her head, trapping her against him. His other hand roamed her body, from the curve of her hip to her waist, up her back, to her face. He backed her against the tow truck, grinding his pelvis into hers, the hard ridge of his erection burning into her.

She was on fire. His mouth left hers, then he nipped and licked along her face, to the shell of her ear, back to her mouth. He seemed to want to devour her, to swallow her whole, and she welcomed his hunger. In that moment, she would have let him take her against the side of the tow truck, would have shed her clothes and ridden him right there. But abruptly, he stopped, pulling back from her so roughly, she might have fallen if she hadn't been leaning against the truck. He gasped in air, eyes burning into her. He looked wild.

'Sorry.' He stumbled back from her.

He turned on his boot heel and hurried for the gate. Kyra swayed as she watched him go, put out a hand to steady herself against the truck. The sound of Randon's pickup engine as it roared out of the parking lot echoed through the night.

Kyra raised a shaking hand to her face, pressed her fingertips against her still-swollen lips. She supposed she should have been angry at Randon's assault, at his abrupt departure. But she understood that what had just happened had been outside of Randon's control. He couldn't deal with his fears about his sister. He'd thought to drive them from his heart with lust, to let his desire for a woman burn them away.

Kyra stood back from the tow truck, let her gaze roam the yard, her mind blank. She'd wanted to comfort Randon, to reach out to him. But when she thought about what she'd been willing to do to achieve that . . . If she and Randon had made love, it wouldn't have been just for him. She wanted it just as desperately, and that frightened her to the core.

A distant glow caught her eyes at the far end of the yard, back where the floodlights didn't quite reach. She realized with a start that the faint illumination seemed to come from the Fairlane. She took a step or two closer. It was almost as if the dome light burned in the old Ford. But the batteries had been removed from every car in the lot. There was no way to power the interior lights. With a shiver, Kyra backed away, then turned toward the exit gate. She locked the gate behind her with trembling fingers and hurried to her car, all the while trying not to look in the direction of the Fairlane.

★ ★ ★

Laura watched Kyra through the Fairlane's passenger window until the junkyard owner drove off. Then she turned to Johnny. '*But who do you think the old man is?*'

Johnny shook his head. '*I don't know.*'

'*He felt me, Johnny. He knew I was there.*'

'*It might not mean anything,*' Johnny said.

'*He was familiar,*' Laura said, pleating her aqua skirt between her fingers. '*I recognized his face.*'

Johnny rested one arm on the steering wheel and turned toward her. '*Maybe you remember him from before. From another time we returned.*'

Laura thought back, to the multitudes of people they'd tried to reach in their times on Earth. '*No,*' she said with certainty. '*Knowing him went deeper than that. I think I remember him from . . . from when we were alive.*'

Johnny gazed at her intently. '*I want to believe you, Laura. That you know this man, that he means something to us.*' He lifted a hand, stroked along the barrier as if touching her face. '*It all seems so impossible.*'

'*You can't give up, Johnny.*'

'*We're running out of time.*' His voice seemed to fade as he spoke, as if he was

226

moving away from her. *'It might be too late already.'*

'It isn't, Johnny, I know it isn't.' The barrier between them seemed to shimmer more brightly, obscuring Johnny's face. *'Johnny!'* Laura called out. *'Johnny!'*

In the next moment, the barrier faded again, but the driver's seat was empty. Laura looked around her frantically, searching for him, frantic with fear.

'Johnny!'

Her scream seemed to echo all around her. She looked beyond the Fairlane out into the dark junkyard and realized with a shock that the wrecked cars had disappeared. She pressed against the passenger window, its glass intact and cold against her palms. She could see where she was now — on a deserted levee road in the driving rain. A swollen river rushed by below her, logs and other debris tossed along within the foam. In the next moment, she was no longer on the levee, but hurtling into the river, the Fairlane bucking and tipping down the bank. She felt her head bang against the window as the car plunged into the icy, swirling water.

Blackness closed around her. Her world turned upside down, the roar of the water driving every other sound from her ears. She groped for Johnny, her fingers scrabbling along the seat. She couldn't find him, couldn't reach him. She heard a crash, and in a heartbeat, something punched through the window. Water filled the car, rising higher. Before she went under, a scream ripped from her lips.

'*Johnny!*'

★ ★ ★

The sound hung on the early morning air, stilling Kyra's hand as she closed the wrecking yard gate. She looked around her, trying to trace the source of what she could swear was a shout of fear, a scream of anguish. Listening intently, she shivered a little in the coolness that the rising sun would soon disperse. There was nothing but silence, sporadically broken by birdsong. She must have been mistaken. Her restless night coupled with rising earlier than usual had fogged her brain. She'd probably mistaken the dim roar of Highway 50 traffic and the soughing of the morning breeze as a human shout.

Closing the gate behind her and securing the padlock, she headed for her office. She wanted to go over Sunday's receipts and run off an inventory report sorted by acquisition number. It was nothing more than paper shuffling, but it gave her something to do to take her mind off Randon and last night.

Running the numbers from the weekend proved to be a distraction, but not a pleasant one. The figures on her computer screen spelled out the precariousness of her financial position all too clearly. With money on hand, she could cover payroll for next week, two weeks at the outside. If she couldn't reorganize her debts by then, she'd have to start laying off.

She drew a weary hand over her face. If she could only sell that damn Fairlane. That would give her some breathing room on the payroll. But she'd gotten few calls in response to her ad in the *Bee*. The ones that did come to look at the car barely gave it a glance before saying no. It couldn't be the price — she'd lowballed it, just to get the thing off the lot. But no one would touch it.

She stood up. Maybe she ought to go take a look at the Ford, see if maybe a little more sprucing up would help. She'd had Mario power-wash it yesterday, and the interior was in good shape. Maybe there was something else they could do to make the car more appealing.

Just as she reached the old Ford, a blast of winter air chilled the sun's pleasant heat. In the next instant, she saw the boy, as if he'd suddenly blinked into existence. All traces of the cockiness she'd seen before in him had vanished. He looked scared and panicked and terribly lost.

He moved toward Kyra, bringing his cold front with him. '*Have you seen her?*'

Kyra couldn't suppress a shudder. 'Seen who?'

'*Laura. She was in the car, right beside me one minute, gone the next.*' He turned in a circle, looking around him. '*She has to be here.*'

'I haven't seen her. I haven't seen Laura.' The boy's desperation added to her own anxieties. 'Who are you, Johnny? When I saw you disappear, I figured it was the heat, or that summer storm, or . . . '

Johnny turned to her. '*I couldn't help disappearing. I don't control it.*' He put his hands out as if to touch her. '*Laura and me, we need help.*'

Kyra gasped at the sharp chill, held herself still with an effort. 'Help with what?'

He looked straight at her. '*With how we died.*'

Kyra heard a roaring in her ears as her brain tried to process Johnny's words. Dead — the boy was dead. A ghost, a spirit, wandering her wrecking yard. 'How you died,' she said weakly.

'We can't remember how it happened. But we have to find out or we'll go back. Maybe for good this time.' He looked frantically around him again. 'Laura must be here somewhere.'

'Johnny, I don't understand.' The snatches of information the boy had given frustrated her.

He focused on her, seemed to calm himself. 'We only come here, to Earth, every few years. When we're not here, we're caught in the black limbo — the in-between.'

'The in-between?' Kyra asked.

'I can't explain it any more than that,' Johnny said impatiently. 'When Laura and I return to Earth, we're trapped in the car. Except this time it's a little different. We're together in the car by night, but in the day, we're out in your junkyard. Separated. We can't see or hear each other.'

Kyra couldn't help herself, she looked around, wondering if the other ghost would pop up from behind one of the cars. 'Then she's here somewhere?'

'She has to be,' Johnny said, the worry returning. 'She can't have gone back to the in-between, not yet . . . '

His plaintive voice faded as he did, not feet first as before, but growing fainter all over as if he couldn't hold himself there in his

231

distress. Kyra watched until nothing of Johnny remained. A mix of sorrow and sheer terror throbbed inside her.

Trembling, she turned toward the Fairlane, staring at the innocent white- and strawberry-ice-cream-pink body. Johnny's chill had dispersed, leaving only a very ordinary morning warmth. Hell, no wonder no one wanted the Fairlane. The damn thing was haunted. Wasn't it just her luck?

*   *   *

It was late afternoon by the time Randon could make it back to the wrecking yard. He'd spent the morning at the location waiting for Mario to bring the Ranchero, then several hours helping the set decorator dress the set to the production designer's satisfaction.

As he headed down the hill in his pickup, the vicious glare of the sun nearly blinding him, Randon wondered why he was going to the wrecking yard at all. There was so little time left in the day, he might as well go back to the motel and get an early start tomorrow morning. But he had to see Kyra. He'd run the images over and over in his mind — the feel of her in his arms, the way her mouth opened beneath his. And last night, after he'd left her and thoughts of Rachelle had crowded in, Kyra had been the only way to drive away the fears.

Damn, he wanted so much to hold her, to have her hold him. He ached for the comfort she could give him as much as his body ached for her touch. He knew he was handling the situation with Rachelle all wrong. He should have promised Tom he'd talk to his sister, should have found a way to help shoulder Rachelle's burden. But he was at a loss to find the right words, to ease her fears when he could barely deal with his own.

When he pulled into the parking lot at the wrecking yard, he stayed in the truck a few minutes trying to order his scrambled thoughts. He wanted to seek out Kyra first thing, pull her close to him, breathe her scent, and feel the silk of her hair against his cheek. But he had no right to expect that of her. He was nothing to her. She was nothing to him.

He climbed out of the truck and forced himself to take his time walking over to the service window. Jackson was there, standing idly at an empty window, reading the *Sacramento Bee*.

Jackson looked up with a smile. 'How you doing, Randon?'

'Fine.' Randon's hands felt shaky; he

shoved them into the pocket of his jeans. 'Kyra here?'

'Took a late lunch. Couldn't get away before now.' Jackson put aside the paper, 'Anything I can do for you?'

'No, no thanks,' Randon said. 'I'll just kind of help myself.'

Jackson picked up the *Bee* again. 'Don't need your camera today?'

Randon pulled his hands free, surprised the Polaroid wasn't in them. 'Forgot it in the truck, I guess.' He nodded at Jackson. 'See you later.'

He retraced his steps to his truck, then looked back out at the yard as he opened the door. For a moment he felt an oppressiveness, like the thick air of a thunderstorm closing around him. The cloudless sky arched above him as the sun beat down on his neck. He closed his eyes against the glare. When he opened them, he saw Laura standing in the back of the yard.

He tucked the camera under the seat and shut the door again. If anything could distract him from his confusing feelings for Kyra it would be this crazy hallucination of a young girl he'd been entertaining. He headed in Laura's direction, found her leaning against a big 4×4 near the chain-link fence.

'*You've got to help me,*' the girl said,

before he could even say a word.

'Look, who the hell are you?' Randon asked. 'And how do you keep appearing and disappearing?'

'*I told you, I'm Laura.*' She moved closer, the air cooling with each step nearer she took. '*And I'm . . . well, I'm . . .* ' She flapped her hands in frustration. '*I'm dead.*'

Randon stared at her. Well, of course — she was dead. What other explanation could there be for a girl who could fade in and out before his very eyes? Unless he'd gone totally mad, driven to insanity by his worry for Rachelle, his persistent lust for the wrong kind of woman.

He chose to believe the girl. 'You're dead.' She nodded. 'You're a ghost.' He felt foolish asking the question. She nodded again.

She stood at about arm's length, slender and pretty in a strapless aqua dress. Unable to resist, he leaned forward and tried to touch her. His hand passed right through her shoulder in a shower of sparks. He snatched his hand back at the sensation of icy heat.

Her expression grew cross. '*I haven't time for games. I need you.*'

He stuck his hand into his jeans pocket. 'What do you need?'

'*We need to know how we died,*' she told him.

'We?'

'*Me and Johnny.*' She gestured off in the direction of the Fairlane. '*We've been stuck in that car for years.*'

'How many? When did you die?'

'*I remember 1955,*' she told him.

He whistled. 'More than forty, then.'

She flapped a hand. '*It doesn't matter. We're trapped. We can't go forward; we can't go back. We only know we have to find out how we died, and we can't do that without your help.*'

A thousand questions whipped through Randon's mind; he narrowed them to one. 'You don't remember anything about how you died?'

Laura shook her head, her ponytail bobbing from side to side. '*We died in the car. There was water — a lot of water. It was cold. But how it happened, why we're trapped here — that's what you need to find out. Soon, before it's too late.*'

'But I don't — '

'*Randon, please!*' she cried, and Randon saw that she'd begun to disappear again, as if the sunlight was swallowing her up. Reflexively, Randon reached out as if to hold her back, but found himself grasping nothing but warm summer air.

* * *

Kyra sat at her kitchen table and rearranged her bills. She switched the electric bill with the phone bill, then placed her credit card statements in a long column off to the right. She wasn't accomplishing anything with her juggling, but since she didn't have the money in her account to pay any of them, it gave her something to do with the intimidating stacks of paper.

She sighed and leaned back in her chair. Where the hell would she get the money for these? She'd cut back on the salary she took out of the business until her personal budget was pared to the bone. Bankruptcy seemed to loom closer and closer, harrying her like a demon.

A faint rap on her door shook her from her dark thoughts and she headed for the living room. She should have looked through the front window to see who it was — even quiet Placerville had its share of trouble. But she knew who she'd see on her front porch — the same man who had danced at the edge of her thoughts all day long.

She pulled open the door and her breath quickened at the sight of Randon. He had that wild look in his eyes, the same look she saw last night before he kissed her. She didn't say a word, just stepped aside to let him in. He kicked the door shut behind him and pulled her into his arms. His mouth was on hers before she could even take a breath, his tongue plunging inside.

He tore off his hat and threw it aside, then his hands moved restlessly over her as if he wanted to touch her everywhere at once. Without taking his mouth from hers, he urged her backwards to the sofa. They tumbled down to the soft cushions, his arms breaking her fall, then his body covering hers. She could feel his erection against her, the hard ridge of it pushing against her belly. She shifted to open her legs, taking him between them, his jeans rough against her inner thighs. A brief moment of sanity surfaced and she wondered what the hell she was doing, where this uncontrolled passion would take them. Then his hand closed over her breast and a flood of heat drove away her good sense.

He circled and rubbed her nipple until it hardened to an exquisitely sensitive peak. He shoved aside the collar of her shirt, popping the top button, and pushed aside her bra. He took her engorged nipple into his mouth, suckling it, pulling at it gently with his teeth.

She shifted, pushing her center into his hard length. With his mouth still on her breast, his hand moved roughly down her body, cupped her at the juncture of her thighs. He stroked the heel of his hand against her denim shorts as if desperate to pleasure her. She gasped for air, tension growing tighter between her thighs, becoming impossibly hot.

Then his fingers thrust against the heavy denim as if to push inside her. He stroked with his hand, his tongue still lapping at her breast. He ground his hips into her while his fingers pushed at her cleft, all the while rubbing, stroking.

She let out a sharp cry, then a long, low moan. He kept touching her, thrusting himself against her, suckling her breast until he'd wrenched every ounce of sensation from her. Then with a panting gasp, he moved away from her against the back of the sofa.

Kyra lay there, stunned, staring at the ceiling. God, what had just happened? The act she'd just shared with Randon had gone beyond intimate into frightening territory. Not just because he had brought her so easily to climax, but because of his desperation, the soul-deep agony that had brought him to do it.

Cautiously, Kyra turned her head to look at him. His eyes squeezed tightly shut, his body as rigid as the lines of his face, he'd found no release in driving her into ecstasy. Nor had he soothed his inner torment. She should feel mortified by what had just happened, but instead she ached for him. Moving carefully, she reached out to him, laying her hand against his cheek. His hand moved up to cover hers and for a moment, she thought he would pull away. Instead, he held her more tightly against him, his face full of emotion.

She grazed his temple lightly with her fingertips. 'Are you okay?'

He dragged in a long breath, opened his eyes to look at her. 'Did I hurt you?'

She had to smile at that. 'You've got to be kidding.'

His lips curved into a brief smile. 'This was not what I intended when I drove over here. But then . . . ' He sighed, the sound heavy. 'I don't know what I intended.'

'What's the matter, Randon?'

He pulled away from her, then rose. Back to her, he stared out the front window. Waiting for him to answer her, wondering if he would, Kyra tugged her bra into place and brought together the edges of her blouse where the button was missing.

He turned to face her, his expression neutral as if he'd donned a mask. 'Tom called. They've scheduled Rachelle's surgery for the day after tomorrow.'

A chill skittered down Kyra's spine as she remembered Rachelle's graphic description of the surgical procedure. She stood, swaying a little. Randon put out a hand to steady her, only a moment before he pulled it away.

Kyra smoothed her hair back, trying to forget what they'd just done on the couch. 'Will you be going over to the hospital?'

'She wants me to.' Randon scrubbed at his face, then looked down at her. 'I don't know if I can, Kyra. If the news isn't good . . . '

'If the news isn't good, then she'll want you there with her.'

'Damn it, don't you think I know that?' He gazed around, as if searching for an answer. 'What could I possibly say to her? What could I do? If the cancer's spread — '

'You'll deal with it,' Kyra said. 'You'll find a way. But you can't just desert her.'

His eyes flashed with anger at that. 'I've never deserted her. I've always made sure she's had everything she's needed.'

Kyra took a step toward him and laid her hand on his arm. 'But now she needs you. You only have to be there, Randon. Nothing more.'

He was silent so long, she wondered if he'd even heard her. Then he pulled away. 'I have to go.'

He strode to the door, hesitated long

241

enough to look back at her briefly. He wanted to ask her something, she could see the question in his eyes. But then he turned away and headed out the door.

She went to the window, watching until he drove away. An emptiness started opening up in her, a gnawing ache. She didn't know if it was empathy for Randon or her own pain, but it nearly overwhelmed her. As she turned from the window, a flash of white in a corner of the living room caught her eye. It was his hat, tipped up against a book-case where he had thrown it. She bent to pick it up and held it close to her for a moment, imagining she was holding him.

What did he want from her? What did she want from *him*? He'd stormed in here, pushed her to a devastating climax, then was gone, leaving her shaken and confused. A part of her felt used, another part felt she hadn't given him nearly enough. Impatient with herself, she set the hat by the front door to take to the yard tomorrow. She wandered back into the kitchen and stared at the stacks of unpaid bills arranged across the table.

Her responsibilities weighed heavily on her. Anger welled up and frustrated tears burned at her eyes. With a growl, she slapped off the kitchen light and headed for her bedroom. The damn bills could wait for another day.

Johnny fixed his gaze on the empty car seat beside him, willing Laura to return. Outside the Fairlane, the junkyard lay in indistinct shadows cast by the tall floodlights. Laura would come back, she had to come back. Doubts crowded him, danced inside him.

When he saw her slip into the car, sparkles of light running along her body, he let out a whoop of joy. As she came to rest on the seat, he grinned at her like a fool, his gaze roaming over her from her blonde head to her bare feet. God he wanted to take her into his arms, to hold her to his heart. It might not beat inside him anymore, but he still loved this girl with every fiber of his soul.

He leaned as close to the barrier as he could. '*I was afraid you were gone.*'

She looked surprised. '*Where would I have gone to?*'

'*The in-between. Or heaven. I don't know. But the way you disappeared . . .*'

A troubled look came into her eyes. '*I don't know what happened. It was like a dream, a dream of what happened back then.*' She raised her hand, matched the position of his on the other side of the barrier. '*But how can the dead dream, Johnny?*'

He pressed his palm toward hers. 'Maybe

243

you're remembering.'

'Maybe.' She worked her hand in closer. *'I talked to Randon. I told him what we needed.'*

'And I spoke to Kyra.' Johnny could almost feel Laura's fingers intertwined with his. *'But I wish you could talk to her. You know more than I do.'*

'I have a feeling, Johnny.' Laura looked up at him earnestly. *'About Randon and Kyra. I think they need to work together. I think they need to fall in love.'*

He had to smile. *'You want everyone to be in love like we are.'*

She shook her head. *'No, it's more than that.'*

Then her gaze fell to their hands pressed against the barrier, and her eyes widened. *'Johnny, look.'*

He followed her gaze, stared at a miracle. Their fingers had penetrated the barrier, lay locked together. He closed his hand slightly and he could feel her, just as he had when they were alive.

'This proves it, Johnny,' Laura said, her tone sure. *'We have to bring them together.'*

As the wonder of her touch flowed through him, Johnny was in no position to disagree. In that moment, if Laura had told him to jump the moon, he would have done it in a heartbeat.

12

When Kyra heard the knock on her office door, she knew who stood on the other side. Her gaze went immediately to the dusty white cowboy hat on her desk and she wondered if she could just stay quiet and avoid the inevitable. But Jackson would have told Randon she was here, having just popped his head in to talk to her, so she doubted that Randon would give up without seeing her.

Besides, she had to give him back his hat. 'Come in,' she called, swiveling her chair toward the door.

He stepped inside and quietly shut the door behind him. Seeing his expression, the phrase 'hat in hand' popped into her mind, except that the item in question sat on her desk. He definitely looked lost without it.

Taking pity, she handed it over. 'You forgot this,' she said, not wanting to think about the circumstances that caused him to toss it so carelessly aside.

He took the hat from her and looked down at it as if searching for courage. He turned it around in his hands a few times before meeting her gaze again.

'I came to apologize,' he said, his gray eyes intense.

'For which part?' Some little devil inside her wanted to goad him. 'For showing up unannounced? For leaving without a good-bye? For . . . ' She couldn't quite mention the in-between part.

A spark lit his gaze, then dimmed. 'It was inexcusable.'

She tried to suppress a smile. 'Your bad manners?'

He didn't seem to see the humor in it. 'Doing what I did to you. Taking advantage of you that way.'

The smile escaped. 'As I recall, I was the one with all the advantages. I don't remember you taking anything.'

That surprised him and for a moment he seemed at a loss. 'Nevertheless . . . '

'Nevertheless, I knew it was something you needed. Nevertheless . . . ' Her voice faltered as she remembered the power of that need. 'Next time ask first,' she said quietly.

She leaned back in her chair, wanting to leave the subject and her mixed emotions behind. 'Was there anything else?'

'Well.' He looked like a man who felt he'd been too easily let off the hook. 'Yes.'

She cocked her brow in query and his attention returned to his hat. 'I wondered if you could come with me for Rachelle's surgery.' He raised his gaze to hers. 'I think it would be good for Rachelle to have another woman around.'

Emotions played across Randon's face, hope and despair chief among them. Kyra knew darn well he wanted her there for his own sake, not his sister's. What that meant about the two of them, she wouldn't dare to guess. But she couldn't turn down his request, even though she could ill afford to be away from the wrecking yard for a day. 'I'll be glad to go with you.'

The gratitude in his smile struck her. In that moment, she would have done anything for this man in her office. The thought terrified her that she'd become so weak, after the Snake's lessons about men.

She turned away from him. 'If you'll excuse me.'

He hesitated a moment, his boots scuffing against the worn linoleum. 'Thank you.'

When the door shut behind him, Kyra sagged in her chair, elbows on her desk, her face in her hands. Oh, Lord, she was falling for this man. Despite every ounce of better sense, he kept reaching inside her and touching her heart. And damn, it was going to hurt when he left.

* ★ ★ ★

Randon strode out into the simmering summer heat. The weight that had roosted on his shoulders since last night was gone. Despite the crudeness of the act he'd subjected Kyra to, she'd said yes.

She was going with him. Thank God. He wouldn't have to face Rachelle's surgery alone, whatever bad news the doctors might have for her. He would have Kyra beside him.

He collected the Polaroid from the service window where Jackson was holding on to it and made his way back out into the yard. He had only four cars left to track down for the production designer and then he'd be done. He still had a few days left on the shoot, assisting the set decorator, but he wouldn't have a reason to return to Kyra's yard. In fact, after Rachelle's surgery, he might not see Kyra again.

It was just as well, he decided as he squeezed between an Achieva and a Cutlass. The more time he spent with her, the more important she became. He could almost feel the ties binding him. He didn't want that kind of commitment. He wanted to be able to pick up and leave at a moment's notice, live his life exactly as he had for the last fifteen years.

Although the thought of leaving Kyra behind opened a hollow feeling in his belly, it had always been hard walking away from friends, starting all over in a new place. This wasn't any different.

And a green-broke colt wasn't any different than a finished cutting horse. None of those so-called friends had ever worked their way as deeply into his heart as Kyra had. Despite only knowing her a handful of days, she meant more to him than he even cared to admit. It would take some time to get her out from under his skin.

He snapped a picture of a late eighties white Cadillac, then moved on, his gaze sweeping the yard. The next time he lifted his camera, someone stepped into his field of view just as he pressed the shutter release. Randon recognized the old man as the one he'd nearly collided with the other day. The codger was just as mean-tempered as before. 'What do you think you're doing, taking my picture?' He grabbed for the photo. 'Give me that.'

The man was several inches smaller than Randon, a little stoop-shouldered with age. Sparse hairs crisscrossed his balding head.

Randon held the picture out of reach, annoyed with the old man's grasping hand. 'Look, mister — '

'Carson, not that it's any of your business.'
He tried again to pluck the photo from
Randon's fingers. 'Give it to me!'

'Mr. Carson, I'll be glad to, if you'll just
give me a minute.' Holding the photo up
high, Randon took a look at it. Mr. Carson
was barely visible, having not quite stepped
into the frame as the shutter released.
'There's not much of you showing, but if you
want it — '

Randon had hardly extended the photo
when Mr. Carson snatched it from him. The
old man gave the picture a cursory glance
before tearing it in two, then again and again,
as small as he could make the pieces.

Tossing aside the scraps, he turned to go.
He hadn't taken two steps before he froze in
his tracks. His back rigid, he raised his arm,
one trembling finger out.

'It shouldn't be here.' Mr. Carson croaked,
waving a hand toward the back fence.

Randon looked to where the old man
pointed, saw the Fairlane gleaming pink
and white in the sunlight. 'What? The old
Ford?'

'It's wrong,' Mr. Carson said. 'It's evil.'

A low moan escaped the old man's throat,
then he wrenched himself around and
hurried toward the exit in a stiff-legged
half-run. When he bumped into a couple

coming in the gate, he pushed past them without apology.

Randon watched him go, puzzling over the old man's behavior. He turned back toward the Fairlane. Laura stood before him, at an arm's length. He edged away from her.

Tearing her eyes from where the old man had disappeared, Laura asked, '*Do you know who he is?*'

'He said he was Mr. Carson,' Randon said.

For a fleeting moment, Randon thought that Laura recognized the name, then she shook her head. '*He scares me. I feel like I should know him, but . . .* ' She looked up at Randon. '*Have you found anything out?*'

It took Randon a moment to understand what Laura was asking. He shook his head. 'I haven't had time.'

She stepped closer. '*You promised. You have to.*' She laid her hands on his arms and Randon stared at the shower of sparks dancing on her fingers. '*We have only days before we go back.*'

'Then you have to tell me more,' Randon said. 'Your last names at least, or your parents' names, or the month you died. I have to have someplace to start.'

'*I can't tell you any of that,*' she said, dropping her hands. '*I don't remember.*'

'Concentrate,' Randon prompted. 'Tell me

what you do know.'

She squeezed her eyes shut, fingertips against her temples. '*We died in 1955 in a storm. We drowned.*'

'In the car?' Randon pressed. 'You drowned in the Fairlane?'

'Yes,' she said. Then, '*No. We were in the car, we were driving, then there was water . . .* ' She looked up at Randon. '*But where did the water come from?*'

'From the storm?' Randon asked. 'Was there a flood?'

She worried her lower lip with her teeth. '*A flood. Maybe. There was water, a lot of it. It broke the window.*'

Randon remembered the bits of broken glass edging the passenger side window. 'I'll see what I can find out.'

'*Today?*'

He ought to keep shooting cars, try to finish the job so he could get on with his life. Still, he told Laura, 'Yes, today.'

She smiled, relief clear in her bright blue eyes. '*You could get her to help.*'

Randon narrowed his gaze on Laura. 'Who?' he asked, although he suspected he knew.

'*Kyra,*' Laura said brightly. '*You love her, don't you?*'

Randon's jaw dropped. 'Excuse me?'

'*I saw you kissing her the other night,*' she informed him blithely. '*Johnny and I used to kiss like that.*'

'You had no business watching us kiss,' he told her sternly.

She ignored his reprimand. '*I wouldn't let him at first. Not until I knew he loved me.*' She tipped her head up at him. '*So you must love her.*'

Dead or not, Laura was still innocent and wouldn't understand how a man could kiss a woman, indeed do more than kiss, without loving her. He chose to sidestep the question.

'I can't work with Kyra. How could I possibly tell her about you?'

Laura smiled. '*Oh, but Johnny* — ' Her eyes grew wide and she looked down at her feet. '*Oh, fiddlesticks!*' she cried as her legs vanished from beneath her.

He'd seen Laura go this way before, but still he reacted. Without meaning to, his hand jumped on the shutter release of the camera, squeezing off a shot.

'*Don't forget!*' she said as the last of her disappeared.

His heart hammering in his chest, he calmed himself with a few deep breaths. Laura didn't frighten him so much as she tilted his world, turning everything he thought he knew upside down.

Kind of like Kyra, he thought as he rubbed at his brow with a shaking hand. He caught sight of the Polaroid in his other hand and the photo jutting from the front. The image was streaked and blurry, not quite finished forming.

He pulled the picture from the camera, turned it over. He wasn't ready to look at it. He knew he'd shot it before she'd disappeared, when half of Laura hung in the air. But could you photograph a ghost? Would he see her pretty face when the picture came clear? And what would that prove?

He flipped the photo right side up and laughed. He had himself a pretty good shot of the front fender and part of the windshield of the Chrysler Le Baron Laura had been standing by. The ponytailed girl in an aqua prom dress was nowhere in sight. He started to crumple the photo, then thought better of it. The Chrysler was white — maybe the production designer would go for it. He started to tuck it into his T-shirt pocket but something urged him to take one last look.

The hair on the back of his neck rose as a prickle of unease coursed up his spine. As if the image had only now become completely clear, he saw what he had missed at first. Not a girl's face, but a few sparkles of light hanging in the air, like the sparks her hands set off along his arms.

He shoved the photo into a back pocket of his jeans and headed for the exit gate. He'd take the few shots he had up to the film shoot, then head down to the university. The library would have to have some back copies of the *Bee*.

He pulled the last photo from his hip pocket before climbing into his pickup and took another long look. Maybe it was a flaw in the film, maybe those glimmering specks meant nothing at all. But it wouldn't hurt to do a little digging.

He couldn't help his sister, couldn't help his own damn self, but maybe this was something he could do. Solve a forty-plus year-old riddle, help a long-dead girl find peace. If he could do that, then maybe he could solve his own problems along the way.

*   *   *

Standing in for Jackson at a service window, Kyra saw Randon leave the yard in a hurry. He didn't even look up at her as he rushed by, didn't even bother to say goodbye. His behavior confused her, kept her so on edge it irritated her.

At the next window, Trish handed over her customer's change, then leaned against the counter and faced Kyra. 'You gonna run that ad for the Fairlane another week?'

The mention of the old Ford brought Johnny's face to mind. 'Have we gotten any more calls?'

Trish nodded. 'Guy came yesterday. I took him back there, but he said no almost before he saw it.'

Kyra gave a weary sigh. Of course not. Who wanted a haunted car? 'The ad's got a couple more days to run, let's wait and see if we get any results.'

Trish chomped on her gum; her brown gaze fixed on Kyra. 'If I ask you something, will you tell me the truth?'

Did she know about Johnny? The thought that someone else might have seen him both frightened and excited her. 'What's that, Trish?'

'Am I gonna keep my job?' the girl asked, concern etched in her young face. 'I hear you and Jackson talking sometimes about how bad finances are and all and I have to know . . .'

A heaviness settled over Kyra. 'I'm doing my best, Trish. That's all I can say for now.'

She glanced out at the yard, back toward where the Fairlane sat. She had to sell that damn car. That was the only spark of light at the end of her tunnel, which meant she had to rid herself of a certain ghost.

She turned back to Trish. 'Do you know if the library at Sac State has back issues of the *Bee*? Like back to the fifties?'

The sudden change of subject obviously confused Trish. 'Sure. On microfilm.'

'When Jackson comes back, I'm going to take a run out there,' Kyra said. 'When's your first class today?'

'Not until four,' Trish said. 'It's a lab.'

'I'll be back in time,' Kyra assured her.

'But what do you need the *Bee* for?' Trish asked.

Kyra glanced back out toward the Fairlane. 'Let's just say I want to do a little research on the old Ford. Maybe find a better way to market it.'

Trish looked dubious, but she didn't comment further. When Jackson returned from his morning errand ten minutes later, Kyra headed out for Sacramento State University.

★ ★ ★

Randon spent more time at the shoot than he'd planned, helping the set decorator and soothing the screenwriter's ruffled feathers. The production designer was blessedly absent, but that meant Randon would have to return later to get the okay on the cars he'd photographed that day.

It was nearly two by the time he made it to the university. He found a parking space in a lot the man at the visitor kiosk swore was near the library, but still he had to ask directions twice before he found it. Up on the third floor, a long-haired male student pointed him toward a cabinet with what seemed a thousand small drawers full of microfilm and microfiche.

Microfilms of the *Sacramento Bee* from the mid fifties were all crowded in a bottom drawer. He crouched down and opened the drawer, running a finger over the rows of boxes. He figured he ought to start at the beginning of the year. Laura had mentioned a storm, so it had most likely been winter.

He located the microfilm for the latter part of January, but the first two weeks were missing. He pulled out the remaining box, then relied on another helpful student to point him in the direction of the microfilm readers.

The readers were in a separate room, bulky machines arranged on desks spread from one end to another. At first glance it seemed the readers were all unoccupied. The lights were low, the dimness eerie in the empty room. Near-empty, Randon realized. Seated at a reader, nearly hidden from view, was Kyra. He couldn't control the grin that spread across his face. He didn't know why it made him so happy to see her so unexpectedly. In fact, it unsettled him. But it seemed like a gift dropped into his lap that she was here.

He moved toward her and touched her lightly on the shoulder. She jumped and gasped, craning her neck so that she could see who stood behind her. She looked surprised to see him, and a little nervous. Her smile seemed forced. 'Hi. What are you doing here?'

'A little research,' he told her, holding out the microfilm box. 'How about you?'

'The same, actually.' She gestured toward the screen. 'Trying to find some information on that '55 Fairlane on my lot.'

Everything went still within Randon. Did she know about Laura? 'Why do you need to know about the old Ford?'

For a moment, she looked stunned at the question, as if he'd caught her entirely off guard. She seemed to scramble for an answer.

'I'm trying to sell it,' she said finally. 'Thought I might have better luck if I knew a little more about it.'

Randon could have sworn she wasn't being strictly honest. Curious, he focused on the screen, at the page displayed. It was from the *Sacramento Bee*, the first two weeks of

January 1955. He looked back at Kyra, saw the evasiveness in her eyes. He burned to know what was going on with her.

Before he could even frame a question, she glanced up at the wall clock at one end of the room. 'Oh my God, I've got to go.' She slapped the rewind button on the reader, held it as the spool rewound. 'I promised Trish I'd be back by three.'

As she pulled the microfilm from the reader, Randon considered asking her to leave it for him. It would save him from having to retrieve it from the drawer. But something kept him from voicing the request, maybe a reluctance to have to explain what he was looking for himself.

She closed the lid of the box, then pushed back the chair. 'All yours,' she said breathlessly.

She didn't step away immediately, just stood looking up at him, head tipped back. He caught a trace of her scent, not so much a cologne as an essence that was Kyra. He wanted nothing more than to cradle her face in his hands and press his lips against hers. She must have read his mind because her eyes widened and she slipped away from him, out of reach. 'I need to know the details about your sister's surgery as soon as possible. So I can arrange with Trish and

Jackson to cover for me.'

'I'll call Tom today.'

She nodded, then turned and left the room. He watched her until she'd disappeared from view.

Settling himself in the chair she'd vacated, Randon studied the posted instructions for the microfilm reader. After a few false starts, he managed to get the spool fed into the machine, then forwarded to the first page. He began the task of scanning headlines, in search of some clue to the deaths of Laura and Johnny.

Back in school, history had never interested him, had never seemed to have a relevance to his life. But reading the paper, seeing these snapshots of people and events, placed the past into a new perspective. The ads especially fascinated him, the styles of dress, the unfamiliar lines of the cars. But searching for even the smallest tidbit of information about Laura and Johnny proved tedious. The sheer volume of text in even two weeks' worth of newspaper made looking for a needle in a haystack seem like a trivial task.

He switched gears, looking for articles related to the weather. Laura hadn't been sure about a flood, but she said there had been a lot of water. If it had been a year of heavy storms with flooding, the paper would say. But beyond some high winds, he could not find anything to indicate that early 1955 had been a particularly bad year weather-wise. He continued doggedly, wanting to have something to appease Laura when he saw her again. But the words started to all run together, to lose sense.

It didn't help that his overloaded brain began parading out images of Kyra. They teased, tantalized, providing him a more interesting diversion. It was too easy to imagine her seated in his lap, her body curved against his, her hands pressed against his chest. He shook his head, pushing aside the fantasies.

He reached the end of the spool and sat back in his chair with a sigh. He felt overwhelmed. If only he had a second pair of eyes to help him search, it might seem less impossible. Of course, he knew exactly which pair he'd want beside him — hazel ones set in a sweet face framed with dark hair.

Rewinding the microfilm, he dropped the spool into its box and contemplated viewing the film that Kyra had returned to the drawer. But the prospect seemed daunting, especially when with every breath he inhaled her scent, and it was her face he saw on the screen.

Maybe he had had enough for the day and should just seek out Laura and try to pull more information from the girl. But to find Laura, he'd have to go to the wrecking yard, which meant he'd see Kyra again. Which was what he really wanted to do. Which was the last thing he should do.

Instead he decided to head back to the location shoot, to try to pin down the production designer. He returned the microfilm to its drawer, then left the library. The afternoon heat settled on him as he traversed the verdant lawns of the campus, passing in and out of the shadows of the trees.

Rush hour had arrived by the time he reached Highway 50, slowing traffic to a stop-and-go crawl. When he reached the Sunrise exit, it was all he could do to not pull off and head for Kyra's yard.

It was past six by the time he reached the location shoot in Camino and the production designer was just climbing into his car to leave. Evans didn't hide his irritation at Randon's interruption. He impatiently flipped through the four photos Randon had shot.

'These two are fine,' he said. 'Get them here tomorrow. And you'd better find the last of them soon. I never expected you to take so long at this.'

I never expected you to be such a total ass. Randon bit back the words, declining to remind the man that if he hadn't been so damned particular, the job could have been finished by now.

What now? he wondered as he headed back to his pickup truck. Go back to the motel? Grab some dinner somewhere? The prospect of eating alone seemed terribly lonely. He remembered the meals he shared with Kyra, the camaraderie mixed with moments of sensual tension.

When he got to Placerville he found himself making the turn toward Kyra's house instead of the one to the motel. The driveway in front of the old Victorian was empty, the front window blinds closed against the summer heat. He considered knocking on the door, but figured she wasn't home. He felt committed to finding her. He continued down the hill into the valley, exiting Highway 50 at Sunrise. When he pulled up at the wrecking yard, Mario was just unlocking the gate to leave. With a quick look at the parking lot, Randon spotted Kyra's car and hurried to catch Mario before he locked the gate behind him.

'Kyra's here?' Randon asked.

'In her office,' Mario told him. The Hispanic man stepped aside, opening the gate. 'Go on in.'

Randon slipped inside, heard the clank of metal as Mario locked the gate. He rounded the corner of the concrete block building that housed the service windows and Kyra's office and caught her just as she was walking away from the door.

Startled, she nearly dropped her purse. 'What are you doing here?'

'I don't know,' he told her. 'I just had to see you.'

'Is it Rachelle?' She gazed up at him, worry darkening her eyes. 'Have you heard something new?'

He shook his head and moved closer. He had to touch her, had to feel her skin against his. He reached out, wrapped his hands around her upper arms.

'Is this okay?' he asked.

She looked confused, made a movement of her head that wasn't yes or no. He rubbed lightly along her arms.

'You told me to ask first next time,' he reminded her.

A slow smile spread on her face. 'I did. So what are you asking?'

'I'm not sure,' he told her, his voice pitched low. 'I know I want to touch you, to kiss you.'

Her eyes fluttered shut a moment, then her gaze fixed on his. 'What else?'

He stroked upward with his palms, resting them against her throat. 'I don't know, Kyra. I don't want to hurt you. I don't want to lie to

265

you. I'm not sure what I need. I only know I need . . . ' He dragged in a breath. ' . . . you.'

She let go of her purse, sighed her response. 'Yes.'

He lowered his mouth to hers. Keeping himself in check, not wanting to repeat the wild loss of control of the previous night, he grazed her lips lightly with his. Her lips parted, but still he held back, only sipping at her mouth, reveling in the feel of her under his hands. Just as he'd imagined, she brought her hands up to his chest, stroked up along it to his shoulders. He could feel the heat of her fingers through the thin knit of his T-shirt, could feel a fingertip resting on either side of his throat. He wanted her hands everywhere on him, stroking against his bare skin. He wanted to take her into her office and make love to her on the tattered sofa, or find a backseat out in the jungle of cars and take her there.

He gulped in another lungful of air, frightened at his crazed thoughts. He'd never wanted to demand so much from a woman as he wanted from Kyra. When he'd had sex in the past, it had always been with a certain detached control, always holding a part of himself back. With Kyra, he wanted to give everything and it scared him to death.

Fighting to take things easy, he let himself

taste her lips, running the tip of his tongue lightly along the seam of her mouth. She sighed in response. He moved his hands, one cupping the back of her head, the other at the small of her back, pressing her closer to him. At the first feel of her soft body against his erection, he nearly lost control again. He pulled his mouth from hers, letting his lips drift across her face, to brush against the shell of her ear.

As he flicked the tip of his tongue in her ear, she released a long, low moan. The sound shattered his control and he gathered her even closer to him, holding her body tightly to his. He took her mouth again, plunging in with his tongue, thrusting as he wanted so badly to thrust inside her body.

He half-lifted her and moved toward her office, an ill-formed idea in his mind to take her inside. Snatches of images flooded him — Kyra naked on her desk or on the sofa or on the floor. He could see himself pushing inside her, her legs wrapped around him as she shuddered with release.

Kyra wrenched back from him, her eyes wild, her breathing erratic. 'What was that?'

His blood roared in his ears, he could hear nothing but his throbbing passion for Kyra. And yet . . . something seemed to echo, to tease him on the periphery of his awareness.

But then Kyra leaned toward him again, standing on tiptoe to brush her lips against his. Her scent, her touch, her body, drove all else from Randon's consciousness.

13

Hidden behind the smashed-in hood of a four-door sedan, Laura watched Kyra and Randon. She would have thought the kinds of feelings twisting around in her now would have died when her body did. But she could so clearly picture her and Johnny doing the things Kyra and Randon were doing, and something burned low in her belly in reaction. She felt something else inside her, too. It started the moment Randon pulled Kyra into his arms. Suddenly, she felt stronger, more solid. Where before she'd felt as if she had no power to control this time on Earth, now she felt capable of shaping her own destiny.

It was because of them, she was sure of it. As soon as they started to love each other, hope had flared so brightly inside Laura. This time, with the help of these two people, they would break free. Maybe this had been their destiny all along, hers and Johnny's. Maybe the other times on Earth had only been for practice, leading up to now and finding Randon and Kyra. Maybe the whole point here was to help the two fall in love, just as they would help her and Johnny escape from the in-between.

She looked around the junkyard. She had to find Johnny. She couldn't wait until nightfall to speak to him. They had to both show themselves to Randon and Kyra, Laura was sure of it.

Something drew her back to the Fairlane. She hurried along the rows of cars, ignoring the fizz of sparks when she brushed up against a bumper or the back of a car. When she reached the Ford, she tried to look inside, but a barrier seemed to enclose the car so that she couldn't see in. But Johnny wasn't here anyway. She only had to be near the car when she called him.

'*Johnny!*' She screamed out the name, heard it rattle around the yard like an explosion. She could just make out Randon and Kyra on the other side of the yard, saw them pull back from each other as if they heard the sound. She didn't want them to stop kissing. It was important that they stay in each other's arms. But she had no choice. She had to call him. '*Johnny!*'

Her heart spoke this time, lending volume and power to her cry. If Johnny was anywhere near, he would certainly hear her. He didn't believe as she did, didn't have her faith. Somehow she had to lend him hers, so that this one time they could come together in daylight.

She shut her eyes, tried to fill her lungs as if she breathed air. Then she shouted out his name again and felt it shatter all the boundaries. And she saw him. Not far from her and moving in her direction. Johnny. Her one true love.

In her exuberance, she screamed her joy and bounded toward him. She flung out her arms, intending to throw them around him. She slammed against the invisible barrier so hard, a phantom pain shot through her.

He reached a hand out toward her. '*How, Laura?*'

She pressed her fingers as close as possible. '*Come with me. We have to talk to them.*'

He looked over his shoulder at Randon and Kyra, still locked in a passionate embrace. '*It might not work. They may not be able to see us.*'

Laura refused to take on his doubt. '*They will. I brought you to me, didn't I?*'

He smiled. '*I love you.*'

Warmed by his words, she put out her hand. '*This is exactly as it was meant to be.*'

He hesitated, then brought his hand next to her. '*Then let's go.*'

Side by side, they walked toward Randon and Kyra.

Kyra felt as if she was drowning in sensation, each point of contact with Randon's hands, lips, body, a blast of heat. In that moment, she would let him do anything, even there on the rough asphalt outside the service room. He fumbled with the doorknob, obviously intent on moving them inside. Kyra cursed the fact that she had locked the door, that she would have to retrieve her purse to unlock it. But that meant she'd have to stop kissing him, something she most definitely did not want to do.

'Randon,' she gasped.

He stepped back, struggling for breath, staring down at her. 'I'm sorry,' he managed. 'Did you want to stop?'

She laughed and shook her head. 'The key. It's in my purse.' She bent to dig for her keys, her hands trembling. Just as she found them, she heard Randon's sharp intake of breath.

'Oh my God,' he murmured.

She looked up at him. He was staring out into the yard. 'What is it?' She followed the direction of his gaze. And she saw them — a young girl, in an aqua party dress, her blonde hair pulled back in a ponytail. A young man sauntering along beside her, a cocky grin on his face.

'It's Laura,' Randon breathed.

Kyra rose, reaching out to Randon to steady herself. 'And Johnny.' She looked up at Randon. 'You see them? Both of them?'

'I do, sweetheart,' he said, the endearment touching her deeply.

She leaned against him, laughing. 'Then I'm not crazy.'

'Unless we both are.' He curved his arm around her shoulder.

The boy and girl stopped a few feet from them. Laura's brilliant smile lit her face with infectious joy.

'*I knew we could do it!*' she exclaimed with youthful enthusiasm. '*Because you love each other now.*'

Kyra could feel the sudden tension in Randon's body, could feel his gaze on her. It was all she could do to not look up at him. She realized she was holding her breath, waiting for him to speak. A ridiculous, unwanted longing bubbled up inside her.

'Kyra and I don't love each other.' He said each word clearly, as if to be certain the girl understood.

Kyra ruthlessly thrust the yearning aside. Of course they didn't love each other. Kyra edged away from Randon, suddenly needing some distance, confused by the disappointment laying like a weight inside her.

Laura tossed away his denial with a flick of her hand. '*You can work together now. I know you'll find the truth.*'

Kyra forced her focus from the tumult inside her to the mystery of Laura and Johnny. 'I went through some back issues of the *Bee* today.'

'I did too,' Randon said.

Of course. He'd gone to the library to look at the *Bee*. Certainly not to look for her. She hadn't even realized she'd harbored that scrap of hope until now.

She kept her voice steady as she spoke to the boy and girl. 'I didn't find anything about two missing teens. Your names didn't turn up anywhere.'

'You don't know your surnames?' Randon asked. 'Neither one of you?'

Johnny and Laura exchanged a glance, then Johnny spoke. '*We hardly remember anything about the time we were alive. I'll see bits and pieces, like how our front door would always stick in the winter or my mother's face . . .* '

The words seemed to be squeezed off by emotion. Johnny looked down at his loafers, looking very much like a young man trying not to cry.

Laura brushed her hand close to his, setting off a waterfall of sparks. '*I remember more than Johnny, like the storm and the*

274

river breaking into the window. But not our last names . . . '

'Don't you think we've tried?' Johnny said bitterly. 'Do you think we're happy in that car, or caught in the in-between? In the in-between I can't hear or see or feel — I just know I'm there, aware just enough to feel the endlessness.' He pushed back a lock of hair that had fallen into his eyes. 'Each time it seems longer. Each time I wonder if we'll ever break free, have another chance. And to think of Laura there, maybe right next to me, or a million miles away . . . '

He took a step closer to Kyra and a dead cold washed against her. 'Maybe I've done something to deserve a hell like that, but not Laura. Not her.'

Laura raised her hand as if to touch Johnny's arm, to comfort him. 'It's not so bad. I know you'll be there when we come through again.'

Silence fell as the sun crept toward the horizon. Johnny looked up at the sky. 'We haven't much time. I don't think we can keep from going to the car when it's dark.'

'Then tell us everything,' Kyra said. 'All over again. Everything you know.'

The two of them began to speak, taking turns with the memories, picking up a thread when the other couldn't recall. Even as young as they'd been when they died, Kyra could see the true love Laura and Johnny felt for each other. It arced between them like the sparks created by their ephemeral touch.

'One more thing,' Randon said when they'd finished. 'You said you died in a storm, which means it had to be winter, or late spring. Can you narrow the time down at all?'

Laura's brow furrowed as she concentrated, then she shook her head. *'I'm sorry. I can't.'*

Watching the girl pleat the folds of her aqua party dress gave Kyra an idea. 'Is this what you wore the day you died?'

Laura looked down at herself. *'I guess so. I never really thought about it.'*

Kyra took in Johnny's white dress shirt and black slacks. 'Then you were probably at a dance or a party. Do you remember where you wore that dress?'

Laura's eyes widened in excitement. *'Yes! This is my prom dress.'*

'So maybe it was after the prom?' Kyra suggested. 'Maybe you went out for a drive or . . . ' Her voice trailed off as she remembered the other things teenagers liked to do in a car.

'Or to do a little sightseeing,' Randon said, his tone amused.

Johnny smirked and Kyra could swear a

blush rose in Laura's cheeks. 'We can start with the spring, then,' Kyra said.

The long shadows in the yard seemed to blur as the sun sank further on the horizon. Johnny's smile fell away.

'*We have to go, Laura,*' he said.

'*One more thing,*' Laura said.

'*Now,*' Johnny said.

With a shock, Kyra realized the two were fading, were being drawn away bit by bit. She glanced at the Fairlane off in the distance and a chill wriggled up her spine at the eerie glow lighting the car.

'*One more thing,*' Laura repeated, her voice as faint as her ghostly form. '*Find out about that man.*'

'What man?' Kyra asked.

'*Randon knows,*' Laura said, the words a whisper of an echo. In the next heartbeat, she was gone, and Johnny with her.

Kyra couldn't suppress a shiver. 'What man did she mean?'

'The old man, maybe,' Randon said thoughtfully. 'I caught him by accident in one of my photos and he was pretty ticked.'

'We have quite a few old men coming in here,' Kyra said. 'I don't suppose you got his name.'

'I did, actually. Was it Martin? No, I'm sure it started with a 'C'.' Randon rubbed at his brow. 'Carson. It was Mr. Carson.'

A picture of the stoop-shouldered old grouch entered Kyra's mind. 'What could Mr. Carson have to do with anything? He's pretty eccentric, but he seems harmless.'

Randon shrugged. 'Maybe he reminds Laura of someone else, someone she knew back then.'

'I'd hate to go nosing into someone's life on the basis of a maybe,' Kyra said. 'I think we ought to focus on Laura and Johnny, see if we can find something on two missing teens.'

'Sure.' His warm hand came up to stroke the back of her neck. 'When you were looking in the *Bee* earlier . . . '

'Mmm, yes?' She shut her eyes at the feel of him.

'Did you find anything about the weather?' Randon asked.

She should have pulled away from his touch, but she couldn't seem to muster the willpower. 'The weather?'

'They died in a storm, Kyra. Was there anything in the issues you looked through about heavy rains, flooding?'

How could he be so matter-of-fact when all she wanted to do was melt in a puddle at his feet? 'No, I didn't see anything about bad weather.'

She met his gaze then and realized he was

anything but unaffected. His eyes dropped to her mouth, and she knew in a heartbeat he would kiss her.

He glanced toward the door leading to her office. She could hear his thoughts — just a few steps away, they could have all the privacy they wanted. His thumb continued to caress her, sending waves of sensation through her body.

But he doesn't love you. Don't forget that.

She tensed slightly, and he pulled his hand away. 'What do you say we get out of here and get something to eat? We can talk it out over dinner.'

She nodded. Dinner was a good idea. If they stayed here, God only knew what they'd end up doing, what she'd end up regretting. Although in that moment she wanted nothing more than to tumble into bed with this man. But if she had sex with him without love, without a commitment, she would hate herself for it. She remembered all too well the hole she'd dug her self-esteem into those last few months with the Snake.

She put on a bright smile. 'Are you buying?' There was barely enough in her purse to cover a cup of coffee.

He smiled in return, and the light in his gray eyes made her melt all over again. 'I'll gladly buy you dinner for the pleasure of your company.'

'The restaurant up the road okay?' she asked. 'That big family place?'

He nodded. 'I've been there. It's pretty good.'

'I can meet you there in about five minutes. I have a couple things to finish up here.'

'Fine,' he said. 'See you there.'

She watched him go, then leaned back against the concrete block wall of the service room. She closed her eyes and dragged in a few deep breaths of the warm, still air. It took some willpower, but she managed to drive away the lingering feel of his hand on her. She headed off to Gertie's dog run.

Before releasing Gertie, she knelt to hug the wriggling, excited shepherd, needing in that moment someone's unconditional love. Gertie delivered in spades, lapping at her face, then resting her massive head on Kyra's shoulder.

When Kyra opened the gate to the dog run, Gertie trotted out, sniffing the air. She froze for an instant and Kyra looked in the direction of the dog's focus. It was the Fairlane, glowing dimly in the growing darkness. Kyra urged the dog out into the yard, then watched her lope off. Even knowing the source of that glow, and the two young ghosts inhabiting the car, Kyra still felt a faint horror creeping up her spine. Johnny and Laura couldn't help being dead, couldn't help being here in Kyra's wrecking yard, but nevertheless . . . Kyra's heart stuttered in her chest as a sound at the edge of her consciousness became something recognizable. A song drifted through the warm summer air. *Unforgettable.*

She turned, trying to pinpoint where the music was coming from. A chill froze her to her core when she realized the song came from the Fairlane. The words rolled over her, as clear as if Nat King Cole stood beside her. She tried not to think about the fact that the old Ford had no battery, and she couldn't be hearing what she was hearing. But waves of fear washed over her anyway.

Unashamed of her cowardice, Kyra rushed for the exit gate, snatching up her purse as she went. As she locked the gate and headed for her car, she did her best to close her ears to Nat King Cole's rich mellow voice. But as she drove the short distance to the restaurant the words wound themselves up inside her, haunting her like a painful memory.

★ ★ ★

Randon saw Kyra the instant she entered the coffee shop. The hostess had already seated him, and he rose from the booth and waved to get Kyra's attention. Still on his feet, he watched her as she crossed the room, his heart doing funny things inside his chest. Every time he'd convinced himself he wanted nothing more from Kyra than a good time in bed, his emotions seemed to persuade him otherwise. It was so damn tempting to listen to that soft, illogical voice inside himself, to forget that he was not a man to stay in one place with one woman. If he wasn't so determined to keep Kyra from getting hurt, he might give in and enjoy what little time he knew they'd have.

He waited for her to sit, then slid into the booth opposite her. He allowed himself a moment of weakness, letting his gaze roam her face, the tousle of dark hair framing it, her wide hazel eyes. Then he opened his menu and buried his nose in it. 'What's good here?'

Kyra flipped through the plastic laminated pages. 'The chicken fried steak isn't bad. Not as good as Mama's, but pretty tasty.'

The waitress came over, the same no-nonsense, matronly woman who had served Randon breakfast. She clunked glasses of ice water on the table, then tugged an order pad from the hip pocket of her black skirt.

Randon ordered the chicken fried steak, although the thought of all that grease made his stomach a little uneasy. Kyra asked for a burger and fries. Not the cheapest item on the menu, but far from the most expensive.

'Is a burger what you really want?' he asked as the broad-hipped waitress walked away.

Kyra's eyes narrowed. 'Why wouldn't I?'

Randon realized he'd stepped out onto mighty shaky ground. 'Just because I'm the one paying, you didn't have to be careful about what you ordered.'

Her lips pressed together. 'I wasn't being careful,' she said tightly. 'I haven't had a burger and fries in a long time. It's what I wanted.'

Although he knew he ought to leave it be, Randon persisted. 'I know it's none of my business — ' He laid his fingers on the back of her hand. 'Is everything okay with you? Money-wise, that is?'

Her expression grew wary. 'Why do you ask?'

He searched for stronger footing. 'Hints here and there. The broken stove and washer you couldn't seem to get fixed on your own. A couple comments I overheard Trish saying.'

Kyra frowned. 'I guess I'd better have a word with her.'

He tightened his fingers on her hand. 'Don't. There weren't any other customers around. I don't think she even saw me.'

Kyra pulled her hand free and lifted her water glass. She took a tiny sip, as if buying time. Then she set the glass down as carefully as if it were the most fragile crystal.

'FourStar is in a bit of a bind,' she said finally. 'Our credit is strung out from here to kingdom come. We have far more debts than we've got the income to cover them.'

He wanted to touch her, to offer reassurance, but he sensed it was the last thing she wanted just then. He linked his hands in front of him instead. 'What happened?' he asked. 'Has business been bad?'

She sighed and slouched in her seat. 'Business hasn't been great. This heat spell has slowed things down, certainly. Other than the hard-core customers, people don't want to slog through a wrecking yard when it's a furnace out there.'

She propped her feet up on the seat beside him. 'But we could squeak by even with the current downturn. The real problem is the loans. The Snake took out a half-dozen loans at God-awful rates not long before he died. I just can't make the payments. At this point I'm having trouble keeping current on anything.'

Money. She needed money. The realization burst on Randon like a revelation. Here was something he could do for her, something he could give her that would involve no emotional entanglements. He tried to temper the excitement in his voice. 'I might be able to help you.'

Kyra looked up at him suspiciously. 'Help me how? Are you a millionaire in disguise?'

He laughed, although it sounded false to his ears. 'No, but I've got some money put aside. Maybe enough to dig you out of your hole.'

'I'm in a pretty deep hole,' she told him. 'No offense, but I find it hard to believe a drifter like you — '

'How much would you need?' he asked. 'To pay off the loans and get back on an even keel?'

She named an amount that nearly took his breath away. It wasn't more than he could manage. With his investments he could pay her debts without batting an eyelash. Anger burned in him at the snake of a husband that had brought her to the edge of financial ruin.

She shifted her sneakered feet on the seat next to him, crossing one ankle over another.

'A bit more than you bargained for, huh?'
She'd obviously misinterpreted his silence.

He flicked his hand in a careless gesture.
'No problem. I can have a cashier's check for
you tomorrow.'

He thought her eyes would fly out from her
head. 'You're kidding, right?' She sat up
straight, dropping her feet to the floor. 'You
are kidding.'

He shook his head. 'I have the money. I'd
be more than happy to give it to you.'

She fiddled with her water glass, swishing it
back and forth on the table. 'Where did you
get that kind of money?'

'Here and there,' he told her. 'Saved from
odd jobs over the years.'

'But what did you live on?'

'I learned early on to live cheaply,' he said.
'I had Rachelle to support, so I couldn't
waste money on myself.'

'Waste?' Her gaze grew soft and she tapped
his linked hands lightly with a fingertip. 'Why
would spending money on yourself be a
waste?'

He captured her finger, curved his palm
against hers. 'I don't need much. When
Rachelle married and didn't need me
anymore, I was just in the habit of being
thrifty.'

He thought she might tug her hand away,

but she didn't. 'So what'd you do, sock it away in a bank?'

'Actually . . . ' He hesitated, feeling somehow uncomfortable with his good fortune over the past several years. 'I've invested it. Stock, a little real estate, even bought a percentage of a cutting horse ranch.'

'So now you want to buy into the auto dismantling business,' she said, her hand warm against his.

'Something like that,' he said, then raised her hand to brush his lips against her smooth skin. 'You'll take the money then.'

He made it a statement, not a question, figuring the issue was settled. So it surprised him when she pulled her hand free and crossed her arms over her chest.

'Absolutely not.' Her chin tipped up, her eyes challenging him. 'I can't take your money.'

Irritation pricked at him. 'Can't or won't?'

'Either way.' She picked up her glass for another sip. 'It wouldn't be right.'

'What's not right about it?' he asked, his annoyance increasing the volume of his voice. A man and woman at the next table turned to look at them and Randon lowered his voice. 'What could be wrong about me helping you?'

Kyra leaned toward him. 'Why would you

help me? Out of the goodness of your heart? Or would you expect a little something in exchange?'

Indignation rose in him at her accusation. 'Of course not. It would be a gift.'

'A gift,' she repeated, skepticism evident in her tone. 'Out of the goodness of your heart, you would be willing to give a total stranger tens of thousands of dollars.'

Certainly she was right. He'd only known her a short time, and although he knew he was generous to a fault, his offer to Kyra went far beyond any other act of generosity he'd committed. But damn it, she didn't feel like a stranger. He rapped his fingers on the table, trying to ignore his wounded feelings. Then he looked up at her.

'If you want the money, it's yours,' he said gently, 'no strings attached. No hidden agendas. If you don't . . . '

She covered his hand with hers. 'Thank you. Truly. But I just can't take it.'

He sighed, frustrated by Kyra's stance. She reminded him of his sister, how single-minded she could be about what she saw as the right way to do things. When Rachelle picked a course, she stuck to it, come hell or high water. Which was why her vulnerability frightened him so. He would have expected Rachelle to face the cancer the way she'd

288

faced everything else in her life — as an enemy with which to do battle.

Kyra drew back as the waitress arrived with their food. 'So tell me about Rachelle's surgery.'

He looked up at her, startled. She laughed. 'Don't worry. I'm not reading your mind. It's just that you get such a sad look on your face when you're thinking of her.'

He picked up his knife and fork and cut the chicken fried steak. 'It's the day after tomorrow at UC Davis Medical Center. There's a gynecological surgeon there who's supposed to be the best.'

Kyra poured a lake of ketchup on her plate, then swirled a french fry in the red puddle. 'They're all supposed to be tops at Davis.'

'They want her there the day before, to run some tests.' He dipped a fork into his mashed potatoes. 'I thought I'd run up there tomorrow evening.' He was relieved that he didn't have to spell out the invitation.

'Can I go with you?' she asked, as if she didn't know full well how much he wanted her there.

'That'd be great,' he said.

The emotional charge dissipated, Randon felt suddenly ravenous. He attacked his food, pausing only long enough between bites to talk over the puzzle of Laura and Johnny. By the end of dinner he and Kyra had a plan of action.

★ ★ ★

Enchanted, Laura listened as the last of the song faded from the radio. She smiled up at Johnny.

'*How did you do that?*' she asked.

He seemed very pleased with himself. '*I just touched the knob and the song started up. Remember how we danced to it?*'

She sighed, leaning back in her seat. '*I do. You held me in your arms and we floated across the gym floor. It felt like we were flying.*'

'*My heart was flying, that's for sure,*' Johnny said. '*That night I knew I loved you.*'

She smiled, feeling as shy as she had decades ago when he'd first admitted his feelings. She gave him a sidelong glance, saw a fierce intensity in his eyes.

'*I love you so much, Laura,*' he whispered.

'*I love you too, Johnny,*' she murmured.

She had to look away; the emotions were too much to bear. Laura's memories ebbed and flowed inside her like an ocean wave.

'*Could you do that again, Johnny?*' she asked dreamily. '*Put another song on the radio?*'

He didn't answer, and she turned her head to look at him. Her smile vanished when she saw the empty seat beside her.

'*Oh, no,*' she moaned.

In the next moment, the dream descended, snatching her into terror.

14

Rain pounded on the windshield of the Fairlane, running down the glass in sheets. Below her, water frothed and tumbled in the channel between two levees, battering its banks on either side. Laura could see only blackness beyond the far levee, the lights of the houses drowned by the vicious storm.

A burst of brilliance blinded her, sent the night scurrying into shadows. There was something evil about the light, something that terrified her beyond reasoning, beyond death. She wanted to turn away, to cower down in the car and hide herself, but the light drew her nonetheless, forced her to look at it.

Mesmerized, she pressed her palms against the window glass, her nose nearly brushing the cool surface. Her breath roiled out like steam, fogging the glass, making it harder to see. She rubbed at the window to clear it, leaving the print of her hand. Johnny wouldn't like that — he always liked to return his folks' car perfectly clean.

Now that she could see better, she tried to make out the source of the glare. But it seemed to be only light, dazzling white, infinitely cold. A shadow loomed out of the light. She had to look away, had to retreat from the window. She couldn't let him see her. It would be terribly dangerous if he recognized her face. But she couldn't move. She seemed glued to the window, her hands frozen to the glass. He was coming nearer and nearer, his dark silhouette growing in magnitude with each step. At any moment he would see her through the glass and he would know her.

Suddenly he was there, his face filling her view, his cruel eyes fixed on her. Recognition sparked in his gaze. Even worse, she recognized *him*, and he knew that, too. Hope washed away from her with the pounding rain as his evil eyes locked with hers.

Suddenly, the car lurched, and she fell across the seat, away from the window. The Fairlane bounced this way and that, tossing her about the car so that she banged her head on the dash, on the door, on the window. One shoe came loose as she whacked her knee on the door handle.

Then the ending all came back to her — the Ford sliding off the levee, plunging into the icy water. The roar of the flood-swollen river, the crash of the window shattering. The water gushing inside the car, shoving her out the broken window as the car turned and turned in the river.

She tried to scream for Johnny, but the water filled her mouth, her eyes. She came up once, struggled for air, but it was too late. The water had filled her lungs, had stripped her very life from her. The leaden sky turned crazily above her as the floodwater tumbled and tossed her in its wake.

* * *

Laura came to with a gasp. Trembling all over, she drank in the morning quiet of the junkyard, the ugly wrecks all around her strangely comforting. She raised fear-weakened hands to cover her face, tried to wipe away the horror of the dream. In her mind's eye she could see the man's enraged eyes, his mouth twisted in an angry snarl. It was as if his rage had lifted the Fairlane and flung it over the levee bank into the river.

She shuddered, wishing she could push the evil face from her thoughts, but she knew it was important to remember. In the dream, she'd known exactly who he was, had recognized him. But the passage into the real world had dulled the images, so that only a tantalizing scrap of memory remained. The man's name danced just out of reach. If only Johnny were with her now. She longed for

him, although she sensed that despite last
night's success, she would not be able to
bring him to her today. The bright summer
light pouring down seemed to dilute her
energy so that the very notion of calling him
exhausted her. She should look for Randon or
Kyra instead. She desperately needed an
anchor, some assurance that the hideous
dream wouldn't grab her again.

She forced herself to move, threading her
way between the cars. She wondered if Kyra
would be able to see her today or if they'd
returned to the way it was before. Laura
hoped that somehow things had changed so
that she could tell Kyra about the dream.

Laura moved close to the front building,
the one with three windows and a big sign
above reading *FourStar*. The Negro man and
the girl with the dark spiky hair stood behind
the counter, but Laura couldn't see Kyra. She
drifted close enough to listen, easing between
the two lines of customers.

'Mrs. Aimes isn't in this morning,' the
Negro man said to the customer at the front
of the line. 'She should be back this
afternoon.'

Laura moved away from the people, looked
at the parking lot. She didn't see Randon's
pickup truck out there, so he wasn't here
either. Uneasily, she made her way back into

the yard. A strangled sound alerted her first, then the clunk of something heavy hitting the asphalt. She looked up and froze in utter terror. It was Mr. Carson. His hands were full of grease and a piece of a car lay at his feet. His pale blue eyes fixed straight on her. He could see her.

'Can't be,' he rasped.

Laura looked down at herself, willing herself to disappear. But just as she couldn't seem to stop it on command, she couldn't start it either. She would have smiled at the man, pretended to be a real girl, but something in Mr. Carson's eyes told her he knew exactly what she was.

She should try to scare him. Reaching out to the nearest car, she swept her hand through it in a cascade of sparks. His rheumy eyes widened and his mouth dropped open. She saw the stamp of fear in his face, changing his features, contorting them. The transformation sent fingers of alarm walking up Laura's spine, a warning she didn't understand. She flung herself clear through the hood of a sedan, the sharpness of it causing her to gasp. He followed her every motion, his blue gaze never leaving her. She expected him to become more afraid, but he didn't. Something else began to brew in his eyes.

Her feet tingled with the first phase of the vanishing. Relief washed over her as the effect swallowed her in a wave, taking her from his view. He watched every moment, a strange look of satisfaction settling on his face. When she'd gone completely, when she was invisible but could still see him, he bent to pick up the car part he'd dropped and walked away. His casualness frightened Laura more than anything else. He acted as if he knew her. Then the realization struck her with the force of a flash flood. Of course he knew her. He was the man from her dream.

★ ★ ★

Kyra watched as Randon threaded the third spool of microfilm into the reader, all too aware of his knees brushing against hers, his arm so near she could feel his warmth. It had been like this from the moment they'd first sat down at the reader, really since he'd first arrived at her house this morning to pick her up. Even as he'd followed her down the hill, him in his truck, her in her car so that she could leave it at the yard, she felt his presence powerfully.

Randon leaned back in his chair as he forwarded the film, the muscles in his arm flexing. Kyra stared at the ropy lines moving under the bare skin of his forearm and itched to feel the movement against her palm. She resisted the temptation as she had thus far, but the resulting tension prickled along her skin, stroked its way persuasively up her spine.

He stopped the film on the first front page and focused on the screen. She would have almost thought him immune to the feelings arcing between them if it weren't for the edgy way he shifted in his seat, the way his fingers worried the arm of the chair in which he sat. He must have felt her gaze on him because he turned toward her. His gray eyes burned into her, setting off a flash point deep inside her.

She gasped in a breath and slid her chair back a little. 'This isn't working.'

'What do you mean?' His attention was back on the screen as he scrolled through the spool.

Our being together, she thought. Feeling the way we feel and pretending we don't. Trying not to want what we both want.

'We're nearly through May and we've found nothing,' she said. 'It hardly rained at all that month, certainly not enough for a flood.'

'We could look at June,' Randon suggested.

Kyra shook her head. 'Too late for a prom, not to mention heavy rains.'

He pushed back from the table, turning in his swivel chair. 'Then what do we do next?'

She blew out a puff of air. 'We could go back to January and make our way forward.' The prospect of combing through the three winter months of *Bee* back issues settled on her shoulders like a weight. 'But she said she wore the dress at her prom.'

Randon tugged off his hat and plopped it down on the table. 'Maybe the dress has nothing to do with it. Maybe it was just her favorite.'

Kyra couldn't suppress a smile. 'So when you die, you get to wear your favorite dress for eternity?'

Randon laughed, dissipating some of the tension between them. 'Maybe so,' he said, then plunked his hat on his head. 'I'd like to have a new Stetson, though.'

Kyra grinned at him, her gaze meeting his. God, she loved his eyes, the depth of them, the kindness. She felt something inside her soften as she gazed up at him, and a warmth spread from her center out, encompassing her. It was a dangerous, dangerous feeling. Lord, it was so close to love it terrified her.

She turned away, deliberately focusing on the image on the screen. 'Her favorite dress,' she murmured, trying to distract herself. She looked over at Randon. 'If the dress was her favorite, she'd certainly wear it again. Maybe she wore it at her junior prom in May, then the next school year wore it again.'

'She's sure of the year, though,' Randon reminded her. 'It would have to still be 1955.'

'Why couldn't it be the tail end of 1955 instead of the beginning?' Kyra asked. 'The winter rains would start up again in November, continue into December.'

Randon pressed the rewind button on the reader, then quickly unthreaded the spool. 'So we need the microfilm from November and December. What kind of school function could she have worn the dress to?'

Kyra rose as he did, helping him gather up the boxes of microfilm. 'Has it been that long since you went to high school? You don't remember the dances?'

He seemed embarrassed. 'I never went to dances. I told you I dropped out, took the GED.'

They dropped the microfilm boxes into a basket to be refiled and returned to the cabinets. 'So you missed out on all that adolescent angst. Wondering which girl to ask to the dance, praying you wouldn't step on her feet.'

They found the *Bee* back issues for November and December 1955, then returned to the reader. 'This sounds like the voice of experience,' Randon said. 'Did your feet get stepped on?'

Kyra laughed, remembering. 'Alan Westhoff loved to dance. Unfortunately, he was a terrible dancer.' At Randon's gesture, she took the swivel chair in front of the reader, he sat beside her. 'But I was in love, and sore toes were a small price to pay.'

'So what happened to Alan?'

'Moved away our senior year,' Kyra said. 'Became a high-powered attorney in L.A., married a college sweetheart. Found someone else's toes to step on.' She smiled up at Randon. 'So, do you dance?'

He smiled back. 'I do a mean two-step. I generally keep my feet off my partner's toes.'

An invitation hovered on the tip of Kyra's tongue, that they go out dancing. The thought of Randon holding her in his arms was altogether too appealing. She turned to the microfilm reader, fumbled with the spool. 'Johnny's and Laura's school would have had a homecoming dance for sure,' she said as she threaded the film into the reader. 'Maybe a holiday dance closer to Christmas.'

'So . . . ' He leaned in close to her, curved arm around the back of her chair. 'What did you wear to your prom?'

Her hands trembled a little as she forwarded the film. 'What does that have to do with Johnny and Laura?'

'Nothing.' He bent forward so his lips nearly brushed her ear. 'I just want to know.'

The low rumble of his voice sent a shiver through her. 'I wore black.'

'I think I need a few more details than that,' he said, then his lips grazed her ear, the sensation a pleasurable shock.

'It was shiny, strapless,' she told him in a near whisper. 'Tight through here.' She gestured down her body from her breasts to just below her waist. 'Loose to my ankles.'

'Was the back cut low?' He stroked the length of her spine, stopped at the base. 'Down to here?'

She nodded, unable to speak. She looked up at him, to ask him to move away, to give her some space. But she couldn't push the words past her throat, and instead her eyes did the talking, asking for something different.

He tipped up her chin, and traced her lips first with his intense gray gaze, then with his thumb. He moved the pad of his thumb from side to side on her lower lip, setting off an ache inside her. Then he lowered his head and pressed his mouth to hers, lightly, the bare contact increasing her urgency. When the tip of his tongue stole out to graze her lips, she brought her hands up to cradle his head, to bring him closer. She wanted more than he was giving her and she couldn't think of how to ask. Finally his tongue thrust into her mouth, the friction against her lips tantalizing. She strained to get closer to him, the throbbing spreading out along her nerves in waves.

A giggle sifted into her awareness, then loud whispers. Randon pulled back, setting her away from him. Dazed, she looked up at him, the lopsided grin on his face urging her to move in closer for another kiss.

'We've attracted an audience.' He gestured with his head back behind him.

Sitting up straighter, Kyra peeked over his shoulder and saw the two coeds over by the change machine staring at them in avid fascination. Ducking back down, she felt the heat rising in her cheeks. She turned back to the reader. 'You're a bad influence on me.'

He drew a fingertip along the curve of her ear. 'Can I help it if you're irresistible?'

She drew back out of reach. 'Please don't.' She paged through the first week of November, barely aware of what was on the screen. 'We can't keep doing this, Randon. Not when we both know where it will end.'

He sobered then, realizing she was serious. 'You're right. It's just that sometimes when I look at you . . . '

'What?' she said softly, looking straight at him.

His gaze locked with hers for a long beat. 'There's no future for us, Kyra.'

She forced herself to keep her eyes on his. 'Of course there isn't.' Why did she keep forgetting that? And what was she doing hoping anyway? A relationship was the last thing she needed — or wanted. Kyra returned her focus to the image on the microfilm reader, but the damage was done. She couldn't keep her mind off Randon and his brief kiss. With only a touch, he resurrected long buried dreams until she could think of little else. She feared that if there was anything in the paper about Johnny and Laura, she'd miss it entirely in her distraction.

Randon kept his hands to himself, was scrupulously careful to give Kyra her space when he leaned in to point out something on the screen. But the tension between them didn't diminish. It lay unseen like a downed tree limb, submerged just beneath the surface of a storm-swollen river.

When they reached the end of the first spool of microfilm, Randon rose from his chair. 'Let's skip ahead to December.' He picked up a box of microfilm. 'I'll look over the first two weeks. You take the sixteenth through the thirty-first.'

He settled himself in front of the reader next to Kyra. The knot between her shoulders easing slightly, Kyra fed in the spool for the last two weeks of December 1955. Anxiety gnawed at her that they'd found nothing that shed light on Laura's and Johnny's fate, adding to the stew of emotions inside her. She forwarded the film, scarcely taking note of the headlines rolling past.

'Finding anything?' Randon asked her.

'Nothing unusual,' she said. 'How about you?'

'Nope.'

The flat, monosyllabic answer irritated her, as if he put aside the feelings that had sizzled between them moments ago. She reached the end of the December eighteenth edition and fast forwarded quickly past the classified ads, determined not to let his curtness get to her.

She positioned the reader to the front page of the Monday paper, registered the headline. 'Wait a minute.'

Randon turned his chair toward her. 'What is it?'

She tapped the screen. 'Looks like things started getting bad here.' She read him the headline. '*Rain, Snow, Gale Batter Valley in Severest Storm of Season.*'

He scooted his chair over, gestured to the

page-one photo of partially submerged cars. 'There was some street flooding at least.'

She scanned the article, read about fifty-mile-an-hour winds and power outages. They continued through that edition and the ones following, scrolling through the spool more slowly. They reached the December twenty-second issue, read about high water driving hundreds from their homes, three deaths in a small dam break. Four local counties had declared emergencies.

Kyra forwarded past the sports section and classifieds, then hesitated. 'I'm almost afraid to read on.'

'We have to,' Randon said softly.

'I know.' Her hand rested on the control knob. 'But something inside is telling me we're about to find the answer and we're not going to like it.'

Despite her unease, she tipped the knob to the right and slowly scrolled to page one of the Friday paper. Randon read the headline out loud.

'*Marysville Evacuation Starts as River Levee Peril Mounts.*' He turned to Kyra. 'Where did the Fairlane come from? Sacramento area?'

'I don't know.' She stared at the screen, at the blaring headline. 'The man who sold it to us had a Sacramento address, but he never mentioned where he got the car. It could have been Marysville.'

'That's only about forty miles north of here,' he pointed out. 'It's possible.'

Kyra read through the article, feeling a chill skitter up her spine. Twelve thousand people evacuated. Only as a precaution — the levees weren't reported to be in danger of breaking — but she could imagine the fear Laura and Johnny must have felt.

They continued through the paper to the Christmas Eve edition. 'Good Lord,' Kyra said softly as she positioned the spool to the front page.

'So the levee did break,' Randon murmured.

The *Bee* was full of evocative photos — Yuba City just west of Marysville, under water; a group of nurses slumping in exhaustion in an evacuation center; a young girl clutching a doll, probably the only treasure she'd managed to bring with her.

'The Marysville evacuees had gone to Yuba City,' Kyra said. 'They would have had to evacuate again.'

'Hell of a lot of confusion,' Randon said.

As Kyra turned pages, her gaze fell on a provocative headline and her heart rocketed in her chest. *'Car Plunges off Levee into River; Pair is Missing.'*

'False alarm,' Randon said. 'It was a married couple.'

'I guess I shouldn't have expected it to be that easy.' She forwarded slowly through the paper, stopping at a page of pictures. She read down a long column of text, scanning quickly.

A name jumped out at her. She dropped her hand on Randon's, said quietly, 'Look at this.'

As he leaned in to see where she was pointing, she read aloud. '*Some families have been separated by the evacuation. Mr. and Mrs. Harold Garvey have apparently lost track of their son, Johnny. 'We're certain he's gone to a different evacuation center,' Mrs. Garvey said. 'He'd better turn up,' Mr. Garvey said jovially. 'He borrowed my brand-new Ford.'* '

Kyra's voice faded to a whisper as she read the last few words. 'That must be him. It has to be.'

'The first evacuation order was broadcast at midnight,' Randon said. 'If Johnny and Laura had gone out that night . . .'

'But how could they?' Kyra asked. 'They would have known about the levee danger. Wouldn't they have stayed home?'

'They might have underestimated the peril,' Randon said. 'They were teenagers.'

'They were in love,' Kyra said.

The hazards of storm or floods wouldn't have meant anything to them. It only mattered that they be together. Agitated, Kyra raked her fingers through her hair. She battled those same desires with Randon. To be with him, to love him. If she gave in to her urges, a flood might not overcome her as it did Johnny and Laura, but heartbreak would drown her just as certainly.

Impatient with herself, she returned her focus to Johnny's and Laura's problem. 'So they went out to a dance, or on a date.'

Randon nodded agreement. 'They could have parked up on a levee afterward. Missed the evacuation call completely.'

'Or maybe they were already dead by then.' Kyra shuddered. 'So do you think that's it? They got caught when the levee failed? Got washed away in the flood?'

Randon rubbed at his jaw pensively. 'I suppose so. But what's the big mystery here? What is it about that unfortunate incident that would keep them trapped in the car, trapped on Earth?'

Kyra leaned back with a sigh. 'Randon, I don't understand half of what's going on here. Hell, I'm still trying to get my mind around the idea that a pair of ghosts are living — make that occupying — my wrecking yard.'

Randon stared at the screen a moment longer, then shook his head. 'We haven't found the answer yet.'

Frustration filled Kyra. 'What other answer is there? They went off a levee and drowned in the Christmas Eve floods.'

'But what made the Ford go into the river?' Randon persisted. 'Was Johnny driving too fast? Is that why he doesn't remember — he feels guilty that he caused the accident.'

Kyra raked her hair back from her forehead again, slumping down in her seat. 'I've had enough for today. The words are all blurring together.' She glanced at the clock, saw it was well past one. 'And I've got to get back to FourStar sometime today.'

'Let's just go to the end of the spool,' Randon suggested. 'See if they mention anything more about Johnny Garvey.'

They scanned the *Bee* through December thirty-first, but if there was an item about the missing boy, both she and Randon missed it. Kyra rewound the spool and returned the microfilm to its box. Randon rose from his seat and stretched, the motion tightening his T-shirt across his chest. Kyra tore her gaze from the tempting ripple of muscles and headed out of the room.

'Maybe we ought to take a different tack,' she said as they left the library, 'and look at back issues of the local Marysville or Yuba City paper.'

'Good idea,' Randon said. 'Where could we get our hands on those?'

'I'll put a call in to the State Library this afternoon. We could go over there tomorrow.'

'Rachelle's surgery is scheduled for tomorrow.'

'Then maybe the day after,' Kyra said.

A muscle worked in Randon's jaw. 'Sure. That's if everything is . . . okay.'

Meaning if the news was bad after Rachelle's surgery, Randon might be too distracted to pursue the mystery of Laura and Johnny. Kyra reached out for Randon's hand, giving it a squeeze. His fingers linked with hers, tightening almost painfully. As they reached his truck in the parking structure, he released her hand.

They didn't talk much on the drive back to FourStar, just desultory comments about the heat, the music on the radio, the column of smoke from a wildfire off in the distance. When he pulled into the parking lot at the yard, he didn't turn off the engine.

'I need to get back to the motel, check for messages,' he said.

'I'll see you tomorrow, then.' She slid out of the truck.

He caught her arm. 'You're still going

311

tonight, aren't you? To the hospital?'

'Yes, of course,' she assured him. 'I'd forgotten.'

His brow furrowed. 'Six okay?'

'Fine,' she said, smiling. 'Just pick me up here on the way.'

He released her arm, returned his hands to the wheel. 'See you, then.'

She slammed the truck door shut and backed away. She waited while he drove off. The lonely look on his face seemed emblazoned in her mind, the stark vulnerability. God, why did he have to need her? It only made the challenge of not loving him all the more difficult.

15

For once, good news awaited her when she returned to the yard. For mid week, the morning's sales had been brisk. Several customers had bought bigger ticket items, including a dad who purchased one of the nicer vehicles on display up front to refurbish for his daughter. A half dozen members of a local car club had made a lunch time pilgrimage down in a search for parts.

Kyra laughed when she saw the full cash drawer. 'Maybe I should stay away more often,' she told Trish.

'I saved the best news for last,' Trish said. 'Some guy took a look at the Fairlane today.'

The Fairlane! She'd forgotten about the ad. 'What did he say?'

Very pleased with herself, Trish grinned broadly. 'He wants to buy it, Kyra.'

Alarm bubbled up inside Kyra. 'How could he? I mean everyone else turned it down flat.' Everyone else had sensed Laura and Johnny and run the other way.

Trish laughed. 'It's kind of funny. He's a minister. He says his dad owned a car just like it.'

Kyra's heart rattled in her chest. 'His name wasn't Garvey was it?'

'Garvey?' Trish looked at her oddly. 'No. Why would you think that?'

'Never mind,' Kyra said, realizing how ridiculous her guess had been. Too much time spent poring over old newspapers. 'You were saying?'

'His name's Reverend Heathman. And he left a deposit, Kyra. He's coming back this afternoon to talk to you.'

Kyra ran a shaky hand over her hair. 'That's great. Let me know when he's here.'

She headed back to her office, thoughts tumbling in her head. She couldn't sell the Fairlane now, not when she and Randon had nearly solved the puzzle. But she couldn't afford to pass up an offer, either. In her office, she grabbed the phone book from under the desk and flipped through it for the number of the California State Library. As she dialed, she tried to work out what to do about the old Ford.

After making her way through a maze of voice mail, she confirmed that the state library carried the local Marysville and Yuba City papers in its microfilm collection. As she hung up the phone, her gaze fell on the stacks of paperwork for the state she had yet to complete. That was it. She could tell

314

Reverend Heathman she wasn't quite finished clearing the title on the Fairlane. That she needed another week before she could turn it over to him. Surely in another week, she and Randon would have all the pieces of the mystery sorted out. Johnny and Laura would be free of the Fairlane and it would be just like any other car. Or, they would solve the puzzle too late and the two teens would return to the in-between. Kyra shivered at the thought of the stark oblivion Johnny had described. What if this was there last chance at salvation? What if only she and Randon stood between them and eternal purgatory?

They *would* discover the answer. Somehow, they would ferret out the truth. She'd promised and now she felt an even greater urgency to deliver. Maybe she should look for them now, Kyra thought. Tell them what they'd found out so far. Maybe that would trigger more memories for Laura.

Kyra headed out to the yard, the sun warming the back of her short-sleeved cotton shirt. The delta breezes had kicked up, cooling the searing temperatures of the last several days. The high might not even reach the nineties today. As she passed between the rows of cars, Kyra realized she had no idea how to find Laura or Johnny. They'd always appeared to her spontaneously. She'd never sought them out. Maybe it just wouldn't work this way.

As she thought of Johnny, a consideration she'd pushed to the back of her mind surfaced. She had his father's name. It wouldn't take much digging to discover if Mr. or Mrs. Garvey were still alive and living in the area. But what she would say to them? I've met your son and he seems like a nice young man? And, oh, by the way, he's dead?

What if Mr. and Mrs. Garvey didn't know Johnny was dead? What if they thought he'd run away and all these years had held out hope of seeing him again? If she barreled into their lives with the news, it might shatter them. And just how would she substantiate Johnny's death? Tell them she'd seen his ghost? That he'd appeared out of nowhere and she'd watched him fade and disappear before her eyes? They'd be calling the men in the white jackets for her. No, she couldn't tell them yet. When it was all said and done, when she and Randon had some hard facts that they could present to the police about the disappearance of Johnny and Laura, then she and Randon could go talk to the Garveys. And to Laura's parents.

Without being aware of the destination

she'd set, she reached the Fairlane. The chrome gleamed in the midafternoon sunlight, and heat came off the fat pink and white fenders in waves. She put a hand on the hood, remembering the chill she'd felt that first day. But now she felt only ordinary warmth. She wondered where Laura and Johnny went when they disappeared. Were they still here somewhere, watching her? Surprisingly, the thought didn't frighten her. She liked the idea of them nearby.

'Johnny?' she called out softly. 'Laura? Are you here?'

She turned slowly, straining to see the blonde girl or dark-haired boy somewhere near her. Nothing.

'Johnny!' she said a little louder. 'Laura! Are you here?'

It worried her that she couldn't find them. They couldn't already be back in the in-between, could they? Maybe that was why the minister didn't sense their presence. They were gone. Brief panic filled her, but she quelled it. No, she didn't believe they were gone. Somehow, she could still feel them here, even though she couldn't see them. At least, she wanted to believe it.

She tried calling their names a few more times, then decided that maybe it just didn't work this way, appearing on command. On the off chance that they were somewhere nearby and could hear her, she began telling them about what she and Randon knew so far, about the flooding, the evacuation, and Mr. and Mrs. Harold Garvey. She wondered how it would feel to Johnny to rediscover his last name, hoped fervently that he could hear her. When she'd finished, she stood a moment more, scouring her mind for any other details she might have left out. The scuffle of feet startled her and she whirled away from the Fairlane.

'Mr. Carson,' she said breathlessly.

The man barely saw her. He stared at the old Ford behind her, shaking his head slowly.

'Why is it here?' he rasped. 'How can it be here?'

'The car?' Kyra asked. 'Why shouldn't the car be here?'

Mr. Carson swung his head toward her. 'Because of them.'

A prickle of fear shot up Kyra's spine. 'You know about them?'

His pale blue eyes burned into hers. 'I know they're dead. I know they shouldn't be here.'

She took a step toward him. 'How do you know? What do you know about them?'

Mr. Carson backed away, shaking his head. 'I don't know anything.'

'Mr. Carson,' Kyra called. 'Wait! Don't be afraid.'

'I don't know,' he said, stumbling into a black sedan, then sidling away. 'Shouldn't be there. Evil.' He turned and trotted off, his shoulders hunched in on themselves.

Evil? Why would the car be evil? Surely there was nothing evil in Laura and Johnny. What did the old man know? Laura had been certain she'd recognized Mr. Carson. Kyra had dismissed it at the time, but now she wondered.

She needed to see the teens, to assure herself they were here and still safe. The encounter with Mr. Carson had unsettled her. She felt a danger in him, a danger she didn't understand. She caught sight of Trish up by the service windows, trying to flag her down. A man stood next to Trish. The minister, no doubt. Still troubled, Kyra put aside the problem of Mr. Carson and headed over to Trish. Time to focus on more practical matters.

★ ★ ★

Johnny had tried to scare the minister away. He'd felt guilty about it, seeing the man's collar and all and knowing he was a man of God. Johnny might not believe in God anymore, but he couldn't help but respect people who did, like the minister, or Laura. Still, Johnny knew it wouldn't be good if someone bought the Fairlane, took it away from Kyra's lot. He feared that moving the Ford would drive him and Laura back into the in-between. Every day, every hour even, he felt his link with the Fairlane grow weaker.

Laura, though, believed so strongly that Randon and Kyra would find an answer, that they would deliver him and her from the half-hell in which they existed. That and her undying faith in God seemed to strengthen her. If she felt the in-between reaching out for her, ready to grab her back into oblivion, she never said. She never lost her certainty of salvation.

Johnny watched Kyra approach with the minister at her side. He'd have to try again to discourage the man from buying the Ford, find a way to frighten him. That wouldn't make Kyra happy — he knew she needed the money, having overheard the girl, Trish, and the Negro man, Jackson. But he and Laura needed more time.

As soon as the minister came near the Fairlane, Johnny crowded in close. He waved his hands in the minister's face, jumped from side to side. It was silly, really — Johnny knew the man couldn't see him. But it had worked with the others.

Johnny watched the man's face, so he could tell when the minister sensed him. The minister's eyes widened a little, and Johnny could swear the man smiled. Angry that the man wasn't afraid, Johnny moved in even closer and swiped a hand clear through the minister's body. *The man laughed!*

Johnny backed away in shock. By the time he recovered, Kyra and the minister were walking away, shaking hands. Kyra gave one last look over her shoulder at the Fairlane and Johnny saw the concern, the worry in her face. She'd sold the car.

Although she'd promised to help them, she'd gone and sold the car right out from under them. This minister would come to take the Ford away, sending Johnny and Laura back into the nothingness of in-between. Their link to this world that had grown so slender with each passing moment would break. Maybe forever.

Despair washed over Johnny, sapping him of strength. He felt himself fading, drifting. He sagged against the Fairlane, only dimly aware of the faint sparks arcing from the car. A desperate need for Laura burst through him. Laura would give him strength, an anchor. He would wait here for dark. He would wait here for Laura. And pray to a

God he'd lost faith in that she would come.

★ ★ ★

As they drove to the UC Davis Medical Center in the heart of Sacramento, Kyra could think of nothing but how good Randon smelled. His male scent filled the pickup's cab, a mix of soap and musk. His hair was damp beneath the worn white cowboy hat, and he'd shaved. Kyra's fingers itched to stroke his cheek, to see if it was smooth or still slightly rough.

He caught her looking, turning away from the light Highway 50 traffic long enough to sear her with his hot gaze. There was a new energy between them tonight, a raising of the stakes, like river water inching toward flood stage. There was still time to turn back the coming inundation. With a word she could channel it in another direction. But somehow she knew she wouldn't say that word tonight.

Kyra swallowed against a dry throat. 'Rachelle's all settled in at the hospital?'

Randon's hands tensed on the steering wheel. 'Tom took her down there this afternoon. He called me an hour ago to give me her room number.'

'How's she doing?'

His jaw worked. 'I don't know. She keeps telling Tom she's fine, but . . . '

'But?' Kyra asked.

'She's scared to death, Kyra,' Randon said, a certain desperation in his voice. 'And there's nothing I can do about that.'

Kyra risked touching him, placing a hand lightly on his arm. 'You can be there for her.'

He glanced at her. 'That might not be enough.'

She stroked him, the comfort in the gesture edging into something far more volatile. 'It won't stop the cancer, if it's there. But it can help the fear.'

He reached over and covered her hand with his, squeezing. They spent the rest of the drive in silence, with nothing but the ever present tension passing between them.

★　★　★

Randon didn't like Rachelle's color. Her gray eyes seemed sunken in on themselves in the stark whiteness of her face. He wondered if the paleness of her skin was a sign that her condition had worsened, but he was too afraid to ask.

He reached out blindly for Kyra. She gripped his hand, her fingers locking with his. Her presence gave him the strength to force a smile, to lean in to give his sister a kiss on the cheek.

'Hey,' he said. 'How ya doing?'

She smiled back at him, a weak effort. 'I'm fine. I keep telling Tom he can go back to the motel and be with the boys, but he keeps hanging around here.'

Randon's brother-in-law hovered over Rachelle on the other side of the bed, his face impassive. Randon glanced over at him, could see the well-disguised tension in the hard set of his mouth.

'Chris and Daniel are fine with my mother, Rachelle,' Tom said. 'They're happy to be with their grandma. And they love staying at the motel.'

Rachelle sighed. 'But you don't need to hang around here all night.'

'What about Randon and Kyra?' Tom asked, his tone faintly bullying. 'They just got here. Are they supposed to go too?'

Her lips compressed as if she were just barely holding back tears. 'Of course not. We'll visit for a bit, then you all ought to leave. I need my rest. I have a big day tomorrow.'

Her voice wavered slightly on the last word and Randon looked over at his brother-in-law again. Tom stared back as if asking for something from Randon, something he wasn't sure Randon could give.

Randon remembered what Kyra had said, felt the power in her words as she stood here beside him. He let go of Kyra's hand, took up Rachelle's in both of his. He tugged a little on her small, cool hand until she met his gaze.

'I'm with you, Rachelle,' he said softly. 'No matter what, no matter where I go.' He swallowed hard. 'No matter how this all turns out.'

Tears welled in Rachelle's eyes. 'I didn't want to have to depend on you again, Randon.'

He brushed away a tear that slipped down her face. 'But I want you to.'

She shook her head. 'It isn't fair to you.'

He squeezed her hand. 'Fair has nothing to do with it. You're my sister. I love you.'

She just gazed up at him silently, letting the tears flow unchecked. Then she pulled her hand free. 'I really am tired,' she said, closing her eyes. 'Would you mind terribly if I asked you to go?'

Unease filled Randon. It was as if Rachelle had rejected what he'd told her or rather, that she'd just not let the words sink in. An air of hopelessness hung over her and Randon wanted to grasp her and shake her.

Kyra stepped closer to the bed. 'No problem, Rachelle,' she said soothingly. 'We'll

325

see you tomorrow.'

Randon leaned over to press another kiss on his sister's cheek, then stepped back. 'We'll be here in the morning.'

She opened her eyes and managed a brief smile. He and Kyra turned and left the room, Tom following behind.

They paused in the corridor outside her room. 'Are you leaving?' Randon asked Tom.

Tom looked at the closed door, then back at Randon. 'In a bit. She does need her rest. She hasn't slept well the last couple days.'

'I'm worried about her,' Randon said.

Tom grimaced. 'Tell me about it. She's the picture of cheer around the boys and my mother, but the few times I've caught her off guard . . . ' He shook his head. 'Damn, I hope this surgery goes well.'

Kyra brushed her fingertips against Tom's arm. 'I'm sure it will.'

Randon put out a hand to shake Tom's. 'We'll see you tomorrow.'

They turned and headed for the elevator, a fountain of suppressed emotion within Randon threatening to break free. He stood on the edge of a sword, Kyra on one side, his familiar lonely existence on the other. He had only to let go to leap into paradise. And now with Rachelle's illness, her terror, his own fear, he felt powerless to resist that surrender.

Standing with Kyra in the small space of the elevator, he felt his control shredding, a fiber at a time. Need had caught up to him with an overwhelming urgency.

When they stepped out of the elevator on the ground floor, Randon took hold of Kyra's arm. She turned toward him, looked up at him expectantly. She knew what was coming without his even having to say a word.

'I don't want to be alone,' he said softly.

Her eyes widened slightly, and she took in a shallow breath. 'I want to be with you,' she whispered.

He stared down at her for another long moment, then with his hand still on her arm, guided her out of the hospital. He helped her up into the truck, then released her arm reluctantly. When he climbed inside the cab, he reached for her hand.

'We'll have to go to my motel,' he said.

She wrapped her small hand around his. 'We could go to my house.'

He shook his head. 'The motel. In case Tom or Rachelle need to call me.'

She nodded agreement. He tugged her lightly, so that she slid across the seat next to him. He set her hand on his thigh and started the engine. The warmth of her hand so close to his groin nearly undid him. It took an enormous effort to focus on pulling the truck out of the parking space and toward the exit.

Several minutes later on the freeway, Kyra said, 'My car's still at the yard.'

'I'll drive you in tomorrow,' Randon told her.

'You'll need to take me home first to change,' she said. 'In the morning, I mean.'

He heard the nervousness in her voice, wondered if she'd already changed her mind. He dragged in a breath. 'We don't have to do this.'

'You talk as if it were a chore.' She laughed, the sound false to his ears. 'Something you're only doing because you have to.'

'I do have to. Not out of duty, but because . . . ' His hand covered hers. 'I need this, Kyra. I need you.'

He felt a sudden fear that his vulnerability would put her off, make her lose her desire for him. He imagined himself balanced precariously in the palm of her hand where the slightest gesture would cast him back into loneliness. He'd made his leap — maybe he'd gone the wrong direction.

She stroked his leg lightly with her fingertips. 'I want to be what you need, Randon.'

Her caress sent sensation shooting up his leg and he struggled to breathe. He scrambled for something to say in response,

328

managed to squeeze out, 'Good. That's good.'

They didn't speak further as they continued up the hill toward Placerville, just let the tension between them fill the cab of the truck. Kyra's scent was a steady presence, a taste on his tongue, a stroking sweetness on his skin. He trembled slightly in anticipation of seeking out the source of her scent and feeling it on his lips, under his hands.

He pulled carefully into a parking slot at the motel and shut off the engine. Everything within him propelled him to culmination, to the coming together he had longed for from the moment he'd met her. But there was something he had to say first, out of honesty, out of conscience. One point he had to make very clear. He turned to her, studied her upturned face. Behind them the sun glowed orange on the horizon, coloring the air, washing Kyra's skin in peach and pink, streaked with shadows. Watching her, Randon felt as if he would burst into flames.

He had to say the words first. 'Kyra,' he said softly. 'If we do this, you have to know — '

'That there's nothing more,' she finished for him. 'I know.'

'Do you?' he pressed, although his body clamored for him to get out of the truck and go inside with her. 'This isn't love. What we do tonight won't keep me here. I'll still be leaving.'

She tipped her chin up, the set of her jaw stubborn. 'I know.'

He curved a hand against her cheek. 'It doesn't mean I don't care for you. That this won't be special.'

He saw her throat work as she swallowed. 'It just won't mean forever.'

She'd said the right words, had agreed with him. But Randon sensed Kyra was hiding something behind her determined face. But then she leaned in close, brushing her lips against his and it no longer mattered what secrets she concealed.

He drew away to climb out of the truck and she waited for him to come around to the other side. Opening the door, he took her hand to help her down. He kept her hand as they walked to her room, only releasing it long enough to let them both in.

The room was dark. Randon raised her hand to his mouth. 'I want to see you,' he murmured.

He guided her toward the bed, snapped on the small lamp on the nightstand. The pale yellow light spilled over her face, softening the lines of it, casting a mysterious shadow on her hazel eyes.

His blood roared in his ears as he looked

down at her. He realized if he listened to his body's demands he would be throwing her on the bed and taking her in a flashpoint of passion. But he didn't want it fast, he wanted to savor every touch, every sigh.

Tossing aside his hat, he scraped in a breath. 'I want to feel you everywhere,' he whispered. He laid a hand against her cheek. 'Here.' He slid his fingers down along her throat, then lower to the first soft slope of her full breasts. 'Here.' He dipped between her breasts, watching her eyes flutter shut, continued down across her flat belly. 'Here,' he said, his lips close to her ear.

He followed the curve of her ear with his mouth, slipping the tip of his tongue out to follow the seashell whorl. She gasped in reaction, her hands flattening on his chest.

Did she want him to stop? He backed away, only bare inches before she clutched at the knit of his T-shirt, pulling him back. 'Come here.' Her fingers drifted up to curl around his shoulders.

'Tell me what you want,' he said, dragging his teeth over the lobe of her ear.

Her fingers tightened on his shoulders. 'You're doing fine so far.'

He moved his mouth along her jaw, trailing kisses. Her hands stroked along his shoulders to the back of his neck, hot against his bare skin. When she threaded her fingers through his hair, his heart stuttered in his chest. He pressed his mouth against hers, reveling in its softness. She parted her lips in invitation and he let himself taste her, moving his tongue along her lower lip. He wanted to plunge inside, to slide his tongue against hers, to taste the honey of her mouth. But he held back, struggling to draw out the pleasure.

Because this was their only night. They would enjoy each other in this room, in this moment. They would make love, once, twice, hell, maybe all night. But after tonight, after these few hours, it would be over between them.

Randon buried his fingers in Kyra's short silky hair, tipping her head to take her mouth more fully. He would have this night and nothing more. Because he didn't want to love her. And he was terribly afraid that it was already too late.

16

Even as Kyra felt a certainty within her that this was exactly what she wanted, a warning voice clamored in her head. Even as a tightening wire of passion strummed inside, her heart ached knowing the final price it would have to pay.

She sighed as Randon brushed his lips against hers again, sensation shimmering through her. She had always known she could not make love to this man if she did not love him. She had just thought she could resist her body's pull by denying her heart's determined message.

She loved him. In only a few day's time, knowing only the small part of him that she knew, she loved him. She should have been suspicious of this headlong rush into love — it was exactly what had doomed her with the Snake. But despite her meager experience with Randon, her instincts told her his precise measure. He was a caring man of honor and dignity, without an iota of cruelty in him.

He had made it as clear as he could there would be no tomorrows for them. She would have to take this, now, and it would have to be enough. She knew it wouldn't be, but in that moment, she had no other choice. So she would extract from this time every ounce of passion.

She tugged at his T-shirt, pulling from the waistband of his jeans. 'Take it off,' she whispered. 'I want to touch you.'

He obliged her, pulling the shirt over his head. Immediately, she pressed her hands to his chest, reveling in the thick curls there. She stroked with her lips, the contrast of warm skin and soft, tickling hair intoxicating. Moving to one flat male nipple, she circled it with her tongue. He gasped in a breath, his hands gripping her shoulders. She flicked his nipple with her tongue, then grazed it lightly with her teeth.

'Good God,' he rasped. He slid his hands to the front of her shirt, fumbled with the buttons.

She covered his hand with hers. 'Not yet. My turn first.'

She felt his quiet laughter against her cheek. 'Yes, ma'am.'

'I've fantasized about you,' she told him as she trailed her tongue across his chest.

He sucked in a breath. 'Have you?'

'Yes.' She teased his other nipple, and felt his fingers dig into her shoulders. 'Indulge me.'

She let her hands roam over his bare skin, down along his ribs, feeling the leanness of him, along his sides. His muscles rippled as she touched the flat planes of his stomach and she heard soft laughter again.

'Ticklish?' she asked.

He seemed to hold himself still with an effort. 'No.'

She grazed an experimental finger around his navel, enjoying the wave of reaction. 'I've discovered your secret.'

He reached for the front of her blouse again. 'Then let me discover yours.'

She captured his hands, replaced them on her shoulders. 'Not yet.'

She moved from the front of him to his back, running her palms along the strong muscles flexing along his spine. She spanned his shoulders with her hands, their breadth a wonder. Then she moved lazily down his arms, stroking and massaging the ropy muscles as she went.

'You're killing me,' he growled.

'You're a big strong man,' she purred. 'You can stand it.'

She took his hands from her shoulders and kissed them, pressing her lips first to the backs, then turning them over. She laved his palms with her tongue, swirling along the intricate network of lines.

'What are you doing?' he gasped out.

'Reading your fortune,' she said.

'What does it say?'

She flicked her tongue between his fingers. 'A night of pleasure awaits you.'

He took control then, cradling her face in his hands, tipping her head up to him. He kissed her, his tongue diving inside her mouth, mating with hers. She stroked along his arms, his shoulders, moved along his back to the waist of his jeans. She dipped inside, fingers pressing against firm skin.

He rasped in a breath, his hands sliding down her body to her breasts, covering them. He teased at her nipples with his palms, the thin cotton of her blouse and lace of her bra a fragile barrier. The tips grew hard and aching, matching the drawing ache between her legs. She pulled him closer to her, his hips pressing against her. The hard ridge of his erection burned along her soft belly and she wanted to stroke a hand along its length. She wanted to feel him deep inside her.

This time when he moved to unbutton her blouse, she let him, shifting so that he could slide it off her shoulders. He bent to her breast, flicking his tongue against a lace-clad nipple, driving an agony of sensation through her. She clutched his head, her fingers tangling in his hair. He wet the lace with his tongue, then nipped lightly with his teeth. She gripped him so hard, she was afraid she'd hurt him.

He reached around her and released the hooks of her bra. Then he straightened and slipped the straps from her shoulders, down her arms in a long caress.

The hot intensity in his eyes as he stared down at her sent a shiver through her. Even knowing most men loved large breasts, she'd always felt awkward in her body, out of proportion.

She waited for him to close his hands over them, to fondle and knead them as the Snake had done. She felt torn between wanting Randon to touch her and hating that reminder of the hurried lust of her late husband.

Instead, Randon set his hands at her waist, and lowered his mouth to hers. He pulled her in closer to him as he kissed her, not crushing her breasts to him, but grazing her nipples lightly against his chest, back and forth in a mesmerizing taunt. She tightened her grip on his shoulders, trying to tug him to her, but he resisted, just keeping up his tease.

The sensation built inside her from that slight contact. His tongue thrust into her mouth, the warm skin of his chest scraping lightly against her nipples, his hands massaging gently at her waist. She felt a wet heat between her legs that begged for contact, ached for his touch.

'Randon,' she pleaded, her nails digging into his shoulders.

He tipped her back against the bed, laying her down on the spread. Now he did touch her breasts, still standing over her, cupping them, stroking them, his palms hot against her nipples. She raised a languorous hand up his leg to the fly of his jeans, pressing as she went.

His hands resting lightly on her breasts, he shut his eyes and dragged in a long breath. 'If I had any damned willpower, I'd tell you to stop that.'

She pressed the heel of her hand against him and he groaned. 'Why should I stop?'

'Because I want this to last forever,' he said, 'and what you're doing will shorten things considerably.'

'We have all night,' she told him and turned her focus to the snap of his jeans. She unfastened it, then slid the zipper down, his erection pushing the fly open. She tugged down, and they worked together to remove his jeans and briefs.

'Now you,' he said.

He undid the button and zipper on her

shorts and shucked them in one smooth move. Then he stood over her, his gray eyes burning. 'Tell me your fantasies.'

She could feel herself blush and wondered if it stained her whole body. 'Wouldn't you rather lie down?'

'In a minute. Tell me.'

She shifted on the bed, restless. 'They were just ordinary fantasies.'

He leaned over her, hands on either side of her body, wrists brushing the sides of her breasts. 'Tell me.'

She squeezed her eyes shut. 'I thought about touching you. Like I did just now.'

'And?' he prompted.

She opened her eyes. 'I imagined touching you . . . ' She reached up, drew one finger along the length of his shaft, from tip to base. ' . . . here.'

He swallowed and his arms trembled. 'What else?'

She smiled at the effect her touch had on him. 'I thought about this.' She stroked farther down, cupped that most vulnerable part of him. A sound got lost in his throat and his head pitched down.

'What else?' he rasped.

'I wanted to do this.' She curved her head up, bringing his shaft down to her. She kissed the tip, then took him in her mouth, laving with her tongue.

His breathing grew harsher, loud in the quiet of the room. After long moments he pulled her hands away, pushed her gently back onto the bed.

'My turn,' he said hoarsely. 'Let me tell you my fantasies.'

His hands on her thighs, he parted them and settled himself between them on the bed. His erection jutted up, setting off an ache to have him inside her.

He caught the direction of her gaze and smiled. 'Not yet, sugar.'

He leaned over her, brushing her lips lightly. 'A hundred times a day I've thought of kissing you, tasting you. Here . . . ' His tongue flicked out and traced the line of her lower lip. 'Here . . . ' He trailed along to her ear, dipped inside. 'And here . . . ' He tasted her pulse point hammering in her throat.

He moved lower, along the smooth skin of her breast, his cheek slightly roughened by his beard. 'But I have to say, this occupied a good deal of my thoughts.' His tongue moved leisurely around her nipple, until it peaked, hard and exquisitely sensitive. He nipped lightly at her nipple while his hand covered her other breast, and his fingers worked a different magic.

Kyra thrashed her legs, unable to keep still,

burning clear down to her center. 'I don't know how much more of your imagination I can take.'

'Just one more fantasy.'

He took his mouth from her breast, pressed kisses down along her body. He paused at her navel, circling it with his tongue. Kyra gripped his shoulders, her heart hammering in her ears.

'Of everything I imagined, this was the best.' He placed his hands on her inner thighs, slid them closer to her soft folds. She felt his fingers brushing, teasing. 'This is the flavor I wanted most to taste.'

At the first touch of his tongue, Kyra's hips bucked off the bed. He pressed them back down, holding her in place.

His soft laughter shivered through her. 'I'm afraid you'll have to just lie there and take it.'

She answered him with a low moan. His tongue circled her sensitive nub, swirling against it again and again. Everything inside her expanded, stretched out, near to bursting.

'Randon,' she whispered, not even sure of what she was asking.

'I suppose you want more.' The wash of his tongue sent shattering waves through her. 'Greedy.'

She felt his clever fingers moving against her, then he thrust them inside. She cried out, throwing her head back. His tongue and fingers worked relentlessly, pleasure exploding out to every cell of her body, lifting, reaching. He held her universe in his hands, delivered her into paradise.

The first wave of climax broke through, tumbling her over and over in its wake. She felt her body convulse around Randon's fingers, felt his satisfied murmur rumble through her. A ruthless lover, he pushed her to a second climax, then a third before finally letting her return to shore, exhausted and sated.

She couldn't have moved if her life depended on it. She felt as if she was in pieces, the parts slowly crawling back to become whole again. She managed to open her eyes, saw him cradled in her thighs, watching her. She laughed. 'You look damned smug.'

His smile broadened. 'I feel pretty accomplished right now.'

She tugged on his shoulders, pulling him up to her. 'You're not finished yet.'

'Just a minute.' He slid from the bed, picked up his jeans and pulled a small square from his pocket. He looked over at her as if to gauge her reaction. 'I bought these today. I figured . . . hell, I don't know what I figured.'

'You figured we both wanted the same

thing, Randon. And you were right.' She held out her hand. 'Give that to me.'

He gave her the condom, watched her with hot intensity as she opened it, then sheathed him in it. Then he knelt between her thighs, his strong erection jutting up.

'It's been a while, Randon.' Heat rose in her cheeks. 'I might be a little tight.'

'I'll go easy.'

She took him in her hand and guided him to her. At the first touch of him between her legs, she wanted all of him. She was greedy, like he'd said. But he went slowly, inching in. She could see the strain on his face, in the tension of his arms on either side of her. She stroked along his body to his hips, held him there to urge him inside her.

'Okay?' he rasped.

'Marvelous.' Her body convulsed around his hard length as if to pull him in. 'Wonderful.'

His head dropped in response and he thrust fully inside her. She gripped his hips to hold him where he was, then wrapped her legs around him, locking them at his back.

She circled him with her arms, pulling him closer. 'You're mine now.'

His gray eyes flared silver. 'I'm not going anywhere.'

He began to move, drawing away, then

filling her. Every nerve sensitized by her orgasms, the explosion inside her built again quickly. She groped down to his hips, urging him to move faster, gratified when he complied.

Climax hit her again, slamming into her like a wall of floodwater. Her body squeezed him, milked him, until his own orgasm pounded into her. His groan of release vibrated through her, scudding over her nerves, heightening her pleasure.

He sagged on top of her, his weight exquisite. His face nestled in her throat, his warm breath soothing. She stroked along his back to bury her fingers in his hair, sifting through the softness.

After a long while, he raised his head and looked down at her, his smile wry. 'You don't play fair.'

She teased at his ears with her thumbs. 'What? You didn't enjoy that?'

He laughed, and she could feel the sound, clear to her toes. 'I'm still waiting for my head to come back down from the ceiling. But that was too damn fast.'

She stroked his cheek bones, brushed his eyelashes. 'Then we'll just have to do it again.'

'Damn right we will.'

She kissed him, letting her lips linger on

his. 'I hope you have plenty of those things in your pocket.'

His tongue flicked out. 'I bought the economy size. If the ones in my pocket give out, the rest are in the truck.'

He gave her one last kiss, then got up from the bed. 'Give me a minute.'

She watched him cross the room to the bathroom, then rose herself. She'd been so involved, she hadn't noticed the scratchy bedspread, but they might as well get comfortable.

As she tugged back the covers, the enormity of what they'd just done overwhelmed her. She sank to the edge of the bed. She'd gone against every instinct of self-preservation tonight, every iota of good sense. She'd let her feelings rule, let her heart take the lead. And her heart would be paying the price.

Even still, she'd made the right choice. She eased herself back onto the bed, tugged the covers to her waist. When Randon returned, she smiled at him in welcome, held out her arms to him. She would extract every drop of pleasure from this night, accept it as the palest imitation of love. She would have the memories to hold forever. Even though she'd hold them in an aching, empty heart.

Randon lay in the darkness, Kyra beside him, her head on his shoulder. She slept, the sound of her even breathing soft in the dark room. The weight of her on his arm felt so right he wanted to hold her there forever. But he didn't have forever. He had only now. Then he would move on as he always had since the first time he left home.

He could stay. He rolled the idea in his head, testing it. But the familiar clutch of panic started up in him, sending tension running the length of his body. Even the feel of Kyra beside him didn't soothe that tension. And yet . . . He dragged in a deep breath, inhaling her scent. The whole room smelled of her, smelled of sex. The sensual aroma teased him, aroused him. He felt his manhood stirring again.

And yet if he left Kyra . . . Desolation sunk in his chest, crushed his heart with its lonely pain. Leaving would quiet the panic; leaving Kyra would break him. Even as he weighed the two options inside him, he knew the older instinct would win out. The long habit of moving on was ingrained and would bulldoze right over those other passing fancies. Although he knew what he felt for Kyra wouldn't easily pass.

He turned a little toward her and lay a hand lightly on her belly. They'd been careful to use protection both times they made love. It had always been crucially important to him with other women to protect them, to prevent pregnancy. And yet . . . In the dark he could see only the faintest suggestion of Kyra's form — the lush breasts, the slim waist, generous hips. And where his hand lay against her belly, he could plant his seed, start a baby. A child to carry on his legacy.

He took his hand away and lay back on the bed. What kind of legacy could he leave? That of a drifter, a ne'er-do-well who'd accomplished nothing in his lifetime?

He thought of the money he'd accumulated in mutual funds and CDs. That was something he could give a child. It might pay for school or a car or maybe a horse and saddle. He'd already planned to put aside some for Daniel and Chris, maybe there'd be enough for a child of Kyra's.

Who was he kidding? He wouldn't be having a child with Kyra. It wouldn't be right because he couldn't stay; yet it'd be downright sinful to leave. So it wouldn't be his baby he'd be giving his money to. It would be some other man's child.

Damn, he wanted to give her something. She'd refused his help with her business, but if somewhere down the road she married again, and had a son or daughter, she might not turn down a gift to the child. But could he do that? Bring himself to give to another man's baby, knowing another man had lain with Kyra after him, another man had rights to her body, her heart. When he himself had had a chance at that paradise and turned it down. He couldn't stay. He couldn't leave. He had to go.

The thoughts tumbled in his mind, battering at him, tearing him in two. He'd found a woman who meant everything to him, but it changed nothing. He still couldn't bring himself to stay.

Without realizing it, his grip tightened on Kyra's arm and she woke. 'What is it?' she asked, her voice groggy with sleep.

He loosened his fingers, stroked her arm where they had dug in. She shifted, reaching up to switch on the light. Squinting against the brightness, she turned her body to face him. Her fingertips trailed lightly down his arm. 'What time is it?'

He pulled her closer on the pretext of checking the bedside clock. 'A little after eleven.' He fitted her body along his, thrusting his hips. 'Very convenient that you're awake.'

He said it playfully, as if he only wanted

more of the mindblowing sex they'd experienced earlier. But his need for her suddenly overwhelmed him until he wanted her with a frightening desperation. He was terrified that he might hurt her and sought a way to ease the intensity of his feelings.

Rolling her under him, he settled himself between her thighs. He kissed her brow, the tip of her nose, her chin. He dipped his head and brushed his eyelashes across her cheek until she giggled at the ticklish sensation. He had to keep things light, had to erase the heaviness in his chest. He drew back so he could see her face. She smiled up at him, her expression wistful, wishful. His eyes met hers and what he saw there made his heart lurch. *Love.*

She loved him. She spelled out her feelings in her eyes, her direct gaze. It shone like a jewel in her face. The enormity of her love rushed through him, a flash flood of emotion. The potential of it danced before him. This could change everything for him, renew him, heal him. He had only to say yes.

Until the day came when he had to leave. It would wait for him, beckon him. Lure him from Kyra's side, make his time with her unbearable. Even now, he could feel the urge to move on drag over his skin in an icy wash like water from snowmelt. He squeezed his eyes closed, shutting out her face. When he opened them again, the light had disappeared from her eyes and he saw only the beginnings of arousal. He could only guess what lay hidden behind that mask.

Leaning over her on his elbows, his erection against the cleft of her thighs, he pressed a soft kiss to her lips. 'You are an incredible lover.'

Her gaze clouded at that, just for a moment before she smiled. 'You're pretty damned decent yourself.'

'What I want to do with you,' he said, his lips grazing her throat, 'is anything but decent.'

She moaned and writhed under him, inflaming him until his thoughts muddied. He knew only Kyra — her body, her scent, the pleasure sounds she made. He kissed her, thrusting his tongue inside her mouth, his hands stroking her. Her breasts filled his palm, her nipple hot and hard against his skin. The taste of her intoxicated him.

'Randon.'

Her voice seemed to come to him from a distance. It was only a cry of passion, he told himself, closing his mouth over her nipple. His hand moved to part her legs wider, his erection pressing against her center.

'Randon.'

This time, despite the haze of passion, he couldn't deny the message in Kyra's tone. She wanted to tell him something, wanted him to stop. But still he pushed at the welcoming warmth of her body, feeling the first entry inside her.

'Randon!'

Her insistent cry held him back, stopped the full thrust of his body. He lay there, poised, the tip of his manhood inside her, heaven just beyond it.

'What is it?' he asked raggedly.

'You're not using protection.'

He tensed, stunned at what he'd nearly done. He felt like an idiot, a complete rat. In all his times with a woman, even as a fumbling teenager, he'd never forgotten to wear a condom.

Except he hadn't forgotten. That thought caromed through him, shook him to the core. Somewhere in the back of his mind, hidden behind the walls of denial, he had wanted to put his seed inside Kyra, to make a baby, his baby.

Appalled, he eased back from her, rose on his knees. 'I'm sorry.' He forced a laugh. 'Got a little carried away.'

Climbing off the bed, he grabbed his jeans, pulled out a foil packet. He sheathed himself, then stood over her. He stroked the silky

351

insides of her thighs, enjoying the way her eyes drifted shut. 'Ready?'

She reached for him and he lowered himself to her. Guilt still nagged at him, but he pushed it aside. He'd caught himself in time. There was no harm done.

He entered her in one long thrust, then stilled, listening to her low moan. Her hands clutched at his hips, urging him in deeper. He complied, feeling as if he would climb right inside her.

'Randon.'

This time his name was a soft whisper of pleasure. The sound sifted along his nerves, heightening sensation. He began to thrust, long slow strokes that lifted him along a sensual spiral.

She groaned, a deep vibration within her, echoed by the clenching of her body around him as she climaxed. He held back, wanting to feel every morsel of her pleasure. He drove her to another peak, and her hips bucked against his. That pushed him over the edge, and his world exploded as he came inside her. He thrust again and again, her legs tight around his waist, her tight wetness closing on him, squeezing him.

When the tremors finally left his body, he eased off and over to lie beside her on the bed. He gathered her close, wanting her there forever, wanting what he couldn't have. Wishing she'd never mentioned the damn condom.

Another shudder ran through him, but this time not in reaction to the passion. He felt an unaccustomed constriction in his throat, a burning in his eyes.

He pulled away and climbed from the bed, keeping his face averted. 'Be right back.'

Shutting the bathroom door behind him, he disposed of the condom, then splashed cold water on his face. Leaning over the sink, hand resting on the counter, he tried to pull himself together.

She opened her eyes as he reentered the room and held out a hand to him. Even as he crossed to the bed, the urge to tug on his clothes and take her home hammered at him. He thought the confusion of his emotions would drive him mad. She slid over to give him room, and he lay beside her. He switched off the light and gathered her in his arms. Now he was lost in her again, as if his compulsion to flee had been an illusion.

He couldn't think about the tumult inside him. He would just hold her to his heart, and in this moment everything would be right. Breathing in her scent, he let himself relax into sleep.

★ ★ ★

The first jangle of the telephone wove itself into Randon's dreams. The second jerked him from sleep, sent his heart racing. With the third ring he grabbed for the phone, dropping the receiver once before getting it in his hand.

'What is it?' he said.

Tom's voice came through the receiver, edgy with fear. 'It's Rachelle.'

Randon rose on one elbow, awakening Kyra. 'What's happened?'

Tom dragged in a breath. 'She's missing, Randon. She's gone.'

17

Randon jolted upright. 'What the hell do you mean, she's missing?'

Kyra sat up beside him. 'Is it Rachelle?'

Randon put out a hand to quiet Kyra. 'How can she be missing?'

'She left the hospital.' Panic roughened Tom's voice. 'We don't know where she's gone.'

Scrubbing at his face, Randon tried to understand. 'How could she leave the hospital?'

He could hear Tom take in a calming breath. 'Sometime around midnight she got dressed, went down to the lobby and called a cab. The cab brought her here to the motel. She took my car — '

'How'd she take your car without you knowing it?'

'This place is packed. Some damn convention. I parked on the other side of the lot to give my mom the space in front of the room.'

'So she's gone off somewhere in your car.' Randon tried not to make the statement sound like an accusation, but it didn't quite work.

'I've damn well beaten myself up enough about this, I don't need you to do it, too.'

'I'm sorry.' Randon looked down and saw his hand linked with Kyra's. He hadn't even realized he'd reached for her. 'Blame won't do us any good, anyway.'

'When the hospital contacted me, I called the cab company, managed to trace her steps to here. The motel manager saw my car pull out of the lot about half an hour ago.'

'She can't have gone far,' Randon said.

'But where would she go? Back home?'

'Maybe. But it doesn't make sense that she'd leave you and the boys behind.'

Tom sighed heavily. 'Nothing she's done lately has made sense. She's scared, Randon. Damned scared. I think maybe in her mind she figures that by running away from the hospital she can run away from the cancer, too.'

Randon understood running away. 'Call the California Highway Patrol. Let them know the situation. Maybe they can keep an eye on I-5, see if she's headed back to Redding.'

'Then what? I can't just sit here.'

'Take your mom's car and check out some of the local places — restaurants, coffee shops. Anything still open at this hour.'

Randon peered at the clock. One-thirty

A.M. The thought of his sister out alone at this hour unnerved him.

'What about you?' Tom asked.

Should he stay put and wait for a call? Hell, he couldn't stand to do nothing any more than Tom could. 'I'll head up I-5, check along that route.' He turned to Kyra. 'Any chance you have a cell phone?'

She nodded. 'There's one at the yard.'

He returned his focus to Tom. 'Keep your mom posted on what you find. I'll keep in touch with her, too.'

Dropping the phone on the cradle, he threw aside the covers. As he grabbed his clothes, Kyra scrambled for hers.

'Tell me,' she said.

He related what Tom had told him. 'I'll drop you at home on my way out.'

She quickly buttoned her blouse. 'I'm going with you.'

'There's no need — '

'I'm going,' she cut in. 'I care about your sister. I care about you.' She pulled on her shorts, tucked in the blouse. 'Besides, you need my cell phone.'

He needed far more from her than that. He put a hand on her arm and rubbed lightly. 'Thank you.'

She stood on tiptoes and gave him a brief kiss. As she drew back, he saw that light in her eyes again, the loving message he had to deny. Then she turned away and finished gathering up her things. In five minutes, they were headed out the door.

*　*　*

Kyra hung up her cell phone and dropped it in her lap. Outside the windows of Randon's pickup truck, black night along I-5 closed in, touched with the faint scent of wildfire. She sagged back against the seat, exhausted.

Randon flicked his gaze in her direction. 'Well?'

'Highway Patrol hasn't seen her,' Kyra said. 'No sign of her in any of the places Tom checked.'

'Other than the gas station where she filled up the car.'

'Right. She turned toward Highway 50 after gassing up, but she could have gone almost any direction from there.'

Randon's expression was grim. 'Tom get a hold of his neighbors?'

Kyra toyed with the palm-sized cell phone. 'Yes. They'll call if Rachelle shows up there.'

The way he gripped the steering wheel, she thought it would break off in his hands. 'Why'd she do this, Kyra?'

She was holding her breath, hadn't even

realized it. She released the air from her lungs. 'She's scared, Randon.'

'I know that much from Tom,' he said impatiently. 'It still doesn't make sense.'

Kyra shook her head slowly. 'It wouldn't. What Rachelle's feeling isn't rational.' She looked over at Randon. 'Did she tell you about the procedure she's to have in the morning?'

Randon shrugged. 'Exploratory surgery, to see if the cancer has spread.'

'Is that all she told you?'

He must have caught something in her tone, because he looked at her sharply. 'What else is there?'

'They have to cut her wide open.' Kyra saw him flinch as she said the words, but she continued. 'From here to here and across.' She gestured as Rachelle had done.

Randon shuddered. 'And then?'

'The surgeon examines her inch by inch, looking for the cancer.' Kyra let that sink in. 'She sees it as a violation, Randon. Beyond the fear of the cancer, of more malignancies, the surgeon's intrusion into her body terrifies her.'

Randon's throat worked. 'How do you know all this?'

'She told me. The day we had dinner with them.'

359

Pain filled his face. 'But she wouldn't talk to me.'

Kyra put out a hand, lightly stroked his arm. 'Sometimes it's easier for a woman to tell something intensely emotional to another woman. Especially when it involves their bodies.'

His arm felt rock hard with tension under her touch. He seemed to want to blame himself, no matter what she told him.

'We have to find her,' he said.

'We will.'

He was silent for several moments, then he said, 'This is impossible. How the hell will we find her?'

'We will,' Kyra assured him, although she felt as much at a loss as he.

He stomped on the brakes, slowing the truck, and pulled off at the next exit. When he'd stopped the pickup, he faced Kyra. 'We can't keep driving aimlessly.'

'You're right.' She set the cell phone on the seat beside her. 'We ought to try to think like Rachelle, get into her head.'

He let out a puff of air. 'I'm the last one to understand my sister.'

'You know her, Randon,' Kyra insisted. 'Where did you two grow up? In Redding?'

'Just outside Marysville, actually. That's where we were living when my folks died.'

At the mention of Marysville, Kyra felt a chill go up her spine. Marysville was where Johnny and Laura had lived their last days. She returned her focus to Rachelle. 'Is there anyplace around there that had a special meaning to her? Someplace she might want to return to?'

He shook his head, but slowly, even as he denied it, he knew the answer. 'There was one place . . . '

A cautious excitement bubbled up in Kyra. 'Where?'

'This little spot by the Feather River. We used to have picnics there. But I don't see how — '

'Could you find it again?'

'I think so,' he said. 'It's been years.'

Kyra picked up the cell phone, fingers shaking. 'I'll call Tom and tell him. How long will it take to get there?'

'An hour.' He started the engine. 'But Kyra, this could be another dead end.'

'It's not, Randon. I know it. I just . . . ' Inexplicably, Laura and Johnny came to mind again and she shivered. 'I have a feeling.'

Randon pulled back onto I-5 and headed south.

★   ★   ★

Rachelle clutched the bridge railing, staring at the Feather River far below her. She'd parked the car in one of the spaces by the picnic area, then walked up here. At this time of night, traffic was nonexistent on this stretch of road. No one would be around to stop her. She held tightly to the rail, the cool metal smooth on her palms, the light breeze tossing her unbound hair. She hadn't bothered to brush it when she left the hospital, just threw on her clothes, grabbed her purse, and ran.

She almost thought Tom wouldn't leave. She'd told him again and again she was fine, that she'd really feel best if she knew he was back at the motel with the boys. He'd kissed her before he left, tenderly pressing his lips to hers. For the first time in months his caress broke through the barrier she'd placed between them and it nearly undid her. She almost begged him to stay, to stop her from the course she'd decided on.

The tumble of water over the rocks below competed with the soughing of wind through the trees, making a lonely sound. When she'd thought of all the ways she could do this, she strove to find an option that would make it impossible for the kids to be the ones to find her. She'd read too many stories of children's lives ruined by finding their mother afterward. She'd spare Chris and Daniel that much.

Pain lanced through her when she thought of her boys. To never see them again — she'd ached to peek inside the motel room when she came for the car, but she just couldn't risk it. She'd had to satisfy herself with imagining them sleeping in the room, the covers a tumble, Chris's hair askew. And Tom in the next bed, his lean body half bare in the summer heat, his face relaxed, dreaming. She did love him. She loved him desperately. But the ice that had closed around her heart in the last few months, made worse by her illness, seemed to have cut her off irrevocably from him.

The river splashed below her on the rocks. The bridge was very high, a good fifty to sixty feet. Would it be enough? She was enough of a coward to take this way out; the thought of lying there broken but not dead horrified her. Or to be saved and to have to face this choice again.

You don't have to. The thought flashed in her mind. She ignored it, despite its seductive tone. She simply could not, would not let the doctors invade her body. It would only allow them to tell her what she feared was true, what she did not want confirmed — the cancer had spread. She could sense its presence all through her body with irrational certainty. It had been her biggest secret from Tom. The weakness in her body, the lassitude, the fevers, the nausea. She'd managed to hide it all so far, revealing her symptoms only to the doctor. Only the oncologist knew the likely extent of the spread. A death sentence either way. She preferred the self-imposed one.

She moved along the rail, edging toward the center of the bridge, its highest point. Looking down at the sturdy barrier under her hands, she wondered how she would do this. She couldn't squeeze through the rail — the space was too small for even a child to slip through. That meant she would have to climb the rail and make her leap from the other side. God wasn't making this easy on her, that was for damn sure. But if he'd had easy in mind, he wouldn't have given her the cancer in the first place. He would have let her go on as before, loving her husband and watching her children grow.

She slammed the lid on that line of thought before the tears returned and made her weak. This was best for everyone. Not just for her own selfish fears, but for Chris and Daniel, who wouldn't have to see their mother eaten up by the cancer, wasting away to a frightening ghost. They wouldn't have to see her pain, her terror at the end. Leaving them now, before it all started, was better for them. She was sure of it.

Backing away a bit from the rail, Rachelle searched for toeholds in the construction of the barrier. The openings in the rail supports were narrow, but her sneakered foot should just fit. She tried the first step, forcing her toe into a space about a foot up from the pavement. She hefted herself up, her weakness making the effort difficult. She had to stop, gather her strength for a moment before trying for another step.

At the top, she gasped in a deep breath and slung one leg over to the other side. The movement nearly tipped her entirely over the edge, and she squelched a scream. When she regained her balance, black laughter rose inside her. She might be set on jumping, but it had to be on her own timetable. It had to be deliberate, not by chance.

She clung with her legs on either side of the rail. Should she just let go here? She might hit her head on the bridge on the way down . . . Would that be worse? Her hands grew slippery with sweat as she dithered, and she had to dig her fingers into the rail to keep her balance.

When she first saw the soft glow in the distance, she thought it was approaching headlights. She squinted into the dark, aware that if a car came this way, she would have to finish things before it arrived. She couldn't risk someone pulling her from the rail. She couldn't bear the indignity of it. But the glow didn't brighten into sharpness as a pair of headlights would. It grew stronger, bigger, as it neared her. As she stared at the light, the rail cold under her sweat-slicked hands, something seemed to resolve from the center of it.

A girl. Hair pulled back in a blonde ponytail, an aqua party dress frothing around her knees. And back behind her in the shadows stood a boy, dark hair slicked back, his shirt a slash of white in the darkness beyond.

'*Rachelle*,' the girl said.

Rachelle's flesh crawled at the sound. The wind picked up again, tossing Rachelle's hair across her face. The girl moved closer and Rachelle stared at her dress. The skirt lay still in the brisk breeze. The wind seemed to blow right through her. A new kind of fear lanced Rachelle. She wanted to back away as the girl advanced, but she was afraid she'd fall. Afraid she'd fall.

'W-who are you?' Rachelle stammered. 'What do you want?'

The girl smiled, moving even nearer, the

glow following. The boy hung back. '*You need to get down from there.*'

Rachelle shook her head. 'You need to leave. This is no concern of yours.'

The girl reached out a hand. Rachelle felt the chill of it clear through her body. '*Please come down, Rachelle.*'

A shock ran through her, sending a tremor through her arms where they braced against the rail. 'How did you know my name?'

The girl gazed up at Rachelle, grief in her wide blue eyes. '*Why would you want to die?*'

In the face of that frank, guileless question, Rachelle was dumbstruck. The answers tumbled in her brain as they had over the last several days, but they seemed nonsense now. They slipped away from her grasp.

Rachelle leaned hard on her arms, exhaustion overcoming her. 'What does it matter?'

'*I didn't want to die.*'

The words seized Rachelle's heart; for a moment she couldn't breath. 'Am I dead already? Is that why I see you?'

In spite of herself, she looked down at the river below, half expecting to see her own body broken there on the rocks.

'*You don't want to die, Rachelle.*'

The girl's soft voice brought Rachelle's attention back to her. Tears spilled from

Rachelle's eyes, falling on the cold metal rail.

'I don't. I don't want to leave them.'

The girl moved closer, sparks scattering where she touched the railing. '*If you do this, you'll break Randon's heart.*'

Her brother's name set off a clamor of pain. 'How do you know Randon?'

The girl tipped her head up to Rachelle. '*You have to stay. For Randon. For the ones who love you.*'

The boy called out, '*Laura! We have to go.*'

'*In a minute, Johnny.*'

Laura crept even closer, put her hand against Rachelle's middle.

'What are you doing?' Rachelle asked, frightened by the cold heat spreading from the girl's touch.

'*Laura!*' the boy shouted.

'*Hold on, Johnny. There's something here.*'

Laura's hand went inside her.

'Oh, God,' Rachelle moaned as the girl's arm went wrist-deep into her belly.

'*I see,*' Laura said softly. '*It's all through here.*'

Terror froze Rachelle. Her arms ached from holding tightly to the rail. Fire burned wherever Laura's fingers trailed.

'Please,' Rachelle whispered.

Johnny called, '*I'm fading, Laura. If we don't go now —* '

368

'*I can fix this, Johnny. I don't know how, but . . .*'

A blue-white flame engulfed the girl, simmering over her skin. And as she moved her hand inside Rachelle, the heat flowed outward, flaring along nerves, searing each cell to its smallest molecule. In another moment, Rachelle would explode in fiery ice, shatter into nothingness.

Is this how it feels to die?

A brilliant burst of light forced Rachelle's eyes shut. She could feel the rail between her legs, under her hands; all else was consumed in flames. If the fire didn't destroy her, it would remake her and a joyous hope replaced her fear.

After a time that stretched to forever, the light eased. Rachelle opened her eyes, searched around her. But the bridge was empty. No girl or boy, no fire. Only the soft glow of light remained. As she stared at the light, it faded, dispersed. And off in the distance, moving closer, a pair of headlights approached.

★ ★ ★

Randon's eyes burned from scanning along the highway for any sign of Rachelle. He thought they were near the picnic grounds,

369

but it had been close to twenty years since he'd been here and everything looked different.

Kyra's hand closed on his arm. 'There's something up ahead. On that bridge.'

When his headlights first picked out Rachelle straddling the railing, his heart pounded. 'What's she doing?' he asked, although he knew.

'Slow down. Ease up next to her.'

He stopped the truck just beyond Rachelle, so that the wash of his headlights illuminated her. He wanted to leap from the cab, run to her and grab her.

Kyra's fingers were light on his arm. 'Easy, Randon.'

Moving slowly, he climbed from the truck. 'Rachelle?'

'Randon.' Tears made her voice ragged.

'Don't move, honey. Just hang on.' Bridling the urge to hurry, he rounded the front of the truck and walked toward her. 'Let me help you down.'

'Please,' she said. 'I'm afraid to let go.'

'You don't want to let go.' He reached her side, wrapped his arms around her. 'Come to me now.'

As he lifted her down from the rail, her frailty shocked him. She buried her face in his neck like she had as a little girl.

'I was stupid, Randon.'

Her tears wet his neck. He began to tremble in reaction and had to support himself against the rail. But he wouldn't let her go. 'It's over now.'

'Not yet.' She backed away a little, met his gaze. 'I haven't told you, about the cancer.'

Randon swallowed, not wanting to hear, grateful when Kyra stepped up beside him to rest a hand on his back. 'Tell me.'

'It's all through me. I don't know for sure, but I've been feeling awful, Randon, weak and sick. And my blood counts . . . '

He held her tightly to him. 'We'll deal with it.'

Pushing away from the rail, he carried her to the truck. Kyra opened the passenger door and Randon set his sister inside. Then he and Kyra climbed in.

'Where'd you leave the car, Rachelle?' he asked.

'Below. The picnic area.'

He started the truck, drove across the bridge. 'I'd like to let her lay down in the backseat of the car,' he said to Kyra. 'Would you mind driving her?'

'No problem.'

Just beyond the bridge, he turned off on a narrow road that wound down to the picnic area. Rachelle's car was the only one in the lot. Beside him, his sister slumped in the seat. 'Maybe it won't be as bad as I think.'

Kyra met his gaze over Rachelle's head. 'Maybe not.'

Rachelle sighed. 'The girl thought she could do something. Maybe she did.'

Something prickled up Randon's spine. 'What girl?'

Rachelle's answer was thick with sleepiness. 'I think . . . her name was . . . Laura.'

Kyra gasped. Randon thought his heart stopped. 'Rachelle,' he said softly, 'what did she look like?'

But Rachelle, exhausted by the night's exertions, had fallen asleep. Randon glanced down at her, considered waking her for an answer.

Kyra reached behind Rachelle to lay a hand on his shoulder. 'Randon?'

He shook his head. 'Let's leave it. Maybe it's best we don't know any more right now.'

A thousand questions hung in the air as he lifted his sister from the truck. She didn't stir as he settled her in the backseat.

Kyra found the key in the ignition and started the engine. 'See you back at the hospital.'

He returned to the truck, emotions churning inside him. With Kyra following behind him, they drove on into the night, returning Rachelle to safety.

★ ★ ★

'*We stayed too long,*' Johnny said.

Laura sagged against the Fairlane's seat, her energy drained. '*I had to, Johnny. She's Randon's sister. I had to do what I could for her.*'

Johnny sat silently. Laura wondered if he sensed her weakness, if he worried for her. If he knew the whole of it, he would be as scared as she.

He turned toward the barrier between them. '*I don't understand how we got there in the first place. One minute we were here, the next . . .*'

'*It wasn't hard to find.*' She gazed up at him. '*We died near there, Johnny.*'

He shuddered. '*How did you know she was there?*'

She had no answer to that. She only knew that time, always their enemy, had nearly finished its miserly measure. And by going to Rachelle, by doing what she could for Randon's sister, she may well have severed her last connection to Johnny.

'*This might be what I was meant for all along,*' she mused, more to herself than to

Johnny. '*Why God put me here.*'

She felt the first of the nightmare come on her. Johnny must have seen her fade because he banged against the barrier, setting off fireworks.

'*Laura!*'

She felt as insubstantial as a puff of air. '*I think I'm finished, Johnny ... God's finished ...*'

'*Damn your God!*' He pounded on the barrier, a sizzle of sparks. '*If He'll take you from me ... damn Him!*'

She pushed aside the pain of Johnny's words. As darkness crowded in, she turned to him. '*I love you.*'

Then the maelstrom snatched her into madness.

★   ★   ★

Kyra heard Rachelle stir restlessly in the seat behind her. She glanced in the rearview mirror, saw Rachelle's gray eyes open, but Kyra sensed Randon's sister still slept.

'I love you, Tom,' she said, then drifted back to sleep.

I love you. The words lodged in Kyra's throat, a gift she ached to give to Randon. A gift he didn't want.

Her gaze fixed on the taillights of Randon's

truck, she followed him down the exit for the hospital and put aside her heart's foolish impulse.

*   *   *

Johnny stared at the seat beside him. Laura had gone again, sucked up into the nightmare. Gone before he could tell her.

'*I love you, Laura.*'

The words hung in the emptiness of the car, banging around in the hole that had once been his heart. A crazy grief overwhelmed him. God had forsaken him. The black limbo awaited.

18

This time, it was real. Laura sat in the Fairlane, the engorged waters of the Feather River rushing alongside the levee where she and Johnny had parked. The rain pounded down just as it had more than forty years ago. The windshield rippled with the water streaming from it. And Johnny sat beside her.

Not the Johnny trapped with her in the prison of the old Ford. This was the Johnny of 1955, the one who had left the Christmas Eve party with her to drive through a storm to the levee. The one who wanted nothing more than a few minutes alone with her, to kiss, to caress, to hold her close.

He reached for her now. 'I love you, Laura.'

He touched her. There was no barrier, nothing to hold him back. Laura nearly sobbed as she felt his hands on her, pulling her close. Tears welled as his lips brushed hers.

'I love you, Johnny.'

Maybe it was all finished. Maybe what they'd waited for all these years had been that moment on the bridge with Rachelle. Not the

376

answers to a mystery that might be better left unsolved.

'Hold me, Johnny.'

She circled her arms around him, her heart filling with joy at his nearness. They were together again, forever joined. The long nightmare was over. Except. A question niggled at her, clamored to be heard. She tightened her grip on Johnny, trying to quiet the imperious query. But it persisted. Why were they still here on the levee? If their bondage to Earth had ended, why would they be here again, caught in a storm on the levee where they died?

The sudden tension in Johnny's body gave Laura her answer. 'What's that?' he asked.

She wanted nothing more than to stay exactly as she was, but the dream's imperative wouldn't let her. She turned to look in the direction of Johnny's focus. This was how it started.

She peered through the obscuring rain, out past a clump of oaks. 'There's a man out there.'

'What's he dragging?' Johnny asked.

Laura stared at the long, dark bundle the man wrestled with between the trees. The burden seemed nearly as big as the man.

'I don't . . . ,' she began.

Then the thing the man hauled across the ground snagged on a tree. Something escaped the wrappings. A hand.

'Johnny, it's a body.'

Johnny pulled her face into his chest. 'We have to get out of here. Before he sees us.'

He released her, turned the key in the ignition. But in his hurry, he must have flooded the engine because the brand new Fairlane wouldn't start.

The man's head went up at the sound of the grinding engine. 'He knows we're here,' Laura moaned. 'Oh God, Johnny.'

Johnny took in a breath, groped for her hand. 'We have to wait, just a minute.'

The man listened a moment longer, then resumed his struggle with the body. Laura watched, mesmerized as the man reached the edge of the levee and rolled his burden into the frothing waters below.

'Now,' Johnny breathed and turned the key again. This time, the engine caught and he put the car into gear. 'We're okay, Laura.'

Johnny turned the car around. To get home, they would have to go past where the man had dumped the body. But if they hurried . . .

The glare of headlights splashed over their faces as a car emerged from the trees. 'He sees us!' Laura cried.

Johnny gunned the engine. 'He won't catch us.'

The Fairlane fishtailed along the levee road as Johnny floored it. Before he could pull away, the other driver got close enough that Laura could glimpse his shadowy face.

She knew him.

She groped for Johnny's arm. 'It's him.'

'Who?' Johnny asked, intent on his driving.

'It's Mr. — '

The first slam of the other car into the rear of the Fairlane jolted Laura into the dash. She screamed and struggled back into the seat. 'What's he doing?'

'He just wants to scare us. He's probably not even sure we saw him.'

Another bang and Johnny had to fight the wheel to keep the Fairlane straight. Laura looked out the back window, but the man's face was swallowed in blackness. 'How much farther before we're off the levee?'

'Another mile.' Johnny reached for her across the seat. 'Who did you say he is?'

The words never formed. Johnny's hand never quite reached hers. Another impact from behind shook the Fairlane, flinging Laura away from Johnny. He shouted as he lost control of the Ford, as the car spun on the rain-slick road. Time slowed, parceling itself out in eternity-long seconds: The

Fairlane skidding to the edge of the levee, the car dipping down as it went over, she and Johnny tossed around the interior like dolls, the final plunge into the cold black Feather River.

She thought at first they would be alright. The Ford didn't turn over, just swapped ends in a dizzy circle as the water bullied them along. 'I can't get the door open, Johnny!'

He didn't answer. She was afraid to look at him, afraid he was already dead. She continued to struggle with the door, pushing and pushing against the weight of the water.

She never saw what shattered her window. A submerged log or other debris hit her a heartbeat after it blasted into the car. It seemed to keep moving after it struck, propelling her out of the car, out of the river, up into darkness. Just as it had before. The man, his dreaded burden, the Fairlane sliding into the river, hers and Johnny's passage into the in-between. This was all of it, all the answers. Except it was too late.

★ ★ ★

By the time he and Kyra met Tom at the hospital and got Rachelle settled in again, it was too late for Randon to even think about driving back to Placerville. So he and Kyra went to Tom's motel to spend the few hours left of the night. They moved the boys to the second double bed in Tom's mother's room. Kyra and Randon took the spare bed in Tom's room.

Randon's sleep was full of jumbled dreams, the few hours rest almost more exhausting than no rest at all. When the alarm startled him awake at six, fragments of images swirled in his mind — Laura and Johnny, the old Fairlane, water pulling him under — but they'd faded by the time he'd showered and dressed.

The boys were up and dressed despite the early hour. The usually voluble Chris was solemn and quiet; his older brother Daniel looked ready to cry. During the quick breakfast at the coffee shop adjacent to the motel, everyone picked at their food. Randon made sure Kyra sat beside him, grateful for her steady presence. After breakfast Tom's mother took the boys back to the motel to wait. He, Tom, and Kyra drove over to the hospital, Tom in his own car.

Beside him in the truck, Kyra pulled the sweater Tom's mother had loaned her more tightly around her. She still wore the short-sleeved shirt and shorts from the day before. The early morning air was cool.

'What time is the surgery?' she asked.

'They were going to prep her at seven.' He glanced at the dash clock. 'They've probably started by now.'

'So we wait.'

'I could probably run you home if you like.' He held his breath, waiting for her answer.

'No. I want to be there. To know . . . '

He reached for her hand, urged her closer to him. She slid across the seat toward him. 'This will work out, Kyra.'

She squeezed his hand in response, her silent reassurance saying more than any words could.

★　★　★

Johnny stood in the junkyard beside the Fairlane, searching. The other wrecks sent out long, soft shadows in the early morning light. He wanted to think that Laura wandered in and out of those streaks of dark and brightness, but he knew better. She was gone, dragged back to the in-between. And he probably had sent her there with his blasphemy, his lack of faith. His unwillingness to believe in God had always distressed Laura. This time it had destroyed her.

She'd never gone to the in-between before him. They'd always been pulled back together, given one last moment of awareness of each other before the nothingness took them. He didn't know what it meant to have her gone with him still here, but he was certain it was bad.

'God.' He squeezed the word from his throat. *'I'm sorry. Bring her back. Take me instead.'*

But why would God listen to him? He'd shot off his mouth, made his doubts clear. God had better things to do than hear the prayers of an unbeliever.

Nevertheless, he tried again. *'God, help me. I'm sorry.'*

He shut his eyes, grief welling within him. *'I'm sorry, Laura: I'm sorry I let the car go off the levee.'*

★ ★ ★

The hours dragged on. Randon spent more time pacing in the small waiting room than sitting in the hard vinyl seats. When he'd sit, Kyra would put a hand on his or slip her arm across his shoulders, giving him a moment of comfort. But then his agitation would drive him to his feet again.

Tom sat with his head in his hands. Randon sensed his brother-in-law didn't want to speak or even look at them out of fear it would somehow change the outcome. He left the room twice, once to call the boys and again to check with the nurse to see if there was any news. Although Tom knew the doctor would speak to them when it was over, Randon figured he just couldn't help asking. Randon wanted to do the same thing.

Through it all, Kyra's presence soothed him. She went to get cups of coffee that none of them drank, patted Tom's shoulder when he seemed on the edge of tears, and pressed a gentle, calming kiss on Randon's cheek when he thought he would explode with worry. She held his hand in hers right now as he sat beside her. 'It can't be much longer,' she said.

No sooner were the words out of her mouth than the surgeon appeared in the doorway. Lines of fatigue stood out on his face, but his lips were curved in a faint smile.

'Mr. Lee?'

Tom looked up, hopefully. 'How is she?'

The doctor took a step into the room. 'It's remarkable. Based on her oncologist's report, I'd expected stage three progression at least.' He grinned. 'But your wife is clear. One hundred percent. Not a trace of cancer.'

The words burst inside Randon and he felt dizzy with relief. 'She's going to be okay?'

'She'll need frequent checkups for a while, but yes, she's fine. Her blood counts are normal. Everything checks out.'

'Thank you.' Tom rose, grasped the doctor's hand. 'Thank you.'

The surgeon seemed bemused as he shook Tom's hand. 'I never would have expected it.'

'Can I see her?' Tom asked.

'She's in recovery. The nurse will take you in there in a bit.'

The doctor left. Tears streamed down Tom's face. Choked up, Randon grabbed hold of Kyra, burying his face in her hair. Then his feelings overwhelmed him, his own sobs shaking him to the core. He clutched Kyra as if she were a lifeline, his only hope to survive.

Later, when the nurse arrived, he'd pulled himself together. They let Tom go see Rachelle first, giving him a few moments alone with her. Randon kept hold of Kyra's hand while they waited, feeling lighter, happier than he had in years. She raised his hand to her lips and kissed his palm. There was something in her eyes, a message that oddly didn't frighten him as it once might have. He didn't want to put words to it yet, but he could feel possibilities opening up inside him.

★ ★ ★

Kyra tried not to make too much of what she'd seen in Randon's face. She'd caught him in a moment of extreme vulnerability, powerful emotions still gripping him. She might have seen only what she wanted to there. To tell him now that she loved him wouldn't be fair. He needed time to recover from his terror over his sister's disappearance and the uncertainty of what her surgery would reveal. If Kyra expressed her love for him now, she would never trust his response. So she sat quietly as they waited for Tom to return, then she went along with Randon to see Rachelle. They spent only a few minutes with his sister. Still drowsy from the anesthesia, Rachelle was only half aware that they were there. Kyra stood back while Randon spoke softly to his sister, gently holding her hand.

As they left intensive care, Randon seemed more at peace than Kyra had ever seen him. With Rachelle's recovery, Kyra realized Randon's violent need for her was gone. Guilt immediately swamped her at the thought.

With his hand at the small of her back, he guided her past the nurse's station. 'Can I take you home?'

'Yes, please.'

Despite her guilt, Kyra couldn't help but

wonder what good her love was to him when he didn't need it. She stared at the elevator door, willing it to come faster.

'Kyra Aimes?'

She turned back toward the nurse's station. 'Yes?'

'There's a call for you.' The woman brandished a phone receiver. 'Someone named Jackson.'

Uneasiness stirred in Kyra's gut as she retraced her steps. 'I can't imagine why he'd call me here.'

As she took the phone, Randon placed a steadying hand on her shoulder. 'What's up, Jackson?'

'It's the damnedest thing,' he said. 'There was someone at the yard asking for you today.'

'The minister?'

'No, not him,' Jackson said. 'A boy.'

Kyra's blood ran cold. She glanced up at Randon, then held the phone out slightly so he could hear. 'What did he want?'

'Wouldn't say exactly. Just that he needed to see you.'

Her hand shook. Randon put his arm around her, pulling her closer. 'Did you get his name?'

'No. In fact . . . ' Jackson chuckled softly. 'Maybe I'm losing my mind a little in my old age, but one minute that boy was standing there and the next . . . '

'He was gone,' Kyra finished for him. 'Jackson, I'll be right there. If you see the boy again . . . well, tell him I'm coming.'

★ ★ ★

Kyra slammed the door to Randon's pickup and headed for the entrance to the yard. 'We should try over by the Fairlane first.'

Randon kept pace with her as she half-ran toward the back row. 'I thought we were the only ones who could see them. How did Johnny appear to Jackson?'

'Probably the same way Laura brought the two of them together so we could see them both. It had to be done, so she did it.'

They reached the Fairlane. 'Johnny!' Kyra shouted, not caring who heard her. 'Johnny, where are you?'

Randon paced beside the old Ford. 'Maybe he can't come because I'm here. Should I leave?'

'No, stay.' Kyra turned in a slow circle, searching. 'Johnny!'

The boy appeared at the speed it takes to switch on a light and no more than two feet from her. Kyra gave a little yelp of surprise.

'Johnny, you scared me to death.' Her own

words sent a chill up her spine.

'It's Laura,' Johnny said. 'She's gone.'

Randon came up beside her. 'What do you mean, Laura's gone?'

Grief hung over Johnny like a curse. 'She didn't come back last night after she helped that woman.' He looked up at Randon. 'Your sister. She kept her from going off the bridge.'

'And I'm grateful, Johnny, more than I can express.'

'It wasn't just that. Laura found something inside your sister. She made a fire and burned it all out. But the fire took the last of Laura's energy.'

Kyra took a step closer to Johnny, put out a hand that she knew couldn't comfort him. 'She might still be here. Maybe she just needs to build back her strength.'

Johnny shook his head. 'God took her back to the in-between because of me. Because I couldn't believe in Him. Because I let the car go off the levee.'

'I know you didn't mean to, Johnny,' Kyra said. 'We haven't given up finding out what happened.'

Johnny backed away, wavering in the bright sunshine. 'I don't care anymore.'

'We're going to make this right,' Randon said. 'She helped Rachelle. I'm damned well going to do what I can to help you.'

'It doesn't matter. If Laura's gone, it doesn't matter anymore.' Johnny seemed to drift away on the faint summer breeze.

Kyra stared at the place he'd been. 'What do we do now?'

Randon drew her into his arms. 'Go to that other library, look through the local papers.'

'We won't be able to today. The State Library's already closed.'

'Tomorrow, then.'

'But what if she's gone?' Kyra rubbed her cheek against his chest, let his scent and warmth soothe her. 'What if she's truly gone to the in-between?'

He was quiet so long, Kyra looked up at him. He pressed a kiss to her brow. 'Then I guess we'll need another miracle.'

★　★　★

Randon drove Kyra back home, then turned to her in the cab of the truck. 'I ought to head back to the motel.'

She took his hand, traced the lines in his palm. 'If you want.'

'I'd rather stay here.'

'I'd like you to.' *I'd like you to stay forever.* 'I'll fix you dinner.'

He closed his hand over her fingers, raised

them to his mouth. 'That stove still working?'

His lips closed around one fingertip and her eyes drifted shut. 'Working fine.'

Picking up her purse with trembling hands, she climbed from the truck. He stayed close behind her as she went up the walk, opened the front door for her after she unlocked it.

'Can dinner wait?' he asked as he shut the door behind them.

'It's early yet. Too hot to eat.'

'Way too hot.' He tossed aside his hat, then tipped his head to slant his mouth across hers. 'You're so sweet. You taste like honey. Especially here.' He grazed one fingertip over her sensitive mound.

Her knees seemed to melt. 'You drive me crazy, cowboy.'

He skimmed his hand across her breast until her nipple hardened in response. 'I could make love to you just about anywhere, but I've had quite a few fantasies about that bed of yours in the other room.'

She hesitated a moment, considered how it would be when he was gone, when she'd lie in that lonely bed by herself. An empty bed would be easier to bear if she didn't have to share it with memories of him. Or maybe the memories would give her something to hold on to. Resolved to take the chance, she took his hand and tugged him toward the bedroom. 'I'd love to fulfill your fantasy.'

He let her lead him, let her guide him to the bed. She pushed him down to sit on the edge. 'I'm in control tonight,' she told him.

She reached for his T-shirt, pulling it from his jeans, sliding it up his body. When he tried to help her take it off, she stayed his hands. 'I'm in control,' she repeated.

He relaxed then, the light in his gray eyes brighter than the room. She pulled off his shirt then dropped it to the floor. Reaching on tiptoes so that her breasts rubbed against his face, she tugged the chain for the ceiling fan, setting the blades in motion.

'Boots next,' she said. He lifted one foot, then the other while she removed his boots and socks. 'Stand up.'

When he rose, she made sure she took a good long time releasing the snap on his jeans and lowering the zipper. She reached into the open fly, letting her palms skim against his erection.

'Kyra,' he moaned.

She laughed low in her throat. These were going to be her memories and she would make them as vivid as she could. Working at his jeans, she lowered them, exquisitely slow. The rough hair on his legs caressed her palms. She massaged the muscles in his long thighs, reveling in his tremors of reaction.

When his jeans were tossed aside, she went down on one knee. She pressed her lips against the front of his briefs, kissing along his hard length. Hands around his hips, she held him to her, nipping lightly with her teeth.

'Oh my God,' he rasped, fingers digging into her hair.

She curled her fingers into the waistband of his briefs and gave a tug. The tip of his manhood caught on the elastic, but rather than pull it away with her hands, she used her mouth to free him.

'Kyra!'

Easing her mouth around him, she lowered his briefs to his knees. His breathing grew heavy as she explored him with lips and tongue.

She urged him onto the bed, stripping his briefs from him. 'Lie down.'

Amusement warred with arousal in his face. 'Yes, ma'am.'

She took her time unbuttoning her blouse, unclasping her bra, removing her shorts and panties. He watched her with hot intensity until a liquid warmth pooled between her legs.

He reached for her, but she pressed his arms back onto the mattress. 'Patience,' she whispered.

Fishing a foil packet from his jeans pocket, she climbed onto the bed and sheathed him with the condom. Straddling his hips, she aligned her cleft with his manhood without taking him inside. Then she leaned over him, brushing her breasts against his chest.

He groaned, a long, low sound. 'You are a wicked, wicked woman.'

'I aim to please.' She stroked her nipples against his hair-roughened chest until her torment turned in on itself. Sensation shot through her, tightening low in her body. She had to have him inside her. But she would do it slowly, drawing out the pleasure. She reached down for him, eased him to her wet cleft.

He thrust deep inside her with a swiftness that robbed her of thought. 'Sorry,' he gasped.

She convulsed around him almost immediately, waves of white heat shaking her to the core. As he continued to thrust, she climaxed again, losing the boundaries of her body until it encompassed his. When he reached his peak, it seemed the world centered on the two of them, exploding out into eternity.

I love you. She said the words in her mind, a silent cry. *I love you, Randon.*

In a slow spiral, she returned to Earth, to awareness of Randon's arms around her, his lips against her temple. She thought of the words locked inside her. Even though she was glad she kept them to herself, her heart grieved.

She slid off him and settled beside him. She smiled and gazed up at him. Her heart pounded as a chill went up her body. She could see in his troubled face that she hadn't been as clever as she'd thought. She hadn't kept the words to herself after all. She'd said them out loud. *I love you.* And the only response in Randon's eyes was good-bye.

19

Randon drove up the hill to the movie location, guilt eating at him. He'd tried to justify leaving in the wee hours. Kyra was still asleep and he had left a note on the pillow. He really had to get back to the motel to change and clean up, then up to the film shoot. There was no reason to wake her.

But the truth was, he hadn't wanted to face her. The words she'd let slip during their lovemaking had sent a shock wave through him, set off a tumult of fear and longing. He'd already suspected she'd fallen in love with him, but the sure confirmation still shook him. Shook him, and forced him to examine how he felt about her. It wouldn't change anything if he loved her — he'd still be gone within a few days. But he'd have to consider which would be the lesser of two evils — to reveal his feelings before leaving or to keep quiet about it.

He wondered if she'd ask him to stay. Begging didn't seem to be in Kyra's nature. She might ask once, then accept his answer without argument. But damn, a part of him wanted her to argue, to push him into something he could swear a week ago he never would have wanted.

He made the turn for Camino and wended his way into Apple Hill toward the location. He didn't have any new pictures to show Evans. In fact it would have made more sense to head down to the wrecking yard this morning, but he needed a little space before he saw Kyra again. He'd pick her up around lunchtime as he'd said in the note, have something to eat, then drive over to the library.

When he pulled up to the trailer, he saw Evans in a heated discussion with Aaron, the screenwriter, over by the aluminum folding tables. The dispute ended with Aaron throwing the script at Evans and stalking off into the woods.

Evans slammed the script on the table. 'About time you showed up, Bolton.'

Randon was determined not to let the man get to him. 'I told you I was with my sister.'

'I tried to reach you all day yesterday.'

'You didn't try very hard. There weren't any messages at the motel.'

Evans flicked a hand at him. 'You're done here, Bolton. I've decided I've got enough cars.'

It took Randon a moment to register what

Evans had said. 'You don't need me on the shoot anymore?'

'Budget's too tight to keep you on. Melinda's got your check.'

As Randon walked toward the trailer, a roiling started up in his belly. He should be relieved right now to be done with the impossible production designer. True, he was out of a job for the moment, but it had never been a problem for him to find another. And he certainly had enough socked away to carry him through a period of unemployment. But this meant he could leave anytime. Maybe he'd stick around a few more days to keep tabs on Rachelle, visit with his nephews. But after that, there was nothing to keep him here. Or was there?

Melinda gave him one last come-hither smile as she handed over his check, but he barely acknowledged her flirting. Opportunities seemed to be opening up for him with each step he took back to his pickup, the same ones he faced every time he finished a stint. Except this time a new option offered itself in the form of Kyra Aimes.

Staying with Kyra was too much to think of right now. He turned the ignition on the truck, and the engine grinded sluggishly. It took a second try and a tad more pressure on the accelerator to start the truck. It was the battery, no doubt. He'd been due for a new one but hadn't taken the time to replace it.

As he drove back down the hill to Placerville, a sense of freedom seemed to chase him along Highway 50. But was it because now he was free to go? Or because now he was free to stay?

★   ★   ★

When Kyra had awakened to Randon's note on his pillow, she didn't know whether to be relieved not to have to face the awkward morning after or mortified that she'd chased him away. Although he'd promised in his quick scrawl to meet her later, she half expected he'd only said that to give himself time to leave the county. But he'd turned up at the wrecking yard after all. And as soon as she climbed into the truck, he pulled her into his arms and kissed her. She didn't know what that meant. She only knew that she loved him. But damned if she'd tell him again.

When he started the pickup, the engine cranked a few times before it caught. Shaken by a dozen conflicting emotions, she forced a laugh. 'Better be careful, your truck might find a home here.'

'Battery.' He pulled out of the parking lot,

399

headed for the freeway. 'I'll have to take care of it before . . . ' He cleared his throat. 'Talked to Evans this morning. He informed me he had all the cars he wanted.' *So I'll be leaving soon.* He might as well have shouted out the words.

'No problem. You're all paid up.' She looked about for something to say, desperate to change the subject. 'How's Rachelle doing?'

'She hurts like hell. Feels like a gutted pig.' He smiled. 'But she's ecstatic — there's not a trace of cancer anywhere.'

'Do you think it was Laura's doing?'

His expression turned serious. 'You heard the doctor. Her blood counts, the CAT scans . . . she was in far worse shape than she let on. She kept it from me, even from Tom. If it hadn't been for Laura . . . '

Kyra pondered what he'd said. 'I looked for Johnny today. Couldn't find him.'

Randon shot her a quick glance. 'You think he's gone, too?'

'I don't think so. I had this feeling . . . '

Randon took her hand in his. 'We're doing this anyway — finding out what happened. No matter how it turns out.'

'Right.'

She supposed he felt committed to Laura and Johnny, to fulfilling a promise. But he hadn't offered her any commitments.

They stopped for lunch at a little diner downtown not far from the State Capitol. Kyra took a few cursory bites of the salad she ordered and picked at the garlic bread that accompanied it. She let Randon pay for the meal without argument.

'If you don't mind my asking,' Randon said as they walked down Tenth Street toward N Street, 'how's the money situation going?'

She supposed that was a safe enough topic. 'Not a whole lot better. Selling the Fairlane will give me some breathing room, though.' She'd told him about the minister and how she'd delayed him a week before picking up the car.

When they reached the California State Library, Randon opened the door and stood aside to let her go first. 'And if we don't solve the mystery before the week's up . . . '

'It won't matter.'

Because Johnny and Laura would both certainly be gone. Back to a strange limbo Kyra didn't presume to understand. As irretrievable as Randon himself would be when he left her. But she could do something about Johnny and Laura. 'The State Library keeps copies of local newspapers representative of each county,' she told him as they approached an information desk. She asked the librarian what the local papers were in 1955 for Sutter and Yuba Counties.

The librarian scanned her index. 'That would be the *Independent Herald* for Sutter County and the *Appeal Democrat* for Yuba.'

They headed for the room where the microfilm was stored. 'Should we read together?' Kyra asked.

'It might save time if we each took a paper.'

What he said made sense, but somehow her heart took it as a rejection. 'I'll take the *Herald*, then.' She walked away from him, searching the rows of drawers.

Kyra had already started on her spool of film when Randon sat at the reader next to her. Focusing on the screen, she skipped ahead to Christmas Eve. She relived the horror of the flooding with photographs of devastation accompanying poignant stories. Right beside her, but somehow far beyond her reach, Randon stared intently at his screen.

Kyra doubled her focus on the newspaper displayed before her, carefully scrutinizing each column of type. But as she reached the December thirty-first issue, despair settled on her. 'Finding anything?'

'Nothing.' Randon slowly forwarded his

film. 'Same coverage we already saw in the *Bee.*'

Kyra finished the New Year's Eve edition, rewound her spool. 'Should we start looking at January 1956?'

'I guess. I don't know. Let me get through this last issue.' He leaned back in his chair, rubbed at his brow, then held out a hand to her. 'Come help me look.'

Kyra scooted her chair toward him. He put his arm around her shoulder, pulling her close as he forwarded the microfilm. 'They would have been gone a week by the thirty-first. Their parents must have declared them missing.'

Kyra watched carefully as he slowly eased the control along. 'Remember, everything was in an uproar with the evacuations. Their parents probably couldn't even get home.'

'Even still — '

'Wait.' Kyra put her hand out to stop Randon from scrolling further. She raised a finger to the displayed page. 'Look at this.'

The small article had been tucked beside a three-quarter page ad, at the bottom of a long column of text. The headline said, *Teenagers' Bodies Found.*

After a quick scan of the text, Kyra squeezed her eyes shut. 'You read it, Randon. I can't.'

His gentle voice rumbled in her ear. ''The bodies of Marysville teens Johnny Garvey and Laura Mills were found on the bank of the Feather River five miles south of Yuba City after a week-long search for the missing Marysville High School students. The teens' parents, Mr. and Mrs. Harold Garvey and Mr. and Mrs. Frank Mills, had thought the two sweethearts had taken refuge at an evacuation center during the flooding, but the discovery of their bodies has dashed those hopes.' '

She opened her eyes and looked up at Randon. 'Then their bodies were found. I'd wondered about that.'

Randon released a long breath. 'This doesn't tell us much more than we already know.'

'Let's keep reading. There's got to be something.'

Shrugging, he continued to scroll. The next page was filled with advertisements, with a few short articles across the top.

'What's this?' Randon asked, tapping the screen.

There in the corner, slightly damaged by a tear in the newsprint, was a headline reading, *Another Flood Victim*. Kyra leaned close to make out the text on either side of the tear.

She skimmed the first paragraph. 'They

found another body.'

'Look at the name of the woman who died,' Randon said.

'Meredith Carson.' Kyra glanced up at him. 'So?'

'Who do we know named Carson?'

'The nutty guy at the yard,' Kyra acknowledged. 'But it's a common enough name. It may not be the same Mr. Carson.'

'True.' Randon studied the article again. 'I wish I could read this last line. The way the paper's torn . . .'

'Zoom it in,' Kyra suggested.

He pressed the controls, magnifying that corner of the paper. 'Can you make it out?'

Kyra leaned closer. "Mr. Carson . . . was questioned earlier in the week . . . about his wife's disappearance." She faced Randon. 'Why would they question him?'

Randon looked grim. 'If they suspected foul play.'

'You mean if he killed his wife. But there's still no way of knowing if this is our Mr. Carson. Or if there's even a connection.'

Randon had left his hat in the truck and now he raked his fingers through his hair. 'Let's rewind the paper a bit. There might be another article about this Mr. Carson.'

He scrolled the paper back, the whirring of

the machine loud in the quiet room. He stopped in the middle of the Christmas edition and moved forward.

It was the photo that Kyra saw first, the face of an eerily familiar young man pictured beside a shot of a sweet-faced woman. The caption identified them as Mr. and Mrs. Richard Carson.

'It's him,' Kyra murmured. 'It's that crazy old guy from the junkyard.'

Randon read the story. 'He reported her missing on Christmas Day. The police suspected him from the start.'

'He was a teacher at Marysville High School.'

'Laura's and Johnny's school.'

'So Laura and Johnny knew him,' Kyra said.

'They still do,' Randon said. 'Or at least Laura does.'

'No wonder he frightened her so.' Kyra shivered. 'What do you think happened?'

'Carson killed his wife, dumped her body in the river. He probably figured with the flooding no one would ever know.'

Kyra nodded. 'But Laura and Johnny must have seen him.'

'And he saw them. But he couldn't risk them reporting him to the police.'

'So he ran them off the levee.'

Randon's gray eyes grew stormy. 'And left them to drown.'

★   ★   ★

They hurried back to the city parking garage at Tenth and L where they'd left the truck. 'We have to do something about Mr. Carson,' Kyra said as she climbed into the cab. She still felt outraged by his wickedness. 'We can't just let him go free.'

He turned the key and the engine ground. 'What would we tell the police? A couple of ghosts told us he killed them?'

'But what if it's not enough to tell Johnny how they died? What if we have to bring Mr. Carson to justice, too?'

The engine didn't catch. Randon twisted the key a second time, but there was only the click-click-click of a dead battery.

He slammed his hand against the wheel in frustration. 'Damn!'

'Why don't I call Mario at the yard? He can bring out the tow truck and jump-start you.'

'Good idea. Thanks. I knew I should have gotten this damn thing replaced.'

They found a phone booth just outside the parking garage and Kyra dialed the wrecking yard. She spoke briefly to Jackson, then hung up and gave Randon the bad news.

'Mario had a family emergency. Trish is off at a class, so Jackson's alone at the yard. We'll have to try something else.'

Randon scrubbed at his face. 'There's got to be an auto parts store around here someplace.'

Flipping through the phone book, Randon located an address, then scrawled it on a scrap of paper he found on the sidewalk. The quickly drawn lines on the paper reminded Kyra of the note he'd left her that morning, setting off a tumble of emotions she'd thought she'd conquered.

As they started down the downtown streets in search of the address Randon had found, she wondered if she ought to say something about last night. But it was obvious her declaration had scared him to death. Maybe it would be best if she just stayed quiet, even though her heart clamored at her to say the words again.

By the time they found the auto parts store, bought the battery, and returned to the truck, it was nearly five. Rush hour traffic teemed in the one-way streets, the drivers' tension palpable. The screeching brakes and honking horns seemed to have affected Randon, because he kept up a steady stream of softly spoken curses as he struggled to replace the battery.

Kyra stayed in the cab and out of his way. When he climbed in to start the truck, she could see his jaw muscles flexing. Unable to help herself, she reached over and lay a hand on his arm.

He stiffened for a moment before he let out a puff of air. 'Sorry for the foul mood. It's just that . . .'

She rubbed his arm lightly. 'What?'

He shook his head slowly. 'I don't know. I just have this feeling about Johnny and Laura . . .'

'What is it?'

Covering her hand with his, he faced her. 'We have to hurry, Kyra.'

He kept his gaze on her another moment, then turned his attention to starting the truck. The engine roared to life. Leaving it running, Randon climbed out to close the hood, then jumped back inside. 'Let's go.'

But the heavy freeway traffic conspired against them. An overturned big rig had blocked three lanes of Highway 50, reducing their pace to a crawl.

Kyra gripped her hands in her lap. 'The yard will be closed by the time we get there.'

Randon stomped the brakes, stopping inches from the sedan in front of him. 'That might be better. It might be easier for Johnny to show himself if everyone's gone.'

They finally crept past the big rig, picking up speed as the lanes opened again. Kyra couldn't seem to take her eyes from the dash clock for long, acutely aware of the minutes passing.

'Thank God,' she murmured when they finally reached their exit. It was nearly seven by the time they pulled up to the locked gates of the yard.

'Johnny!' Kyra shouted as she fumbled with the lock. She got it open and she and Randon pushed through.

They ran to the Fairlane. 'Johnny!' Kyra called out again, Randon's deeper voice echoing hers. She circled the old Ford, running her hand along it, searching for the chill that preceded Johnny's appearance.

She felt only the heat of sun-warmed metal. 'He can't be gone yet. He can't be.'

'Let's split up, search the yard.'

She nodded agreement. 'I'll take the south side, you take this side.'

As she walked off, she called out to Gertie, figuring the sensitive dog might lead her to Johnny. But the German shepherd didn't come, and she wondered if Jackson had forgotten to let her out into the yard. Squinting into the setting sun, she walked toward Gertie's dog run.

The gate hung open. Unease prickled the back of her neck. She called the dog again, listening intently for a bark, the sound of claws on asphalt. She heard nothing except Randon's voice shouting Johnny's name from the other side of the yard.

Gertie would turn up. She put aside her concern for the dog and continued on through the yard, calling Johnny's name. The stillness in the yard set her on edge. She'd been out here by herself many times after closing, but an oppressiveness clung to the air tonight. A cloud had drifted over the sun, occluding it, hinting at the possibility of another summer storm.

The silence nagged at her. She realized suddenly that she could no longer hear Randon's voice. He'd simply stopped calling out to Johnny, that was all. There was no reason to be concerned.

She went up on tiptoes, looking off in the direction she'd seen him last, but she couldn't see the battered white cowboy hat moving between the ranks of cars. In fact, nothing stirred in the yard but her.

She swallowed back a moan, telling herself she was being ridiculous. But she couldn't shake the feeling that there was something wrong. She felt a sense of urgency to find Randon. She threaded through the wrecks toward the Fairlane where she'd seen him last, calling his name.

She nearly missed seeing Gertie. The dog lay underneath an Econoline van, a hundred yards from the old Ford. Only the barely perceptible rise and fail of her side indicated to Kyra that the dog was alive.

Kyra crouched down to check on the shepherd, reaching under the van's back bumper. Gertie's eyes opened briefly, then shut again. 'Oh, Gertie, what happened?'

'She'll be okay.' The man's voice jerked her to her feet, brought her around to the side of the Econoline.

Mr. Carson sat sideways in the back of the van, legs out through the open slider door. 'I pulled her into the shade so she wouldn't get too hot.'

Kyra tried to suppress the trembling in her voice. 'What are you doing here, Mr. Carson? The yard is closed.'

'I know. I hid.'

'You shouldn't be here, Mr. Carson. You'll have to get out of that van.'

'Okay. It's time anyway.' He slid down from the high seat, dragging something behind him in his hand. A crowbar.

Kyra's stomach clenched. 'Did you hit my dog with that, Mr. Carson?'

The old man shook his head vigorously.

'I wouldn't hit *her*.'

The emphasis on the pronoun sent alarm coursing through her. He wouldn't hit a dog, but his own wife . . . Oh, God, had he hit Randon? Was he lying out there somewhere hurt and bleeding?

'I just gave her something to make her sleep.' He gestured with the crowbar. 'I would never hurt an animal.'

'Mr. Carson,' Kyra said carefully, praying she was wrong about Randon. 'You have to leave the yard.'

'I can't. I have to do something.'

Wary of the crowbar, Kyra kept her distance. 'No, Mr. Carson. You have to go, now.'

'I can't.' Keeping his gaze on her, he reached inside the van. 'I have to take care of that car first.'

When he straightened again, he clutched a can of gasoline.

20

Kyra stared at the red metal can. 'What car?' she asked, stalling.

'That old Fairlane.' He thrust the heavy can toward the Ford behind her, at the end of the row. 'It's evil. It shouldn't be here.'

'Mr. Carson, why don't you set down that can? We're not allowed to put gas in the cars.'

He grinned, a cheerless stretching of his lips. 'Not going to put it in the car. Going to put it on the car.'

'I can't let you do that.' She edged closer to him, toward the hand holding the crowbar. 'That's against state regulations. They could close me down over that.'

For a moment, his grin faded as he considered what she said. Then he released a rusty chuckle. 'I won't tell anyone if you won't, Mrs. Aimes.'

He turned to go past her; she stepped back into his path. 'What are you going to do with the gasoline?'

'Told you.' He took another step, she parried. 'Put it on the car. I have to burn it.'

'Burn the car?'

414

'I have to destroy it. Destroy them. To keep them from coming back.'

She'd known already — read the newspaper reports, seen his picture. Still, the confirmation sent a thrill of fear through her. *Randon, where are you?*

'I can't let you burn one of my cars.' She measured the distance between herself and the crowbar, eased closer. 'It's my property.'

He gave that some thought, the furrows in his brow deepening. 'I'll pay you for it, how's that? You tell me a price — '

'The car's already sold.' She was almost near enough to try for the crowbar. 'I took a deposit.'

Irritation clouded his face. 'Then I'll pay you for that, too. But I got to burn that car.' He made a move to stride off.

Again Kyra stopped him. 'But why?' She gestured behind her at the Fairlane. 'It's just an old car.'

His gaze narrowed on her. 'I thought you knew.'

She gulped in air. 'Maybe I do. Or maybe I know something different. Why don't you tell me?'

His hard look nearly stole her remaining courage, but she couldn't let him destroy the old Ford. It was Johnny's and Laura's only link to Earth, and if it burned, they would be trapped in the in-between forever.

God, she wished Randon were here. She couldn't even risk a quick glance around to search for him. She had to keep her eyes on the evil old man before her.

'Tell me, Mr. Carson.'

His hand shifted on the crowbar and Kyra thought it was over. 'You know about them, don't you?'

Relief washed over her. 'Johnny and Laura?'

He didn't like hearing the names. 'They shouldn't have been there.'

'Where?'

His throat worked as if he wasn't sure he wanted to say the words. 'On the levee.'

She wasn't sure how much she could push the man, but she had to stall him until Randon showed up. And Randon would, soon. That he hadn't turned up yet meant that Mr. Carson must have hit him with the crowbar, left him unconscious.

Oh God, what if Mr. Carson hit Randon too hard? What if he was dying out there, or already — She wouldn't think that way. She returned her focus to Mr. Carson. He'd set down the heavy gas can and held the crowbar in his other hand. Kyra shuffled her feet a bit so that she moved closer to the side holding the iron bar.

'What happened on the levee?' she asked casually.

Mr. Carson's gaze sharpened on her. 'How do you know about the levee?'

'You told me,' she said quickly. 'Just a minute ago.'

He nodded. 'I did.' He switched hands again, the crowbar back in his right. 'I didn't know they were there, until after.'

'After what?'

He ignored her question. 'They were parked up there, lights off, doing God knows what. Biggest damn storm of the year and those two kids are parked on a levee.'

'Maybe they didn't know how bad the storm was.'

'Maybe they just didn't care. Ever think of that?' He brandished the end of the crowbar at her. 'Kids just don't care.'

Kyra took in another breath. 'What happened on the levee, Mr. Carson?'

The point of the crowbar dropped. 'She was already dead, you know.'

A chill crawled up Kyra's spine. 'She was?'

He ran the fingers of his left hand along the iron bar. 'I didn't really mean to kill her.'

'I'm sure you didn't.' She could barely force the words out.

'It was an accident.' His gaze fell to the bar in his hands. 'But I was glad after.'

417

The sinister words twisted inside her. She swallowed against a dry throat. 'What happened at the levee?' she asked a third time.

'She was in the kitchen cleaning up from a Christmas Eve party. I was busy in the garage when she yelled out to me to come help her.' His expression grew dark. 'I didn't like it. I told her I was busy, she shouldn't talk to me that way.'

Kyra held her breath, waiting to hear the rest of it.

'She yelled something else and I ran inside.' His fingers stroked the bar. 'I didn't know I had it in my hands until . . . '

He raised his pale blue gaze to Kyra. 'There wasn't much blood. It was easy to clean off the kitchen floor.'

'And then?' Kyra whispered.

'I wrapped her in the bedspread, I didn't much like that bedspread. I knew the river waters were near flood stage. It would be easy enough to claim she'd gone for a walk, had fallen in . . . '

Kyra wondered if she could just reach in and grab the crowbar from him. She wondered if his wife's blood still clung there, alongside Randon's. 'But the police still questioned you.'

He shrugged. 'The neighbors had heard us

arguing that day. And other days. But even when her body washed up, no one could say if she'd hit her head on a rock or a log or . . . something else.'

Her fingers tingled with the urge to snatch the iron bar. 'So you took her to the levee. In the storm, in the dead of night, where no one would be watching, except — '

'Except those damn kids were there!' His pasty skin flushed red. 'Doing God knows what. And the damn bedspread came undone, so her hand flopped out, and those kids knew exactly what I was doing.'

The image he'd painted stayed in her mind. 'You couldn't let them go to the police.'

'Of course not. They shouldn't have been there in the first place.' Agitated, he slapped the crowbar against his left palm. 'They started off the levee and I went after them. Not sure what I meant to do, maybe stop them, scare them into keeping quiet. But when I rammed the back of their car, the boy lost control, went over the bank.'

'You didn't help them,' Kyra stated flatly.

'Why would I? They shouldn't have been there in the first place.'

Anger and outrage burst inside her. This damn small, petty, evil man had driven a young man and woman to their deaths and felt not the least regret. She lunged in, her hand closing over the center of the crowbar. Mr. Carson pulled it away with both hands. She refused to let go, grappling with him, her rage over what this man had done giving her strength.

All his evil seemed to distill in his cruel blue eyes. 'What the hell are you doing?'

'I won't let you destroy the car!' She struggled to wrest the bar from his grip. 'I won't let you kill them again!'

He growled viciously. He had surprising strength for a man so old, but she was determined to keep her grip.

Keeping her eyes fixed on him, she lifted her head. 'Randon!' she screamed. 'Randon!' She filled her lungs. 'Johnny!'

She nearly had him; she could feel his fingers loosening. But with a power lent by madness, he flexed his arms and flung her to one side. She stumbled over the gas can, letting go of the crowbar to break her fall.

The thud of the crowbar against her back jolted through her. She crouched on hands and knees, her vision swimming from the pain, her stomach clutching in waves of nausea. He stood over her a moment and she wondered if he would finish her off as he had his wife, as he may have Randon.

'Randon,' she moaned, swaying.

Blackness flirted with her, danced along at the periphery of her vision. If she came through this, she swore she would tell Randon she loved him. She prayed she would tell a living man.

'Can't let you go,' Mr. Carson said. He raised the crowbar.

The sound of an engine roaring to life stayed his hand. As he stood with the crowbar still poised to strike, confusion whirled inside Kyra. The tow truck was the only working vehicle in the yard. Had Randon started it up? Was he driving over here to rescue her? But the tow truck was locked in Mario's mechanic's bay, the keys to it inside her office.

The engine roared again as if the driver had punched the accelerator. Mr. Carson made a strange gurgling sound in his throat. From the corner of her eye, Kyra could see the crowbar loose in his hand. Fighting against the pain, she raised her head.

The Fairlane was moving. It backed slowly from its place along the chainlink fence, gleaming pink and white in the setting sun. It had no tires, no battery, no fuel in the gas tank. Still, the wheels spun; the engine rumbled in the quiet of the empty yard.

'No,' Mr. Carson rasped.

The Fairlane turned toward them. The sun

glared on the windshield, opaquing it, but Kyra knew she wouldn't see anyone inside. The car glided along the aisle, wheels suspended above the ground as if the old white walls still cushioned them, the engine purring.

'No!' the old man shouted, raising the crowbar. He planted himself in the path of the oncoming car, swiping the air with the iron bar.

The Fairlane picked up speed. It seemed to grow in size as it came closer. Slumped behind Mr. Carson, Kyra struggled to rise. She couldn't quite get to her feet. The ground vibrated with the approach of the old Ford.

Her face pressed against the asphalt as she tried to gather strength to stand up. She thought the first cold touch was a breeze brushing against her skin. Then she felt the shape of fingers closing around her arm. Randon? But no, he still wasn't here. Nevertheless, hands gripped her, helped her to her feet and out of the way of the Fairlane.

She tried not to shiver from the chill, suppressed her reaction to the sparks skittering along her arms. She laughed, giddiness the only response left to her.

The sound tore Mr. Carson's attention from the oncoming car and back to her. 'This is your fault.' He advanced on her, swinging the crowbar. She heard it whip through the air, inches from her head. He closed on her, swung again.

The blare of the Fairlane's horn startled the old man, upset his aim. Then he cocked back his arm, ready to deal a final blow. A roar of rage drowned even the sound of the Fairlane's engine. Leaping from between the cars, Randon threw himself at Mr. Carson, knocking the old man to the ground. Mr. Carson still gripped the crowbar as he fell, tried to raise it to strike. But Randon slammed his hand over the old man's wrist, pinning him.

Mr. Carson pounded with his other hand, beating Randon in the ribs. Randon tried to evade the blows as he struggled to wrest the crowbar from the old man.

One last roar of the Fairlane's engine and the front fender of the car struck against the flailing iron bar. Terror took the last of Mr. Carson's strength and his fingers lost their grip. He stared at the car looming over him, eyes wide, mouth agape. A low, frightened moan escaped from his throat.

Tossing aside the crowbar, Randon rose, jerking the old man to his feet. The Fairlane's door opened and Mr. Carson nearly sagged back to the pavement. His eyes bulged in fear as Johnny stepped from the car.

Johnny moved closer, the lines of his body shimmering. '*I remember it all now, old man. What you did on the levee. The way you chased us.*'

Mr. Carson shook so hard, Kyra could hear the clack of his teeth. 'You shouldn't have been there in the first place.'

'*You banged into the back of the Ford.*' Johnny slapped his palm against the old man's chest, throwing off sparks. '*You pushed us off the levee.*'

Gibbering, Mr. Carson sank toward the pavement, and this time Randon let him go. His face grim, Randon stripped the old man's belt from his waist. None too gently, Randon used the belt to tie Mr. Carson's hands behind him.

Kyra took a shaky step toward them. Randon closed the distance, pulling her into his arms. She looked past him to the boy. 'He told me everything, Johnny. We'll go to the police. They'll make it right.'

Johnny nodded. '*It's what we needed. I won't be going back now, to the black limbo. I only wish . . .*' Emotion seemed to close off his throat.

Kyra put out a hand, wishing she could comfort him as Randon's arms did her. 'We'll watch out for her. I'll keep the car and maybe next time . . . '

Johnny's face told her he didn't believe there would be a next time. '*If you see her,*' he said, '*please tell her how much I love her. That I'll always love* — '

'*Tell me yourself, Johnny.*'

She arrived in a shimmer of light, a joyous smile on her face. Her arms outstretched toward Johnny, she repeated, '*Tell me yourself.*'

Johnny ran to her, and this time no barrier stood between them. He threw his arms around her, lifting her and spinning her around, shouting out his delight.

'*I love you!*' He turned her one last time, then settled her on her feet. '*I love you. Forever, Laura.*'

Laura tipped her face up. '*And I love you, Johnny. Forever.*'

A glow seemed to light the boy and girl from within, growing in brightness. The brilliance shot skyward in a blinding column reaching to the heavens. Kyra's eyes filled with tears as she watched as long as she could. But when the light burned too brightly to bear, she had to look away, burying her face in Randon's chest.

She felt Randon's hand in her hair, stroking, soothing. 'They're gone.' His voice was barely more than a whisper.

She raised her head, looked where she'd

seen them last. There was nothing to suggest they'd ever been there. The old Fairlane rested back on its wheels, as inanimate as the other wrecks in the yard.

Pulling away from Randon, she approached the old car. She ran her hand along the open door. 'It feels . . . different. They're truly gone now.'

Randon moved to stand beside her. 'But where they wanted to be.'

Unable to resist, she lowered herself behind the wheel. 'How did he do it, Randon?'

He leaned into the car. 'It was like you said before. He had to. That gave him the strength.'

She sat another moment, running her hands along the steering wheel. Then she shifted her feet, ready to climb from the car. Something bumped her heel and she reached for it under the seat. 'Something's stuck here.'

She worked at the shape wedged in the seat mechanism, finally managing to wrench it free. 'Oh, my God,' she breathed as she gazed down at what she'd retrieved. Tears pricked at her eyes.

She felt Randon's hand on her shoulder. 'Are you okay?'

Rising from the car, she set the mud-stained, aqua-colored item on the seat. She imagined Laura's terror, Johnny's anguish.

'Kyra?'

She swallowed back her tears, turned to Randon. 'I'm fine. What about you?' Pushing aside the dark hair curling at his temples, she found blood, still softly oozing. 'You ought to see a doctor.'

He sucked in a breath at her light touch, pulled her wrist away. 'There's no need.'

At their feet, Mr. Carson moaned. Kyra glanced down at the old man. 'What do we do about him?'

'We call the police. But in a minute.' His arm around her, Randon guided her well out of earshot of Mr. Carson. 'I'm really more concerned with what we do about you and me.'

Kyra dipped her head, afraid to meet his gaze. 'Is there a you and me?'

He cradled her face in his hands, tipped her head back. 'There's nothing more to keep me here.'

Although she'd expected his good-bye, hearing the beginnings of it cut her like a blade. 'I suppose not.'

'My sister's fine. The job is finished. And Johnny and Laura . . . they're where they need to be.'

She nodded, too miserable to speak. He stroked her brow, his fingertips exquisitely tender on her forehead.

But his gray gaze seemed troubled. 'So what do we do now?'

Her throat closed and she couldn't have spoken a word if her life depended on it. And yet . . . she remembered her silent prayer earlier, her vow. Now was the time to fulfill it, even if it didn't change a thing.

'I have to tell you something, Randon. Before you . . . ' She cleared her throat. ' . . . before you go.'

He brushed a kiss on her cheek, then drew back. 'Tell me.'

She gripped his arms, as if to take strength from him. 'I love you.'

The clear-spoken words seemed to hang in the air between them. Pain washed over his face.

'I have to leave, Kyra.'

She nodded, feeling more miserable than ever. 'I wanted you to know. I love you. No matter how you feel about me.'

His fingers worked in her hair and a thousand emotions seemed to burn inside him. 'But I . . . oh, my God, I . . . ' He squeezed his eyes shut and his hands trembled. Then his eyes flew open and he did the last thing she might have expected. He laughed. A short burst of sound, and then, grinning, laughter poured from him. He pulled her to him, squeezing her so hard she could hardly breathe.

'I'm an idiot,' he finally said.

Irritated now with his private joke, she scowled up at him. 'I'm inclined to agree. What's so damn funny?'

He dropped to one knee, astounding her even more. 'Kyra Aimes, will you marry me?'

She thought her jaw might hit the rough asphalt. 'What?'

He took her hand. 'I love you. I want to marry you.' He pressed his lips to the back of her hand, almost reverent. 'I love you.'

She gazed down at him, his dark head bowed over her hand. 'Yes,' she whispered.

He climbed to his feet again and lifted her off hers, holding her tightly. 'I love you,' she said to him, joy exploding inside her. Then she nudged against him so that he let her slide to her feet. She looked up at him sternly. 'Just one question, Mr. Bolton. What were you laughing about?'

His loving expression touched her deeply. 'I realized I don't have to leave you.'

'Of course you don't. You can stay — '

He shook his head, stopping her words. 'I can't. It's just not in me to stay in one place. But ... ' He stroked the back of her neck, sending shivers through her. ' . . . I can take you with me.'

She could see the hope in his expression,

coupled with worry. As if she would ever consider letting him go without her. She ran her palms up his chest to rest them on his shoulders. 'Randon Bolton, I will go anywhere with you.'

He grinned, exultation lighting his face. 'You will?'

'Of course, you idiot.' She whacked him on the chest. 'I love you.'

He captured her hand. 'What about your business?'

'I'll work something out. Jackson can run this place as well as me.'

He looked down at her sternly. 'I'm paying off your debts. You damn well better not tell me no.'

'I wouldn't dream of it.' With her free hand, she drew lazy circles on his chest. 'I will need to come back every once in a while.'

'And I'll want to visit Rachelle and my nephews. I won't stay away like before.'

A giddiness filled her and she felt as if she could float to the heavens as Johnny and Laura had. 'We'll work it out, Randon.'

He laughed. 'Hell, if we can help two lost souls find peace, we can do anything.'

She rose on tiptoes to kiss him. 'I love you, Randon.'

'I love you.' His lips closed on hers, warm with promise.

As she lost herself in his arms, she thought she heard a girl's soft voice, a shred of a whisper in her ear. *Thank you*. Then she heard only Randon's breath, Randon's heartbeat, and the softly spoken words blew away on a breeze.

Epilogue

With Randon beside her, Kyra knocked on the door of the old wood frame house on X Street. She heard movement inside, and then the door opened. A white-haired woman, who Kyra knew must be Laura's mother, stood before them.

Kyra smiled. 'Mrs. Mills?'

'I'm so glad you came.' Mrs. Mills pushed open the screen door for them, calling over her shoulder, 'Frank, they're here.'

As they stepped inside, Mr. Mills came in from the kitchen, drying his hands on a towel. Tossing the towel on a chair, he shook Randon's hand. 'Have a seat.'

Kyra and Randon sat side by side on the flowered chintz sofa. Mrs. Mills perched on the edge of a matching easy chair, but her husband seemed too agitated to sit.

Mrs. Mills locked her hands together in her lap. 'You said you had something for us.'

'Yes.' Kyra reached for the bag she'd set beside her.

'First,' Mrs. Mills said, her voice wavering, 'I wanted to thank you again. It was difficult finding out what really happened, but still . . . '

'We were glad to know,' Mr. Mills added. 'It helps to lay Laura to rest.'

She and Randon exchanged a glance, then Kyra turned her attention back to Mrs. Mills. 'The police told you everything?'

Mrs. Mills nodded. 'Everything that evil old man told them.'

Blessedly, Mr. Carson had pled guilty to the three counts of manslaughter. Kyra hadn't looked forward to testifying if it had gone to trial.

'So what is it you have for us?' Mrs. Mills asked.

Kyra reached into the paper bag. 'I found it under the seat.'

She pulled out the aqua pump and held it out to Mrs. Mills. The woman's blue eyes immediately filled with tears. Mr. Mills sank down on the arm of his wife's chair.

'Oh, heavens,' he murmured.

Mrs. Mills took the shoe from Kyra. 'I remember when we bought these.'

'The police let me take it when they were done with it,' Kyra said. 'I had it cleaned.'

Mrs. Mills nodded. 'Thank you.'

Mr. Mills lay his arm around his wife's shoulder and they sat silently for a long time. Then Mr. Mills turned to Kyra. 'We lost track of the Garveys. Were they notified?'

She let Randon answer. 'Mrs. Garvey died

433

ten years ago. Mr. Garvey's in a nursing home.'

'How did he take the news?' Mrs. Mills asked.

'I don't know how much he understood,' Kyra said. 'He has Alzheimer's.'

She and Randon had visited Mr. Garvey the day before, to give the nursing home the proceeds from the sale of the Fairlane for his care. He remembered his son clearly, but had chosen to forget that he'd died.

Mrs. Mills shook her head in sympathy. 'Poor man.'

She and Randon stayed a few minutes more, refusing Mrs. Mills offer of a glass of lemonade before they left. Kyra had one more loose end to tie up, one more bit of the past to resolve today.

They had only a few blocks to drive. The old pickup pulled up to another wood-frame house on a tree-lined street much like the one the Mills lived on. But this one held memories almost too intense to bear. Randon took her hand, the gold band on his finger gleaming in the summer light. 'We don't have to do this today.'

She squeezed his hand. 'We do. I do.' She opened the door. 'Let's go.'

As they moved up the walk, she clung to Randon like a lifeline. Her hand trembled as she raised it to knock.

At first she heard nothing from inside and thought he might not be home. Then the door scraped open.

As she gazed up at the man standing on the other side of the screen door, her eyes filled with tears. She struggled for breath to speak.

'Dad,' she said, then swallowed and tried again. She pulled Randon forward. 'Dad, I want you to meet my husband, Randon Bolton.'

His face splitting into a wide grin, her father pushed the screen door open and welcomed her inside.

Other titles published by
The House of Ulverscroft:

THE MIDWILLOW MARTYRS

Janet Mary Tomson

The year is 1830 and Martha Cavanagh, the minister's daughter, is experiencing the first pangs of love. Gabriel Lawless, the object of her affection, has returned home after seven years but not only is he a common labourer, he is also a rebel. When the landlords cut their workers' wages, the labourers form a friendly society. Their oath of allegiance is treated as treason. With the line drawn, the time has come to take sides. Can Gabriel be the hero Martha dreams of? Or the villain her father seeks to destroy?

THE HIGHCLOUGH LADY

Melinda Hammond

Governess Verity Shore longs for a little adventure, but when Rafe Bannerman arrives to carry her off to Highclough she soon discovers that life can be a little too exciting! An estate on the edge of the wild Yorkshire Moors, Highclough is Verity's inheritance, but the land is coveted, not only by her handsome cousin Luke but also by Rafe. With her very life in danger, whom can she trust?

LOVE THROUGH A STRANGER'S EYES

Jan Springer

Chance Donovan returns home with a new face, new identity, a burning desire for revenge and good timing. His wife, Emily, is about to marry his best friend, the man Chance suspects is behind his nightmare imprisonment for the past few years. The minute Emily catches the ragged stranger stealing food from her lighthouse kitchen, she feels a strong attraction to him. Resisting the urge to send him packing, she decides to hire him. But will she break through the painful walls surrounding this quiet man? And why does his welcome touch make her forget the man she's about to marry?

A DARING DISGUISE

Gillian Kaye

At the outbreak of the French Revolution, the de Charnay family escape from Paris to their Welford cousins in Sussex. However, several complications arise. First, Marianne Welford quarrels with her fiancé, Harvey Burrage-Smith MP, when he refuses to go to help her French cousins; then, when the de Charnays arrive, there is an immediate attraction between Marianne's sister Lucy and Edouard de Charnay — an attraction not easily resolved. As the tension rises, Marianne and Harvey travel to Paris amidst turmoil and conflict, but there must be many adventures before the two families can finally settle down to their new lives.